PRAISE FOR CHRISTINE GUNDERSON

"Deliciously readable. Funny, smartly observed, and impossible to put down, *Behind White Picket Fences* is a pitch-perfect take on modern motherhood—and how long-buried secrets can unravel a perfect suburb."

—Aggie Blum Thompson, author of *The Neighbors Are Watching*

"Wise, subversively witty, and absolutely unputdownable, *Behind White Picket Fences* is the story of an unlikely group of women who discover that sometimes bad fences make for the best neighbors. Christine Gunderson is a truly gifted novelist, and I can't wait to read what she writes next."

—Camille Pagán, bestselling author of *Dog Person*

"*Behind White Picket Fences* will have you arriving early in the carpool pick-up line to race through every last twist and turn. An unputdownable, laugh-out-loud, and heartwarming read that will keep you guessing until the last page."

—Sharon J. Wishnow, author of *The Pelican Tide*

"A captivating dive into an idyllic community where the manicured hedges mask danger. Once again, Gunderson crafts strong female characters who readers will root for and wish were part of their circle of friends."

—Jennifer Jabaley, author of *What's Yours Is Mine*

"What modern mom hasn't secretly dreamed of dropping out of the childhood rat race and returning to the days when kids simply played outside? With layered, relatable characters and a suspenseful plot, *Behind White Picket Fences* explores the intensity, chaos, and isolation of modern motherhood while simultaneously questioning whether that mythical 'simpler time' ever existed. I wish I could gift this book to every exhausted parent I know!"

—Hadley Leggett, author of *All They Ask Is Everything*

"At the heart of Gunderson's compelling sophomore novel, *Behind White Picket Fences,* is an exploration of the frontline of motherhood versus the impossible expectations of modern society. Readers will cheer on her cast of endearing and quirky characters as they band together to navigate parenting, stalkers, real estate developers, lifestyle influencers, bullies, and the local PTA in a novel that is equal parts fast-paced and timeless."

—Kristin Kisska, Agatha Award-nominated author of *The Hint of Light*

BEHIND WHITE PICKET FENCES

OTHER TITLES BY CHRISTINE GUNDERSON

Friends with Secrets

BEHIND WHITE PICKET FENCES

a novel

CHRISTINE GUNDERSON

LAKE UNION PUBLISHING

This is a work of fiction. Names, characters, organizations, places, events, and incidents are either products of the author's imagination or are used fictitiously. Otherwise, any resemblance to actual persons, living or dead, is purely coincidental.

Published by Lake Union Publishing, Seattle

www.apub.com

EU product safety contact:
Amazon Media EU S. à r.l.
38, avenue John F. Kennedy, L-1855 Luxembourg
amazonpublishing-gpsr@amazon.com

ISBN-13: 9781662533082 (paperback)
ISBN-13: 9781662533075 (digital)

Cover design by Emily Mahar
Cover images: © Mr.Music, Priya Rahman20 / Shutterstock

Printed in the United States of America

For Erik, Mark, and Kari, with all my love

Chapter One

KIERSTEN

Kiersten Cleaver looked down at the plastic teeth arranged across the reception desk at the orthodontist's office. The straight, beautiful teeth of disciplined people who wore their retainers *every night* for the rest of their lives.

Unlike her son, Matt, who'd accidentally thrown his upper retainer away in the middle school cafeteria yesterday. The orthodontist referred to the plastic-and-wire contraption as an *appliance*. It sounded like a washing machine for his teeth and cost about as much too.

"When would you like to make your next appointment?" the receptionist asked.

A simple question, but Kiersten could not formulate an answer.

This happened more and more often lately. Brain fog. Inability to concentrate. Trouble remembering the ten thousand trivial yet somehow vitally important things she had to keep track of each day. Was it perimenopause? Lyme disease? Or perhaps just low IQ?

The impossibly young receptionist stared up at her with clear eyes and luminous, unwrinkled skin. She looked like she was eleven, and this made Kiersten feel like she was forty-two going on eighty-three.

"Mrs. Cleaver?" The receptionist cleared her throat and frowned, obviously unsure of the protocol for interrupting parents in the middle of some kind of senior moment. "When would you like to bring Matt in for his next appointment?"

Never. Was never an option?

She dreaded coming to the orthodontist, which always included a lecture on the importance of brushing *along the gumline*, as well as dire warnings about the discoloration of teeth if patients failed to *brush thoroughly* while wearing braces.

Her thirteen-year-old son routinely failed to do this, and of course, his poor dental hygiene was her fault because she was his mother, and when you are a mother, everything is your fault.

"Wednesday, October 22 at four thirty is available," the receptionist prompted.

Kiersten glanced down at the calendar on her phone, where all the new activities and appointments of a fresh school year loomed. Her mind ran through the logistical ramifications.

If she took Matt to the orthodontist on Wednesday, October 22 at four thirty, she'd be unable to take Luke to the Orton–Gillingham dyslexia tutor. Or drop James at hockey practice. Or pick up Johnny from LEGO Robotics Club.

They'd moved to the DC suburbs in late July. School started in August. Now she found herself drowning in mid-September, swimming against a tidal wave of games, practices, clubs, parent meetings, back-to-school nights, and appointments.

She didn't know the other parents yet and had been unable to join the elaborate trade network of car pools mothers relied on to get children from point A to point B. Plus, she had no family nearby to help with the driving, like she had back home in Minnesota.

"I'm so sorry, but I'm afraid that won't work," Kiersten said. Obviously it was her fault they were too busy to schedule an appointment at a time the orthodontist found convenient. "Is there anything available on a Friday?" She'd come to think of Friday as Freedom Day, because it was the only day without lessons, practices, games, or meetings.

"Sorry, we aren't open on Fridays."

"How about Monday?"

The receptionist shook her head. "We aren't open on Mondays either. And we reserve Tuesdays for putting on and removing braces. But you could come in on a Wednesday or a Thursday."

The orthodontist was like a restaurant where you could have anything you wanted, as long as it was a hamburger.

Kiersten massaged her forehead. She'd have to pull Matt out of school because there was absolutely no time to squeeze in an orthodontist appointment later in the day. And that would likely annoy Mrs. Bile, the terrifying school secretary with intimidating eyebrows who she'd met at Classroom Sneak-a-Peek before the first day of school.

She scheduled the appointment for 11:00 a.m. on a Wednesday and left with her son and his new retainer trailing behind her across the parking lot.

"You seem kind of cranky," Matt observed when they got in the car.

"I'm not cranky," she said, immediately aware that she sounded cranky.

He shrugged and turned to the window. "Just sayin'."

She took a deep breath. "I'm so-rry if I sound cranky. It's just frustrating when we can't make a simple orthodontist appointment because we have so many after-school activities."

"I could quit baseball," he volunteered quickly.

She frowned. "You love baseball. And you're really good."

"I used to be," he said, his voice bitter.

The ever-present knot of worry inside her stomach twisted a little tighter. "That's not true."

He'd said this yesterday too. She cleared her throat and assumed a neutral tone, like a sportscaster on TV. "This new travel team is just . . . well, it's a higher level of play."

Higher level of play. She'd learned that phrase from her husband. She still wasn't sure what it meant. Or if it was even true.

"I'm the worst one on the team," Matt mumbled from beneath the fringe of bangs obscuring his eyes. She hadn't had the energy to fight about haircuts while still submerged under the chaos of moving boxes, pediatrician appointments, school forms, and an ongoing battle with the cable company about the subpar Wi-Fi at their new address.

"But you made the team!" she pointed out. "Most of the kids who tried out didn't."

"And I'd rather be playing with those kids, in the rec league. All the kids on this new travel team are assholes."

"Matthew!" She gasped. Her boys never swore, at least not around her. "Language."

He gave a sulky shrug. "It's true."

"It's only been a few weeks. Give it some time."

He slumped lower in his seat and stared out the window. She glanced at him, worry spreading through her body like a virus.

Had it been a mistake to sign him up for this extravagantly expensive travel team? But her husband was convinced that Matt would go from talented to extremely talented if he played with other extremely talented kids.

And if Matt became extremely talented, he could get a baseball scholarship and play in college.

Then she and Garrett could stop lying awake at night wondering how they were going to afford college tuition for four boys on her husband's new government salary. Plus the money she earned working part-time from home as an on-call advice nurse for a giant HMO, where every call seemed to end with her telling people to go to urgent care, just in case, for liability reasons.

She stopped at a red light and glanced at her son. "Let's see how things go at the tournament in Pennsylvania this weekend, okay?"

"Is Dad coming?" he asked.

She stifled an irritated sigh. It had been Garrett's idea to sign Matt up for travel baseball, yet he was never home to help with the travel part.

"No." She tried to keep her voice free from spousal judgment. "He's flying home on Saturday. But obviously I'll be there, and so will your brothers. We'll leave after school, then drive back right after your game on Sunday morning because Luke has a soccer game in Ashburn at two, and Johnny has hockey practice at the rec center at four thirty."

Matt sighed. "I feel like we live in this crappy car."

She bit back a snappy retort. *He's a child,* she reminded herself, *and none of this is his fault. Or his choice.*

She felt like she and Garrett had committed a form of child abuse by pulling their quiet oldest son away from grandparents, cousins, and a close-knit group of friends just a few weeks before he turned thirteen.

She couldn't imagine anything harder than moving halfway across the country for seventh grade, away from a school filled with blue-and-gold Future Farmers of America jackets, to a school where most kids would be hard pressed to identify which farm animal produced the bacon in their refrigerator.

Yet she and her husband had done this to their sons.

"I miss the farm," he said in a small voice, still looking out the window, facing away from her. "I hate that our neighbors are so close we can see into their backyards. I miss Grandpa and Grandma."

She fought to keep her voice steady. "I miss them too."

In Minnesota, they'd lived on a farm ten minutes from the dairy operation Garrett managed, with both sets of grandparents just down the road. Healthy, involved grandparents who drove the kids to activities, cheered them on at games and school events, and helped with homework and projects.

Now the boys only saw their grandparents during random FaceTime calls while Garrett traveled constantly for his new job as an undersecretary at the Department of Agriculture.

This week he was in Kansas . . . or maybe Nebraska? And she was stuck here, a stranger in a strange land, a married single mom trying, and failing, to raise four boys by herself.

"Luke got in a fight the other day," Matt said in a small voice, still facing the window. "At recess."

Her stomach curdled in shock. *"What?"*

He shrugged. "He's in the lowest reading group, and some kid called him a dumb hick. So he slugged him."

"Why didn't I hear—"

"The bell rang, and recess ended, and everybody went inside," he said. "The teachers didn't see."

She gripped the steering wheel in stunned silence, forcing her mind to focus on the rudiments of driving, yielding to a bicyclist crossing the street before making a left-hand turn.

"Don't tell him I told you, okay?" Matt said.

"Okay." She paused. "Is Luke *okay*?"

Matt shrugged again. "He hates this new school, just like I do. And I think he's already flunking math. And maybe English. And science too. But otherwise he's fine."

How could Luke be failing when the teachers hadn't even had time to give out *tests*?

She eased her minivan into the school parking lot and took a deep breath, trying to slow her racing mind. Matt shouldered his enormous backpack and groaned softly.

She shot him a sharp look. "Is your shoulder—"

He raised his palm, cutting off all further questions. "I gotta go, Mom. I have a science test."

Kiersten swallowed her next question and followed him into the school. She flashed a warm smile at Mrs. Bile, the school secretary, which was not returned. Then she signed her son in and reached for a goodbye hug. His young face contorted with pain when she touched him.

"Do you need some Tylenol?"

"I already took two this morning." He shrugged. "It's just sore from pitching yesterday."

The knot inside her stomach expanded again, like a malignant anxiety tumor. He'd been diagnosed with something called Little League shoulder a few weeks ago. He was supposed to rest his arm, but he'd pitched four innings yesterday.

"I'll make another appointment with the orthopedist."

He rolled his eyes. "Great. Another appointment."

"I love you," she whispered, forcing herself not to reach in for another hug. "Today will be better, I promise."

"Yeah, right," he muttered softly as he turned away. "Bye, Mom."

He disappeared down the hallway, thin shoulders slumped in defeat as her heart flooded with pain.

Chapter Two

PIPER

Piper Mondello entered the "Stinky Room" at the sprawling Hollin Terrace Elementary and Middle School complex, taking note of the exits, the windows on the north and south walls, and the extra-large purse belonging to a woman sitting in the first row.

Incendiary device? Grenades? Or just a metric ton of Target receipts and broken crayons?

Probably just crayons. But you never knew for sure. Piper sat in the empty seat behind the woman with the purse. Best to keep an eye on her.

Mr. Vex, principal and overlord of both the kindergarten through grade five elementary school and the grades six through eight middle school, stood beside a folding table at the front of the room, swiping on his iPad. Young and nattily dressed, he referred to this space in all written and spoken communication as the *Presidential Room*.

But this name didn't stick, probably because of the mysterious odor that sometimes permeated the area, which seemed to come from either a perpetually malfunctioning water heater or an unmentionable issue in the boys' bathroom next door.

Piper wasn't crazy about the smell, but she objected to holding PTA meetings here for different reasons.

The windows had no shades, and in the winter when it grew dark early, anyone could lurk outside and peep at the people seated within. The room had only one exit, and the long, narrow dimensions provided little space to maneuver if things went south.

Plus, all forty-five US presidents gazed down at her from the walls, and that didn't help either. She gazed back, wondering if Rutherford Hayes had been as difficult as he looked. Chester A. Arthur must have been a stinker. And Warren G. Harding allegedly had two mistresses. Every protection agent's worst nightmare.

Speaking of stinkers and nightmares, Mr. Vex, whom she suspected of having lofty ambitions, impatiently cleared his throat and glanced at his watch, a smug smile curving his mouth.

She'd already scheduled an appointment with Mr. Vex on Monday. But maybe she should accost him after today's meeting. This issue couldn't wait.

She rubbed her eyes, more exhausted now than she'd been after her three-mile predawn run.

She knew too much; that was the main problem. Too much about security threats, predators, criminals, bombs, online scams, human trafficking, pornography, weapons, violence, and the strange things people did with reptiles.

Everything will be fine.

She just needed to relax. That's why they'd put her on administrative leave after the Incident. So she could *relax*.

Her fingers crushed the meeting agenda into a ball.

Stop it.

No. Wait. She wasn't supposed to talk to herself using that kind of *tone*.

You are a beautiful woman of invincible strength. Calm your mind. Calm your body.

She silently repeated the words of her therapist.

Breathe in. Breathe out. Center yourself.

She inhaled and exhaled slowly, then uncrumpled the paper ball and attempted to iron out the wrinkles with her flattened hand.

See? Everything is fine.

But it wasn't fine. Not even close. Once again, her mind went back to the message she'd found on her daughter's iPad last night. She'd read it again this morning, right after her run, hoping it had been a bad dream, that it wasn't real.

i want to do things to you

A wave of nausea had washed over her as she squinted down at the words. She'd read them over and over again, hoping the letters would somehow realign to reveal a less ominous meaning.

i want to do things to you

Her brain had screamed questions into the early-morning silence. Leaning against the kitchen island, she'd wiped the sweat from her eyes as she looked down at the iPad sitting on the quartz countertop. The girls were still asleep, her husband still out of town, the house dark and quiet.

As far as she could tell, the message had come from one of her daughter's classmates, Alex Orlov, a boy known for causing trouble.

He'd sent the message two days ago. Her daughter hadn't replied.

i want to do things to you

She and her husband had tried so hard to shelter the girls from things like this. No cell phones until Christmas of eighth grade. No social media accounts until high school. No Snapchat. No apps like Facetune to make them question the natural beauty of their own features.

You couldn't be too careful as a parent. Her career as a Diplomatic Security agent protecting State Department personnel around the globe had taught her that danger lurks everywhere, especially if you're female.

Her time detailed to the FBI, where she dealt with human trafficking, followed by her job focused on domestic terrorism at the

Department of Homeland Security all led to the same anxious conclusion: Bad guys were everywhere, doing bad things all the time, and you had to remain vigilant to protect those you loved from harm.

And now in spite of all her precautions, her just-turned-thirteen-year-old daughter was getting messages on her school-issued iPad from a sick boy who wanted to do things *to* her.

Not *with* her. *To* her. That one word made all the difference in the world.

She'd heard about this boy. He'd been kicked out of at least two private schools, and now he'd ended up at Hollin Terrace, the local public school.

She knew she should muster some compassion for this child, but instead she felt a blind rage. She wanted to drive over to his house and lock him in a closet until her daughter turned sixty.

Or she wanted to call her friend Caleb on the SWAT team, dispatch him to the boy's house, and have him carried away in handcuffs.

But she no longer had that power or any power at all. And rightly so. Because of the Incident. An epic, front-page-of-*The-Washington-Post*, *Saturday-Night-Live*-parody-level incident.

She'd assessed a threat. And she'd been wrong. Epically, spectacularly *wrong*.

She'd been placed on administrative leave, pending an investigation, and would likely be fired at the end of it.

In the meantime, she was required by the Office of Employee Assistance to attend weekly sessions with a therapist to deal with the anxiety that had allegedly led her to make such a catastrophically bad call.

She was quite possibly the only person in America who had a federally mandated *therapist*.

Her fingers curled into a fist. And what if she was wrong now?

Maybe this boy wanted to take her daughter to a movie. To mini golf. To Chipotle for a burrito. Maybe he really did want to do things *with* her, not *to* her. Maybe it was a typo.

But the sick feeling inside her gut told her she couldn't dismiss this.

When the squeaking floorboards overhead had signaled that the girls had begun to stir, she'd headed upstairs and knocked softly on her oldest daughter's bedroom door.

No answer.

She opened the door a crack. Dark silence. She entered and turned on the bedside lamp.

Caitlin threw an arm over her eyes. "Already?"

Piper smiled and pushed the wild tangles from her daughter's face. Her beautiful face.

Piper was attractive. Pretty enough for all practical purposes. But her oldest daughter was stunning. Not pretty. Not cute. But full-on, no-exaggeration *beautiful.*

So beautiful that people stared in restaurants and the grocery store. Caitlin had just started seventh grade, but she'd skipped the awkward stage, going from adorable child to gorgeous teenage girl.

And every time someone turned to stare, especially if they were male, Piper found herself wishing her daughter were plain. Unremarkable. Average. *Safe.*

She gazed down at her daughter's full lips and long lashes. Should she bring it up now? Or wait?

She couldn't wait.

"Can I talk to you about something?"

Her daughter croaked out a groan. "Seriously, Mom? It's like four o'clock in the morning."

"No. It's 7:00 a.m., and you have to get up for school."

"Ugh." A dramatic sigh emanated from under the pillow she'd pulled over her head. "What is it?"

"This." Her mom opened the iPad and showed her the text.

Her daughter scrambled into a sitting position, outrage emanating from every limb. "You're reading my *texts*?"

"I'm *not* reading your texts. But maybe I should be. Your sister told me about it."

Caitlin's mouth curled into a scowl. "That little snitch."

"She's not a snitch." When had her daughter started talking like a prison inmate? "She's worried about you. And so am I."

Caitlin rolled her eyes. "That's why I didn't tell you. I knew you'd make it, like, a *federal case*."

Piper ignored the eye roll. "It's a very weird text, don't you think?"

Her daughter rubbed the sleep from her eyes. "Yeah," she finally conceded. "He creeps me out."

"Then why didn't you tell us?" Piper tried and failed to keep a note of reproach from her voice.

"Because I knew you'd go all, like, DEFCON five or something," Caitlin said. "And you'd talk to the principal and get him expelled, and then everyone would hate me cause he's like, you know, *popular*."

Piper forced herself to stay calm. To pretend that her daughter was just like any other witness she'd ever interviewed in the course of an investigation. "Has he done this before?"

"No. I mean, he hasn't texted me before but . . ."

Goose bumps rose on her skin. "But what?"

"Well, he says things sometimes . . . like . . ." Her daughter looked down and lowered her voice. "Like *sex* things."

Bile rose in Piper's throat, and she swallowed, hard. "What kinds of *sex things*?"

Caitlin blushed to the roots of her blond hair. "I don't want to repeat them . . . they're sick."

"Okay." She'd circle back to that when her daughter felt more comfortable. "How often does he say these things?"

"Like . . . I don't know . . . once a week maybe . . . in the hallway. Or standing in line in the cafeteria."

"Does anyone else hear him say these things?" Piper asked. A witness always bolstered any claim.

"No." Caitlin's fingers twisted the pale-pink sheets as she spoke. "He just, like, whispers them really low and fast, then walks away."

Piper reached out and smoothed her daughter's hair before asking one final question. For now. "Are you afraid of him?"

Caitlin looked at her for a long moment. Then her eyes filled with tears as she nodded.

She pulled her daughter into a hug as her heart shattered into a million pieces. Piper could send a bullet into the center of the smallest circle on the paper target at the gun range. She'd taught self-defense classes. She traveled all over the world protecting diplomats from harm. Yet her own daughter went to school every day feeling *unsafe*.

"Okay." She took a shaky breath and gave her daughter a reassuring squeeze. "That's all I need to know. For now."

They sat like that for a minute or more. Her daughter had gone limp, melting into Piper's arms as she stroked her hair, as though she were a little girl again, instead of a young woman dealing with all the fears that came with being female.

"What are you going to do, Mom?"

"I'm going to request a meeting with the principal."

"Mommm . . ." Caitlin's voice held a note of warning.

Piper held up her hand. "I'm just going to ask them to speak with . . ."

"Alex," her daughter supplied.

"Right. Alex. And they'll tell him to stop sending texts and saying creepy things. They'll tell him to stay away from you."

"That's all?" Caitlin's eyes narrowed. "You're not going to, like, throw him into juvie or something?"

I would if I could, Piper thought.

"That's all." Piper crossed her heart. "I promise."

"Do you *really* have to do this?"

"Do you want him to stop saying these things and sending you inappropriate texts?" Piper asked.

Caitlin gave her mom a duh look. "Of course I do."

"Then I have to talk to the principal. Because Alex won't stop on his own." *And if he thinks no one is watching, it will get worse.*

Unfortunately, she knew this from experience.

"Okay." Caitlin nodded slowly. "But Mom . . . you need to know that . . . this is like . . . this is just what school is *like* now. Some girls get . . . videos . . . from boys."

"What kinds of videos?"

"Like, sick videos they make at home . . . in their bedrooms."

Her mother sighed, wishing she could unknow so many of the things she knew. "This is not normal, Caitlin. It's not acceptable. You should not be threatened and harassed at school. You have a right to feel safe. All girls have a right to feel safe."

She could feel herself launching into lecture mode and steered herself back to the matter at hand. "Write down the things he says. I'll call the principal today and quietly put an end to this, okay?"

Caitlin crumpled into her mother's arms again as fresh tears spilled down her cheeks. "I'm sorry I didn't tell you. I just . . . I don't want it to become this *big thing* where everybody knows and I'm like, the bad guy for telling on him."

"I understand," Piper said. "We'll handle it quietly, and we'll make it stop. Okay?"

Her daughter had given her a weak smile as she wiped the tears from her cheeks. "Okay."

The sharp rap of the gavel startled Piper, thrusting her back into the Stinky Room as the PTA meeting started.

"Thank you all for coming today." The PTA president, resplendent in head-to-toe athleisure wear, gave a queenly smile to all the mothers in the room.

Yes. Mothers, Piper noted. They wrote the bills up for debate on the House and Senate floors, negotiated trade agreements, and were members of the Council on Foreign Relations, but somehow they were still the only members of their two-parent households who attended PTA meetings. Even this one, the inaugural meeting at the start of the school year, scheduled for maximum inconvenience in the middle of a workday.

Piper's gaze wandered from the woman holding the gavel to the principal, who sat beside her.

His complacent smile triggered another flash of anger, and she sat up a little straighter. She would *not* wait until Monday. She'd accost him today, as soon as the meeting ended.

Her daughter's safety depended on it.

Chapter Three

KIERSTEN

Kiersten climbed into her car, exited the school parking lot, and drove her minivan to a nearby park, where she turned off the engine and sat staring ahead at a small cluster of moms sitting on a picnic blanket, holding infants.

She glanced at the clock on the dashboard and grimaced. She'd planned to attend the first PTA meeting of the year after the orthodontist appointment.

She didn't necessarily *want* to join the PTA, because how much could she realistically volunteer, with her HMO Call-an-Advice-Nurse job, and travel sports, and her husband always gone, and a giant pile of unpacked boxes in the basement? But she did want to make friends in this new place, and the PTA seemed like a good place to start.

Her gaze traveled to the rearview mirror, where she took in her unwashed hair and naked face. All the energy leaked from her body, and she sagged in her seat like a three-day-old helium balloon. She couldn't go to the PTA meeting looking like *this*.

Some of the moms out here in the DC area were . . . intense. A little intimidating. She'd met a few of them at Sneak-a-Peek the day before school started. They looked like the kind of people who discussed battleground polls on CNN after a presidential debate. Half of them seemed to run vitally important government agencies, and the ones who didn't wore head-to-toe Lululemon and looked like former Olympic athletes.

One of the women she'd run into had casually mentioned that she'd gone to Harvard. Kiersten was still trying to figure out how the woman had managed to insert this fact into a two-minute conversation about whether or not her fourth grader really needed the mini stapler she'd been unable to find at Target. In her mind, the conversation went something like this.

Were you able to find the mini stapler?

Yes. I went to Harvard.

She took a giant swig of coffee from her stainless steel travel tumbler, then closed her eyes and exhaled. She would attend the *next* PTA meeting, after she'd taken a shower, put on under-eye concealer, and found a way to disguise the fact that she only had a bachelor's degree from Mankato State.

Through the windshield, she watched as one of the mothers on the picnic blanket dangled brightly colored plastic keys in front of a baby who reached out with chubby hands to grasp the toy.

Little kids, little problems. Big kids, big problems.

Someone had told her this, years ago. It felt condescending at the time, and she'd resented the person who said it. When Matt had colic and refused to sleep, it was a huge problem. But now she felt like she understood.

She couldn't fix her son's distress with a fresh diaper or a bottle. These big-kid problems seemed far beyond her abilities, above her pay grade. Fitting in at a new school, dyslexia, ADD, flunking, fighting.

She marveled, not for the first time, at a world where you had to pass an elaborate series of tests to drive a car, but even people who had never changed a diaper could walk out of the hospital with a new baby, no questions asked.

Digging into her purse, she searched for her cell phone. She needed to talk to her husband.

Though he couldn't plan a birthday party or be trusted to buy the right kind of chicken nuggets at the grocery store, they were volunteers in the same two-person army, sharing the same almost-impossible mission: to raise healthy, kind, emotionally balanced humans in an often unhealthy, unkind, unbalanced world.

She was pretty sure God had created Adam for this purpose. So he could lie and tell Eve the kids would be just fine, even when they were both positive their offspring would end up in jail, in a cult, or running an illegal Bitcoin-mining operation from the family basement, where they would still be living at age thirty-five.

She punched Garrett's number into her phone, and he picked up on the fourth ring. "Hey. Just heading into a meeting. What's up?"

"Luke got into a fight."

A beat of silence. Then, "Hold on." She could hear his voice, muffled now, telling someone he'd be there in a second. "A fight? You're sure?"

"Matt told me. Just now."

A slow exhale on the end of the line. "Okay. We'll deal with it when I get back."

"Garrett."

"Yes?"

"What if this move was a huge mistake?"

Another pause, followed by an impatient sigh. "Look, I'm about to head into a meeting with fifty ranchers who are terrified they won't be able to feed their herds or their families next year because it hasn't rained in six months and their pastures are burnt to a crisp. I can't talk about this right now. I'm sorry."

"I just . . . I didn't know it would be like this." The admission filled her with shame. She felt like a homesick child, instead of the capable woman she wanted to be, the strong adult her husband and sons needed her to be.

A long pause on the other end, then her husband's voice, gentle now, but with the faintest hint of an accusation. "Look, we knew this transition might be hard. But we said we'd give our family this opportunity for two years. Museums. A chance to live fifteen minutes from the nation's capital. Exposure to different people and cultures and a different way of life. We made this decision *together*."

She wanted to reach through the phone, through time and space, and wrap her hands around his neck and strangle him.

Because he was right.

She desperately wanted to blame him for this decision, but she couldn't because they had made it together.

She'd encouraged him to take this job.

The arguments came flooding back, arguments that came from her own mouth. *You'll be in a position to make policy that helps farmers and ranchers and small towns. We'll be living five minutes from Mount Vernon and twenty minutes from the Capitol. So much history! Such a great opportunity for the boys.*

Think of all the good you can do in this position.

She'd actually said that. She'd been so stupid.

And it was a chance to break away, for just a couple of years, from the grandparents and aunts and uncles and in-laws who dropped in unannounced at all hours of the day and night, who helped enormously but also made constant well-intended suggestions, criticisms, and observations.

James spends an awful lot of time playing that Minecraft *game.*

Maybe Luke doesn't have dyslexia. Maybe he just eats too much sugar.

When I was their age, I had chores. These boys don't do enough to help around the farm.

This move to DC was supposed to provide a break from all that. A chance to parent without the peanut gallery.

But as it turned out, the peanut gallery provided an awful lot of free, high-quality childcare. Not to mention homecooked meals, rides to practice, help memorizing the multiplication tables, and love.

"I gotta go," Garrett said, breaking into her thoughts. "I'm sorry, honey. But we'll deal with it when I get home, okay?"

"Okay," she whispered. She knew she should utter the two quick words that normally ended their calls, should force herself to mutter *Love you* even if she didn't mean it, especially if she didn't mean it.

But she couldn't do it, and apparently neither could he.

Garrett disconnected the call. She tossed her phone into the passenger seat.

They'd gone to a museum exactly once, the Smithsonian Natural History Museum, back in July, to give themselves a break from the boxes and unpacking. They'd seen the Hope diamond and a mummy and an enchanting exhibit with live butterflies. It had been their best day so far.

Then school and sports started in mid-August, and Garrett began traveling, and they hadn't set foot in a museum since.

And that thing about being *minutes* from the nation's capital? That was only true at 10:23 a.m. on a Friday morning in August when there was no traffic. At other times it could take almost an hour. Or longer. She'd learned that the hard way.

She rested her head against the steering wheel and fought back tears. She would *not* cry. Crying never helped.

"I just wish . . ." She whispered the words, then stopped. It was more of a *feeling* than a wish. Nostalgia and longing wrapped in frustration. A desire to give her own children the very best of what she'd had growing up.

But what was that exactly? What did she really want?

To go back home to Minnesota?

No. That wasn't the answer. Because even if they moved back home, she'd still have four kids in five million activities. She'd still have a son with dyslexia and ADD who struggled in school. She'd still be driving around in circles at top speed in a minivan, going nowhere, except maybe crazy.

I wish we could go back in time.

Yes. *That's* what she wanted. Life wasn't like this when she was a kid. She didn't start playing sports in earnest until high school. She didn't have loads of homework every night.

She rode her bike around the neighborhood after school in her tiny hometown with a pack of kids. At dusk, she pedaled home to a balanced and nutritious dinner made by her stay-at-home mother.

Then she watched *Little House on the Prairie* and *The Love Boat* with her whole family, all in one room, together, on a device that looked like a piece of furniture, and went to bed.

She wanted to go back to *that* world. To a place with no social media. No cell phones. No arguments about screen time and *Fortnite* and *Minecraft*. No PowerSchool portal to check grades in real time. A place where the telephone clung to the wall like a barnacle, and a long curling cord held the world at bay.

She shook her head, banishing these memories and the soft yearning they generated.

A ridiculous wish. Also impossible. Impractical. And a little bit sad.

You can't go home again. And you can't go back in time.

No point in fantasizing about a different way of living. She'd chosen to have four children, and this wild, frenetic existence was the price of modern motherhood. Everyone was busy. Everyone had a million activities. She just needed to buck up and stop complaining. *Embrace the suck,* as her brother, an army veteran, sometimes said.

She sighed and ran her fingers through her unwashed hair. Things would get better once they got settled.

Plus, she only had to live this way for another decade or so, until her third grader turned eighteen and left for college . . .

She'd figure this out. Because that's what mothers did.

And as for that other issue . . .

She shuddered at the memory of what she'd found this morning.

The flutter of movement had caught her eye as she gazed out the window at dawn, thinking existential thoughts while nursing her first cup of coffee.

Something white peeked from the trunk of the massive sweet gum tree in the front yard.

She slammed her coffee cup down on the counter. How many times had she told the boys not to leave their socks, their shoes, and inexplicably, sometimes even their underpants, *in the front yard*?

She bolted into the mudroom, put on her flip-flops, and approached the tree, eyes narrowed.

Not a sock. Or underpants.

Instead, a page of lined notebook paper quivered in the early-morning breeze, spiked to the tree trunk with a large nail.

Stepping closer, she scrutinized the paper without touching it.

Dark-brown streaks crisscrossed the page like a child's attempt at finger paint.

Her eyes narrowed; then she inhaled sharply.

Dried blood. A substance any nurse could identify.

She'd removed the paper and zipped it into a plastic bag. Another fun thing to discuss with her husband when he returned home.

What if . . .

She slammed her mind shut, refusing to go there. Then she took a deep breath, sucking air into her lungs, wishing she could also inhale hope, strength, wisdom, and sanity.

Things would get better. They had to get better. Because surely they couldn't get worse.

Right?

Chapter Four

PIPER

When the PTA meeting ended, Piper maneuvered through an archipelago of small conversational islands, skillfully avoiding Cameron Schultz and her recruitment efforts for the Roaring Twenties School Gala planning committee.

Piper knew from experience that Cameron's committees often devolved into nasty civil wars. Last year, the moms who wanted appetizers from Wegmans got into a big argument with the moms who preferred Costco, and now this year they were all room parents together and the whole thing was very awkward.

Like a cheetah, she slipped past the gala-planning moms and into the little group surrounding Mr. Vex.

Their last principal had ruled the school with an iron fist and finally retired to spend more time with her new grandbaby after fourteen years at the helm.

Mr. Vex was her opposite in every way, and many of the moms, particularly the younger ones, liked this new approach. He also happened to be thirty-five years old and unusually good looking, which the mothers of Hollin Terrace Elementary and Middle also appreciated. No one had ever before experienced a PILF or even known that such a thing could possibly *exist.*

Piper patiently awaited her turn, listening without smirking or even raising her eyebrows as Abigail Morton, a kindergarten mom, discussed the many difficulties involved in parenting her gifted son.

"I just want Benjamin to be *challenged*," she told Mr. Vex earnestly. "He's so bright, and he's already been exposed to *algebraic thinking*."

Piper bit down hard on her lower lip. Had her girls ever been exposed, unwittingly and as kindergartners, to *algebraic thinking*? It sounded harmful, like exposure to lead, or Agent Orange.

Mr. Vex assured her that Benjamin would receive *extra enrichment* in math so he could continue to learn at an accelerated pace rather than merely learning to count like his less gifted classmates.

One by one, the other moms slipped away, and finally, it was her turn.

She introduced herself with a firm handshake. "Piper Mondello. I emailed your assistant this morning to set up a meeting on Monday, but I'd prefer to talk now, if you don't mind."

He glanced down at his Apple Watch and frowned. "I have five minutes before my next meeting. What can I do for you?"

She took a deep breath and plunged ahead. "It's about my daughter Caitlin. She's in seventh grade, and she's being sexually harassed by a boy in her class."

He raised an eyebrow. "By whom?"

"Alex Orlov." She pulled out her phone and showed him a picture of the message she found on her daughter's iPad.

His expression didn't change, but his posture did. Almost imperceptibly, she sensed him pulling away.

"It sounds like he's asking her out on a date," he said, his voice neutral. "Kind of retro. But seems harmless enough."

"No." She shook her head vehemently. "Read it closely. It says *I want to do things to you*. Not *with* you. *To* you."

"How many of these messages has he sent?" Mr. Vex asked, eyes narrowed as he looked down at her phone.

"This is the first one."

He stroked his chin. "I see."

He had the same perfectly manicured five-o'clock shadow she'd noticed on male celebrities the last time she looked at *People* magazine while getting her hair cut.

"But he says things too," she added quickly. "When she's in line in the cafeteria, and in the halls."

"Like what?"

"It's explicit and inappropriate." Heat spread across her cheeks, and she wanted to shake herself. She'd testified in court more times than she could count, repeating phrases far worse than this one, out loud and under oath, for judges and juries. But these words felt different. Uglier. Dirtier. Because they were directed at her daughter.

"What does he say, Mrs. Mondello?" Mr. Vex asked again.

She cleared her throat and repeated the words her daughter had finally shared with her before leaving that morning. "He said, 'I want to tie you up and . . .'" She lowered her voice and spelled the f-word.

He raised an eyebrow. "That is explicit."

"It's explicit, inappropriate, and threatening."

"It is, but unfortunately, it's also fairly common in this day and age." He suddenly looked much older than thirty-five, and she felt a tinge of compassion. "Thanks to the internet, boys are exposed to things they weren't exposed to in the past, and at much younger ages."

"And that's unfortunate," she said, working to keep her voice calm. "But what are we going to do to protect our girls from the things these boys are exposed to?"

He shrugged. "Well, I can talk to this boy and ask him not to do it again."

Her self-control evaporated. Words exploded from her mouth like shrapnel. "That's *it*?"

"I can't expel him for a first offense. But if it continues, we can talk about other interventions."

She shook her head in disbelief. "Can you at least speak to his parents so they know what's going on?"

Once again, his expression remained neutral, but something changed in his posture. He stood up a little straighter, seemed to stiffen.

"If I feel the message isn't getting through to the boy, then I'll involve his . . . parents."

There it was again. An almost imperceptible pause before the word *parents*.

She frowned. "Look. If my kid were doing something like this, I'd want to know."

He gave her a weary smile. "Not everyone feels the same way. I wish they did. But many parents expect us to handle school issues at school. They don't want to be bothered."

"Bothered?" She inhaled sharply. "Isn't being *bothered* a fundamental part of parenthood?"

He sighed. "It used to be. I'm not sure that's the case anymore."

She said nothing for a moment, weighing her options. Should she argue? Push back? Demand the boy be suspended? But she could tell this man believed her and even seemed slightly sympathetic. At the moment, this appeared to be the best he could do.

It wasn't enough. Not by a long shot. But it might be enough to scare Alex Orlov into leaving her daughter alone.

And if he didn't, she'd come at Mr. Vex again, harder next time. And she'd talk to the boy's parents herself if she had to.

"Okay." She allowed her tone to convey her unhappiness. "I guess it's a start."

"I'm sorry I can't do more." His handsome face radiated sincerity. "Please keep me posted. If it continues, we'll escalate our response."

Was she being dazzled into acquiescence just because he looked like a young George Clooney?

"I will."

As she walked to the car, she pondered the strange small-town dynamics of elementary and middle school.

Even if you had only one child, you could be tied to a particular school for *years*. Especially if it was a K–8 school. And if you had two or three or four kids, you could be trapped at a school for a decade or more as your children slowly worked their way up from kindergarten.

Every decision became a calculation. If you had three or five or eight years left at a school, did you really want to get on the administration's bad side by fighting this particular battle *now*? Or did you keep your powder dry and save your complaints for some really big issue that may or may not crop up down the road?

As she drove home, she couldn't ditch the feeling that she hadn't fought hard enough. That she'd pulled her punches because she still had years ahead of her at Hollin Terrace with Mr. Vex at the helm. Because even though Caitlin was in seventh grade, she had younger siblings coming up behind her, with Olivia in fifth grade and Bella in second.

Piper pulled into the driveway and sat in her car, trying to identify the uneasy feeling lodged in the center of her gut. There was a dynamic at play here, an undercurrent she could sense but didn't understand.

She just wanted to keep her girls safe. Was that so much to ask?

Chapter Five

KIERSTEN

While the good, civic-minded mothers of Hollin Terrace Elementary and Middle attended the PTA meeting, Kiersten ran errands and felt guilty.

Growing up in a small town had given her a deeply ingrained sense of community responsibility. There was a special circle of hell reserved for freeloaders who didn't sign up for a shift with the volunteer fire department, take their turn mowing the Lutheran church cemetery, or serve on the Bergen farmers' elevator board.

She tried to push these thoughts away as she dashed to Costco and the grocery store to lay in supplies for the impending road trip to Pennsylvania for Matt's baseball tournament.

Then she girded her loins for one final chore before picking the boys up from school and hitting the road.

She'd been dreading this all week. She'd even cleaned the toothpaste-encrusted hellhole the boys called a bathroom as a procrastination tactic to avoid this task. But now, after her conversation with Matt, she couldn't delay it any longer.

She took a deep breath, ate four Ghirardelli chocolate squares to fortify herself, and logged into PowerSchool to check her children's grades.

Kiersten was always telling her sons not to use the word *hate*. But she hated the student grade portal with the white-hot fury of a thousand burning suns.

In the olden days when she was a kid, report cards provided moments of pride mixed with terror and disappointment four times a year when her parents opened the white envelope that came in the mail from school and learned that she had an A-plus in English, but also a C-minus in Algebra.

But now, thanks to technology, PowerSchool allowed her to have these terrifying and disappointing moments *multiple times each week*.

Taking a deep breath, she opened her laptop and eased into things by starting with Matt, who personified all the oldest child stereotypes. Diligent. Hardworking. Responsible. Her shoulders relaxed as she looked at a short column of grades in the nineties. No tests yet. Just graded homework assignments, all completed and turned in on time. She moved on to James, then Johnny.

And finally Luke.

Squinting through one eye, she scanned the columns as her stomach clenched. A string of zeroes denoted missing homework assignments. After only a few weeks of school, he'd already managed an F in math. A D in science. A C-minus in English and social studies.

She slammed the laptop shut and tried to identify the emotion that ravaged her body every time she checked the portal.

Not disappointment. Or even anger.

No. It was fear. Flat-out, heart-pounding, adrenaline-pumping fear.

Fear of a future she couldn't predict and didn't fully understand. A place where the old occupations had fallen away and new ones had yet to materialize.

A future where only those kids who turned in their homework on time and did well on standardized tests would survive. A future where kids who got B's and C's lived in shipping containers in a *Blade Runner*–style dystopian hellhole where they served AI Robot Overlords in plutonium mines on Mars and ate dehydrated bread pellets and Soylent Green.

She suddenly felt an overwhelming urge to down a bottle of whiskey or smoke a pack of cigarettes, even though she rarely drank and never smoked.

Instead, she opened the pantry, hunching her shoulders as she prepared for a soup can or a cereal box to fall on her head from the crammed shelves above.

She stepped on a stool and reached for the top shelf, where she found the box of Pepperidge Farm Milano cookies she'd hidden from her husband and the boys in case of an emergency such as this. She ripped it open and popped a cookie into her mouth.

It wasn't fair that Luke, who was just as smart as his brothers, had to work twice as hard to get half as far. It wasn't fair that his brain was wired in a way that made every moment he spent in school miserable and difficult.

It wasn't fair, but it was also a fact.

She stuffed another cookie into her mouth.

She needed to spend more time working with him at home. She needed to read aloud the books assigned for his English class. She needed to sit beside him and make sure he not only completed his assignments but actually remembered *to turn them in*. She needed to create a system.

But she also needed to make dinner, do laundry, and drive four boys to ten different games, practices, and activities between the hours of 3:30 and 8:30 p.m. every day after school. And on weekends.

So when exactly was she supposed to quiz him on the periodic table? When they stopped at a red light? Because that was the only time they could realistically squeeze it in.

Plus she had *three other kids* who also needed her time and attention. Like Matthew, a deep thinker and quiet perfectionist who had a harder time making friends.

And James, the social butterfly who tended to be attracted to the rowdiest kids in his class.

And then Johnny, who had less athletic ability and was having a hard time finding his place in the world, which meant he needed to try *all* the sports, plus every activity from LEGO Robotics to Scouts to chess club to Odyssey of the Mind as he searched for his "passion."

Because as a modern mother, she was expected to help her children find their passion, preferably in time to write a compelling essay about it for their college applications.

She ate four more cookies, then printed the list of missing assignments. She would sit down with Luke on Sunday night and try to get a handle on things. If they worked hard, they could get his grades up before the end of the quarter.

They. As in she and Luke together. She would be repeating sixth grade as a forty-two-year-old woman.

She reached for another cookie. Shame flushed her cheeks as her fingers brushed the crumbs at the bottom of the empty bag.

Stop.

She crumpled the bag. This needed to stop right now.

How much did she weigh? Did she even know anymore?

She hadn't seen the scale since the move. It had become one of the many mysterious objects that disappeared into a packing box in Minnesota but had not yet emerged on the other side of the moving black hole here on the East Coast.

She tossed the cookie bag into the trash and headed for the unfinished part of the basement, a no-man's-land of unpacked boxes, in search of the bathroom scale. They'd shoved everything in here after unpacking the essentials like underwear, pots and pans, the Nintendo Switches, and the TV remote.

Her gaze roamed over the canyon of cardboard stacked almost to the ceiling, each box labeled with her husband's messy print or her own neat cursive.

She frowned as her gaze came to rest on four boxes in the far corner, behind the hot-water heater, marked with unfamiliar handwriting.

She moved closer. A thick layer of dust covered the boxes, and they looked older than the packing boxes that held the rest of their belongings. They must have been left behind by the old couple who'd sold them the house.

They were lovely people, Henry and Myrtle DiLorenzo, the grandparents of her husband's best friend from college. He'd grown up in this area and helped her and Garrett find a place to live.

They'd brokered the deal without using a real estate agent, and the DiLorenzos had asked less than market value because the house hadn't been updated since it was built in the 1960s. They'd replaced the roof and windows and appliances as needed. But everything else remained the same. Tiny kitchen and tiny closets. Popcorn ceilings. Wood paneling.

The old couple had been told their home would be torn down if they put it on the market, so they were delighted to sell to a family with children who planned to live in it instead of demolishing it.

Now Henry and Myrtle lived a few minutes away in a retirement village. Kiersten had intended to pay them a visit and bring a housewarming gift, but of course, she hadn't actually found time to do this yet.

Another thing to feel guilty about. But now she'd *have* to pay a visit, if these boxes belonged to them.

She crouched on the cold concrete floor and unfolded the cardboard flaps. Dust rose in the air, making her sneeze as she peered down at a neat stack of large hardback books covered in green and cream-colored leather.

A wave of nostalgia washed over her as she removed the one on top and ran her fingers over the letter *C* embossed on the cover.

Encyclopedias.

A flash of recognition made her smile. Her grandparents had owned a set just like this. As a girl she'd sat on the floor for hours, looking at the pictures and reading about Africa, bats and cougars, Lichtenstein, Mount McKinley, and zebras.

She lifted the volume into her lap and opened it.

Her breath caught in her throat.

What in the world?

The inside of the book had been hollowed out, the pages cut away.

Instead of words, she found a book hidden between the covers of the encyclopedia.

Her heart pounded inside her ears as she removed the small book from its hiding place inside the larger one.

A black leather-bound volume with the word **DIARY** embossed across the cover in gold. A thin black strap with a tarnished lock ran across the front. She pressed the tiny gold button on the lock and tugged gently.

It remained locked. Shut tight.

She leaned back on her haunches, chewing on her lower lip.

Who did this belong to?

She put the locked diary back into the *C* encyclopedia and removed the rest of the volumes from the ancient cardboard boxes, stacking them in alphabetical order, *A* through *Z*.

Sitting cross-legged on the floor, she began to open each volume, starting with *A*. She broke into a smile.

There, inside the hollowed-out center, she found a key, threaded onto a blue ribbon.

Fingers fumbling with excitement, she rushed to lift the cover on the next volume. The letter *B*.

A pang of disappointment stabbed when she found pages of smooth encyclopedia paper describing Babylon, bacteria, Barcelona, and bonobos.

She scrambled to open the rest.

M had been hollowed out and contained another small black diary. The next volumes contained regular pages . . . until she got to the letter *S*. That one contained another diary.

She opened the last volume, *WXYZ*, and felt her mouth drop open.

Cash.

Gently, she brushed her fingers over a thin wad of ancient bills, held together with a rubber band.

What the heck?

She slumped back on her heels, staring in wonder. Could those nice old people who used to live here have been geriatric drug dealers?

Only one way to find out.

She inserted the key into the lock, opened the first diary, and began to read.

Chapter Six

DOTTIE

March 3, 1965

I had my last day at the office yesterday. They've called three times to ask me how the mimeograph machine works, and I miss it already. Not just the machine and the oddly comforting scent of the ink and the damp feel of the new copies. I miss Big Red, my IBM Selectric typewriter, too, whizzing my fingers over the keyboard faster than any other girl in the office. I even miss making the coffee on Monday morning when the account execs file in, except that the smell of freshly brewed coffee now makes me queasy.

I took one last run at Daddy yesterday morning. I went into his office by the sales floor and closed the door. He knew what I wanted before I even opened my mouth.

"Dottie. Please don't."

I sat down in the chair in front of his desk and tried to keep my voice steady. "But Daddy—"

He shook his head emphatically. "I should have made you quit the day you got married like we do with all the other girls."

I smiled. "But you couldn't because I'm indispensable."

"You know the policy." He brandished his gold pen at me. "We can't have pregnant secretaries running around a car dealership. How would that look?"

"Please Daddy, just a little longer." I felt like I was six years old again, begging to stay up past my bedtime.

"Absolutely not. Today is your last day, just like we planned. We'll give you a nice send off." His face softened. "Then you go home and take care of your new husband and my future grandson."

I rested a hand on the not yet visible bump on my belly. "Or granddaughter."

He shook his head and chuckled. "Nope. It's a grandson. I feel it in my bones."

I gazed through the window overlooking the showroom floor and spotted Dickie, my brand-new husband who supposedly requires so much care. His big hands caressed a powder-blue 1965 Chevy Impala. They remind me of sharks, those Impalas, the way the hood hangs over the grill.

Dickie spoke to a dazed-looking young couple, charming them with his wide grin and square jaw. Just like Paul Newman. That's what all the girls in the office say. "You're so lucky, Dottie. Your husband looks just like Paul Newman."

The next part is implied. What's a gorgeous guy like that doing with a girl like me? Because I'm plain. Unremarkable. And a little . . . different.

Mechanically inclined. Those are the worried words my mother used to whisper to her friends as I built towers with Tinkertoys instead of playing with dolls like a normal girl.

Daddy didn't have a problem with it, though. In those terrible days after Mother died, he let me spend my time at the dealership with him, or out in the garage with Oscar and Herman and all the other mechanics, learning about spark plugs and carburetors.

Daddy indulged me, I suspect, because he knew I had a broken heart, just like he did. He let me stay out there doing oil changes until I turned fourteen. Then he put his foot down, and said I could only help out if I worked in the secretarial pool.

So I learned to type and run the mimeograph machine and take dictation. I loved working in the office with the other girls, typing up sales contracts and purchase orders after school and over the summer.

And that's where I met Dickie, the day after I graduated from high school. He came into the break room to get a celebratory cup of coffee after selling a car.

He leaned against a file cabinet, tall and lanky with those bright blue eyes. "You must be the boss's pretty daughter I've been hearing so much about."

I blushed, stammered, and fell in love right there on the spot, standing next to the Bunn coffee machine.

And he does look like Paul Newman, which is why I should be over the moon right now. A handsome husband with a job working for my dad at the biggest car dealership in the mid-Atlantic. A couple months pregnant and carrying a healthy baby, according to Dr. Carlyle.

But . . . I thought we'd have more time before the baby. We went to Florida for our honeymoon, we came home, and now I'm expecting. I wanted to try that new pill that keeps you from getting pregnant. Not forever, of course, but just to delay things for a little while, just for a year or two.

I asked Dr. Carlyle about it before the wedding and he told me I had to bring Dickie to my next appointment, that I needed my fiancé's permission before he'd write me a prescription.

And when I told Dickie, he looked at me like I was crazy.

"But honey, don't you want to be a mother?"

"I do but . . . I just turned 19. And you're only 23. Maybe we should wait . . . just a couple years. Maybe I don't want to share you yet," I added, pulling him closer.

He kissed me then and whispered in my ear and I forgot all about that pill until after the honeymoon and then it was too late.

There are . . . other things too . . . about Dickie. But maybe this is all just part of being married.

Like The List.

He says it's designed to help me be a better wife, to make our house run more smoothly. He sits me down every Sunday night in the den and we go over it together.

For example, on Fridays I'm supposed to wax and polish the linoleum, dust the baseboards and clean every silver, copper, and brass item in the house as well as the insides of the windows. On Mondays, I'm supposed to wash all the floor mats, in addition to laundering and ironing the sheets and all our clothes.

In the evening, I like to read. But instead I'm supposed to plan out my menu for the next day and make my grocery list so I'm never without the ingredients I need to make a proper three course meal for dinner each night. Not to mention all the baking I'm supposed to do.

I did all the cooking and some of the cleaning after Mother died, but we also had a housekeeper, so I guess I never realized how much work it takes to run a household.

I offered to give Dickie a list of things he can do as well. For example, he could put his underwear and dirty socks in the hamper instead of leaving them in the middle of the floor, and he could fix that little hole in the corner of the garage, so mice don't get into the fallout shelter underneath and eat up all our supplies. But Dickie just laughed and told me I'm hilarious. The list of household chores is for *me*, not him.

"Your dad gave us this beautiful home on this brand-new cul-de-sac. Don't you want to keep it nice?"

And then I felt guilty. Of course I want to keep a nice house. Of course I want to create a clean, comfortable home for Dickie to return to after work each day.

I guess I just didn't realize how much work is involved in being a new bride with a husband and a house to care for.

But maybe all married couples go through a period of adjustment. I just need to figure out how Dickie likes things, and then it will be easier.

Sometimes he gets so mad when things aren't the way he expects them to be, and I never know what might set him off. Like when I didn't fold his undershirts the way he likes. He ranted and raved for ten minutes. It reminded me of Danny's final letter from Viet Nam, where he talked about how the jungle was filled with hidden traps, how he had to watch every step when he went out on patrol.

But the rest of the time Dickie is so charming. To me, and everyone else too. Daddy thinks he hangs the moon.

Anyway, the whole gang had a nice little party for me on the sales floor over the lunch hour yesterday, and that was the end of my career at the dealership, where I've spent summers and weekends for as long as I can remember. I did a good job too. I've kept the books since I graduated from high school. I handled payroll. I even sold a car, once.

I guess they'll survive without me. But the mimeograph machine and my old Selectric might not make it. That new girl they hired to replace me doesn't seem very bright.

But maybe being bright doesn't matter as much as people think.

Danny was the smartest mechanic in the garage, and he died in Viet Nam because he couldn't afford to go to college and got drafted instead.

And I'm a math whiz. Valedictorian of my class at good old SMA. And look where I ended up. Right here in the kitchen, just like my mother. Pregnant and making pot roast.

Pot roast is #9 on Dickie's List of suggestions.

Chapter Seven

PIPER

Piper got in her car after the PTA meeting and glanced at her dashboard. Nineteen minutes until pickup. Not enough time to go home. Not enough time to make a full run at Target or the grocery store.

It always seemed to work out this way. She felt like she spent entire days killing odd amounts of time.

Seventeen minutes to kill between the end of school and Olivia's tap class. Twenty-three minutes to kill between voice lessons and the epic commute out to Caitlin's Irish dance class. Thirteen minutes to kill between Bella's ballet class and *SpongeBob* rehearsal.

Heaving a deep sigh, she put the car into gear and headed for the school pickup line.

She pulled in behind a gray minivan emblazoned with Minnesota Twins and Minnesota Vikings decals, a Hollin Terrace Elementary and Middle School bumper sticker (**WHERE LEARNING IS FUN!**) plus an assortment of busy badges for a dizzying array of hockey, baseball, and soccer teams. They even had a bumper sticker advertising their *orthodontist.*

She rolled her eyes. Did these people never think about security?

The rear of her car remained naked and unadorned. Political bumper stickers were an invitation for people on the opposite side of the ideological spectrum to cut you off in traffic. School and activity stickers told everyone who you were and where you were going. Why would anyone in their right mind do that?

"Because they have nothing to fear and nothing to hide."

That's what Trina, her federally mandated therapist, had said when she'd mentioned this particular form of vehicular insanity.

"Nice people support their school and their soccer league by giving them free advertising space on the back of their car," Trina had explained.

But of course, Trina could afford to think this way, because Trina didn't receive death threats from insane people on X.

Unlike Piper.

I have a special knife in my pocket right now. It's one I plan to use when I skin you alive.

Her muscles clenched as the latest message he'd posted on X last week echoed through her mind.

I can't wait to kill you slowly and watch you die. I'll start by removing your clothes. Then your fingers. You will feel the same pain you've inflicted on me.

She closed her eyes, took a deep breath, and visualized a box. She placed each word inside the box, shut the lid, turned a giant key, and locked it tight.

Then she opened her eyes, pulled out her phone, and typed a quick text message to Mike Rodriguez, her old boss.

Just checking in . . . anything new on Hawkeye Slaughter?

A few minutes went by; then the response came back. Call me.

Her heart dropped. This couldn't be good.

She punched in the number, and he picked up on the first ring.

"Here's the deal." Mike always cut right to the chase. She took a deep breath and steeled herself for whatever he was about to say. "Hawkeye is gone."

"What do you mean, he's *gone*?" The question came out an octave too high, shrill and laced with panic.

"He disappeared. He was last seen at an urban prepper expo two weeks ago in Virginia, taking selfies with his many YouTube fans. He said something about going dark to prepare for the 'Great Unraveling.' No one has seen him since."

"So we have no idea where he is?"

Mike sighed. "We think he purchased a property in the Shenandoah Valley, but he did it through an LLC, so it's harder to trace. He's much smarter than your average doomsday prophet slash posse comitatus nutjob."

"Great." She rubbed her hand across the back of her neck. "In a world filled with psychotic conspiracy theorists, I manage to piss off the smart one."

"He's well funded too. Don't forget that. He sold his check-cashing business right before his wife died, and he now has millions to play with."

"This is really disturbing, Mike."

"I know . . ." Mike admitted. "But maybe he's—"

"Taken up yoga and joined an ashram?" she offered hopefully.

"It's possible."

"But not probable," she said, her heart sinking.

"We do have one lead . . ."

She heard the pause in his voice, and it made her heart stop. "Yes?"

"Well, we think he may have joined forces with an antitechnology militia with ties to a violent domestic terror group. They just tried to burn a 5G cell phone tower near Richmond."

"What?" She stared up at the pen marks one of her children had somehow managed to scribble on the ceiling of her SUV. "Are you serious?"

"Yeah. I know. It's not good," Mike admitted. "We think this extremist group is running a training camp on the property he purchased. Based on some of the people he follows on Twitter—I mean X—and some of the things he's posted . . . well, we think he may have invited these groups to join him physically this time, not just ideologically."

She rubbed her temple, an ineffective attempt to ward off the early pricking of a massive stress-induced headache. "What kind of militia?"

"Oh, you know, garden-variety insanity. Anti–law enforcement. Anti–federal government. Anti-technology. Preparing for the coming revolution. That kind of thing."

"But I still don't understand why—"

"He lost his wife," Mike said gently. "They were married for twenty-eight years. Six months before she died, he lost his only child in a car accident. The kid was texting while driving. And as far as we can tell, those losses kind of . . . put him over the edge. Now he's an angry, violent man with a lot of money and nothing left to lose. And he blames technology for his son's death. He's started threatening tech-company CEOs. And he blames you for the loss of his wife."

"But I didn't—"

"Kill anyone?" he interrupted. "Of course you didn't. But you work for the federal government, and he needs a target for his rage. His wife could have had that heart attack sitting in her driveway. Instead she had it while sitting in the traffic jam we created by shutting down the Fourteenth Street Bridge."

"The traffic jam *I* created," she said bitterly.

"*We* created," he insisted. "There were at least fifteen people involved in that decision. You just happened to be the one sitting in the chair when the music stopped."

She leaned back against the headrest. "And now people are offering to weaponize his anger."

There was a beat of silence as Mike acknowledged the truth of this statement. Then he said, "I'll keep you posted. Try not to worry."

"That's like telling a fish not to swim."

"I know."

She ran a hand through her hair. "My girls are about to get in the car so . . ."

"I understand," Mike said. "Listen, we all know what this guy is threatening to do . . . and we're on it. I promise."

"Thanks, Mike."

"And we're keeping your seat warm. It's not the same without you . . . and those cupcakes Olivia makes."

She smiled. Olivia had discovered baking last year, and her experiments had kept the office well supplied with treats.

"I appreciate that. Talk to you later."

She pressed the red button on her phone, ending the call. Then she tossed it into her purse in frustration.

How was she supposed to protect her girls when she couldn't even protect herself?

Shouts, screams, and scratching noises brought her attention back to more immediate concerns.

She glanced out the window, where an ocean of children surrounded her SUV. The sounds of a zombie apocalypse and the sounds of children attempting to get in the car at the end of the school day were remarkably similar.

She pressed the unlock button, and Bella and Olivia climbed inside, both chattering like magpies.

Caitlin approached from the middle school side of the parking lot. She said nothing as she climbed into the car. Piper shot her a worried look. She'd seemed quieter since the conversation about Alex Orlov. More withdrawn.

But her sisters flooded the car with noise.

"Mom, did you order my new tap shoes?"

"Colton Lindenhurst *pulled his pants down* in PE today."

"*I'm starving.* Did you bring snacks?"

"I left my water bottle at home, and I was *dying of thirst all day.*"

Piper's conscience prickled with guilt. She had seen the forgotten water bottle on the kitchen counter after school drop-off that morning and pretended like she hadn't.

"Teddy Maxwell got a new pair of Nike tennis shoes that cost *$400*, and Gabriel Adelson smeared ketchup all over them at lunch. He was *so mad*."

She'd heard a mother of boys once complain that her sons didn't talk about their day. She'd jokingly asked Piper to provide a transcript of everything she heard in her car on the way home from school so she'd know what was going on.

A quiet car . . . What would that even be like? With self-reproach in her heart, she pushed away this temporary longing for silence. She wouldn't trade her beautiful, funny, chatty girls for anything on the planet. But sometimes . . . well, sometimes they were *a lot*.

"Move over, Bella, you're sitting on my *tiara*."

She headed left out of the school parking lot, and into an afternoon and evening of logistics calibrated down to the minute. Dance. Voice. Piano. Pick up sandwiches at Subway. Eat in the car. Then the big event of the day, Bella's opening night performance as a scallop in *SpongeBob: The Musical*.

Piper closed her eyes and tried to quell the anxious tension roiling her gut. Then she asked the universe to open the emergency supply of patience she would need to get through the rest of her day.

Chapter Eight

KIERSTEN

Questions about the diaries absorbed Kiersten's thoughts as she raced home from school pickup with the boys in the back of the minivan. *Who was Dottie? Why were her diaries hidden inside a set of encyclopedias? How did they end up in her basement? And where did all that cash come from?*

It was 4:32 p.m. before she finally managed to feed the boys, then hustle them out of the house and back into the minivan for the trip to Pennsylvania. She'd often wondered why the words *get in the car* weren't *strong enough* on their own, and why she always had to augment this phrase with amendments like *right this minute* or *now* or *before I lose my patience*.

A missing uniform shirt eventually found balled up under Matt's bed ensured that she would now leave just in time to hit peak rush hour traffic on the Beltway. A penalty administered by the universe for her many organizational failures, both in the laundry room and in life as a whole.

"Mom, why do *I* have to go to Matt's baseball tournament?" asked James, one of her perpetually aggrieved middle children.

"Because Dad is gone, and I cannot leave you home alone overnight at the age of nine or the police will come and charge me with a crime."

He squinted up at his mother, clearly unsure how much of this explanation was true and how much was hyperbole.

His eleven-year-old brother, Luke, snorted in derision as he climbed into the coveted third row. "You're too little to stay home alone."

"But I don't *want* to go to Pennsylvania," James said plaintively.

She flipped open the back hatch and inserted the many items piled beside the car: baseball bats, cleats, coolers, snacks, and overnight bags filled with goggles and swim trunks—because the team hotel had a pool—plus uniforms, one of which was *white*, for stunningly impractical reasons she would never understand.

As she finished, a flash of color in her neighbor's yard caught her eye.

"Mom, who's *that*?"

She turned to look, and her mouth dropped open.

In the yard next door, a tall blond woman raised her arms to the heavens like a priestess performing a powerful incantation and unfurled a blue-and-white-checked picnic blanket. She spread it under the enormous sweet gum tree in front of her beautifully restored mid-century home, tastefully decorated for fall with autumnal gourds.

Two little girls scampered onto the picnic blanket, clad in white eyelet dresses. The younger held a bouquet of wildflowers, which seemed to match the little crown of wildflowers adorning her head. The older girl unpacked what appeared to be a vintage china teapot with matching teacups and set them on a tray.

Like their mother, the girls were lovely. Hair so blond it looked white, with rosy cheeks and blue eyes. It looked like a Fairy-Tale Princess Convention. Perhaps the small woodland creatures were stuck at the registration desk waiting for their name tags and would show up later.

Kiersten realized she was staring. "Good afternoon!" she called out in her friendliest voice, to prove she wasn't a stalker.

Of course, her neighbor probably had lots of stalkers. Kiersten would be happy to have stalkers, too, if she could be six feet tall and skinny, with lustrous blond hair and children who could lay out an entire picnic basket without breaking anything, fighting, or shooting each other with Nerf bullets.

Her neighbor stepped gracefully over the teapot and crossed the yard toward her.

They hadn't actually met, but this neighbor had left a basket of delicious muffins on her front steps the day they moved in, along with a handwritten note on engraved stationery welcoming them to Beaverbrook Lane.

Kiersten racked her brain, trying to remember her neighbor's name before she reached the driveway. It was something vaguely horticultural. Camilla? Azelea? Jasmine?

"Hi!" the woman said in a cheerful voice. "I'm Aspen Davis."

"Kiersten Cleaver," she replied, extending her hand.

Aspen didn't shake her hand. Instead she embraced it, making a sort of hand sandwich between her own soft and manicured fingers.

Aspen looked her directly in the eye. "It is *so wonderful* to meet you."

Kiersten felt a little stunned by this earnest welcome. "It's a lovely day for a picnic," she finally managed, recovering the ability to speak.

Her neighbor squinted at the horizon. "It is. The light is perfect."

"We're heading to a travel baseball tournament, but maybe we can get together when we get back. If you have time," she added hastily. Perhaps spa treatments and shopping for picturesque aprons took up a large portion of her neighbor's day.

"Oh, I have lots of time," Aspen said with an airy wave.

"Where do your girls go to school?" Kiersten asked.

Aspen made an expansive gesture. "Here."

"Hollin Terrace?" Kiersten asked. "That's where the boys go too."

"No. I mean *here*. At home. We homeschool Felicity Grace and Ella Joy."

Kiersten felt herself blinking stupidly at these compound names and immediately felt inadequate for unimaginatively naming her children after their uncles and maternal and paternal grandfathers. Matthew. Luke. James. And Johnny. Sometimes she felt like an Uber driver for the apostles.

"Oh wow," Kiersten said. "That's impressive."

"It's actually so much easier." Aspen shaded her eyes with her hand and squinted up at the late-afternoon sun. "We used to run around to preschool and dance lessons and all those things. Then we decided to slow down and live with *intention*, you know?"

Kiersten didn't know, but she nodded as if she did.

"We summered in Scandinavia a few years ago," Aspen said, as if this explained it all, "and we sort of fell in love with the culture."

Kiersten wanted to be the kind of person who *summered.*

Instead, she was the kind of person who cleaned the walleye her husband caught at his family's mildewed lake cabin in northern Minnesota, while swatting away mosquitoes the size of baby flamingos.

"And we just decided, why not live this way all year round?" Aspen continued, eyes wide, radiating a sort of butter-churned earnestness. "You only get one life. Why not live the way you *really* want to live?"

Her question hit Kiersten between the eyes like a rock from a slingshot. *Why not live the way you really want to live?*

But before she could ponder this philosophy more fully, angry shouts from the minivan pulled her attention away from this prophet in ballet flats.

"You stole my charger," one of the boys hollered at his brother. Kiersten stifled a sigh. Time to hit the road.

She glanced at her watch. "I have to get going, but it was so nice to finally meet you. And thanks for the muffins when we moved in."

As she turned to leave, a strikingly handsome man approached and rested his hand on Aspen's shoulder. He wore a perfectly tailored sports coat with pressed khaki pants and a white shirt with no tie. He looked like a Brooks Brothers model at a party on someone's yacht.

He turned to her with a charming smile.

And you must be Ken. "I'm Kiersten," she said instead, extending her hand.

"Trey Davis." He squeezed her hand in a tight grip and flashed a dazzling smile, exposing arctic-white teeth. "Great to have you in the neighborhood. It's good to have another family with young kids here on the cul-de-sac."

"We didn't even know that house was on the market." Aspen stooped to adjust her daughter's flower garland.

"That's probably because it wasn't on the market," Kiersten said. "We met Henry and Myrtle DiLorenzo through a family friend. We did the whole transaction without a real estate agent."

"Saints preserve us." Trey spread his hands across his chest in mock horror. "We can't have any more of *that.*"

"Babe, let it go." Aspen punched her husband's shoulder playfully. "Trey and his dad are developers and home builders," she explained, turning back to Kiersten. "Trey also does real estate. He hates to see a great property sold to anyone but him."

Trey grinned down at his wife. "True. And if you ever decide to sell, let me know. You have a huge lot. With water views, if you cut down all those trees." Then his eyes narrowed. "I know how much you paid for it. The very definition of a steal."

Kiersten felt her face flush. Was he implying that they had somehow *defrauded* Henry and Myrtle?

"Grammy, Grampy, come say hello," Aspen called out, waving to an elderly couple making their way down the sidewalk.

They moved slowly, the husband tall and erect, while his wife, white haired and stooped with osteoporosis, clutched his arm for support.

She reminded Kiersten of a butterfly—fragile but lovely. Wrinkles creased her face, but high cheekbones and wide eyes hinted at beauty in her youth.

"I'm Margaret Davis," she said, giving Kiersten a faint smile.

The older man beside her didn't share his grandson's dimpled chin and chiseled jawline, but his white hair and erect posture gave him a courtly air.

"And I'm Richard Davis." He extended his hand. "Trey is our grandson, and Aspen is our granddaughter-in-law. And these beautiful little girls are our great-granddaughters."

"Nice to meet you," Kiersten said.

"We're about to have a tea party with Grammy here." Aspen gestured at the teapot and macarons the little girls had spread across the picnic blanket.

"As long as you help me up once I sit down," Margaret said. "Getting up is harder than it looks when you're eighty-one years old."

"Of course, Grammy. You know we will." Aspen turned to Kiersten with an adorable shrug. "Grammy is *super popular* on the 'Gram."

Kiersten blinked, suddenly feeling stupid. Was Aspen talking about Instagram? Or some entirely new form of Substack, Slack, Signal, Bluesky, WhatsApp, Discord, Snapchat, or Threads? Sometimes she wished people could go back to sending postcards and clipping articles from the newspaper, like her grandmother did. "Well, I don't want to keep you from your tea party," she said, manufacturing a smile.

"We're *super* glad you're here," Aspen said, radiating warmth. "And we'd love to get to know you and your boys. And your husband too. Come say hi when you get back. We're always home. Stop by anytime."

Kiersten nodded. "I'll do that."

"Nice to meet you," Trey called out without looking up from his phone.

Kiersten gave a cheery goodbye wave as she retreated through the border of hydrangeas marking the property line.

She hauled herself into the driver's seat of her minivan, and her smile evaporated when a rolled-up sock flew through the air and bounced off the back of her head. One of the boys had chucked it at Matthew, who as the oldest brother had claimed the right to sit in the front passenger seat.

She tossed the sock behind her as her mind replayed the conversation she'd just had with her new neighbors. She wasn't entirely sure about Trey, the husband. He reminded her of Garrett's boss, the secretary of agriculture, who she'd met at her one and only Washington cocktail party, a man who constantly scanned the room, looking for someone more important to talk with.

But Aspen and the old couple seemed lovely.

She cast an envious glance at her neighbor as she left the cul-de-sac and began her interminable rush hour journey toward the Mystic Hills baseball complex in Pennsylvania, where she would spend the weekend with hundreds of other baseball-obsessed parents and kids.

What would it be like, to drop out of everything? To be home all the time manifesting abundance in a cotton apron while your children played harmoniously in the backyard?

A Nerf bullet whizzed past her ear. She swore under her breath and yelled, "Knock. It. Off."

She glanced in the rearview mirror. The back of the minivan looked like a homeless encampment. Each boy sat huddled under a blanket to block out the light, watching movies or, far more likely, inappropriate YouTube videos on their iPads.

When she looked away, one last Nerf bullet sailed toward the front of the car. She sighed. How many times had she told them not to fire weapons inside a moving vehicle?

Normally at this point, she'd stop the car and threaten to turn around and go home *right this instant* if they didn't stop.

But that only worked if her passengers actually wanted to reach their destination. If she threatened to turn the car around now, everyone would cheer.

Why was she always driving to places no one wanted to go?

Was Aspen Davis right? Could her family really travel a completely different road?

Chapter Nine

PIPER

Late Saturday afternoon, Piper collapsed onto her sofa after surviving the second of six performances of *SpongeBob: The Musical.*

She'd been a green room monitor for today's matinee performance, and the sardines would *not* stop talking. She'd aggressively blinked the lights in the classroom where everyone collected "backstage" between scenes, and tried to restore order.

Then a member of the sea anemone chorus lost one of her tap shoes right before the big number with Squidward. They found it in the prop bag about thirty seconds before she had to go onstage.

Piper had witnessed coups and international incidents that were less stressful than one afternoon as a children's theater volunteer. She didn't know how the directors and producers not only survived but rose to the occasion and volunteered to put on a new show again year after year.

She'd changed into sweatpants and settled onto the sofa with a cup of tea, preparing to enter the safe and peaceful world of the *Great British Baking Show*. She personally did not enjoy baking, but she loved visiting a place where tragedy consisted of a Victoria sponge with a soggy bottom.

But it took her a full five minutes to find the show using their incredibly complicated television / remote control system. Was it on

BritBox? Hulu? Or Netflix? And why did they have both Disney+ *and* Paramount+? And what exactly was Pluto? And Roku? Did they need that too?

Just when she finally settled down to watch regular British citizens create four-layer cakes incorporating six kinds of buttercream, her daughter Caitlin hurtled into the family room with tears streaming down her face.

Piper's stomach clenched. She clicked off the TV and reached for her daughter. "Honey? What's wrong?"

Caitlin tossed her iPad into her mother's lap and threw herself down on the couch beside her. "Look."

Piper glanced down at a grainy image with the words *Caitlin's Ass* superimposed over the picture.

Her heart dropped. "What is this?"

"It's my *butt*," Caitlin wailed.

Piper shook her head, trying to understand why her daughter's butt was on the internet. *"What?"*

"From PE yesterday." Caitlin's voice trembled, thick with tears. "We were playing volleyball. I bent over to serve, and Alex Orlov took a picture of me from behind. And then he texted it to all the boys in my class. It's everywhere. Someone took a screenshot and sent it to me. People are posting it on Instagram with the caption 'Caitlin's Ass.'"

Piper's mouth dropped open. Then rage tore through her. "This is the most inappropriate, unacceptable, rotten—"

Caitlin's beautiful tear-stained face silenced her.

She doesn't need anger. She needs love. And protection.

She wrapped her arms around her daughter and took a deep breath. "I'm sorry this is happening, Caitlin. It isn't fair. It isn't right, and I am going to end it. Right now."

Silently berating herself for not being tougher on the principal yesterday, she rose from the couch and headed for the small office she shared with her husband.

She should have done this the moment that boy started texting Caitlin. Bullies didn't stop until you made them stop. Hadn't she learned that lesson herself at nine years old?

She yanked open a desk drawer, pulled out the school directory, grabbed her purse, and returned to the family room.

"Where are you going?" Caitlin asked, her voice pitched high in alarm.

"To have a conversation with Alex Orlov's parents."

"Mom. *No.*"

"Caitlin." She sat down and clasped her daughter's hands, looking her straight in the eye. "This situation is escalating. The picture is bad enough, but at least you're wearing long PE shorts and we can't see your face, and no one is using your full name."

But what if he starts posting deepfakes? What if he superimposes Caitlin's face on a porn star's body? What if he posts her full name and date of birth and address?

Her daughter's future imploded before her eyes. Images like this could destroy a woman's life. College admission, denied. Job interviews, withheld. And when she got old enough to start dating, the images would repel decent men and attract sick ones.

"We need this to stop *now*," Piper said firmly.

Tears streamed down Caitlin's face. Finally, she nodded. "Okay."

Piper pinched the bridge of her nose, forcing herself to stop reacting and start *thinking*.

Should she call? Or show up unannounced on their doorstep and have this conversation in person?

Knowledge was power, and she needed to know more about these people. Did they have a Toyota in the driveway or a Maserati? A modest home or a mansion? Maybe they were hardworking immigrants. Or conscientious federal employees like her and her husband and almost everyone else she knew here in the DC suburbs. Maybe they were Hill staffers or lobbyists or lawyers.

Or maybe they were something else.

Piper rose from the couch and headed for the mudroom. "You're in charge of your sisters until I get back," she called to Caitlin as she pulled on her shoes. "Text me with your iPad if you need anything. Or call on the landline. I'll be back as soon as I can."

If only she knew her neighbors better. At age thirteen, Caitlin was old enough to babysit other people's kids, but it still didn't feel right to leave the girls alone right now.

Especially after what she'd found last night when they got home from the opening night performance of *SpongeBob*.

She tried to push the image out of her mind as she grabbed the school directory and got in the car.

But it lingered. A piece of notebook paper smeared with what looked like blood, nailed to the trunk of a tree in front of the house. **I KNOW WHERE YOU LIVE** written in block letters with a black marker. She'd taken a picture and texted it to Mike Rodriquez. Wearing gloves, she'd zipped it into a plastic bag. He asked her to bring it into the office on Monday.

Disgusting. Deliberate. And just out of range of the Ring camera.

Hawkeye Slaughter's most recent threat echoed in her mind.

I can't wait to kill you slowly and watch you die.

Shuddering, she slammed the car door. She only had the bandwidth for one crisis at a time.

Her stomach twisted in a knot as she squinted down at the address in the directory: 783 Potomac Shores.

An exclusive neighborhood, overlooking the river. She'd heard the governor lived near here, in a huge house with his wife, Ainsley, and their kids.

The former owner of the Washington Commanders had a home down there too. It was on the market for something like $35 million. She and her husband had joked about putting in an offer before they bought their house on Beaverbrook Lane four years ago.

She swallowed a sigh. If only he were here right now. Brendan's height and build were average, but he had *presence*, and he radiated quiet intimidation when necessary.

Like on their flight to Orlando for that Disney trip last spring. The obnoxious man sitting across the aisle made the flight attendant cry. When the drink cart passed, Brendan stood, put a hand on the man's shoulder, and whispered a few words into his ear. The man turned pale and did not speak another word for the rest of the flight.

Of course, none of this mattered because Brendan wasn't here. As usual. Leaving her to handle yet another domestic drama alone.

She punched the address into the GPS and tossed the directory into the passenger seat.

Then she squared her shoulders. She could handle this. She'd once negotiated with a mad doomsday prophet in Idaho and gotten him to release the twenty-three women and children locked inside his compound, unharmed. She'd protected diplomats from terrorists in war zones.

But she'd also brought the entire DC metro area to a standstill. All because she chose to believe the schizophrenic man who said his white panel van was filled with explosives when he parked it next to the Lincoln Memorial and refused to move.

She'd looked at the information, made a determination of threat, and been wrong.

And maybe she was wrong again now.

Maybe Alex Orlov's parents were lovely, responsible people who had no idea what their son was doing.

Maybe they'd understand, even be grateful she was bringing the issue to their attention.

Thus armed with a positive attitude instead of her service weapon, she headed for the big houses overlooking the Potomac.

Chapter Ten

KIERSTEN

On Saturday afternoon, Kiersten herded her children to a lonely corner on the left side of the dugout for Matt's second game of the day and set up camp. The other team parents sat together in a little cluster of lawn chairs on the right side of the field, a settlement that did not welcome outsiders.

Most of the kids on this travel team had been playing together for years, and their parents had apparently decided they didn't have space in their lives for new friends.

She didn't blame them. How many times had she done the same thing? Engrossed in a conversation with her buddies, failing to notice, much less include, someone new, someone she didn't know.

She'd tried to focus on the game but found no comfort there either. Matt had pitched four perfect innings in the first game; then he fell apart. In the second game, he struck out early and missed an easy pop fly. The coach benched him and put someone else on the mound as he sat in the dugout, icing his shoulder.

Gratitude stole over her, followed by a sharp pang of guilt as she realized the combination of a second loss and torrential rain in the forecast meant tomorrow morning's game would be canceled. If they won, they'd have to stay over. But if they lost, they could go home tonight.

Was there a German word for this parental mixed feeling of relief and guilt, like *loserfreude* or *guiltenschnapple*?

With her other boys playing happily with a gang of younger siblings and a soccer ball a few yards away, and Matt sitting on the bench, she gave up all pretense of watching the game and reached into her purse for the diary she'd found in the basement.

After a furtive glance at the loyal and committed baseball parents who cared deeply about the outcome of the game, she managed to shield the open diary with her purse and began to read.

Chapter Eleven

DOTTIE

March 15, 1965

I have every modern, time saving appliance a woman could possibly want in this lovely new house Daddy bought for us. I have a clothes washing machine and a dryer and a new Frigidaire.

But there still aren't enough hours in a day to do all the things necessary to keep this house clean. Or at least up to Dickie's standards for cleanliness.

When he puts on his white glove and runs his finger over the top of the kitchen cupboards, he somehow still finds dust, even though I dust religiously. It feels like all I do is wax and scrub and iron and clean, all day long.

There are lots of other nice young couples in this new neighborhood, but most of them are busy with children. I'd like to get to know them, but Dickie says I can't waste time having coffee with the neighbors until all my chores are done, and my chores are never done.

He makes me keep track of how I spend my day in a little notebook. I have to account for every hour. Sometimes I write down something like this:

1 to 2 p.m. Washed the baseboards

And then I sit down, put my feet up on the hassock and read a book for a whole damn hour instead, just to spite him.

I know I shouldn't feel this way, wanting to spite my husband. But I can't help it. I told him I don't need his advice on how to run our household.

And he told me I'm young and new to all this, so I need *direction*. Like he's a wise old man who's been married for forty years or something. He's only four years older than I am.

Anyway, there's a whole army of women home all day on our cul-de-sac, and I'd love to get to know them better, but in addition to all my chores, I've got pretty bad morning sickness, which should really be called All Day Sickness because I feel like upchucking *all the time*. But maybe I'll work faster and be able to join the ladies for coffee when I'm a little further along and feeling better.

Ruby says the morning sickness should end in a couple weeks, when the first trimester ends. I wish my mother were here to answer questions about things like this, but she isn't, so I'm awfully glad I have Ruby.

I finally went and saw her last week and brought a gift for her beautiful new baby. Now that Dickie and I are living on the other side of town, I don't see her as much as I used to. Dickie drives the car to work, so I have to take the bus.

Daddy offered to give us a second car, but Dickie says we have to stand on our own two feet. I notice that he was happy to take this house Daddy offered, and the country club membership, and the car *Dickie* drives, but when it's a car for *me*, well, then Dickie suddenly wants to hold the line and be independent.

Anyway, this is one of the ways Dickie makes it difficult for me to get together with Ruby. Last time I saw her, she lent me her copy of *The Feminine Mystique*, that new book everyone's talking about. Dickie saw it sitting on my nightstand and he picked it up, walked out to the garage and tossed it in the trash can.

Now he calls her "Radical Ruby" and told me I shouldn't talk to her anymore. Dickie gives everyone little nicknames. When he's unhappy with me, he calls me Dottie the Dimwit. Makes me feel about two feet tall.

So I might have given Dickie the impression that I was at the dentist this morning . . . when I was actually visiting Ruby.

I don't like lying to him, but Ruby's been my best friend since second grade, and I'm not going to stop seeing her just because Dickie disapproves of her taste in books.

But at least he's excited about the baby. That seems to be the only time we get along lately, is when we talk about the baby, plan for the baby, discuss names for the baby. If it's a boy we'll name him Gerald, after my dad, and if it's a girl we'll name her Priscilla, after Dickie's mom, who passed away a few years ago.

I can't wait to be a mother. And I'm sure everything will be better between Dickie and me, once we have a baby in the house.

Chapter Twelve

KIERSTEN

"Mom. Can we go now?"

Kiersten squinted up at the circle of boys staring down at her, disoriented to find her body at a baseball game in Pennsylvania 2025 while her mind remained on Beaverbrook Lane in 1965.

Who was Dickie, and why was he such a jerk? And how had Dottie's diaries ended up in *her* basement?

Matt tossed his glove onto the picnic blanket and sprawled down beside her lawn chair.

"Did we lose?" she asked, trying to keep the hopeful note from her voice.

His mouth puckered in irritation. "Yeah, thanks to me, and the first baseman, and the three other guys who struck out. We sucked. It was a slaughter."

"I'm sorry, honey."

As she folded up the blankets and lawn chairs, she considered the end result of this expedition.

She'd driven three hours in a minivan with four kids so her son could lose to neighboring teams from Falls Church and Arlington. They could have skipped the drive and the hotel and played each other on a field fifteen minutes from home instead. With a sigh of resignation, she herded the boys back to the car.

She punched "Home" on the GPS and then watched in dismay as the roadways on the fastest route available turned from blue to red. An accident somewhere.

She said a prayer, then leaned forward in the driver's seat, shoulders hunched around her ears, fingers gripping the steering wheel, and plunged into the sea of cars.

"Mom, I'm hungry," Johnny called from the third row.

She ignored this and grasped the steering wheel tighter.

Driving through rural Minnesota on a summer day felt like a form of *meditation*. Wide, sparsely trafficked highways winding through neatly planted rows of corn and soybeans under the cobalt dome of an endless sky, like a road trip through the Elysian Fields.

But *this* . . . this East Coast driving felt like hurtling through a vortex into the opening montage of *The Sopranos*. Careening down six lanes of traffic at seventy miles an hour, surrounded by smokestacks and concrete, boxed in by eighteen-wheelers. It induced a sort of vehicular claustrophobia.

An hour later, Matt frowned at her from the passenger seat. "Mom, I have to go to the bathroom."

These were the first words he'd spoken since getting into the car. His brooding silence spoke volumes about the game and his performance.

She answered, gaze firmly glued to the highway. "I'm trying to find that truck stop we heard about with the Subway *and* the Burger King."

Because no one could possibly be expected to agree on one fast-food restaurant. They needed to stop at the travel plaza with options for every palate in the car.

"Mom. Are we there yet? I'm *starving*," James called from the row directly behind her.

She turned off at the next exit, as directed by the GPS, and pulled into the parking lot of a massive truck stop called Big Jim's.

"We're here," she called in a cheery voice for the benefit of Luke, who had not complained about hunger, thirst, or a full bladder, and must therefore be asleep beneath his blanket tent. After another reminder, he emerged from his cocoon, groggy, with his hair sticking up.

She climbed out of the car, limbs stiff with tension. She needed this break for food and drink even more than the boys did.

They entered the crowded truck stop, and she clutched Johnny's hand. At age eight, he was the only child who would still condescend to hold her hand in public.

Anodyne '80s music washed over them, then faded into the background as they entered the food court, where tired travelers queued up for pizza, Doritos, and caffeine.

She spotted two families from Matt's team seated at a cluster of tables near Auntie Anne's pretzels. They gave a half-hearted wave but did not issue an invitation to join them.

Kiersten bit her lip and herded the boys around the travel plaza with her credit card. Burger King for Matt, Roy Rogers for Luke, Subway for James, Pizza Hut for Johnny.

They sat down at a little cluster of scratched metal tables and ate in tired silence.

"Does anyone need to use the restroom again?" she asked when they finished.

They shook their heads.

"Okay," she said. "I need to use the ladies' room."

The boys had used the bathroom when they first arrived, while she kept watch just outside. It still creeped her out to send her boys into the men's restroom alone, even though Matt was responsible enough to look after his younger brothers. She'd stood sentry at the entrance, with a Those Boys Have a Mother Who Is Paying Attention look on her face, as a warning to prospective kidnappers, pedophiles, and fugitives from justice.

She gave Matt the keys to the minivan. "You boys throw away your trash while I use the ladies' room. I'll meet you in the car."

She used the facilities, then caught a glimpse of herself in the mirror as she washed her hands.

The dingy fluorescent light accentuated the dark circles under her eyes. Her gaze traveled from her limp hair to her squashy midsection, and then to the pizza stain on her T-shirt.

She had *wanted* to eat something healthy, she really and truly had, but the three carrot sticks with hummus in the "healthy" section of the truck stop convenience store were no match for her screaming hunger pangs. So she'd eaten the remnants of the french fries and pizza left by her offspring.

She examined her face more closely. Was that facial hair? On her *upper lip*?

She'd become a crone. A *death* crone. She'd reached the age when, according to a History Channel special she'd watched one night when her husband was out of town and she was too tired to get up off the couch and go to bed, her Stone Age tribe would march her out to the tundra and urge her to take the Long Walk.

Given that she was the most decrepit member of the clan, her death would allow the others to successfully ration the remains of the wooly mammoth they'd just killed and survive the winter.

Leaning forward, she looked at herself again. Really looked this time.

What had become of her? The witty person who excelled at Scrabble and loved Jane Austen novels and had friends to sit with at children's sporting events? The emergency room nurse who specialized in making trauma patients feel both safe and comfortable? The high school basketball star who'd led her tiny hometown to victory in the state tournament so many years ago?

Where had that person gone? And how had this become her life?

No friends. No hobbies. No profound thoughts on books, movies, politics, religion, war, peace, AI, or the future of humanity. Just damp, stringy hair in a pizza-stained T-shirt and jeans that no longer fit, listening to "Jessie's Girl" play through tinny speakers at a truck stop on the Pennsylvania Turnpike at five o'clock on a Saturday night.

Heaving a sigh that emanated from the very marrow of her bones, she left the restroom and walked back to the minivan. An indecisive rain began to spit down from the sky, casting a fine mist that shrouded the world in gray.

She got in the car and glanced in the rearview mirror. The little blanket settlement was back up again. She couldn't see faces. Just lumps.

"Everyone ready?"

Now it began to pour, fat drops thumping the roof of the minivan.

She called out again, louder this time, pitching her voice above the pounding rain.

The boys didn't respond, probably because they were wearing headphones.

Too tired to harangue them for a response, she pulled out of the parking lot, headlights cutting through fine needles of rain, and headed home.

Chapter Thirteen

PIPER

Piper turned off the GW Parkway, then turned right again, onto a smaller road that twisted downward, toward the Potomac.

The road ended abruptly at a cul-de-sac where six massive homes sat side by side, fronting the river. She slowed her car and took in the scene, trying to figure out where to park.

Tasteful landscaping lights illuminated five of the homes. A homey yellow glow emanated from somewhere deep inside each one, probably a family room or a kitchen with river views on the backside of the house.

But the home in the center blazed like a sparkler at midnight on the Fourth of July, every door and window open, spilling wanton light into the rising dusk of a mid-September sky.

And not just light . . . but sound too. She cocked her head and listened as thumping bass notes infiltrated her car.

A suburban block party . . . or a rave?

She opened the driver's side door and stood on the running board of her SUV, craning her neck as she tried to see around the corner of the house, searching for the bouncy house, or the Build-A-Bear mobile workshop, or the American Girl doll tea party, or even just a lone magician.

Instead her gaze landed on a tiki bar beside the pool and a woman wearing a vintage cigarette girl costume with an ostrich plume in her hair, handing out Jell-O shots in small plastic cups.

Piper gripped her purse a little tighter. This was *not* what she expected when she set out to speak to the fellow parents of a Hollin Terrace Middle School student.

She glanced at the number above the front door: 783 Potomac Shores.

The right house, but everything felt wrong.

In her experience, people with school-age children did not have the energy to attend, much less throw, wild parties with thumping bass music.

Wild parties were tossed overboard the moment parents arrived home from the hospital with their first child and sleep suddenly became the single most important survival tool in the parenting lifeboat.

Maybe that's why this party was happening at 6:00 p.m.? Maybe these people had found a way to combine the pleasures of youth with the responsibilities of middle age? Maybe their parties began after the last youth soccer game of the afternoon ended and wrapped up promptly at 10:00 p.m., when it was time to take the babysitter home?

She glanced up at the stone-and-stucco house as a blond woman in a low-cut sequined dress waved energetically from a turret and hollered to someone named Trey.

Were Italian villas supposed to have *turrets*?

Admittedly, she was not an architectural critic. But the scale seemed off somehow, the proportions wrong. Like a Disney version of an Italian villa, rather than an *actual* Italian villa.

Or maybe this house was perfect in every way and she was just jealous because it probably had massive closets *and* a walk-in pantry, while she had to share a closet with her husband and keep half her wardrobe in plastic bins under the bed and switch everything out when the weather changed.

She got out of the car, straightened her shoulders, and clicked her key fob. Party or not, she needed to go inside and get this over with.

She wove through the cars that lined the cul-de-sac, an odd assortment of high and low, with BMWs, Mercedes, and Teslas parked beside Ford Fiestas, Dodge Darts, and a Honda Civic that had clearly seen better days.

Her eyes narrowed. Not a single minivan.

None of the cars sported bumper stickers, either, touting the Mount Vernon Soccer League, the Potomac Landing Gators Swim Team, or Ollie the Owl, the Hollin Terrace school mascot, who sat on a pile of books clutching in his talons a scroll emblazoned with the words **LEARNING IS FUN**.

Ahead of her, a very attractive couple in their early twenties climbed the steps to the front door, which stood wide open.

She followed behind them and stepped into a raging party.

Either Alex Orlov lived in the Barbie Dreamhouse or her daughter was being harassed by the Great Gatsby of Hollin Terrace Middle School.

Had she somehow wandered into one of those really hip whiskey commercials that ran during NFL games? Or an old Benetton ad?

The young people were an arresting mix of global beauty, like a Miss Universe pageant for men and women. Even the White people didn't look like *domestic* White people. They looked European somehow—Scandinavian or possibly Russian.

Maybe one of the Bright Young Things could help. She tapped the shoulder of an elegant woman with lush dark hair in a strapless dress. "Excuse me, I'm looking for the people who live here."

"You mean Bruno?"

Did she mean Bruno? Bruce and Irina Orlov were listed in the directory as Alex's parents. Bruce could be Bruno.

"Yes. I think so," she said, almost shouting to make her voice heard above the music.

The woman raised a bare shoulder in a half shrug. "Try the basement." Then she turned back to her partner and continued her conversation.

Piper gave her a tight smile. "Thank you."

She'd faced armed and dangerous people over the years, but she'd never realized before that beauty could also be a weapon. She hoped that when her own daughter grew up to be impossibly gorgeous, she would also be kind.

Maneuvering through the crowd, she made her way down the stairs and into a rec room with a billiard table in the center of the room. Six television screens hung on the main wall, each displaying a different sporting event.

A soccer match took pride of place on the biggest screen, in the center of the wall. Her eyes narrowed as she glanced at Cyrillic lettering on the back of the jerseys. A team with a lion logo played a team with an ornate letter *D* on their uniforms.

She approached a group of men clustered in front of the screens, picking up snatches of conversation peppered with phrases like "parlay" and "over-under."

Sports betting. Not illegal. Necessarily.

She cleared her throat. "I'm looking for Bruno."

The group went silent; then a large man with small eyes stepped forward. "I'm Bruno."

He had the face of a boxer. His nose had obviously been broken, possibly more than once, and his features were thick, as though he'd been drawn with a Sharpie instead of a pencil. Blond, with sharp blue eyes, he looked like a henchman in a Bond movie.

He wore a blue polo shirt with an ornate *D* embroidered over his heart, the same *D* worn by the soccer players running across the TV on the wall.

"Lovely party," she said, fabricating her most disarming smile.

He moved closer. "I don't think we've met."

The alcohol on his breath tickled her nose, but she couldn't read his tone or his expression.

"Sorry for crashing," she said with a little shrug. "But our kids go to school together, and I need to speak with you . . . privately."

He gave her an appraising look. Then he said, "Follow me."

She could feel the men in the basement watching as they left the room. Weaving through the partygoers, he led her up the stairs to an office on the main floor. He opened the door and gestured her inside.

A whisper of fear caressed the back of her neck as he pulled the door shut with a soft click.

How many times had she told the young women taking her self-defense classes to read Gavin de Becker's book *The Gift of Fear*? How many times had she told them to listen to that prickle of unease?

And now here she was, in an enclosed space with a man she didn't know, failing to follow her own advice.

She reached inside her purse and surreptitiously removed her keys, and the Mace attached to her key chain, fisting them inside her closed palm.

She'd had this key chain for years. Did Mace degrade over time? Did it have an expiration date, like canned tuna? Expired Mace was such a poor substitute for the Glock she'd always carried for work.

Focus, Piper.

She took a steadying breath as Bruno moved to a table beside the empty fireplace and filled a crystal glass with amber liquid from a decanter.

"Drink?" he asked, raising the glass.

She'd addressed this exact situation when she taught self-defense classes. *Never accept an opened drink from a strange man.*

"No, thanks."

"Suit yourself." He took a sip, then moved to the leather wingback chair behind an enormous mahogany desk in the center of the room.

"Please, sit." He gestured to a leather chair in front of the desk. Smaller. Lower. The supplicant's chair.

She sat with her purse on her knees, keeping her fist hidden behind it. Suddenly she felt silly, like a little old lady gripping her handbag to ward off pickpockets.

Relax. He's a fellow parent. Not Pablo Escobar. Or some guy trying to roofie a coed in a college bar.

She glanced around the room. Dark wood paneling, a chess set in front of the window. Bookshelves lined one wall, but she noticed the shelves held no actual books.

"So," he began. "You are a mother . . . from the school?" He spoke with an accent, but she couldn't place it.

"Yes. My name is Piper Mondello. Your son Alex and my daughter Caitlin are classmates."

"How nice." He gazed at her under heavy-lidded eyes. "So what can I do for you?"

His accent tugged at her mind. Azerbaijan? Valletta? One of the former Soviet satellite states?

She relaxed her grip on the keys and pulled out her phone. She held up a screenshot. "Your son took a picture of my daughter's butt during PE class and posted it on Instagram. Then he made an account called Caitlin's Ass."

He looked at her evenly. Then he shrugged. "Boys will be boys."

She tossed the phone back into her purse and clenched her fist around her keys again. "What he's doing is illegal. It's online harassment. We could have him expelled. We could take him to court. He could be charged with disseminating child pornography."

She wasn't entirely sure if this was true. The law hadn't caught up with the technology in most states. Penalties were sketchy when it came to adult online harassment, and even murkier where juveniles were involved. But it could be true—it *should* be true, damn it. She threw it out there so he'd take the situation seriously.

It didn't work. He looked completely unfazed. "I will tell him to delete this. Is that what you want?"

"It's a start," she said, keeping her voice cool, unemotional. "I also want him to stop speaking to my daughter, to stop texting her, to stop taking her picture, and to leave her alone. He's sexually harassing her. And it needs to stop."

He tilted his head. "You look familiar."

Oh no. Not this again. He didn't look like the kind of person who read *The Washington Post*. He looked like the kind of person who got his news from scantily clad women in TikTok videos. But still. He probably watched cable TV, and they'd had a field day with the Incident on Fox and CNN.

"I very much doubt we've met at a PTA meeting."

His eyes narrowed. "I never forget a name. Or a face."

Was that a threat? The fear rose first, skittering across her skin like an insect, followed by a sharp stab of anger. She lifted her chin, nostrils flaring.

"You will tell your son to stay away from my daughter and delete the account and the picture, correct?"

"Yes. I will ask him to do this."

"No. You will *tell him* to do this."

His face remained expressionless. "Fine."

"Good."

"So what's the occasion?" she asked, breaking a silence that grew more menacing the longer it continued.

"What do you mean?"

She jutted her chin in the direction of the noise outside the door. "The party."

"My wife and I are social people. We run a business, and this is just a little gathering, for our special friends."

"Is it legal?" she asked sweetly.

He threw his head back and laughed. "Mostly."

"Money laundering? Uranium smuggling?" she suggested with a bright, false smile.

"Property development."

Property development, my ass.

She'd seen a lot of shady characters in her career. And she'd found that shady characters were almost invariably flashy as well—an odd, but reliably consistent combination of traits. And this Bruno character screamed shady, from the gold chain at his throat to the expensive Ferragamo loafers on his feet.

"Property development." She rose from her chair. "Right. Of course."

She was done listening to this man. She'd call in some favors and learn everything she could.

"I understand you have a small but lovely home, Mrs. Mondello."

She froze.

"A lovely home on Beaverbrook Lane, if I'm correct," he continued, gazing at her over the rim of his glass.

The back of her neck prickled. "How do you know where I live?"

"The same way you know where *I* live." He made an expansive gesture with his arms. "The school directory works both ways, you know."

"Is that a threat?" she asked quietly, heart thudding so loudly she was afraid he could hear it.

"On the contrary." He spread his fingers over his chest in an expression of innocence. "It's a compliment. You have lovely river views."

Her eyes narrowed. "Only in the winter."

"Yes," he said softly. "Only in the winter."

Silence filled the room again as her mind raced. He didn't know she'd be coming. He couldn't have looked her up in the directory. *So how did he know where she lived?*

Then he stood. "Thank you for coming, Mrs. Mondello."

"Have a good evening," she said stiffly. Then she turned and left the room. Pushing through the party, she made her way back to the car. She climbed inside and locked the door. Her foot trembled as she slammed down on the accelerator, spun out of the driveway, and raced home.

Chapter Fourteen

KIERSTEN

Kiersten pulled into her driveway at a little after 7:00 p.m. The rain had let up as they crossed the Woodrow Wilson Bridge and entered Old Town, where Mother Nature decided to atone for the harrowing drive through a downpour by treating them to a brilliant sunset, complete with a rainbow over the Potomac, as they drove south on the George Washington Memorial Parkway toward home.

"Guys," she ordered as she pulled into the driveway, "you must help carry things into the house."

She'd seen this movie before. Her children would bolt from the car and run upstairs to their bedrooms, leaving her to make nine trips back and forth to the house, carrying blankets, pillows, snacks, and gear inside.

As she opened the rear hatch, an almost paralyzing wave of anxiety washed over her.

Something isn't right.

This feeling of unease had dogged her for miles. Ever since that pit stop at Big Jim's Travel Plaza.

Something isn't right.

Her mind had repeated these words over and over again as she'd dodged eighteen-wheelers in the sheeting rain.

Something isn't right.

The boys emerged from the car like slugs and stood stretching in the driveway.

She looked at the boys.

One boy. Two boys. Three boys.

Three. Boys.

When she had four sons.

"Guys, where is Johnny?"

The boys all looked at each other.

"I dunno." Luke gave a sullen shrug. "I'm not my brother's keeper." Years of Lutheran church and Sunday school, and this was the only Bible verse that had made an impression.

"Stand still." She felt all the blood drain from her face. "No one move."

She ran into the backyard, calling Johnny's name. She ran into the garage, filled with empty packing boxes. "Johnny? Johnny, are you *here*?"

Her voice rose an octave each time she shouted his name as panic shot up her spine.

He couldn't be in the house. Because the house was locked. But she unlocked the front door anyway, threw it open, and ran through each room, shouting his name.

"Johnny? Where are you?"

Silence.

She flung herself back down the stairs, through the mudroom, and into the driveway, where the boys stood, their faces pale and horrified. She hurled the minivan door wide open and plunged inside, ripping apart the blankets and pillows.

Corn chips. Water bottles. iPads.

But no Johnny.

She climbed out of the vehicle and sank to her knees in the driveway. Was this real? Or was it a nightmare?

She pressed her hands into her skull, felt the pinprick of pain as her nails dug into her scalp.

Wide awake. Not a nightmare.

Dear God. What have I done?

"Mom, where's Johnny?" Matt's thirteen-year-old voice cracked with emotion.

"Where's Johnny?" Luke repeated, his voice thick with fear.

"Did we leave *without Johnny*?" James shrieked, every syllable pitched with horror.

She had forgotten many things in her life. Car keys. Sunglasses. Her phone. Even her purse.

But now she had actually lost *an entire child.*

Johnny had no phone. Johnny was only *eight years old.*

And she'd left him. Left him at a truck stop on the Pennsylvania Turnpike.

She cast her mind frantically over their last stop. They finished eating. She told the boys to get in the car while she used the restroom.

Then she just got in the car and drove away. She thought he was under the blankets. But she didn't check to make sure.

And that—

She looked at her watch.

That was TWO HOURS AGO.

She struggled to her feet, clutched the side of the minivan, and vomited.

Chapter Fifteen

PIPER

Piper pulled into her driveway, stopped the car, and then stared, perplexed at the strange little tableau next door.

Three boys stood beside a minivan with all the doors flung open. The older boys wore a catatonic expression while the youngest openly sobbed.

Meanwhile her neighbor . . . what was her name? Cathy? Caroline? She'd only met this neighbor once, briefly, the day they moved in.

Whatever her name, this woman stood beside her minivan, bent at the waist, shoulders heaving as she . . .

Vomited?

Piper squinted. Yup. That's right. Her neighbor was vomiting all over the driveway.

The woman's face was paper white with a clammy sheen. Piper had seen that look before on diplomats attempting to power through state dinners while suffering the double whammy of jet lag and a don't-drink-the-water stomach bug.

She opened the center console of her SUV and grabbed the paper towels, trash bags, and first aid kit stashed inside.

Scenarios whizzed through her mind. Could her neighbor be a day drinker? A drug user? A microdosing tech bro? Had she traveled to the Congo recently and contracted Ebola?

Piper ran across her own impeccable green lawn, maintained with pride and joy by her husband on the days he was actually home, and crossed the border into the Land of Boys, where everything from the baseballs in the flower beds to the bin of hockey sticks and Nerf guns on the front porch screamed *This is why we can't have nice things.*

She approached her neighbor warily.

The woman leaned against the car, bent at the waist, hands resting on her knees. She'd stopped vomiting, but a malodourous puddle pooled on the concrete between her feet.

Three boys who shared the woman's blond hair and blue eyes stood beside her, helpless and wide eyed, the youngest with tears streaking his face. Must be her sons.

The oldest boy rested a hand on his mother's back, and Piper's heart softened. He had not yet learned that when women puked, you held their hair back, but he'd make a wonderful boyfriend someday.

The woman looked at Piper with a thousand-yard stare and pulled her cell phone from her back pocket. "I left him."

Ah. Divorce. Infidelity. Possibly domestic abuse. She'd seen it all before in her long law enforcement career.

Piper ripped a paper towel from the roll and stooped to mop up the pile of vomit in the driveway. "Your husband?"

"My son," the woman said softly. "I left my son at a truck stop on the Pennsylvania Turnpike."

Piper stopped cleaning. "You did *what*?"

"I left my son at a truck stop on the Pennsylvania Turnpike," her neighbor repeated in a hollow voice. "Accidentally," she added as an afterthought.

"You're sure?" Piper knew the question was stupid the moment she uttered it, but she couldn't help herself. How exactly did a person manage to leave a child at a *truck stop*?

"He isn't here, is he?" The woman sounded argumentative.

"I see three boys," Piper conceded as she rose to stand. "Is there . . . another one?"

"Yes. Yes, there is." Her neighbor wiped her mouth with the back of her hand. "And I *forgot* him."

"Where?"

"Big Jim's Travel Plaza," the woman repeated in a robotic voice. She sounded like a slightly deranged Alexa.

"Have you called the police?" Piper asked.

The woman shook her head. Then she bent at the waist and threw up again.

Piper stepped quickly out of the vomit-shrapnel radius. Her neighbor was obviously in shock.

"I'll call the police," she said firmly.

She pried the woman's cell phone from her hand and called the truck stop, then dialed 911 with her own phone, while also texting a friend who worked for the Virginia Highway Patrol.

Meanwhile her neighbor had begun to babble incoherently, muttering the name of the truck stop under her breath, and something about blankets. With both phones held to her ears, Piper used her elbows to guide her neighbor toward the front porch. She instructed one boy to clean up the vomit and told another to get his mom a glass of water.

Then Piper turned to the oldest son, who sat beside his mother on the porch, helplessly rubbing his hand across her back in tiny circles.

"Where's your dad?" she asked.

The boy looked startled by the question. "He was in Kansas. Or maybe Oklahoma. I'm not sure. He's supposed to fly home tonight."

"Do you have a phone? Can you reach him?"

The boy shook his head. "I tried. But I think he's in the air."

"What's your mom's name?"

"Kiersten," the boy said. "Kiersten Cleaver. And my brother is Johnny."

"Hold on," Piper said to the 911 dispatcher on the other end of the line. Then she knelt in front of Kiersten and looked her directly in the eye. "Kiersten, can you spell your son's first, middle, and last name for me."

Kiersten nodded. "J-o-h-n C-o-l-i-n C-l-e-a-v-e-r."

"What was he wearing?" Piper broke off before adding, "When you last saw him." But it didn't matter.

Kiersten burst into tears, choking out the words between sobs. "A red . . . Minnesota Twins . . . T-shirt. Blue Adidas running shorts . . . and . . . white Nike tennis shoes."

Piper relayed the information to the dispatcher and gave the same information to the person who answered the phone at the truck stop.

Relief flooded her body as she broke into a wide smile.

Thank God.

"They found him. He's sitting behind the counter with the cashier. They've been trying to reach you, but he didn't know your cell phone number." She handed the phone to Kiersten. "You can talk to him."

Kiersten took a deep breath and closed her eyes. Piper watched as her neighbor pulled her frayed nerves back together and injected her voice with a note of cheerful calm.

"Hi, honey. Are you okay?"

She couldn't hear the answer on the other end of the line, but whatever he said brought a smile to Kiersten's ravaged face.

"You can eat as many powdered donuts as you want," Kiersten said, wiping away the silent tears streaming down her cheeks. "And I'm just going to stay right here on the phone with you while you eat them, okay?"

A moment later the 911 dispatcher came back on the line. The highway patrol had arrived at the truck stop. Piper gave her phone to Kiersten, and Kiersten spoke with the officer.

After a short conversation, she hung up Piper's phone. Then she spoke to her son again on her own phone.

"The officers will drive you home now, okay? I'll be waiting right here. See you soon, okay?"

The moment she disconnected the call, Kiersten burst into a fresh round of sobs and threw her arms around Piper. Her oldest son leaped from the porch with a whoop of joy and went to tell his brothers.

Piper repressed a groan as Kiersten clung to her. Just her luck. A *hugger*.

She endured Kiersten's damp embrace for a full minute before attempting, gently, to disentangle herself.

Then she looked up to find her across-the-street neighbor, Rosamund, approaching.

She didn't know Rosamund well . . . they'd had a few pleasant conversations by the mailbox since Rosamund moved in a couple of years ago. They'd even made vague plans to carpool home from school, which never materialized because of conflicting after-school activities.

The tight feeling in her chest loosened as Rosamund approached. Because Piper could make phone calls and find lost children, but the hugging and the tears and the *crying* . . . well, this whole situation was way beyond her emotional pay grade. She needed some help here. And maybe Rosamund could provide it.

Chapter Sixteen

KIERSTEN

Kiersten wiped the tears from her cheeks as a neighbor she'd never seen before strode toward them on long legs, her caftan flowing in colorful waves as she moved. Tall, with red hair and scarlet lipstick, she looked sort of . . . dramatic.

If this woman were a state, she would *not* be Minnesota.

Her house across the street looked dramatic too. Instead of a tidy front yard like Piper's, or an attempt at a tidy front yard, like hers, this neighbor had a sort of wildflower meadow sprouting on her lawn.

Wind chimes hung from her front porch, and she had little signs tacked up on the wall beside the front door, including one that said **In this house, we believe the Force is with us, always.**

Kiersten rummaged through her exhausted brain, trying to remember what Henry and Myrtle had told her about this lady who lived across the street.

She wrote geology textbooks or something? And she had a daughter in middle school.

A thirteen- or fourteen-year-old girl trailed after the woman, clad in some kind of cape, her short hair dyed blue. Behind her large round glasses, the girl's eyes were rimmed with red.

Had this child been forgotten at a truck stop too?

"Is everything okay?" the woman asked, casting an anxious glance at Kiersten.

"Hi, Rosamund." Piper rose and greeted the woman. "Thanks for coming over. This is our new neighbor, Kiersten. She's had an . . . eventful . . . evening."

"Can I help with anything?" Rosamund asked.

"Actually, would you mind ordering some pizza?" Piper asked. "And then maybe come outside and join us?"

Rosamund looked surprised. Perhaps she'd been hoping for a more dramatic mission . . . battling a grease fire in the kitchen or performing the Heimlich maneuver.

"Sure." Rosamund nodded. "I can do that."

"I'm gonna stay here with Kiersten until the situation is resolved. But my girls haven't eaten dinner yet, and Kiersten's kids are probably hungry too," Piper explained.

Kiersten could read the desire to be helpful and the desire to know what the heck was going on wrestling across Rosamund's face. "But is everything—"

"Everything is fine," Piper assured her. "It's a long story." Then she gestured at her own three girls standing at the edge of the driveway, looking worried and at the boys clustered on the porch. "But the police are on their way," she said, lowering her voice, "so if you could take all these kids out in the backyard and keep them occupied with pizza, that would help a lot."

Rosamund opened her mouth, then closed it again, obviously making a heroic effort not to ask more questions. Instead, she nodded and waved her phone in the air. "C'mon, kids. Tell me what kind of pizza you want."

Piper glanced at Kiersten as the crowd of kids surged into the backyard. "Do you want to go inside?" Piper asked.

She shook her head vehemently. "No."

Her arms and legs felt heavy, as though sand filled every pore. She wasn't sure she could walk inside even if she wanted to.

And she didn't want to. She needed to see the patrol car the moment it appeared. And she wanted Johnny to see his mother the moment the police car pulled into the driveway.

They sat in silence for a few moments as Kiersten tried to absorb the terror and relief of the last twenty minutes. Slowly, the numbness paralyzing her mind and body gave way, and the horror of what she'd done flooded through her again.

"I left my son at a truck stop on the Pennsylvania Turnpike." How could she have *done* such a thing? "I am a terrible, terrible, *terrible* mother."

Piper shot her a sideways glance and flashed a wry smile. "But you remembered to bring the other three home."

Kiersten looked at her neighbor for a long moment. She found no judgment in Piper's brown eyes, just compassion. For a split second, her anxiety retreated, like the moon passing behind a cloud. Then a bubble of laughter rose up from somewhere deep in her gut. She tried to hold it back.

You remembered to bring the other three home.

She snorted. She chuckled. Then the dam broke and a torrent of hysterical laughter washed over her body. She laughed so hard she cried, shoulders silently heaving, until the gush subsided into a sort of hiccup-sob.

"This is impossible," she said, wiping her eyes.

"What's impossible?" Piper asked.

"Raising four boys in a place where I have no friends and no family to help me and a husband who travels all the time. Luke is dyslexic and flunking all his classes and got into a fight. Matthew has Little League shoulder and no friends. And on the rare occasions when I actually see my husband, we don't talk, we discuss *logistics*. My family is falling apart. And do you know what I think the solution is?"

"What?"

"Driving." Kiersten gave a bitter laugh. "Driving to Sports. Activities. Practices. Games. I seem to think that my children exist to

be coached. Tutored. *Driven.* It's all I do. It's all we ever do. Drive to school. Drive to practice. Drive to games. And to what end?"

The corner of Piper's mouth twisted in a rueful half smile. "At least you're driving your kids *to* something that might lead to a college scholarship someday. I'm driving to Irish dance."

Kiersten had heard of this, but they didn't have Irish dance in her part of rural Minnesota. They had ice fishing. And hockey. Scandinavian culture didn't seem to lend itself to the more exuberant forms of self-expression, like dancing.

"What is Irish dance exactly?" Kiersten asked.

Piper sighed. "It's an extremely complex, highly technical, and very entertaining form of dancing. And you do it all without moving your arms."

Kiersten worked to keep her expression neutral. That did sound a little . . . impractical. But she wouldn't say that out loud to this incredibly wonderful neighbor who had just orchestrated the return of her lost and found son.

Instead she nodded, as though this made perfect sense. "Okay."

"It's really difficult to master," Piper explained, resting her chin on her hand. "You have to be both smart *and* athletic. And one of my daughters is really good. She's a perfectionist, and she likes that it's exacting and difficult. But there's no big payoff for Irish dance. The best we could hope for is like"—she paused and waved a hand in the air—"a touring company of Riverdance or something. There are no Olympics. No Division I college scholarships. And yet, here I am, spending thousands of hours and dollars, driving my daughter to Irish dance at a studio in Reston on I-66, going west, *at rush hour*, three days a week."

Kiersten shuddered. She'd lived in the DC region long enough to experience the vehicular horror of westbound I-66 at rush hour.

"Do all your girls do Irish dance?"

"Of course not," Piper snorted. "That would be too easy. One does tap and ballet. The other one sings and plays piano. They do musicals. Children's theater. And where does it all lead?"

"Anorexia and madness?" Kiersten asked.

"Possibly," Piper conceded. "Or if they are very lucky, they could grow up to be Dallas Cowboys Cheerleaders."

"What about Broadway?"

Piper shrugged. "My girls are talented. But I don't know if they're *that* talented."

"So why do it?"

"Because what if they *are* that talented?" Piper asked, her voice plaintive. "Am I going to be the person who sabotages their Broadway dreams? All because I was too lazy to do a little driving? And they enjoy it. Most of the time. Even Bella, who's started to pull her hair out the night before auditions."

"Do *you* enjoy it?" Kiersten asked.

"Does it matter?"

"Maybe it does matter," Kiersten said slowly. "Is your family happy?"

Piper paused and seemed to consider the question. "Happy enough? But I mean . . . happier than what? Amish people?"

Kiersten chewed on her lower lip and tried to find the right words. "I wish . . . I wish we could just drop out for a while and see what it's like. To have something to compare our modern insanity with."

"Didn't we all do that during COVID?"

"That was different." Kiersten shook her head. "I'm not talking about isolating and avoiding people. I'm talking about slowing down and finding a different way to do things. Like our neighbor." She jutted her chin in the direction of the home next door, with its charming window boxes and a tasteful pumpkin display.

"You mean the Influencer?"

Kiersten's eyes widened. "She's an influencer?"

Piper nodded. "Half a million followers on Instagram. Hygge Mom, or Urban Chicken Mom, something like that."

"What does *hygge* mean again?"

"It's like Scandinavian, for cozy and shit."

"Well then, yeah," Kiersten admitted. "Like her, but without aprons and a chicken coop."

"Just quit . . . everything," Piper repeated in a soft voice.

Kiersten nodded dreamily. "All of it. No school. No sports. No tutors. No screens. No so-called 'enrichment activities.'" She made air quotes with her fingers. "An experiment. For the rest of the school year."

Piper looked grave, as though Kiersten had suggested robbing a bank or going to Walmart on Black Friday. "No screens?"

"No screens," Kiersten repeated. "We recreate our own childhood. We use our imagination. We play outside. We read."

"What do you think would happen?"

Kiersten shrugged. "I don't *know* what would happen, and that's why I'm afraid to try it. Maybe we'd still be stressed out and disconnected. Maybe that much time with our children would make us even crazier. Maybe they'd go into withdrawal if we took away *Minecraft*. Or maybe we'd be relaxed. Happy. Free."

Silence settled over the front porch as she considered the implications of the word *free*.

Free from the rush of getting ready for school in the morning. The rush of after-school activities. The rush of being somewhere at a certain time in a certain uniform. The rush of weekends spent driving from one game or activity to another.

Free from the arguments and yelling about screen time. Free from homework and school projects. Free from the terrible rush of negative adrenaline when she checked the PowerSchool portal and found that Luke had all those missing assignments.

Or when she dug in the bottom of Johnny's backpack and found the dreaded red homework folder and realized that she hadn't checked it *all week*.

What would it feel like to be liberated from all that?

Free from expectations and competition and labels. Who's in advanced math? Who's in the gifted and talented program? Who's starting? Who's on the bench? Who has learning "issues"? Who's "talented"? Who's popular? Who's not?

A beat-up Kia pulled up, and a young man exited with three boxes of pizza. Rosamund emerged from the backyard, paid him, and took the pizzas back to the kids. Then she returned to the porch and sat down beside them.

"Thanks for the pizza," Kiersten said. "Let me know how much I owe you."

Rosamund dismissed this with a wave of her hand. "Happy to help. We've had a rough day. And being with your kids back there . . . well, it's been nice for Guinevere."

Kiersten turned to examine her neighbor more closely, and this time she noticed smudged mascara under her red-rimmed eyes.

"Are you all right?" Kiersten asked.

"No." Rosamund's shoulders slumped. "I am not."

Chapter Seventeen

KIERSTEN

Kiersten laid a tentative hand on Rosamund's arm. "Well, as it turns out, my front porch is the place to be if you're having a bad day of epic proportions."

"It's my daughter's birthday. She's thirteen today." A wistful tone laced Rosamund's words. "And she invited four girls to her party. We got everything ready. And none of them showed up. They sent her this text instead."

She raised her phone, showed them a photo of a text.

Kiersten squinted at the screen. Happy Birthday, Loser. She gasped. The casual cruelty of the words jolted her, like touching the electric fence back home. "Oh, Rosamund. I'm so sorry."

Rosamund bit down on her lower lip. "Guinevere has always had a hard time fitting in. Probably because I saddled her with a name like *Guinevere*."

"This is not your fault," Piper said gently. "But I'm sorry it's happening."

Rosamund gave her a wistful smile. "She's a wonderful blend of sophisticated and childlike. Super smart. Reads all the time, but she can be a little . . . socially inept. She's not on the spectrum. Nothing with a diagnosis . . . just different. You know, *quirky*. We had some issues with bullying last year. I thought that was behind us . . . but it turns out, it's not. It's started up again. This time a boy is involved, and he's meaner than the girls."

Kiersten squeezed her hand. "We were just talking about how great it would be to drop out."

It sounded so radical when she said it out loud. But maybe there was safety in numbers. She wouldn't have the courage to do this alone, but if her neighbors joined in . . . well, then maybe it wasn't such a crazy idea after all?

Rosamund frowned. "What do you mean by 'dropping out'?"

"We quit everything. School. Sports. Activities. We drop out of the rat race," Piper explained.

"We go back in time," Kiersten added. "It would be like when we were young. Our kids would play outside. Roam the neighborhood unsupervised and play with firecrackers."

"And no more iPads or phones or devices," Piper added. "No more screen time."

Rosamund's mouth dropped open. "But what would you actually *do*? Homeschool?"

"We'd drink Tab and smoke Virginia Slims and go to Tupperware parties," Kiersten said. "Isn't that what moms used to do?"

Rosamund fixed her gaze on Kiersten. "I'm serious."

"We hadn't gotten that far yet," Piper admitted. "We hadn't gotten beyond dropping out."

Rosamund was silent for a moment. Then she looked Kiersten in the eye. "I don't think it's *entirely* crazy."

Kiersten felt a spark of terror, like she'd somehow become responsible for leading a group of climbers to the top of Mount Everest, blindfolded. And naked.

"You don't?" Kiersten asked cautiously.

"What we're doing right now isn't working." Rosamund's voice had a hard edge. "I talked to the school last year. They said they'd fix it, but they didn't. Maybe they can't. I don't know. I'm ready to try something new."

"My daughter is being bullied too," Piper said slowly. "I mean, not bullied exactly. More like . . . sexually harassed, at the vast age of thirteen."

She told them about her daughter's iPad and her meeting with the principal and Bruce Orlov.

"And the school is doing nothing?" Rosamund asked, outrage etched across her face.

"Like with your situation, I don't know if they can't or they won't, but I don't think—"

"He's here!" Kiersten shouted, springing to her feet as a highway patrol car pulled into the driveway.

Two officers in tan uniforms emerged from the car, one male, the other female. The female officer opened the rear door of the patrol vehicle.

Johnny sprang from the back seat and dashed into Kiersten's arms. She pulled him into a hug so tight she was afraid she might crush him. He clung to her for a moment, then squirmed to pull free.

"MOM. It was SO COOL. I got to ride in a POLICE CAR."

She swallowed, working hard to keep her voice steady. "I know, honey. That's really awesome. Are you okay?"

He nodded vigorously. "I'm fine. When I couldn't find you, I told this nice cash register lady who looked like Grandma that I got forgotted, and then she called the police, and you called the police, and they came, and then they brought me home. And I got to use the scanner gun and help Verna check things out."

She needed to send a massive bouquet of flowers to Verna. "That's great. But are you *okay*?"

"I was kinda scared at first when I couldn't find you," he admitted. "But then Verna let me help with the scanner gun, and then I wasn't scared anymore. But she wouldn't let me use it on cigarettes and beer. Just candy and pop and chips."

"Okay." She resisted the urge to pull him into her arms and hug him again, allowing herself instead to plant a kiss on top of his head.

"You can go have some pizza while I talk to the officers. What do you say to the police?"

He turned to the officers standing behind his mom. "Thank you for bringing me home when my mom forgotted me."

Her face burned with shame. If she lived to be a hundred, she would never forget this moment and she would never forgive herself for what she'd done.

"We had a nice long talk with your son on the drive here," the male patrolman said.

Kiersten's heart dropped. Oh my God. What had Johnny told them? That she yelled in the morning when they were trying to get to school on time? That they'd once driven all the way to the airport for a family vacation before they realized Luke wasn't wearing any shoes? That on rare occasions when she was very tired, and the day had been very long, she gave them Lucky Charms and scrambled eggs for dinner?

Were they going to call social services? Would they take her boys away?

"I understand you have four boys in travel sports," the male patrolman said.

She swallowed. "I do."

The female officer gave her a wry smile. "We're parents, too, and we understand. Try not to be too hard on yourself. And next time, maybe do a head count when you get in the car."

Relief made her heart stop, and she exhaled softly. "I will, Officer. Thank you."

But there wouldn't be a next time, Kiersten thought as the patrol car drove out of the cul-de-sac on Beaverbrook Lane.

She was done running on a hamster wheel and calling it a life.

Chapter Eighteen

PIPER

"Come inside and have some pizza. If there's any left." Kiersten opened her front door and beckoned Piper and Rosamund inside.

Piper entered Kiersten's house, relieved to find it even messier than her own. Balled-up socks and Nerf bullets littered the floor. LEGOs covered the dining room table, and unzipped backpacks seemed to vomit worksheets across the tiny mudroom, where the washer and dryer also lived.

She followed her neighbor into the kitchen and family room on the backside of the house. The roar of eight kids laughing, talking, and shouting drifted into the kitchen from the screened-in porch and the backyard.

Guinevere and Matthew played cornhole while Caitlin hovered nearby, not part of the action but near it. Piper's middle daughter, Olivia, and Kiersten's son, Luke, were engaged in a lively discussion about whether or not Jedi could fly, and her youngest, Bella, jumped on the trampoline with Kiersten's two youngest sons, James and Johnny, where all three screamed with laughter.

Her heart clenched at the sight of her daughter rising and dropping in the air, hair flying behind her in a smooth blond sheet.

The girls desperately wanted a trampoline, but she'd done the research.

They were unquestionably *dangerous*. She'd seen the statistics, even though her husband claimed that modern trampolines were much safer than the ones they'd had when they were kids.

She forced herself to turn off the part of her mind that remained constantly attuned to danger.

Just listen.

The corners of her mouth lifted in a nostalgic smile. It sounded like the neighborhood where she grew up in Michigan. Kids in someone's backyard, completely unsupervised, screaming with joy.

"Help yourself." Kiersten carried a pizza box into the kitchen, then scattered napkins and paper plates across the table.

"Can I get you something to drink?" she asked. "I have Gatorade, milk, and water. These are your only options."

"I'll have a lovely glass of water," Rosamund said. Piper requested the same. Kiersten rummaged in her pantry and also found a package of Oreos. For dessert.

Piper examined the layout of Kiersten's kitchen and family room.

"You have a Jefferson," she told Kiersten as she pulled a chair up to the battered kitchen table. "We have the Franklin."

"I have a Jefferson too," Rosamund said.

"What's a Jefferson?" Kiersten asked through a mouthful of pizza.

"A lot of these homes in the Washington, DC, suburbs were built in the baby boom after World War II," Piper said. "Because we're near Mount Vernon, the developer named the models after the founding fathers. I think you guys have a bigger foyer than I do, and a den. Someone built an addition onto ours back in the '80s—otherwise ours would be smaller than yours."

"How do you know all this?" Kiersten asked.

"Lillian Landry, the lady next door. She's been here for like sixty years." Piper grabbed a napkin. "She used to give tours at Mount Vernon. She's sort of an amateur historian. And we have a former mayor at the end of the cul-de-sac too. Richard Davis. Nice old guy, knows all the local history."

"I met him yesterday," Kiersten said as she reached for the purse she'd set on the kitchen counter. "And speaking of local history. I found something interesting hidden in a box in my basement."

She pulled out a small book encased in black leather.

"A diary?" Piper asked.

Kiersten nodded. "From 1965. A woman named Dottie who lived right here on Beaverbrook Lane. I found three of them, hidden inside an old set of encyclopedias. Plus a wad of cash."

Rosamund's eyes lit up. "I love old books."

"This one is definitely interesting." Kiersten pressed the button on the side and opened it. "She was pregnant and a newlywed. Here's where I left off."

She handed it to Rosamund, who started to read aloud.

Chapter Nineteen

DOTTIE

March 22, 1965

It's Monday, so I'm doing the washing today. I love the smell of sheets when I bring them in from the clothesline late in the afternoon.

I'm very grateful for all of this . . . for everything. But I just . . . I don't know. It's hard to realize that the pattern for the whole rest of my life is already set. Right here, right now, at age 19. Washing clothes, cooking food, having babies, taking care of Dickie. This is my life for the next . . . 60 years or so.

It's strange, but I feel a little bit erased now that I'm married. The country club membership Daddy gave me when I turned 18 is in Dickie's name now, not mine. Dickie also has the title to the car, and the deed to the house, even though my father bought them for both of us. And now that we're married, Dickie has access to my checking and savings accounts too.

He and Daddy and the bank just went ahead and did all these things without asking for my opinion, much less my permission. And I was too naive to ask in those early weeks after the wedding.

I know that if I ever need money or anything else, Daddy will be there. But . . .

I'd just like to have something of my own . . . something to remind me of who I was before I got married.

Even my name isn't mine anymore. It's an odd practice, when you think about it, referring to a woman by her husband's name with the word Mrs. tacked on the front. Sometimes I feel like an appendage, rather than a person.

But I have lots to keep me busy. I guess I should be grateful for that.

Dickie suggested I use this time before the baby to learn how to become a better cook. I think I'm already a pretty good cook because I took over all the cooking after Mother died.

But I only know how to make normal meat and potatoes style food. Dickie wants me to learn fancy French dishes like that lady on TV. He wants us to host dinner parties. He's even given me a deadline. I have two weeks to learn to make boeuf bourguignon from Julia Child's *Mastering the Art of French Cooking* cookbook and it's awfully complicated. He also wants me to learn to make Lemon Chiffon Pie for dessert. Then he wants to have a banker and a state senator and their wives over for dinner.

He says it's important, and I need to get all the details right, which makes me even more nervous. I never realized it before, but Dickie is awfully ambitious. He says he wants to run for public office.

Which is fine, I guess. I just never thought I'd end up as a political wife. So I've been working on the boeuf bourguignon.

But what I really want to do is work on Dickie's car. It's making an odd sound and I'm pretty sure it's the fan belt. On Saturday, I'm going to drop him off at the club so he can play golf all day, and then I'm going to drive the car back here so I can sneak under the hood and poke around.

I don't have all the tools I need, but our garage is a good size. It's a little bigger than normal because Daddy paid the developer extra to build a nuclear fallout shelter underneath. He even outfitted it with shelves and cots and blankets. I use it as a root cellar and keep my tulip bulbs and all the canned goods down there.

There's an extra door, too, on the backside, facing the yard, so I can come and go without anyone knowing the lady of the house is out in the garage changing spark plugs.

Anyway, time to bake buns and bread and pineapple upside down cake. Dickie likes a dessert with his evening meal. He says it keeps him sweet.

I sure wish that were true.

Chapter Twenty

PIPER

A hushed silence fell over the room when Rosamund stopped reading.

"This is amazing," Piper whispered.

"And terrifying," Kiersten added. "Doesn't her husband sound *awful*?"

"It's like someone speaking to us *from beyond the grave*," Rosamund said in an ominous voice.

Piper resisted the urge to roll her eyes. "It's definitely a period piece. Do you know anything else about her?"

Kiersten shook her head. "Just their first names, Dottie and Dickie. But I've only read the first few entries. Hopefully as I read more, I'll be able to figure out who they belong to so I can return them."

"But do you think it's right to read someone else's diaries?" Rosamund asked.

"Well, no." Kiersten reached for another slice of pizza. "But it doesn't feel right to keep them either. And I can't return them, or the money, if I don't know who wrote them."

"True," Rosamund conceded. "I wonder which house she lived in?"

"Beaverbrook *is* sort of a time capsule." Piper took a thoughtful sip from her red Solo cup. "People who live here rarely sell."

Rosamund wiped her hands on her napkin. "I think it's because our yards are so huge. They're way more valuable than our houses."

Piper nodded. "Our lot is over an acre. Huge by modern standards."

"And your backyards face the river," Rosamund pointed out. "It must be nice to have water views."

"Only in the winter." Piper repressed a shudder as she thought back to her conversation a few hours earlier with Bruno Orlov.

Kiersten snagged a napkin. "What's the deal with the two houses going up across the cul-de-sac, between your house and Richard and Margaret's place?"

"A widower lived there," Rosamund said as she grabbed an Oreo. "Nice old guy, but I guess he was starting to have cognitive issues. Chip Davis tried to be helpful and sort of watch over him from afar, but I think it got to be too much. The old guy sold his house to Chip last year when he entered assisted living, and now Chip and Trey are building two new homes on that lot."

"So Chip is Trey's dad?" Kiersten asked.

Rosamund nodded. "They're both developers. Trey's also a real estate agent."

"Who's going to live in those new houses they're building?" Kiersten asked.

"We don't know yet," Rosamund said. "They're planning to put them on the market when they're finished. I hear they're planning to ask $2 million."

Piper let out a low whistle. "Wow."

"This house is far from perfect," Kiersten conceded, gesturing to the popcorn ceiling with a slice of pizza. "We could only afford it because it's never been updated. The bathrooms and closets are tiny. And so is the kitchen. But the neighbors are second to none."

"Hear! Hear!" Rosamund raised her Solo cup in the air.

"I don't know what I would have done without you guys today." Kiersten's voice wavered, and Piper stiffened. Was she going to start hugging people again?

"Thank you both." Kiersten blinked rapidly, then dabbed her eyes with a napkin. "For everything."

"Don't mention it." Piper waved away these heartfelt expressions of gratitude with an Oreo.

"I wish that were an option," Kiersten said. "I'm not sure how to tell my husband I left our last-born son at a rest stop."

"Where *is* your husband?" Rosamund asked, looking around the kitchen.

"Kansas, I think." Then she shrugged. "I'm never sure where he is, honestly. I can't keep track."

"I know what that's like." Piper snorted. "My husband is somewhere in Europe. Brussels, I think."

"He travels a lot?" Kiersten asked.

"He's a DS agent."

Kiersten looked confused, and Piper apologized. "I forgot you're new to the area and have not yet learned the many acronyms of the DMV."

"DMV?" Kiersten frowned.

"DC, Maryland, Virginia," Piper explained. "And *DS* stands for *Diplomatic Security*. It's like the Secret Service, but for ambassadors and the diplomatic corps. He's currently assigned to the secretary of state. Where she goes, he goes."

"And she travels a lot?" Rosamund asked.

"Fortunately for America, and unfortunately for me, she's very energetic. Twenty-six countries since she was sworn in. Brendan is never home. And when he is, he's jet lagged."

And she had to resist the urge to ask him to do all the things she needed him to do but couldn't. Shouldn't, because he was exhausted.

Sometimes she found herself wishing he were deployed again, as they'd both been over the years on various assignments. Because then she wouldn't resent him for being physically home but mentally checked out.

"That sounds rough," Kiersten said, picking up another slice of pizza. "At least my husband's travel is mostly domestic. What about you, Rosamund? Does your spouse travel a lot?"

Rosamund paused just a moment before answering. "I'm a single parent. Guinevere's father isn't in the picture."

"That must be hard," Piper said.

"It can be." Rosamund pulled an Oreo apart. "Especially when things aren't going well. You don't have anyone to share the worry, so to speak."

They sat in silence for a moment; then Kiersten said, "I was serious, you know, about dropping out."

Piper gnawed on a pizza crust. The conversation they'd had on the front porch felt unreal, like a dream. The more she thought about it, the more impractical it seemed.

"This is a wake-up call," Kiersten said, her voice thick with emotion. "Something needs to change."

Rosamund reached for her hand and gave it a gentle squeeze.

Piper flexed her jaw, working to keep her own emotions in check. During that phone call yesterday about Hawkeye Slaughter . . . she'd felt so *powerless.*

She hadn't felt this way in a long time . . . but now without her job, without the authority that came with it, she felt powerless again. Just like that day when she was nine years old.

She pushed the memory away and forced herself to focus on Kiersten.

"What's the worst that can happen?" Kiersten asked. "We try something new and we're still miserable? Then we ask the universe to refund our insanity, and we go back to the way we were before."

Piper glanced at Rosamund to gauge her reaction to this proposal. Rosamund stared down at the Oreo in her hand as though it were the Rosetta stone. Then raised her chin and looked Kiersten in the eye.

"I could help," Rosamund said quietly. "I have a PhD in English literature. I could teach grammar, writing, and history. I know a ton about history."

Kiersten frowned. "I thought you wrote geology textbooks?"

Rosamund smiled. "Have you heard of Diana Gabaldon?"

Piper nodded at this mention of her favorite author, then blushed. She'd had a secret crush on Jamie, the kilt-clad hero of these novels, for many years now.

"I'm the Diana Gabaldon of Viking romance. I write under my pen name, Rosamund Thorvaldsen."

Kiersten's eyes widened. "You write *romance novels*?"

Rosamund inclined her head regally. "Do you remember a series on Netflix a few years back called *Shield-Maiden of Stamendahl*?"

"I *loved* that show," Piper gushed. Actually she'd loved the extremely muscular actor who played the show's hero, Ragnar the Bold.

"It's based on one of my early novels," Rosamund said modestly. "It paid off my mortgage and filled Guinevere's 529 account with enough money to fund four years of college, plus my own retirement. I'm still writing a novel a year, but I'll make time to help with homeschooling."

Piper's heart did a little flip. These women were basically strangers. She knew Rosamund but didn't know her well. And she'd only really met Kiersten an hour ago, when she saw her vomiting in the driveway.

But she knew their struggles and understood their fears because she shared them. They were moms, too, attempting to raise kids in an anxious, competitive, technology-infused world, hurtling toward an unknown future. And that created a shortcut straight to the heart of what really mattered.

"Look, I need to think about this," Piper finally said. "But . . . I'm on administrative leave for the foreseeable future, so hypothetically, I have lots of free time at the moment. Plus I'm pretty good at math and science."

Kiersten grabbed a trash bag and began to clean up the paper plates and napkins. "I realize this seems kind of sudden, and maybe a little crazy."

Piper raised an eyebrow. "*A lot* crazy."

"Okay. A lot crazy," Kiersten conceded. "And maybe I'm in shock and I'll wake up tomorrow morning and think this is a ridiculous idea . . . but let's just pretend for a moment that we were going to do this. What subjects are left?"

"Art. And music. Everyone always focuses exclusively on the importance of this STEM *nonsense*." Rosamund made a dismissive gesture with her paper plate. "But the fine arts are vital to a well-rounded education."

"We could go to the National Gallery. And free concerts at the Kennedy Center," Kiersten said. "I looked into things like this before we moved, before I realized we'd spend all our time at travel baseball tournaments and hockey games."

Piper thrust three empty pizza boxes into the trash bag. "But what about things like grades and transcripts . . . and college?"

"It's one year," Kiersten said. "Our oldest kids are in seventh grade. I don't think one year of homeschooling in middle school will ruin their lives."

Piper looked skeptical. "Don't tell that to my mother-in-law."

"Maybe they will actually learn *more* this way." Kiersten raised her shoulders in a hopeful shrug. "Because it will be, you know, hands on."

"We could go to Mount Vernon and learn about colonial history . . . about carding wool and churning butter," Rosamund said. "I've done a lot of research there."

"We could go to the Smithsonian Air and Space Museum to learn about torque . . . and thrust . . . and"—Kiersten gestured upward with the Oreo package—"the vastness of space."

"And we could go to the Natural History Museum and learn about dinosaurs and mummies." Rosamund tossed a wad of paper napkins covered in pizza sauce into the trash bag.

Piper tied a knot in the bag and reached for a new one. She'd once had a conversation with someone on an airplane who assumed that working in law enforcement meant chasing bad guys around on foot, Jason Bourne–style, with a gun in your hand, or playing baccarat at a casino in Montenegro like James Bond. In reality, working for the Drug Enforcement Agency or FBI was much harder and far more tedious than it looked in movies or TV shows.

She had a feeling teaching was like that too. Everyone thought they knew how to be a teacher because they'd once been a student. But she suspected it was incredibly difficult to teach kids things they didn't actually want to learn.

"I hate to state the obvious here, but none of us are teachers," Piper said. "I mean, we don't *know* anything about homeschooling."

"Our neighbor does," Kiersten opened the dishwasher. "We could ask her."

Rosamund raised an eyebrow. "You mean the Trad Wife Influencer next door?"

Kiersten started loading silverware into the dishwasher. "She *is* actually homeschooling her kids."

Piper and Rosamund shot each other a skeptical glance. "I don't know if feeding chickens while wearing a $300 dress from Anthropologie really counts as teaching," Piper said.

"But she must know *something* about it. Like how to make a lesson plan and what kind of paperwork you have to file with the state, things like that."

"Maybe." Piper attempted to soften her skepticism with a polite smile. Glamorous Chicken Apron Influencer Lady did not strike her as someone with practical life skills.

"I'll talk to her," Kiersten said. "Get some advice and tips. And then I need to talk to my husband."

"I need to do that too," Piper said. "And I want to talk to my girls. I need a little more time to think through the . . . ramifications."

"I'd like to talk to my daughter." Rosamund dried her wet hands on a dish towel. "And make sure she's on board with this."

"Why don't we take the next few days to talk to our families," Kiersten suggested. "See if they find this whole idea workable. And then if we decide to move forward, we take a couple weeks to do some research and make lesson plans and get our supplies and things in order. We could start in October."

A moment of silence settled over the kitchen, a silence that told Piper they were all, to use the appropriate law enforcement term, *scared shitless* by this idea.

"Guys, we can *do* this." Kiersten's voice was so earnest, her eyes so wide and blue, that Piper felt guilty for her lack of faith. She looked so wholesome and Midwestern, like Little Bo-Peep trying to lead a revolution.

"All right." Piper squared her shoulders. "If you're sure, then I'm at least willing to consider it."

"I'm sure," Kiersten said decisively.

Piper gave her a tentative smile. A million potholes, pitfalls, and obstacles took shape inside her mind. A million reasons to say no and walk away.

But while she wanted to walk away from the *idea* of dropping out, not to mention all the work involved, she didn't want to walk away from these moms, these neighbors. She wanted to try, for their sake. And for the sake of her girls.

She glanced out at the kids in the backyard. Caitlin tugged on the bottom of her shirt, pulling it lower, as though trying to hide her hips, her midsection, all the things that made her female.

Piper gritted her teeth. She wanted her daughter's confidence to return, wanted her to be brash, happy, unafraid again. Maybe pulling her out of school and away from Alex Orlov would help.

Maybe this idea wasn't so crazy. After all, she'd been wrong before. Famously wrong.

Under her breath, she muttered a little prayer, hoping to be wrong again.

Chapter Twenty-One

KIERSTEN

After the neighbors left, Garrett called from the airport, his voice hoarse and tired. His flight had been rerouted to Dulles, and he'd be home in an hour. Kiersten said something cheerful about seeing him soon and hung up without telling him that she'd accidentally left one of their children at a truck stop. She'd share that news with her husband when he was sitting down, at home.

She puttered around the house, attempting to restore order and put things away, but she felt jittery, unable to focus.

In the past few hours, she'd lost her son, found new friends, and promised to drop out of everything. Was this idea sane or crazier than her current life?

She gave up on cleaning and reached for the diary Rosamund had left open on the kitchen table. Maybe the past could shed light on how to live in the present.

Chapter Twenty-Two

DOTTIE

April 5, 1965

I found the perfect hiding place for my diary today. Though it was painful to desecrate such an expensive gift, I used a carpet knife to carve out the inside of that set of encyclopedias I got from Daddy for my 16th birthday. Dickie would never willingly open any book, much less one as dense and full of facts as an encyclopedia.

Peggy, my replacement at the office, called again yesterday about the mimeograph machine. She was polite enough, asked me when my due date is and how I'm feeling and all, but it was difficult to explain how to fix the machine over the phone. It would be easier just to go down there and fix it myself. I suggested that to Dickie and he was horrified.

"Absolutely not," he said, shaking his head.

"It would be a lot more efficient."

"I don't want you talking to her," he insisted. "She shouldn't be bothering you."

"Why not? I'm happy to help."

He shook his head vehemently. "It's not appropriate for the daughter of the owner and the wife of the general manager to be the typewriter and mimeograph repair man."

Daddy just promoted Dickie to General Manager and there's some grumbling about this, or so I hear from Oscar. Even though Oscar works in the garage, he knows all the front office gossip. He came by yesterday to bring me a set of socket wrenches.

"Some of the other account execs say he just got the job because he's married to the boss's daughter," Oscar said with a pointed look at me. "But according to the girls in the front office, he's a damn good salesman. They say he could convince Henry Ford to buy a Chevrolet. Charming guy, your husband."

I gave Oscar a weak smile. The line between charm and manipulation is thin and hard to see, even when you're looking right at it.

April 9, 1965

I did it! I fixed Dickie's car. As I suspected, it was the fan belt. I took care of that, then I cleaned the spark plugs and checked the alternator. I changed the oil too.

Then I made the mistake of telling Dickie. He screamed at me for a half hour straight.

"Who do you think you are? You could have ruined the engine or damaged the oil pan."

I tried to keep a straight face. Dickie couldn't find the oil pan if it bit him on the nose.

But there's no point trying to argue with him. I've learned that the hard way. Now I just hang my head, pretend to be sorry, and let my mind go somewhere else until he's done hollering.

But I'm not sorry. Not one little bit. That was the most fun I've had in weeks. I can hardly wait for Dickie's transmission to go out.

For a number of reasons.

Chapter Twenty-Three

KIERSTEN

On Sunday night, Kiersten glanced over at her husband and gave him a nervous smile. She'd wanted to have this conversation alone in a quiet restaurant where they'd be undisturbed.

But the boys had reached that awkward stage where Matt could theoretically babysit his younger siblings, but not in actual practice, because they would stage a bloody coup if he told them to brush their teeth, change into their pajamas, or go to bed.

However, hiring a fifteen-year-old girl to babysit a thirteen-year-old boy and his younger brothers also seemed weird. As a result, they hadn't been out to dinner alone since moving away from the grandparents.

Instead, they'd have to talk while breaking down packing boxes in the garage. The boys sat sprawled around the kitchen table inside the house, ostensibly doing homework. She'd just helped Luke turn in seven missing assignments, and she now knew far more than she cared to about igneous rocks, *The Outsiders*, dividing fractions, and the many tribulations of America's thirteen original colonies.

Garrett stuffed packing paper into a black trash bag. "Remind me again why we're doing this when we have four boys inside who are perfectly capable of doing it themselves?"

Garrett always felt the boys should be assigned substantial "chores" like he'd had growing up on a dairy farm. But their children couldn't do chores around the house because their homework and duties as under-age minor-league baseball and hockey players consumed all their time.

"This isn't the farm, circa 1902." Kiersten stacked the boxes they'd already broken down into a neat pile. "They have homework to do before school tomorrow. Which is one of the things we need to discuss."

Garrett looked stoic, resigned to a conversation he didn't want to have. He'd gotten back from Kansas last night, and the boys had excitedly told him all about Johnny's left-behind adventure on the Pennsylvania Turnpike. After they climbed into bed, he'd turned to her and asked, "Do you want to talk about it?"

She hadn't. "Tomorrow," she'd said. "We need to talk tomorrow. Without the boys."

He'd nodded, rolled onto his side, and fallen immediately asleep while she stayed up half the night imagining horrible things that *could* have happened at the truck stop, but didn't.

They'd left the boys inside and retreated to the garage, armed with box cutters and plastic trash bags, ready for their first serious conversation since they'd moved. She realized with a jolt how long it had been since she'd actually talked to her husband about anything deeper than transportation logistics.

She ran the slender blade along the seam of a cardboard box, took a deep breath, and plunged ahead. "So. Yesterday during the crisis, the neighbors came over, and they were really helpful. They're great people."

He picked up a wardrobe box, placed it on the concrete floor, and stomped it flat with a whomping sound.

She paused.

He looked over at her. "I'm listening."

He wore cargo pants and work gloves. Muscles bulged under the sleeves of his gray T-shirt, and his short hair and square jaw made her heart go soft. Still handsome after all these years.

He'd been her high school crush, but they'd run in different circles. He was preoccupied with hockey and cheerleaders, while Kiersten was quieter, preferring to blend in, except on the basketball court, where she stood out.

They didn't start dating until they ran into each other in the library at Mankato State. He wore a massive white cast over the broken femur that ended his scholarship as well as his hockey career at the University of Minnesota, and he'd transferred to a school closer to home.

Kiersten could not resist when she emerged from a row of illustrated anatomy volumes to find her handsome high school crush struggling to reach a book on an upper shelf from the seat of his wheelchair.

Once they started dating, they fell hard and fast. They got married in the Lutheran church where they'd both been baptized, a giant hometown wedding one month after they'd graduated from college.

Garrett took over the family dairy operation with his dad, and she became a nurse at the small hospital in town, working with the doctor who'd delivered her and Garrett just a couple of decades earlier.

Now as they stood in this garage, a thousand miles from their true home, she felt the distance that had grown up between them over the last few months. It slid around the room like an insidious fog, making her feel like she was embarking on an awkward conversation with a stranger, unsure where or how to begin.

"So you met the neighbors," he prompted as he slashed the box cutter across a cardboard spine.

"Right. The neighbors. And as it turns out, they're all having some . . . issues at school. Rosamund's daughter is being bullied. Piper's daughter is being harassed. They're all run ragged and never home, like us, which is why this thing on the Turnpike happened in the first place."

"Okay." He made no further response as he stacked the carcass of a box on a growing pile of cardboard.

"And Luke is flunking three classes and getting into fights, and Matt hates baseball, and his shoulder is acting up again, and so I was thinking that maybe we should just . . ."

She paused.

He stopped what he was doing, wiped the sweat from his forehead, and looked at her. "We should just . . . ?" He lifted an eyebrow expectantly, waiting for her to finish.

She plunged ahead. "We should just drop out. Of everything. For the rest of the school year."

Silence filled the garage, broken only by the sound of an acorn dropping on the roof. A deep frown creased his face. "Drop out?"

"Yeah," she said. "Like, go on sabbatical. Take a break. Try an experiment to see if we're happier and the boys are happier when we aren't stressed out and running around to seventy-five different activities all the time."

He rested his hands on his hips. "I see."

Anger rose inside her like a wisp of smoke from a newly started fire. She needed to smother it, keep it from spreading to her voice, to her limbs. She needed to stay calm. Histrionics never worked with her rational, stoic husband.

"Actually, you *don't* see." She crumpled a fistful of packing paper. "You don't see because you're *never here*."

"Oh c'mon, Kiersten." He ripped another trash bag from the Hefty box. "That's not fair, and you know it. It's not like I'm off hunting or fishing. Or playing golf. Or jetting off to Vegas for bachelor parties. I'm *working*."

She took a steadying breath. "I know you're working. But this whole *arrangement*"—she made a frustrated gesture toward the packing boxes, the trash cans, and the riding lawnmower, as though the contents of the garage were somehow to blame—"it isn't *working*."

"Fine. I agree. It's not working," he said, aggressively shrugging his shoulders. "But dropping out of everything isn't the solution either. In fact, it's completely insane."

"Why?" She could hear her voice rising an octave, getting defensive again. "Why is it insane?"

"Because our boys are talented athletes. If they quit baseball and hockey for a year, they'll be completely behind. And what about school? Who would teach them?"

"*I* would teach them. And the neighbors would teach them. One of them is a writer." She omitted the word *romance* from Rosamund's résumé. "And the other one is . . ." She faltered, suddenly aware of how amateur it all sounded. "The other one is really good at math and science."

He ran his hand over his close-cropped hair. "I don't think that's going to work, Kiersten."

She hurled her box cutter to the floor and stalked across the garage to where he stood. "Listen to me, Garrett. The boys are miserable, and I'm doing all of this *by myself*. And I am telling you, I can't do it anymore. Do you understand what I'm saying?"

"I know it's hard when I travel, but—"

"But what?" She stepped closer, inches from his face. "But it's okay as long as I don't leave any more kids on the Pennsylvania Turnpike?"

He held her gaze for a long moment, then looked away. She could see his jaw tighten as he took a slow, deliberate step back. He pulled a wad of packing paper from a box and stuffed it into the trash bag. "Look, I understand that you're upset about what happened. But what you're proposing here is radical. It could affect their ability to get into college. To get a baseball or hockey scholarship. All because you're tired of driving."

Her mouth dropped open as the injustice of this statement hit her like a punch.

"I don't like driving? *You don't like raising your own kids.* You're never here! They have no father, and I have no husband."

He smashed the overstuffed garbage bag against the floor with a loud *thwap*. "What do you want me to do, Kiersten? Quit the job that pays our mortgage? Or maybe you want to support the six of us with your part-time paycheck from *1-800 Call an Advice Nurse*?"

His contempt for the words *advice nurse* cut her to the core. Suddenly she felt a flash of hatred for the person she'd always loved most in the world.

"I would be happy to work full-time again if you can find me a boss who likes employees who leave in the middle of a shift to take people to the orthodontist and the pediatrician and the dyslexia tutor and batting practice. Or maybe you'd like me to work nights again and leave the boys home alone while you travel?"

He hung his head. His shoulders rose and fell as he inhaled and exhaled slowly. Then he reached out and gently touched her arm. "I'm sorry. I didn't mean that."

She flinched and pulled away. "Yes, you did."

She sat down on a plastic lawn chair and buried her face in her hands. "This isn't *a life* . . . it's an endless series of appointments and auditions for some kind of terrifying future where our kids will only succeed if they're professional athletes or tech geniuses who graduate from Harvard. I can't live this way anymore. And neither can the boys."

It felt good to say it out loud. To surrender. To admit defeat. To speak the fears that drove her to drive her kids, literally and figuratively, every single day.

He pulled up another lawn chair and sat beside her. "Do you want to take the boys and move back home? I could get an apartment and commute back and forth between DC and Minnesota. I could probably be home one weekend a month, but my parents and your parents would be there, plus all the aunts and uncles, to help with the boys. You wouldn't be alone."

A shiver of fear passed through her. His proposal felt like a prelude to something far worse.

"But they'd never see you," she said. "*I'd* never see you."

His shoulders slumped. "You never see me now."

"But then we'd see you even less. We're a family. Not a collection of people who happen to live in the same house. And the boys need you even more than I do. Especially now, as they get older."

He pinched the bridge of his nose and went silent for a long moment. Finally he spoke. "Tell me how this . . . experiment would work."

A faint smile tugged at her mouth. She wanted his opinion because she valued his judgment, and if he truly thought the Experiment was crazy, then it probably was.

But she also wanted him to give the idea a fair hearing. For the first time since they'd started talking, she felt like he was willing to discuss it with an open mind.

She explained the basic outlines of the plan. "So we do school here at home," she concluded. "But we also do so much more because we live in this incredible place filled with some of the finest museums and historical sites in America."

"Sounds like more driving," he said with a wry smile. "And what about sports?"

"We quit sports for one year, and they play baseball in the backyard and basketball in the driveway. Like we did."

He looked into the distance. "Matthew is an exceptional athlete . . ." His voice trailed off.

She finished the sentence for him. "But not exceptional enough."

"Like father, like son," he said with a faint trace of bitterness. "Even without the injury, I wouldn't have made the jump from Division I college hockey to the NHL."

She looked at him in surprise. He'd hinted at this before but never said it out loud.

"I wanted the boys to do what I wasn't able to do. But deep down I know it's not going to happen for them either."

"When did you realize this?" she asked softly.

"When Matt started playing on this travel team. He's every bit as good as the best kid on that team. But to go pro, he'd need to be *better* than the best kid. Way better. And he's not. He's very good. And that's not good enough."

She wrapped her arms around him. Maybe this was how the Mensa parents of academically gifted kids felt when they realized their child did not have the SAT scores to get into Princeton.

"But he's still so good that I think he can afford to take a year off in seventh grade and play in high school, and that's all I want for him, to have the camaraderie of a team when he gets older. Plus his shoulder needs to heal, and that will never happen if he keeps pitching."

"I agree," she said. "I was never going to play in the WNBA, but I loved the Lady Spartans."

Her husband smiled. "And you led them to a state championship."

"I'm so old that I come from an era when girls' sports teams had the word *lady* added to the name."

He removed his work gloves and took her hand. "I'd rather be old with you than young with someone else."

"I appreciate that." She rested her head on his shoulder. "And I'd rather be married to you than Wayne Gretzky."

"You'd have walk-in closets if you were married to Wayne Gretzky."

"I'd rather have you."

He kissed her temple. "Thank you."

"And now we need to talk about Luke."

He sighed. "I know."

"Luke is the one who needs this most," she said.

"Do you think . . ." He paused. "Do you think he got his dyslexia from me?"

She lifted her head and turned to face him. "Honey, it's dyslexia, not COVID."

"I know, but I've been reading about it, and some researchers think there's a genetic component. Now I'm starting to wonder if I have dyslexia. In school I always felt like I had to work twice as hard to get half as much as my siblings."

Her husband's grades were the stuff of family legend. Mr. D Minus, his mother had called him.

"Which is why sports were so important?" Kiersten asked.

"Exactly." He stood and extended his hand, pulling her up from the lawn chair. "But on the ice I could work half as hard for twice as much."

She picked up her box cutter. "The poor kid *is* working hard. And that's why his grades are so frustrating . . . and heartbreaking."

"I see how he's struggling . . . I see him feeling like he's stupid." Garrett reached for another box. "I don't want him to go through what I went through. If there's a way to help him catch up . . . help him learn without hating every minute of learning. If we can give him that, then I think we should do it."

"He can still work with his reading tutor," she said. "But he'll have more time now. He can meet with her more often."

"This still means a lot more work for you." He gestured toward her with the empty box. "The boys will be home *all the time*. Are you sure you want this?"

She forced herself to really think about what he was asking.

Returning to a quiet, empty house every morning after she dropped the kids at school felt like a reward after those long, hard years when she couldn't have five minutes alone in the bathroom, when little toddler bodies sat outside the shower door, pressing their noses to the glass, as though she were a wax figure in a museum exhibit called *Mommy Washes Her Hair*.

Did she really want to be home with her kids twenty-four hours a day, seven days a week?

An image of her own mother flashed through her mind, pulling bread from the oven while darkness tinted the windows of their old farmhouse at 5:00 a.m. on a cold Minnesota morning.

Her mother rose before dawn each day to make pancakes, bacon, and eggs for five kids, her husband, and the hired man who helped with spring's work and harvest. After breakfast, she weeded her massive garden, pickled and canned the produce she grew there, cleaned the house, baked pies and cookies, and did laundry for seven people, moving around the house like a domestic spirit long after everyone else was asleep.

Her mother could butcher a deer, pluck a pheasant, clean a walleye. Kiersten's family never had anything extra, but her mother always made sure they had enough.

Are you sure you want this?

Garrett was asking the wrong question. Motherhood wasn't about what you wanted. Motherhood was about what your kids needed most.

Her kids needed this. She needed it too.

"I want my kids to have what we had growing up . . . I want them to have space and time . . . time to play . . . time to read . . . time to be bored."

He hesitated for a moment; then he said, "Do you *really* have to take away the electronics? They'll mutiny."

"When it comes to electronics, our kids are like alcoholics trying to drink socially. One drink is too many, and a thousand aren't enough."

"You think you can hold the line?" he asked, clearly skeptical.

"I can try," she said. "And if it's impossible, we can return to our current arrangement where we all live in the minivan subsisting on Happy Meals while I literally drive myself and everyone else crazy and then when we come home, I shout at everyone to stop playing *Fortnite* long enough to do their homework."

"People will think we've joined a weird cult." He handed her another box. "They'll think we've become crazy religious right-wingers."

"Or crazy environmental left-wingers," she said.

"Or . . . maybe we're going sane while everyone else is staying crazy?"

She grinned. "It feels dangerous almost, to go against the flow, to do something no one else is doing. But at this point, I'm beyond caring what other people think. I just want the boys to have at least one or two childhood memories from a place other than the back of our minivan."

"Okay." His hands went still, and he looked her in the eye. "I trust your judgment, Kiersten. If you think this is the best thing for the boys right now, then I'm on board. When do we start?"

"We." She took a step closer and smiled up at him. "I like that."

"From now on, I'll take the boys every Sunday afternoon to give you a break," he said. "We'll go to a Capitals or a Nationals game or go hiking or visit a battlefield. I might still have to do a few work calls on Sunday nights, but I'll tell them weekend travel is a hard no. I'm sorry I didn't do it sooner."

"That would be huge."

"I have a degree in animal husbandry, you know. I can teach them about the miracle of the many cow stomachs."

She clinked her box cutter against his. "To cow stomachs."

He leaned over and kissed her softly on the mouth. "To cow stomachs."

Chapter Twenty-Four

PIPER

Piper had expected the pushback to come from her kids. But when she and her husband pitched the idea, the girls were surprisingly open to the Experiment, especially Caitlin, who quietly said school made her stomach hurt and she'd be happy to stay home for a while.

Her heart crumpled when Caitlin spoke these words. Her daughter had been more impacted by Alex Orlov than she had realized.

However, a screaming, tear-filled, door-slamming fight accompanied the pronouncement about dramatically limiting screen time. She felt like they'd taken one step forward and two steps back.

And then her mother-in-law weighed in.

"Perhaps this isn't a completely rational idea," Brendan's mother said over lunch at Le Petite, an adorable French restaurant in Old Town, on a chilly Monday at a few minutes after noon. Piper had always wanted to try this place, and the food was fantastic, but Sylvia was giving her indigestion.

Piper swallowed her sole and tried to formulate an answer.

Her father-in-law was a college administrator, and her mother-in-law taught English at a prestigious all-boys prep school in Connecticut.

Brendan and Piper had intended to speak with Sylvia, to get her advice and thoughts, but the girls beat them to it. They'd called Grandma right away to share the news about the Experiment.

Sylvia had immediately taken two days off and made a special trip down from Connecticut to speak with Piper and Brendan about this decision. And, of course, as fate would have it, Brendan was called out of town at the last minute, leaving Piper to face her mother-in-law *alone*.

Piper knew it had almost given her mother-in-law a heart attack when her son joined the Marine Corps after college instead of pursuing a PhD or attending law school. And then when Brendan went on to join the diplomatic corps, not as a diplomat, but as the gun-toting person who *protected* the diplomats, it almost caused an irreconcilable rift in their relationship.

And now *this*, her own grandchildren removed from their excellent blue-ribbon public school to be homeschooled by their hapless mother. It was clearly too much for this well-dressed, highly educated woman with a PhD in elementary education from Columbia. Piper could read all this in the way her mother-in-law clenched her fork.

"I just don't understand what you're hoping to *accomplish* here," Sylvia said.

"We're hoping to accomplish sanity." Piper patted her mouth with her napkin. "And peace. Balance. Togetherness."

"Yes, and that's all very nice, but what about their *education*?"

Piper toyed with her delicious sole meunière. Part of her wanted to confess the truth, to admit that she knew teaching was the hardest job on the planet and that deep down she was terrified she and other mothers didn't have what it took to educate their own kids.

But Sylvia was *not* the kind of person to whom one admitted deep-seated insecurities.

Instead, Piper kept her answer vague. She felt like a politician answering a question without answering the question. "We are working hard to prepare, and I'm confident we can handle it."

Her mother-in-law raised an eyebrow and lifted her wineglass to her lips, taking a small judicious sip. "These elementary and middle school years are vitally important. Did you know that a recent study has shown a *disparity in pay* between adults who had an experienced kindergarten teacher and adults who had a first-year kindergarten teacher?"

Piper clenched her napkin. "Really."

Sylvia leaned across the table. "Look, Piper, I know you mean well, but I'm not sure you see the *big picture* here."

"And what's that?" Piper asked, her voice tight.

"I routinely see boys with a 1580 or 1590 on the SAT with a million extracurriculars get wait-listed at second-tier schools. The college-application process gets more competitive every year, and to pull these girls out of a perfectly good public school during these critical elementary and middle school years, well, it's just *irresponsible*."

"I'm sorry you feel that way," Piper said stiffly.

"Let's talk about what's really going on here, Piper." Her mother-in-law leaned back in her chair.

Piper blinked. "Something else is going on here?"

"It's your *job*." Sylvia put her fork down with a sharp clink. "Your lack of *direction*. Have you considered going back to school, getting your master's? They have an excellent program for working adults at Georgetown. It would fill this void you have in your life right now that you seem to be filling with *trad wife nonsense* like homeschooling."

"Trad wife nonsense?" Piper almost snorted. And how did her mother-in-law even *know* about trad wives? They must have done a story on NPR.

"That's what this seems to be about." Sylvia waved her wineglass in the air. "Some sort of *back-to-the-land* movement."

Piper sighed. "All we want is to keep the girls safe and happy. So we're going to keep them home, just for the rest of the year, and then we'll reevaluate."

Sylvia leaned across the table and hissed in a low voice. "You young women today have no idea how good you have it."

Piper's shoulders rose a few inches as she braced for a lecture. "What do you mean?"

"The women of my generation fought hard so that women like you could work outside the home, have a career. We fought for girls to get a college education, just like their brothers. And now you want to throw it all away." She made a wild gesture with her napkin. "You're retreating back into the kitchen, like these advances mean *nothing*."

Piper frowned, slightly alarmed. Her mother-in-law wasn't usually so *strident*. "I'm not tossing anything away. I'm just saying we need to slow down a little bit and smell the . . ." Well, not roses. She'd somehow killed all the Knock Out roses she'd planted in her front yard. "And smell the daisies."

"What if the girls grow up to be Soft Girls?"

Piper gave her a blank stare. "What's a 'Soft Girl'?"

Her mother-in-law huffed an impatient sigh. "Don't you *ever* listen to NPR?"

"Well I—" Piper began.

"It's a new trend," her mother-in-law explained, rolling her eyes. "Instead of working and building a career, young women are becoming stay-at-home girlfriends. They spend their days cooking and cleaning for their boyfriends and focusing on their complicated skin-care regimes and making TikTok videos. In Sweden they call them Soft Girls."

"Well, that's not very smart."

"Of course it isn't smart!" Sylvia raised her voice, and the other diners cast a concerned glance in their direction. "No economic security. No career. Utterly dependent on a man for support. And when he gets tired of her, she's both homeless and jobless until the next man comes along."

"Look." Piper felt a surge of anger and worked hard to keep it from her voice. Of course she didn't want her girls to become some kind of cautionary tale on *All Things Considered*. "That's not what this is about.

My girls are strong and independent. But they're also stressed out and exhausted. That's why we're doing this."

And because Caitlin was being harassed at school. But she didn't want to burden her mother-in-law with those worries on top of everything else.

"But who will teach them the things they need to learn?" Sylvia asked.

"Each mom has expertise in a certain area," Piper said, drawing on the emergency supply of patience she normally reserved for trips to the DMV or the fifth consecutive showing of a children's musical. "For example, one of the moms is a writer. She'll teach English."

Her mother-in-law narrowed her eyes. "What *kind* of a writer?"

"Well, she writes novels," Piper said uneasily.

"What *kinds* of novels?"

"Well." Piper wiped her clammy palms on her napkin. "She writes historical fiction."

The color drained from her mother-in-law's face. "What *kind* of historical fiction?"

"Well . . ." Piper stammered. "She writes . . . historical romance novels, but they're *very good* historical romance novels. So good they made them into a series on Netflix."

Her mother-in-law's mouth dropped open. "You're allowing a woman who writes *genre fiction* to teach my granddaughters *English literature*?"

"Look, it will be like . . . *Little Women*," Piper said before taking a big swig from her wineglass.

"How could this *possibly* be like *Little Women*?" her mother-in-law asked icily.

"Well." Piper swallowed and wiped her mouth with her napkin as she tried to construct an answer. "Remember when Amy brought the limes to school and her teacher confiscated them and then the teacher beat Amy's hands with a stick as punishment and Marmee found out and she said . . ."

Piper paused, trying to remember what Marmee could possibly have said. "And Marmee said, 'Enough is enough. *I will educate my girls at home.*'" She thrust her fork in the air to emphasize these words. "If it was good enough for the March family, it's good enough for us."

Sylvia raised a skeptical brow. "This is not 1863, and you are *not* Marmee."

"Perhaps not," Piper said stiffly. "But I'm a mom in 2025 who feels like the way we're doing things isn't working. I've talked to my husband and my daughters, and we all want to try something different. And maybe it will be great and maybe it will be a disaster, but we need to try because it is my responsibility as a parent to keep my daughters safe and happy. And right now, they are neither."

Sylvia rolled her eyes. "Don't cry to me when the girls end up at some college no one's ever heard of because of what you've done."

Piper sighed. Her mother-in-law had forgotten, or perhaps she hadn't, that Piper had actually attended a college no one had ever heard of. She'd had the time of her life, met the people who were still some of her closest friends to this day, and also managed to get an excellent education at the same time.

"We appreciate your support," Piper said with the biggest, falsest smile she could muster. "Do you want to order dessert?"

Chapter Twenty-Five

KIERSTEN

Monday morning Kiersten dropped the boys at school and returned to the disaster awaiting her at home. The house on Monday mornings always reminded her of a hockey arena after a game, when everyone goes home, leaving behind an empty building strewn with half-empty cups, ketchup packets, and lone mittens.

Would her house look like Monday morning *every day* once they started homeschooling?

Probably. But the idea still made sense. She and Garrett planned to speak with the boys tonight. If they were on board, the Experiment would move ahead.

In the meantime, she needed to learn more about how to homeschool. And she needed to make more progress unpacking the remaining boxes in the basement.

Her fingers caressed the diary on her kitchen counter.

But first she needed to find the owner of these diaries so she could return them, and the cash, to their rightful owner. She felt a sense of urgency about this. Whoever had written them must be in her eighties by now.

She picked up her phone and called Henry DiLorenzo, the previous owner of her house. He answered on the sixth ring, just as she was about to hang up. After reminding him of who she was and how she knew him, she explained why she was calling.

"Oh gosh," Henry said. "I'm sorry you got saddled with those boxes. We organized a garage sale on Beaverbrook about ten years ago. Someone in the neighborhood donated a set of encyclopedias. But they didn't sell, so I lugged 'em back inside with some other junk I planned to take to Goodwill. Then I forgot all about them."

"I found some diaries hidden inside," Kiersten explained. "They belong to a woman who lived on Beaverbrook in 1965."

"That was a lifetime ago." Henry gave a wistful sigh. "We moved to Beaverbrook in June of '67. All the homes were new then. State of the art. Myrtle knew all the ladies on the block, of course. They were always getting together for coffee. Lots of nice families. Most of the men worked at the Pentagon or the State Department. The wives stayed home, took care of the house and the kids. Beaverbrook was a great place to raise a family."

"Does the name Dottie ring any bells?"

"No," he said slowly. "Not with me, but I didn't know the ladies the way Myrtle did. But Myrtle, well . . . she's not so good with names anymore . . ." His voice trailed off, and suddenly Kiersten felt terrible for asking him questions.

Henry and Myrtle had sold their house because Myrtle developed Alzheimer's and needed to move into a memory-care unit. Henry had moved into an assisted living apartment in the same complex. Garrett's old college roommate said it broke his grandfather's heart to live apart from his wife of almost sixty years.

She thanked Henry for his time and hung up as the dishwasher hummed in the background. Then she sat down in the tiny breakfast nook off the kitchen, picked up the diary, and began to read.

Chapter Twenty-Six

DOTTIE

April 12, 1965

We went to a dinner party last night at Clara and Howard's house. Clara looked lovely as always, and she served a beautiful pimento cheese dip appetizer, Steak Diane, which she flambeed perfectly at the table without setting any of her guests on fire, stuffed peppers and Baked Alaska for dessert. I have to say, it was pretty impressive.

Dickie was wonderful, while we were there.

But as soon as we got in the car, he started up again. Why can't I arrange flowers like she can? Why isn't our house decorated like theirs? Why don't I wear my hair in a bouffant, like hers?

"You could never pull off a dinner party like that. You'd probably serve boiled carburetors and spark plugs à la mode. I should have married someone else, someone more . . . feminine."

I bit down on my tongue so hard I tasted blood. If he were married to someone else, he wouldn't know Howard, whose father is the president of the bank, or my godfather, Roy, who's the majority leader of the state Senate and was also there last night. Without me, Dickie would never have been invited to that dinner party in the first place. Without me, Dickie wouldn't be driving a new car to a new house while wearing a fancy watch and an expensive suit.

"A man could go far with a wife like that," Dickie said, looking thoughtful. "I should have married someone like Clara."

A little piece of my heart flaked off and fell away when he said that. But anger flashed through me too. I could feel it, loosening my tongue, burning my cheeks.

"Maybe I should have married someone who doesn't scream at me all the time," I shot back.

"No one else would want you." His tone was so matter of fact that a tiny part of me wondered if it was true. "A woman who works on cars in her spare time? Who wants a wife who can change the oil but can't make a decent pie crust? If I hadn't come along, you'd die an old maid."

"I'd rather be an old maid than live with someone who criticizes everything I do." The words flew out of my mouth before I could bite them back and the moment I said it, I realized it was true.

"Careful, Dottie." His tone was soft, but menacing, too, like a hammer wrapped in velvet.

"Why did you marry me, if I'm so deficient?" I hated the plaintive undertone in my voice, the pain that I couldn't quite scrub from my words.

He shrugged. "I thought I could teach you to be a good wife. But unfortunately for me, you're not as smart as everyone said you were." Then he gave me a charming smile. "But don't worry. I won't give up on you."

He reached over and touched my belly. "At least you can supply me with a son."

I flinched and scooted closer to the window. He scowled. "But you'll probably screw that up too and give birth to a girl."

I stared out the window, watching the world go by. He's like Dr. Jekyll and Mr. Hyde.

And I wish I wasn't married to either one of them.

April 28, 1965

I lied and told Dickie I needed the car today because of a baby appointment with Dr. Carlyle. But I didn't have an appointment. Instead I drove over to see Ruby again.

I wanted to ask if I could stay with her for a couple days, until I figure out what to do, until I work up the courage to leave.

I wanted to tell her everything.

But as we sat there in her tiny kitchen with her beautiful baby sitting on her lap, babbling and waving her chubby little hands, I just couldn't do it. The words stuck to the roof of my mouth like peanut butter.

Dickie doesn't hit me or beat me. He's not violent. He's just . . . mean. He says I'm too sensitive, and that everything he does and says is for my own good, to help me improve, to help me become a better wife.

And what if that's true? What if he's doing all this out of some twisted, distorted sense of *love*?

I honestly don't think he can help it. He's wired this way. Or he learned it from his own parents, who had a very unhappy marriage before his mother died. At least, that's the impression I've gotten from Dickie.

I thought about all this as Ruby sat across from me, giving her baby a bottle.

"Does your husband ever . . . give you advice?" I asked tentatively.

She laughed. "Oh gosh, yes. He's full of terrible ideas. Like he thinks we should plant hydrangeas on the south side of the house, even though they would absolutely *fry* in the heat. I've told him, but he won't listen. So I'll let him plant them where he wants, and then they'll all die, and he'll see that I was right."

I gave her a weak smile and kept my mouth shut.

I can't tell Ruby. She wouldn't understand. And I have the baby to think about.

Those years after Mother died were so hard. I was always the only girl who didn't have a mom to help her pick out a prom dress or give her advice about boys. I don't want my baby to be the only child without a father, or worse yet, to be the only child in the class with divorced parents.

Lots of women have it worse. Lots of men have it worse too. Like poor Danny, getting shot at every day and then bleeding to death in the jungle before the medics could arrive. All I have to do is clean my house and cook some meals. I need to keep things in perspective.

And maybe Dickie is right. Maybe I *am* too sensitive. Plus, I'm sort of ashamed. If my marriage isn't working, don't I share half the blame for that? Maybe I just need to have a better attitude. Maybe I just need to try harder.

Chapter Twenty-Seven

KIERSTEN

As she loaded the dishwasher that night, Kiersten's mind returned to Dottie and 1965.

He's like Dr. Jekyll and Mr. Hyde.

And I wish I wasn't married to either one of them.

What would it be like to live in an era when divorce was considered a scandal, with real social consequences for leaving a husband, even an abusive one? She'd always believed that her mother and grandmother had grown up in a time similar to hers. After all, they had the right to vote. It's not like they were Mary Poppins–era suffragettes.

But now she was starting to wonder if she'd taken some things for granted. Like the right to pursue any career she wanted and to keep working, even after she got married and had children. Or the right to be Kiersten Cleaver after marriage, instead of *Mrs. Garrett Cleaver*, with her name and identity subsumed by her husband.

Those old black-and-white *Leave It to Beaver* reruns she'd sometimes seen on TV had given her an impression of a wholesome, more innocent past. But now she felt like she'd stumbled onto the bad side of the good old days.

She'd done some creative googling that morning after reading the next entry, but she still couldn't figure out Dottie's last name or her maiden name. But if she could find an old newspaper, she could look for local car-dealership ads from 1965. And she could only find those at the library. That was the next logical step. That and speaking to Lillian, her eighty-seven-year-old neighbor who was currently in Chicago, visiting her son.

But first she had to make sure the boys were on board with the Experiment. The family room went quiet for a moment as Kiersten's husband turned off the Monday Night Football game playing on TV. The room erupted in howls of protest.

"We need to talk, guys," Garrett said. "Family meeting."

The boys groaned. "Is this about chores?" Matt asked.

"I'll bet it's about grades. Mom's been checking the portal again." Luke shot Kiersten a resentful look.

"Sit down, boys." She set a bowl of popcorn in the middle of the kitchen table. "We have some news."

The boys gathered around the table and began to shovel handfuls of popcorn into their mouths.

She took a deep breath and looked at her husband. He gave her a reassuring smile, and she cleared her throat.

"Okay. So, your dad and I have been talking. And I've also been talking with Mrs. Mondello and Ms. Hensler across the street. And we'd like to pull you guys out of school for the rest of the year."

Silence enveloped the room. Then wild whoops of joy exploded through the kitchen, making her ears ring.

"Are you *serious*?"

"This is the best news *ever*."

"No school? *At all?*"

Her husband raised his hands in the air to silence the whooping. "Please, guys. Let your mother finish."

So far so good. Kiersten squared her shoulders and launched into the rest of the proposal, the part they might not be so enthusiastic about. The school-at-home part. The no-sports-or-activities part.

When she finished, Matt shrugged. "I'm okay with that."

Kiersten couldn't hide her shock. "You are?" She'd expected an argument, or at least a negotiation of some sort.

"Baseball isn't fun anymore, since I'm not playing with my friends. And my shoulder aches all the time. I don't mind taking a break."

"Me too," Luke said.

Johnny ran around the table, waving his hands in the air like a joyful berserker. "This is *awesome*."

Garrett gently steered him back to his seat. "There's more. Your mom's not done."

"Yeah," Kiersten said, bracing herself for the reaction to the rest of her announcement. "Wait till you hear the next part."

The boys looked at her warily. "Are you going to make us do IXL?" Luke asked, naming the hated online "tool" the school assigned in addition to homework.

"Or CK-12?" Matt asked, naming the other online education app the boys most loathed.

"The opposite actually." Kiersten took a deep breath. "No school also means no electronics. No devices. No phones. No iPads or video games."

The reaction was swift and outraged. *"What?"*

"Mom, you can't *do* that."

"That's like . . . not *constitutional*."

Garrett smiled. "There is nothing in the Bill of Rights about an inalienable right to *Minecraft*."

"So no video games *ever*?"

"I talked to the other moms, and you guys can have your devices for one hour on Wednesday nights," Kiersten said. "You can use that time to text or FaceTime friends. You can play video games. But that's it. The rest of the time we keep all your devices locked up in the fire safe with the passports and the birth certificates."

They absorbed this terrible pronouncement with wide eyes.

Then Matt asked, "What about TV? Like, you know, watching shows?"

"We only watch shows and movies together, here in the family room, on Saturday nights," Kiersten said. "And we have to agree on the show. If we don't all agree, we don't watch anything."

She'd gone too far. A chorus of outrage met this pronouncement.

"Mom. This is *wrong*."

"This is *uncivilized*."

"This is, like, how . . . *cave people* lived."

"Do we have to do this?" Matt asked.

"No." Kiersten shrugged. "We do not have to do this. That's the purpose of this meeting. We'd like to try it, but ultimately it's up to you guys. It's your childhood and it's your decision."

"So we really get to be the ones who decide?" Luke crossed his arms, his voice heavy with suspicion.

"Yes," Kiersten said. "I'd like to see if we're happier when we aren't running around like crazy people. But this won't work if Dad and I are leading and you guys aren't following. You have to want this, too, or the Experiment will fail. So it really is up to you."

A deep line appeared on Matt's forehead, and Johnny looked the way he did when he attempted to write in cursive, the tip of his tongue protruding, completely absorbed in thinking hard. She could see they were taking the proposal seriously, weighing the pros and cons.

Finally, Luke spoke. "I'm in," he said, sitting up in his chair. "You can take my phone. I don't even care as long as I don't have to sit in school all day long, bored out of my mind, listening to teachers go on and on about stuff I don't care about."

Matt looked at his brother with a thoughtful expression. "If we were back in Minnesota, I'd say no, 'cause I'd miss my friends. But I haven't really made any friends here yet, so I don't have anyone to miss. And maybe if I take a break from baseball, my shoulder will stop hurting."

"James? Johnny?" Garrett asked.

"I want to try it," James said. "But I don't want to do school with *girls*."

Kiersten stifled a smile. "I'm sorry to hear that, but the girls next door are part of the package."

"Why can't we just do it by ourselves?" James asked.

"'Cause Mom can't teach us math," Luke pointed out.

Unfortunately, this was true. "Mrs. Mondello will teach math and science. Ms. Hensler will do English and history."

"I'll do it," Johnny said. "'Cause then I can be with Mommy all day." Her heart melted. "Even if she doesn't know anything about how to be a teacher."

"Thank you, Johnny. Your confidence is heartwarming."

"I guess I'll do it too," James said.

Garrett gave him a nod of approval. "Glad to hear it."

"So we don't have to go to school in the morning?" Luke asked hopefully. "Can I skip my homework?"

"You stay in school for one more week. We'll get everything ready, and then we'll stop going to school and we'll start the Experiment."

"What's an experiment?" Johnny asked.

"An experiment is when you do something to see how something works, even if you aren't sure how it's going to turn out," Matt said.

His brothers nodded gravely, and Kiersten's chest tingled. They had so much faith in her. Even though she had absolutely no idea what she was doing.

"Thank you, Mom," Luke said.

She looked at him, eyebrows raised in surprise. Of all her sons, Luke was the most like her. As a result, they butted heads all day long. Kiersten was the Bad Cop in his life, the person who made him do all the things he didn't want to do. But he had a wry sense of humor and a core of compassion that often made him her secret favorite.

"For what?" she asked.

"For being, like, *brave.* I don't think most moms would try something this . . . you know . . . off the chain."

True. But most moms had not forgotten a child at a truck stop on the Pennsylvania Turnpike.

"Desperate times call for desperate measures," she said, ruffling his blond hair. "Hopefully this will be great. And if it isn't, you'll know what *not* to do when you have kids."

This year would either go down in family lore as the happiest year of their life, the year their mother made learning fun . . . or it would be forever known as that lost year when they learned absolutely nothing, making each subsequent year of school harder and harder until they finally flunked the SAT and failed to get into college.

Inspirational dream or cautionary tale. They were about to find out which path they'd chosen.

It was sort of like Dottie's marriage, she thought as she climbed into bed that night, and reached for the diary on her bedside table. The Experiment could be a dream solution to all their problems . . . or it could twist into a nightmare.

Chapter Twenty-Eight

DOTTIE

May 4, 1965

To hell with trying harder.

He *took my shoes.*

Dickie called Dr. Carlyle's office and found out I didn't have an appointment. He screamed at me until I admitted I lied and visited Ruby instead.

He says I'm dishonest and untrustworthy and I spend too much time running around and not enough time at home, being a good wife.

Then he took my shoes and locked them in the nuclear fallout shelter underneath the garage.

And now I can't leave the house because *I have no damn shoes.*

This is all because I didn't iron the sheets. I knew there'd be trouble if I didn't iron the sheets, but I just . . . I don't know. It was like an act of rebellion. Sometimes I just want to yell, "you're not the boss of me," like a child. But in reality, Dickie *is* the boss of me, because that *bastard* is my husband.

I can't believe this is happening.

When we got into bed last night, Dickie saw the wrinkles and he lost his mind. He screamed and screamed. Then he threw all my shoes into a laundry basket, carried them down to the basement, and locked them in the fallout shelter with a padlock. He even took my bedroom slippers. And now I can't leave the house, unless I want to walk down the street barefoot.

Then he made me sit down with a pen and a notebook and take notes while he dictated more rules I need to follow. Another list. In addition to the expectation of a spotless house and a three-course meal when he walks in the door each night at 6 p.m. I also have to:

1. Prepare for his homecoming by making myself more attractive. He suggests adding a ribbon to my insufficiently bouffant-ed hairdo, applying lipstick, and changing into a nice dress, thus creating even more laundry to wash each week.

2. Be carefree and interesting. Yes, that's right. I've spent the entire day scrubbing and baking and cleaning, plus vomiting from the morning sickness, but when he returns home from a long, exhausting day in the office, I'm supposed to be cheerful, funny, and *lighthearted*.

3. Make sure the baby is quiet when he gets home from work. Not sure how I'm expected to accomplish this once the baby actually arrives, but he says he does not want to return home to a screaming baby and a strung-out wife after a "long, hard day" at the office

(where I also once worked, I might add, and found each day to be interesting and stimulating).

4. In the coming months when the weather cools, I'm supposed to light a fire and welcome him with a warm drink, like a hot toddy. On warm days, a gin and tonic should await him on the back porch.

Rules 5 through 18: Don't question him, argue with him, voice opinions to him, or complain. In other words, he told me I need to shut up and smile. This home is his castle (purchased by my father) and apparently I'm the deaf, mute, and blind princess relegated to walking the parapet with him for the rest of my natural life.

Then, after dictating these rules for a happy marriage and stealing all my shoes, he left. He didn't come home until 5 a.m. I pretended to be asleep when he came in.

Not questioning his whereabouts or activities when he's been out all night is Rule #19.

Then he showered and went to work without saying a word.

Now he's gone and I'm sitting here, literally barefoot and pregnant, in my kitchen.

I know what I need to do now. I just have to figure out how to do it. Because I almost forgot to record rule #20.

If I try to leave, he'll kill me.

Chapter Twenty-Nine

PIPER

Piper's feet pounded out a cadence of unanswerable questions as her shoes hit the pavement over and over again on the bike path along the George Washington Memorial Parkway.

Are we safe? Are we safe? Are we safe?

But the answers were as elusive now as they'd been three miles ago when she started her run.

She needed this. She hadn't been sleeping, thanks to the news about Hawkeye Slaughter's disappearance, her disturbing visit to Bruno Orlov's house, the bloody notebook paper nailed to the tree, Caitlin's desire to spend more time alone in her room and less time with the rest of the family. And her mother-in-law had started emailing academic studies intimating that her granddaughters would have "suboptimal social and emotional outcomes" and wind up making DIY porn on OnlyFans if Piper pulled them out of school.

And then she'd awoken to the latest threat from Hawkeye Slaughter, posted on X at 3:00 a.m. The revolution is coming. First person up against the wall with a bullet in her head: Piper Mondello #FascistsMustDie

She glanced at her Apple Watch and slowed her pace as she jogged off the bike path, crossed over the stone bridge, and turned onto the wide street that fed into her neighborhood.

Time to cool down and head home. She'd asked Kiersten and Rosamund to keep an eye on the house while she was gone, but she wasn't comfortable leaving the girls home alone when Brendan was out of town, even for a short run.

She slowed to a walk as she approached Haskel Avenue and the massive construction project underway on this street two blocks down from Beaverbrook Lane. A new sign had just gone up. She moved closer to take a look.

A year ago, this corner of Haskel had held a single home, a beautiful old brick mansion set back from the street on a four-acre lot. Now the trees were gone, and the skeletal frames of six homes under construction stood on the lot. With the trees uprooted and hauled away, the Potomac sparkled in the late-afternoon light behind the partially constructed homes.

She approached the sign and stopped to catch her breath.

Potomac Crest

4 Bedroom homes with river views, starting at $2.5 million

She frowned at the sign, conflicted. If these new homes were selling for $2.5 million, then surely her own home a couple of streets over had risen in value as well?

But if they sold their current home, she'd have to live in a shipping container because she and Brendan could never afford to buy another one in their current neighborhood, given these prices.

She squinted at the words running across the bottom.

This project brought to you by The Dynamo Development Corporation, Davis Homebuilders, and The Davis Real Estate Group.

Dynamo Development sounded vaguely familiar. And Davis Homebuilders and Davis Real Estate must be the Influencer's husband, Trey Davis, and his father, Chip.

Interesting. They were doing this project, plus the two homes under construction on Beaverbrook. Business must be good.

She walked the rest of the way home to finish cooling down. As she turned onto Beaverbrook, she stumbled, almost tripping over a small pile of crumbling bricks that had fallen away from the curved sign announcing the entrance to the cul-de-sac.

She bent and moved the bricks away from the sidewalk, closer to the sign, so no one else would trip. The **Beaverbrook on the Potomac** sign had clearly seen better days. Maybe they could take up a neighborhood collection and hire someone to fix it.

As she approached her own house, she squinted at the front porch, where a package sat.

She sighed. How many times had she told the girls they had to *ask* before ordering fancy blow-dryers, sparkly headbands, and inflatable unicorns on Amazon?

She jogged up her front steps and examined the package.

Emblazoned across the box she read the word **PERISHABLE**, along with the logo for Pet Lovers' Depot, and her name and address.

But their dog had died six months ago . . . they didn't have any pets.

She carried the package into the kitchen and contemplated it for a long moment.

Taking a deep breath, she slid a knife under the flap and opened it.

Chapter Thirty

KIERSTEN

Kiersten wiped the sweat from her brow as she finished unpacking one of the last boxes in the basement. She'd made excellent progress today, and now it was time for her reward.

She made a cup of coffee, grabbed a Milano cookie from her secret stash, and sat down with Dottie's diary.

The diary felt a little bit like a soap opera. Or a series on Netflix. It took enormous self-discipline not to binge all the entries at once. But she resisted this impulse, forcing herself to read slowly and carefully, absorbing all the little details that might help her figure out who'd written them.

Each day she felt a little more anxious to learn the ending to Dottie's story . . . to find out if that ending was happy.

Or not.

Chapter Thirty-One

DOTTIE

May 5, 1965

Dickie returned home last night after work and pretended like nothing had happened. I was waiting at the door (barefoot) with a smile, a gin and tonic, and a Goddamn ribbon in my hair.

We ate dinner and then sat out on the back porch together. He asked me how I'm feeling. I asked if he had a nice day. He then proceeded with a long monologue about everyone in the office, complete with belittling nicknames for people I know to be smart, capable, and kind, including my father, who he now calls Gerald the Magnificent in a sneering voice.

He also said I can earn my shoes back if I live by his rules and demonstrate that I can be a perfect wife for the next two weeks. He said I'm off to an excellent start.

So by God, I will. And then I will put on those shoes, walk out the door, and never come back.

I thought about calling Daddy, but he's down at the house in Florida for the next few months and we're all on a party line here on Beaverbrook Lane. Half the neighborhood listens in. You can always tell from the subtle clicking sound in the background in the middle of a conversation.

So if I tell Daddy what's going on while he's down in Florida, everyone will know.

Or I could walk out of the house right now, barefoot, and ask the lady next door for help. But honestly, I'm not sure she'd believe me. Everyone loves Dickie. Handsome, charming Dickie. And even if she did believe me, he's still the father of my child. I don't want to destroy his reputation. I just don't want to be married to him anymore.

So I'll bide my time and earn back my damn shoes. Then I'll leave quietly and head down to Daddy in Florida. I'll have the baby there and return home after Daddy fires Dickie and sends him packing. Being a divorced single mother will cause a scandal, and it won't be easy, but anything is easier than living like this.

May 12, 1965

Dickie says I'm continuing to make excellent progress. It took all the self-control I had not to spit in his eye.

He likes an elaborate dessert with the evening meal every night. And he gets really angry if I make the same meal two nights in a row, but he also has me on a tight budget. He's arranged to have the groceries delivered and he doesn't give me much to work with, because he's so damn stingy.

So I've found ways to create entirely new meals using leftovers from the night before, including dessert. A Bundt cake on Monday becomes strawberry shortcake on Tuesday and a trifle on Wednesday. Mashed potatoes on Wednesday become potato croquettes on Thursday. Pot roast on Thursday becomes pulled pork BBQ sandwiches on Friday. It's kind of like a mechanical problem. I take the inputs I'm given and then I combine the components to build something completely new the next day.

One more week until I have my shoes. And my freedom.

Chapter Thirty-Two

PIPER

Piper's hand flew to her mouth as she bit back a scream. Her toes curled in her shoes as a wriggling, writhing mass of live worms undulated inside the box.

Piper jumped back from the counter as the girls trooped into the kitchen.

"Mom. Are you okay?" Caitlin asked, peering at her mom.

"Did you cut yourself on the mandolin again?" Olivia asked.

"I'm . . . I'm fine." Piper took a steadying breath. She had to stay calm, for the girls. "I just . . . um. I think we got a delivery intended for someone else."

They all turned to stare at the box on the kitchen counter.

"What is it?" Caitlin whispered.

Piper swallowed. "Worms."

Olivia, always the most excitable of her three children, began to dance up and down on her toes, shrieking. "Where? Where? I *hate* worms!"

"Calm down," Piper hissed. "They're contained."

"Are you going to return them?" Bella asked. "Like when we order tap shoes and they're too small?"

"That's a good idea." Piper forced a smile. "You girls go back down to the basement and keep watching your movie. I'm going to call the company now and ask them to come and pick up their worms."

"Can I see them first?" Bella asked. She had a higher tolerance for squeamish things than her sisters did.

"All right."

They all moved slowly toward the island. Bella climbed onto a counter stool and looked down into the belly of the beast, or the box as it were.

"Ew . . . they're alive . . ." she said, wrinkling her nose. "They're *moving*."

Piper shuddered and forced herself to look inside the box again. Her skin began to crawl as she gazed down at a container filled with hundreds of small, plump yellow worms.

"Okay. That's it. Show's over. Go back to your movie. I'll handle our . . . delivery."

She glanced at the paper that had come with the box and found a customer-service number for Pet Lovers' Depot, purveyor of live insects for birds, chickens, geckos, and other exotic pets.

After waiting on hold for ten minutes, a real live human customer-service representative named Angel came on the line.

Piper explained what had happened. Angel asked her to spell her first and last names, followed by her address.

"That's weird," Angel said. "Your address is correct. I mean, your address is the shipping address we have on file."

"But I never ordered this," Piper said.

"Would you mind giving me the last four digits of your credit card?"

Piper complied and heard the clatter of a keyboard on the other end of the line.

"Hmm. We have a different credit card on file. So it's your name and address, but someone else's credit card."

A sick feeling settled over Piper, like she'd eaten something bad, bad like a box of mealworms.

"Angel, can you give me the name attached to the credit card you have on file?" she asked.

"I'm really sorry, but I can't. I'm not allowed to share credit card information."

Damn. Of course she couldn't.

"Listen, could you do me a favor?"

"Sure," Angel said cheerfully.

"If anyone tries to have something sent to this address again, can you call us first to verify before shipping?"

There was a pause. Then Angel said, "You think it's a prank?"

"I do."

"That does happen sometimes," she conceded with a sigh. "Given the nature of our products."

"I understand, and I appreciate your help," Piper said.

"You can return them, though," Angel said helpfully. "Just drop them off at your nearest Pet Lovers' Depot."

"I'll do that right now. Thanks for your help, Angel."

She hung up the phone and rubbed her hands over her face.

This had to be Hawkeye Slaughter. Middle school boys didn't have credit cards.

She heard a sound and looked over to find Bella standing in the corner, staring at her with big brown eyes.

"Mommy."

"Yes, honey?"

"The worms are scary."

"Well, they're kind of yucky, but they can't hurt you."

"But Mommy, what if robbers sent them? Or that mean boy from Caitlin's class?"

She pulled her daughter into a hug and kissed the top of her head. "Robbers and mean boys steal things. They don't *give* people things, right?"

"Right," Bella admitted. "But who wants a box of worms?"

"Lots of people. You know those neighbors a couple houses down, the ones with the little girls a few years younger than you?"

Bella nodded.

"Well. I've heard they have a chicken coop in their backyard. I'll bet this delivery was meant for them."

"You think so?" Bella asked.

"I do, because chickens *love* to eat worms. Mealworms are like . . . gummy bears for chickens. I'll bet that's what happened."

"So they sent the worms so the chickens can eat gummy bears. Instead of being robbers?"

She nodded. It was a convoluted explanation, but it seemed to make her daughter feel better.

"And guess what little girls like to eat?"

"What?" she asked, sticking her fingers in her mouth, despite the ten million times she'd been asked not to do this.

"Ice cream. How about we drop these worms off at Pet Lovers' Depot and then get some ice cream?"

"Guys, we're getting ice cream!" Bella screamed as she ran down the stairs to deliver this glorious news to her sisters in the basement.

Piper taped up the box, mouth set in a grim line. Hawkeye Slaughter's post from this morning glowed inside her mind like a neon sign.

> First person up against the wall with a bullet in her head: Piper Mondello #FascistsMustDie

Chapter Thirty-Three

PIPER

"I feel like I'm not contributing enough," Kiersten said as she and Piper pulled her dining room table apart. Rosamund inserted the wooden leaf to expand it.

"You're contributing your *entire house*," Piper said. "Now push."

"True." She grunted as they pushed the table back together. "But I have the most kids."

Piper had just returned from having coffee with Mike, her old boss. She'd told him about the worms and given him the plastic bag containing the bloody notebook paper. He told her they still hadn't found Hawkeye Slaughter, and he'd found no arrest record for Bruce Orlov. However, he had managed to confirm that Alex Orlov was asked to leave a private school last year, though the school declined to provide any details.

In light of all this, it had been a wonderful distraction to spend the remainder of the day at Kiersten's house, helping to convert her dining room into a classroom.

The worm delivery had swept away all Piper's reservations about the Experiment. She needed to keep her girls close to keep them safe.

"Can you help me move the sideboard?" Kiersten asked.

Kiersten had volunteered to sacrifice her formal dining room to the Experiment. The room had good light and a lovely wood-burning fireplace.

Her kitchen would turn into a cafeteria, her basement would serve as the art room and science lab, and her backyard would become a playground and gymnasium.

They'd just finished mounting a dry-erase board next to the china cabinet, which felt oddly momentous. Drilling holes in the wall meant they were committed, for better or for worse.

"Let's go over the division of labor again," Kiersten said.

"Okay." Piper grabbed a notebook. "I've got math and science."

"I have English, grammar, writing, and history," Rosamund said.

"And I have home economics and life skills," Kiersten said. "I'll teach them the Heimlich maneuver, CPR, and first aid and how to use the washing machine, load the dishwasher, and clean the bathroom. And I'm the school nurse, the lunch lady, admin person, field trip coordinator, state-and-local-home-school-paperwork-filing person, and purchaser of supplies. And I'll head up the Project."

The Project was Garrett's idea. Kiersten's husband had been curious about their new neighborhood and suggested the kids interview the older residents on Beaverbrook to create a living history project.

"Do you want PayPal, Zelle, Venmo, cash, or check?" Rosamund asked.

"I'm retro," Kiersten said. "I would like cash, please."

As a final exercise before launching the Experiment, each family had tallied up the money they'd been spending on tutors, dance classes, costumes and uniforms, sports equipment, travel costs, and batting coaches. They were stunned to learn that they'd save a significant amount of money by dropping out.

They decided to use some of this money for books and school supplies, lunches and snacks, and to pay for admission to museums and field trips.

Now the dining room table lay covered with textbooks purchased on Amazon, plus notebooks, pencils, art supplies, whiteboards, and dry-erase markers.

Piper used scissors to open a cardboard box and removed a grammar workbook and a biology textbook.

"What's all this?" Rosamund pulled a pile of books from the middle of the table and began to read the titles aloud. "*Happy House Life: Ten Rules for a Happy Home and Fulfilling Marriage*, *The Happy House Life Schedule*, *The Happy House Life Workbook*, *The Happy House Life Cookbook*, *The Happy House Life Table of Sustenance*?"

"Our neighbor wrote them," Kiersten said.

"The Influencer?" Piper asked.

Kiersten nodded. "She's been texting me book recommendations to get started. She has this whole Happy House Life system, and she promised to stop by and show me how to implement it."

Piper rolled her eyes and paged through *The Happy House Life: Ten Rules for a Happy Home and Fulfilling Marriage*. "When your husband arrives home after a long day at work, make him feel like the king of the castle. Greet him at the door with the beverage of his choice. Put on his favorite music and give him an hour or so to relax with his feet up in the family room while you finish making dinner."

Piper frowned. "I'm not sure this would work. My husband likes Metallica."

They crowded around her. "What else does it say?" Rosamund asked.

"Send your kids outside or to their rooms when your husband arrives home from work to create a buffer of peace as he manages his reentry from the combat of the workday to the tranquility of his home."

"I think I need a wife," Piper said wistfully. "I wish someone had given me that when I was working."

"Oh dear." Kiersten squinted down at the book, reading over Piper's shoulder. "There's a rule here about *exercise*. Rule number three. Keeping up appearances."

"Try on your wedding dress on each anniversary," Rosamund read aloud. "If you can't fit into it, consider this a warning sign and a wake-up call. Exercise, nutrition, and a healthy diet are important not just for maintaining your body, but for maintaining your marriage. Don't let yourself go. If you lose interest in your body, your husband will too. And he might find something more interesting at the office, in a bar, or on a business trip."

"It's like paying someone to make you feel bad," Rosamund said.

Kiersten frowned. "This sounds a lot like the advice Dickie gave Dottie back in 1965."

"Don't 'let yourself *go*'?" Piper snorted indignantly. "Who in the world would pay *money* for this?"

Kiersten glanced at the front cover. "A lot of people, apparently. It's a *New York Times* bestseller."

"Let me see that." Piper grabbed the book and paged through it. "Listen to this one. 'Never argue with your husband unless it's truly important. Let him believe that he guides you when it comes to masculine topics like politics and money.'"

Piper tossed the book onto the table. "This is such a steaming pile of—"

The doorbell rang, interrupting her words. She glanced out the window.

And there on Kiersten's front porch, as though summoned by these disparaging words, stood the Influencer.

Chapter Thirty-Four

KIERSTEN

Kiersten glanced at Piper and Rosamund as she opened the door and invited Aspen inside. They all looked guilty, like people on *Law & Order* who claimed they were home watching television alone on the night someone murdered their archnemesis.

"We were just getting organized for our first day of homeschooling," Kiersten explained.

"Then my timing is perfect!" Aspen lifted her shoulders in a perky shrug. "I just wanted to bring you some muffins for luck, and this too." She handed Kiersten a canvas bag filled with the same books they'd just been looking at. "To help you get started with your new way of life."

"Gosh, thank you so much." She gestured to the books on the dining room table. "But I already ordered them."

"That's so cool! You can give the extra copies to your friends." Aspen gestured to Piper and Rosamund. "Good to see you again."

"Lovely to see you too," Rosamund said with a gracious smile.

Aspen clasped Rosamund's hand in hers. "I'm so glad you've decided to live your lives with *intention*."

"Oh, *absolutely*," Rosamund said firmly as she disentangled her hands from Aspen's clutching fingers.

"Look, I don't want to interrupt you," Aspen said. "I just wanted to drop some things off to help you get started. I recommend starting with *The Happy House Life*, and then *The Happy House Life Workbook* and *The Happy House Life Schedule*. Do the workbook first, to figure out your core values."

"Our core values," Piper repeated. "Right."

Kiersten glanced at her. Piper looked polite, but she could swear she saw the corner of her mouth twitch.

Aspen nodded. "We use our *core values* to make our Happy House Life *serenity schedule*. Then we go through *The Happy House Life Cookbook* to make our weekly meal plan, which I call the *Table of Sustenance*."

They gave her a blank look, and she elaborated. "It's a play on words. *The Table of Sustenance* workbook is set up like a *grid* or like, you know, a sort of mathematical *table*, but it's about food, and you eat food *at a table*," she finished, looking pleased with herself. "I came up with that one morning in the shower."

Rosamund gave her a brilliant smile. "I love a good double entendre."

Aspen frowned, obviously unfamiliar with the term, then gave a cheerful shrug. "Anyway, we incorporate the Table of Sustenance meal prep into our serenity schedule."

"Got it." Kiersten nodded enthusiastically to make up for Piper's decidedly more muted response.

"I know it sounds like a lot." Aspen wrinkled her adorable nose. "But if you have any questions, you can always ask me, since I'm, like, right next door."

"Would you like to join us?" Kiersten asked. "For homeschooling, I mean?"

Piper shot her a look of horror that clearly said this whole Minnesota-nice thing had gone *too far*.

But it seemed rude, mean even, to start a home school on Beaverbrook Lane and not include all the neighbors . . . even if this particular neighbor *was* skinny, blond, and perfect, with hundreds of thousands of Instagram followers and talked about things like the Table of Sustenance. It sounded like something Bilbo Baggins might sell in the housewares section at Target.

Aspen smiled. "You are *so sweet*. But we create a lot of content while we're doing school, so I don't think that would work. But I'd be happy to be your Happy House Life *mentor*, you know? I do this for a lot of people, and I'm happy to waive my normal $2,500 fee, since you guys are *neighbors*."

Rosamund exchanged a glance with Piper. "How very . . . *kind*," she said.

Piper emitted a sort of moan-grunt of faux gratitude but only succeeded in sounding like she had peanut butter stuck to the roof of her mouth.

"That would be great," Kiersten said, once again attempting to radiate the enthusiasm her neighbors lacked. "We'd like that so much."

"Great!" Aspen smiled back, white teeth gleaming.

"So tell me." Piper gestured to the pile of books. "How did you come to develop this . . . Happy House Life thing?"

"My husband's grandmother is the inspiration," Aspen said, tossing her luxuriant hair over one shoulder. "We were going through a rough patch after our second child was born, and Grammy gave us this retro advice from back when she was a young bride. We thought it was, like, *genius*. So we decided to totally *embrace* her 1960s trad wife lifestyle. It, like, *transformed* our marriage and our home."

"Transformed it how?" Piper asked.

"Read my book first," Aspen said, "and then we can talk about it."

"I can't wait to . . . dive in," Rosamund said with a polite smile.

"But the book was just the *starting point*." Aspen clasped her hands to her chest, glowing like an evangelist. "I also went rummaging around in Grammy and Grampy's attic, and I found all these recipes written on index cards. So I started cooking Grammy's meals while wearing some of her really cool vintage dresses and posting it on TikTok and Insta. Then I started following her schedule, with laundry on Monday, baking on Tuesday, cleaning on Wednesday and so on."

"And you turned that into a book?" Piper asked.

"Once we hit 500,000 subscribers, a publisher reached out and asked us to turn our content into books. We sold, like, a billion copies. Then we did *The Happy House Life Cookbook*, and that has sold, like, a billion copies too. I'm going to be on the Channel Nine morning show next month doing a segment on Thanksgiving prep if you'd like to watch."

Rosamund frowned. "Which one is Channel Nine again?"

"It's the one with Nikki Lassiter," Piper said.

"We'll be *sure* to tune in," Rosamund promised.

"It must be great," Kiersten said wistfully, "to have family nearby."

"It's wonderful for the girls," Aspen said. "We love having Grammy and Grampy and Trey's dad right next door."

"Grammy sounds like a remarkable woman," Piper said politely.

"She's, like, really modest," Aspen said. "She doesn't like to toot her own horn, even though she invented all these amazing recipes. She was way ahead of her time when it came to things like carbs and cholesterol, stuff like that. She's really, like, *scientific*."

"By the way," Kiersten said, "I found some old diaries in a box in my basement. They belong to a woman named Dottie who lived on Beaverbrook in 1965. I'm trying to figure out who they belong to so I can return them, but I haven't had much luck. Do you think your Grammy and Grampy could help?"

"I can ask," Aspen said.

"That would be great. And thank you for all of this." Kiersten pointed to the books.

"Why don't we meet next week to discuss your Happy House Life action plan? That'll give you some time to read my books and get your thoughts down on paper."

"I would love that," Kiersten said, and she meant it with every cell in her body.

Here at last was the thing she'd been looking for her entire adult life. A plan. A schedule. A magical system to end multiple trips to the grocery store each week for forgotten items, a cure for the inexplicable anger that rose each time someone innocently asked what's for dinner. A way to ensure they never ran out of toilet paper, trash bags, or laundry detergent again.

And all she had to do was fill in the blanks and complete a workbook, and then a Disney princess, like Rapunzel with more manageable hair, would come to her house and show her how to implement it all.

"Sounds like you've launched an empire," Rosamund said brightly.

Aspen nodded. "We're actually in talks with HGTV about a show."

"Seriously?" Piper asked.

"Yeah, it's just preliminary right now and it's a secret, so please don't share on your socials, but it's looking really promising."

Kiersten nodded. That was an easy request. The only things she ever shared on social media were first-day-of-school pictures, with the boys standing stiffly on the front steps, clutching new backpacks.

"I'm waiting to hear back from my agent now about their latest offer," Aspen said.

Kiersten suddenly felt deeply inadequate. "All this, plus you're raising two little girls and homeschooling and baking muffins for people. It's impressive."

"I'm not here to make money," Aspen said. "I'm here to turn back the clock and return to a simpler time."

"Amen to that," Kiersten said quietly.

"Anyway, I need to get going," Aspen said. "But I have one favor to ask before I go."

"Name it," Kiersten said, ignoring the look of alarm Piper shot her from across the room.

"We'd like to have an Autumn Harvest Festival here on Beaverbrook," Aspen said. "In early November, with traditional games like pin the tail on the donkey, and burlap sack races and hayrides and a bouncy house. Old-school fun. My husband's real estate company will cover all the expenses. And I was wondering if you guys could help organize it."

Rosamund frowned. "We're terribly busy getting the homeschooling up and running."

"But it would be *educational*," Aspen said, blinking her big blue eyes, as though this should be obvious. "Your kids could run a hot-apple-cider stand and learn about entrepreneurship."

Piper raised an eyebrow. "Like a lemonade stand, but with third-degree burns?"

"Fine." Aspen sounded a little sulky. "Maybe they could run cornhole and pin the tail on the donkey instead?"

"Actually," Kiersten said, "I think it's a great idea."

This is exactly what she'd missed most about home. County fairs and parades and small-town festivals like Bergen Days, with a street dance and sidewalk sales and hot dogs sold by the high school booster club. Some of her happiest childhood memories involved showing her red-and-white Herford 4-H calf at the county fair. And now her kids could have something similar, albeit without livestock, right here on Beaverbrook Lane.

"And maybe you guys could help some of the older people with decorations?" Aspen said. "We want to make sure all the front porches look . . . you know . . . *festive*. And maybe you guys could organize a potluck dinner and also bake some brownies and cupcakes, but with like, a fall motif, like pumpkin spice with cream cheese frosting? And maybe you could also—"

"Excellent ideas," Rosamund said firmly, cutting off all further demands. "Please share all the details when you have them."

"Awesome. I'll send around a Google Doc with a list of responsibilities, okay? And let me know if you'd like to meet next week to go through the workbook."

"I'll do that," Kiersten said. "Thank you so much."

"Welcome to the Happy House Life revolution," Aspen said as she moved through the foyer and onto the front porch. "You've made a wonderful decision for yourselves and your family. You'll never go back to the rat race."

They stood on the porch and waved goodbye to their neighbor as she crossed the cul-de-sac, white skirt fluttering in the breeze like a flag.

Chapter Thirty-Five

PIPER

Piper shut the front door and leaned against it, just in case Aspen tried to force her way back inside and issue more edicts about the Harvest Festival.

"What have we *done*?" Rosamund hissed in a low voice.

"Apparently we've joined *a revolution*," Piper whispered back. "Or a *cult*."

"Why are we *whispering*," Rosamund asked, still whispering.

"Because we're saying mean things about a person who just brought us homemade muffins and promised to show us how to manifest abundance. For *free*," Kiersten said, shooting them a reproachful look.

"We're not being mean." Piper reverted to her normal voice. "We're just being . . . skeptical."

"I'm not skeptical at all," Kiersten said firmly. "I think she's lovely."

Piper rolled her eyes. "It sounds to me like she's either started a cult or she's running a pyramid scheme."

"Or both," Rosamund said. "Regardless, I have a book to write, and I need to go check on my daughter. But we will be here at the crack of 9:00 a.m. tomorrow for the first day of school."

Rosamund returned to her own home across the street while Kiersten and Piper wandered back to the dining room to continue sorting through school supplies.

"That woman cannot be trusted," Piper said as she opened a pack of highlighters. "Mark my words."

Kiersten's mouth dropped open. "You mean Rosamund?"

"No. Of course not." Piper shook her head. "I love Rosamund. I'm talking about the Trad Wife."

Kiersten looked at Piper, opened her mouth, snapped it shut, then opened it again. "I know it's none of my business or anything, but . . . well . . . you seem like you're . . . I don't know . . . but maybe you're a little paranoid . . . maybe?"

Piper smiled in spite of herself. "Are you scolding me in Minnesotan?"

Kiersten hunched her shoulders, looking sheepish. "I might be. A little . . . yes."

"Just because you're paranoid doesn't mean they aren't out to get you. In my experience."

"I think most people are good," Kiersten said gently. "I mean, not *all* people, of course. Not serial killers . . . and telemarketers. But most people."

"That's because you're a nurse from Bergen, Minnesota, who enjoys bringing sick people heated blankets and morphine to make them more comfortable. You're a good person, so you think everyone else is a good person too." Piper crushed the packaging from a pack of glue sticks.

"But you're a good person too." Kiersten paused; then a look of worry creased her face. "I mean, aren't you?"

"Look." Piper turned to her, brandishing a box of colored pencils. "I've spent my entire career trying to protect good people from bad people. And it tends to make a person suspicious. And Aspen makes me suspicious."

"Why?"

"Because I feel like she's trying to sell us something," Piper said, struggling to explain herself. She couldn't articulate why she didn't trust Aspen. It was a feeling, not a set of facts she could recite.

"She gave us all her books and workbooks for free. Plus muffins." Kiersten opened a box of No. 2 pencils, then stood them upright inside an empty coffee mug.

"I feel like she's trying to sell us a philosophy, a way of looking at the world, like a politician."

She didn't like politicians, with the exception of their current governor, Ben Bradley. He seemed like a decent guy. And his wife ran some kind of shelter for runaway teenage girls. She approved of that.

"That might be true," Kiersten conceded. "But she's selling serenity, peace, and organization. I mean, I don't know how to do *any* of this"—she swept her arms toward the tangle of school supplies scattered across the dining room table—"and she does. So I'm going to do her workbook and make her recipes and meet with her once a week and let her be my coach, even though she looks like she's about eleven years old. Because the only thing we're manifesting in my house is stress and anxiety and chaos. If she has a better way, I'm open to it."

Piper looked at her. If only she could be more like Kiersten. Optimistic. Trusting. Nonjudgmental. "I'd like to be you when I grow up."

Kiersten shot her a look of surprise. "You'd like to be fifteen pounds overweight, unable to fit into any of your pants, and live in a house with no pictures on the walls?"

"You're kind and generous. And trusting."

"Well . . . you do seem a little . . . suspicious," Kiersten conceded. "But maybe it's because you used to chase actual bad guys for a living. The only people I've ever chased are little children who don't want to get vaccinated for chicken pox."

Piper sighed. "You're right. I am suspicious. And paranoid. And I'm working on it. I really am. My suspicious mind is the reason I'm on administrative leave."

"I don't know the whole story," Kiersten said quietly. "And you don't have to tell me if you don't want to. But if it would help, I'm here to listen."

Piper looked back at this neighbor who was honest, funny, real, and kind. Suddenly she felt a surge of gratitude to the universe for bringing Kiersten and her family to Beaverbrook Lane. For bringing her a friend when she really needed one, a friend she didn't have to text or make complicated arrangements to see, because she was literally right next door, just a few yards from her own kitchen table.

Piper opened her mouth, and the words poured out. "A homeless man parked a white van in front of the Lincoln Memorial and told us it was filled with explosives, and I believed him. When he asked to be connected with aliens from the Andromeda Galaxy, I still believed his van was filled with explosives. Because people can be both crazy *and* dangerous. But when they finally lured the guy out of the van with a cheeseburger and looked inside, they found an old Atari and a bunch of black-and-white TV sets. And no bomb. No explosives. I was wrong. Spectacularly wrong."

"I'm so sorry, Piper," Kiersten said softly, shaking her head. "That sounds awful."

"It was awful for the thousands of innocent people stuck for hours in a traffic jam of epic proportions. People were late for work, late to pick up their kids, late for colonoscopies and open-heart surgeries. Cabinet secretaries were late for meetings with the president. Then everyone was late to get home again, all because of me."

"Sounds like a lot of angry commuters." She'd been on the Beltway often enough to see how people reacted to traffic jams.

"Not just anger," Piper said softly. "Threats. Violent threats. Against me personally. There's one guy in particular, Hawkeye Slaughter. He talks about all the ways he'd like to torture and kill me on X."

Kiersten's mouth dropped open. "Seriously?"

Piper tapped her phone and began to read in a monotone voice. "I want to peel your skin off, layer by layer while I listen to you scream. I will destroy your life the way you destroyed mine, you evil, fascist bureaucrat."

Kiersten's hand rose to her mouth. "Oh Piper," she whispered.

Piper pressed her lips together, forcing herself to remain steady. Strong. Composed.

Talking about it with a normal person like Kiersten suddenly drove home how abnormal this was . . . and yet she knew so many people who lived with similar threats. Election workers. Public health officials. Diplomats. Members of Congress. Judges. Cops. It was part of being a public servant in the age of rage, in the era of the internet.

Piper tried to muster a smile. "Most of the time, nothing comes of these threats . . . but this guy is smart . . . and he has money . . . and a lot of followers . . . and sometimes . . ."

"Sometimes things happen?" Kiersten asked.

Piper nodded.

Kiersten let out a low whistle. "No wonder you're paranoid."

Piper shrugged. "I made a bad call. And these are the consequences."

"But it sounds like the kind of mistake anyone could make," Kiersten protested. "I mean, the crazy guy in the van said he had a *bomb*."

Piper shook her head. "But he didn't. I failed to accurately assess the threat."

"So how do you fix the problem?"

"I'm working with a therapist." Piper tossed a highlighter into a plastic pencil case. "She keeps telling me to do the opposite of what my mind tells me to do. But trust is just really hard for me."

Kiersten frowned. "Why, exactly?"

She sighed. Only her husband and the people from her hometown knew the whole story. She'd never shared it with the girls or anyone else. "My mom died when I was nine. Breast cancer."

"Oh Piper, I'm so sorry."

"It's okay." She smiled. Kiersten should be a therapist. She had the same patient, nonjudgmental tone as Trina, her federally mandated shrink. "I was an only child, and I was raised by my dad, who happened to be the county sheriff."

"Is that why you went into law enforcement?"

"Partly. Yes."

"What's the other part?" Kiersten sat on a dining room chair, giving Piper her complete attention.

Piper took a seat across from her. "After my mom died, we needed to find a sitter who could take care of me after school and whenever my dad got called out in the middle of the night for an accident or a burglary. We had this neighbor, Mrs. Claussen, and she became my babysitter."

Images flooded her mind when the name crossed her lips. Mrs. Claussen's liver-spotted hands. The silver chain around her neck holding her "spectacles," as she called them. Memories of warm cookies, cold milk, and kindness.

"She was wonderful," Piper said with a small smile. "Her kids were in their early twenties, married but without kids of their own, so she sort of treated me like the granddaughter she one day hoped to have. I stayed at her house next door when my dad worked nights or weekends or holidays, plus after school. Anytime he was at work, I was next door at Mrs. Claussen's house. She was like a grandmother to me."

"She sounds lovely," Kiersten said.

Piper nodded. "She was. But Mrs. Claussen was married to an abusive husband."

Even after all these years, her stomach gave a little lurch when she thought of Dwight Claussen, a man so tall and thick that she'd wondered if he was the giant in "Jack and the Beanstalk." Heavy work boots caked with mud. The sharp scent of nicotine with a pungent frill of alcohol around the edges. Huge hands with a crescent of dirt beneath the nails.

An involuntary shudder crawled up her spine as she continued. "When she turned sixty, Mrs. Claussen finally worked up the courage to leave him. And that's when she moved into the little house next door and started babysitting me. But one time when I was staying over at her house, I woke up in the middle of the night and heard shouting and breaking glass. I tiptoed downstairs and out to the driveway, and I saw her husband beating her with a spade."

Kiersten gazed back at her with wide eyes. "Oh. Piper."

Piper exhaled. "Yeah. It was awful."

"What happened?"

The pictures from that night never seemed to fade. She struggled to remember her mother's face, but Dwight Claussen's crimson cheeks and gashing scowl remained vivid and clear, as though it happened yesterday.

"Mrs. Claussen was screaming, blood dripping down her face. I snuck out the back door to our house and called 911. Then I climbed on a chair and grabbed the loaded .22 my dad kept on a gun rack in the garage and ran next door."

Kiersten drew in a breath. "How old were you?"

Piper met her gaze across the table. "I was nine."

Kiersten gasped. "Nine?"

Piper swallowed the thickness clogging in her throat. "I clicked off the safety, and I pointed that loaded rifle at Mr. Claussen and told him to put the shovel down. And I kept the rifle pointed at him until my dad arrived in his patrol car five minutes later. It was the longest five minutes of my life."

"Did they arrest him?"

"Yeah," she said grimly. "They threw him in jail, but he didn't stay there long. And sometimes when he got drunk, he'd come over to our place and pound on our door. We had to get a restraining order. Mrs. Claussen ended up moving in with us and became sort of a housekeeper for my dad and a live-in nanny for me because she wasn't safe living alone. It was the right thing to do, inviting her to live with us."

She paused. Of course it was the right thing to do. Mrs. Claussen would be dead if they hadn't. But now that Piper was older, now that she'd been forced to work with a therapist, she could acknowledge the price of providing that sanctuary.

"But it also sort of . . . brought the threat inside our house, so to speak. I spent years terrified he'd break in and, you know, shoot us all. He finally wandered out of the bar one night on Christmas Eve and froze to death my senior year of high school. Dwight Claussen's funeral was the first time I'd felt safe in years."

"That's awful."

"I should have had therapy," she said with a wry smile. "But you know how it was when we were young. No one had therapy back then."

"And that's why you went into law enforcement?" Kiersten asked.

"Yeah. I wanted to protect good people, like Mrs. Claussen, from bad people, like Mr. Claussen. And now I want to protect my girls. I want to protect the people I care about. And even though I just met you, I feel like I've known you forever, and I care about you and your boys. I want to protect you. And Rosamund, too, and her daughter. I just don't trust easily. And I don't trust that Influencer."

"Which is understandable," Kiersten said gently, "given what you've just told me."

Piper shook her head. "It's an explanation, but it's not an excuse. The incident with the crazy man in the panel van showed me that I need to change. If I want to get my job back, I need to demonstrate that I can assess threats appropriately. And this is a good place for me to start."

Piper squared her shoulders and took a deep breath. "So I'm going to trust the Trad Wife over there"—she jerked her shoulder in the direction of Aspen's house—"and see where it takes us."

"It is kind of scary, isn't it? This thing we're doing."

"It's absolutely terrifying," Piper admitted. "But most things worth doing are terrifying, in my experience."

"True." Kiersten clutched a pack of loose-leaf paper to her chest. "Getting married is terrifying. Having children is terrifying. Moving to a city where you don't know anyone is terrifying. Anytime you do something without knowing the outcome, it's scary."

"Exactly." Piper nodded. "So I'm going to jump in wholeheartedly with this experiment thing and trust that I'm not destroying my children's future by doing something different from what everyone else is doing. No matter what my mother-in-law says. I'm going to trust that this Harvest Festival is going to be fun, and not just a pain in the ass.

And I'm going to trust that I still have some investigative skills in my toolbox and help you find the woman who wrote those diaries."

"I appreciate that," Kiersten said with a smile. "Because while I know how to investigate things like a persistent pain in your knee, or a cough that won't go away, I have no idea how to find someone from 1965."

"I'm on it," Piper said. "When you finish reading, hand the diaries over to me, and I'll see what I can learn."

"By the way, Aspen is not a name," Kiersten said, scooping up a handful of markers. "It's a deciduous tree."

Piper grinned. "I don't know you well, but I do trust you. And if you trust Aspen, then I will too."

Kiersten smiled. "Trust by proxy?"

"Trust with training wheels." Piper stacked a pile of spiral notebooks in the center of the table. "You know, this is kind of nice."

"Turning my dining room into a one-room school?"

"Having a friend who lives right next door," Piper clarified. "I have friends, of course, old friends who live in the area, but I never get to see them. Between traffic and work and the kids' activities, we never manage to get together."

"You're the only friend I've made since we moved out here." She opened a package of gold star stickers and stuck one to Piper's sleeve. "You are my official First Friend."

Piper smiled. "I've always wanted a gold star."

"And now you have one."

Piper's chest tingled as she touched the star on her sleeve.

She'd always felt intimidated by the other moms at the dance studios where she spent so much time, maybe because she'd been a tomboy who rarely wore makeup and had never been a dancer herself. She wasn't naturally equipped for the sequins and eyeliner and complicated buns of the dance world. So she'd always held the other moms at arm's length, even though they were perfectly nice.

But with Kiersten, she felt comfortable. With Kiersten, she felt like she was enough, exactly as she was.

"I don't think parents are meant to raise their kids alone . . ." Piper said slowly, attempting to explain how she felt. "It's like Rosamund said once, about the Vikings sleeping around the ancient firepit together, or wherever the hell she was talking about."

"Welcome to my feasting hall." Kiersten gestured at the dining room. "My Viking name is Kiersten Dirty Sock."

"I'm Piper Anxiety Leotard."

Kiersten burst out laughing. "I'm glad you're in my clan."

Piper smiled and sank back in her chair, grateful to finally have a clan.

Chapter Thirty-Six

KIERSTEN

Kiersten triple checked her alarm before getting into bed. She'd had two cups of chamomile tea, but it hadn't helped.

A flutter of nervous anticipation about tomorrow's first day of "school" had her feeling wide awake at her normal bedtime. And there were other issues that made her mind race when she should be settling down for the night.

Just before she turned out the light, Garrett had called from somewhere in South Dakota to say good night and wish her luck.

"This is going to be harder than I thought," she told him.

"Why?"

"I just got a text. Luke's Orton–Gillingham tutor is moving to Florida."

"Remind me again . . . Orton Gillingham is . . ." her husband asked.

"A teaching method for kids with dyslexia. You have to be certified, and she was wonderful. And now she's moving. She won't be able to work with Luke."

"Can you find someone else?"

"I'll have to," she said. "But it could take a while. They don't grow on trees. And it's expensive."

"I'll ask around the office, see if anyone has any recommendations."

"Thanks."

"Anything else going on?" he asked. "You sound . . . tense."

"Do you remember that piece of paper I showed you, the one I found nailed to the tree out front?"

"The one smeared with what looked like blood?" he asked.

"Yeah. Well, I found another one tonight. This one had writing. It said 'I watch you.'"

She heard his quick intake of breath. "Seriously?"

"Yeah."

"Did you check the Ring camera?" he asked.

"This note was out back. Our Ring camera only covers the front yard, remember?"

He uttered a curse word under his breath. "I'll install a second one when I get home. Have you talked to the neighbors? Maybe they saw something? Or the boys . . ."

"I'll ask them," she said. "It does sound like their idea of fun, doesn't it?"

"You mean *Let's create secret messages written with bodily fluids and then communicate with each other by leaving blood-smeared papers all over the yard*? Yeah. It sounds right up their alley."

The tightness in her chest eased. He wasn't wrong. That absolutely sounded like something the boys would do.

"I'm still nervous about this Experiment," she admitted.

"Channel your inner Miss Beadle," he said, referencing her deep and abiding love for *Little House on the Prairie*. "You can do this."

"I know. I just . . . I hope the boys like it."

"Johnny and that little Mondello girl are thick as thieves. They've formed a crime syndicate, and they're teaming up to steal ice cream bars from the freezer." She could hear the smile in his voice through the phone. "I think they'll like it."

"I hope you're right."

"I love you, and I'm proud of you. And I'll be home on Friday to give you a break, okay?"

"Okay. Love you too."

Gratitude flooded her chest as she hung up the phone. She'd married young, just like Dottie. Her husband could have been another Dickie.

Instead, Garrett had actually turned out the be the loving and supportive man she suspected him of being, without a whole lot of evidence to support this theory on the day they got married when they were both only twenty-two years old.

So much of life came down to luck, she thought, punching her pillow in frustration as sleep continued to elude her.

After ten more minutes of tossing and turning, she turned on the light, padded down the stairs in her nightgown, and retrieved Dottie's diary from her purse. She couldn't make herself fall asleep, but maybe she could keep reading and try to figure out who Dottie was and how she'd ended up married to a monster.

Chapter Thirty-Seven

DOTTIE

June 9, 1965

Dickie woke me this morning with a kiss and told me he has a wonderful surprise.

I pasted a smile on my face and tried to hide my dread. "What kind of surprise?"

"I'm taking you to San Diego!"

I blinked stupidly in the early-morning light. "For a vacation?"

"For political training!" he sang out, like that's the same thing. "It's run by the national party. For men interested in running for local office. And their wives. I'm one of ten men selected from the state of Virginia. That means they think I have *a lot* of potential. The party is investing in me. They're investing in *us*."

"I see."

He reached for my hands and pulled me out of bed. "We're going shopping today. You need to look your best, for your future career as the wife of a state Senate candidate."

"That might be hard to do. Barefoot." He'd extended the shoe ban when he caught me rolling my eyes at something he said.

He planted a tender kiss on my forehead. "Of course you can have your shoes back, darling. And when we come home, things will be different. I promise."

"Different how?" I asked warily.

He knelt beside the bed, took my hand, and gazed up at me. "I've expected too much from you. I see that now. This trip will be like a second honeymoon for us, a chance to start over."

His gaze held mine as I stared into his beautiful blue eyes. I want to believe him. I really do. But it reminded me of the year I got out of bed at midnight and found my parents stuffing Santa gifts into my stocking. The next morning I desperately wanted to believe those presents came from an omniscient, bearded fat man in a red suit who slid down my chimney.

But I'd seen reality, and I couldn't believe again.

June 14, 1965
San Diego

I can't write the words because that will make them true.

June 16, 1965
San Diego

I wish I could stay here forever. The nurses take turns sitting beside my bed. They hold my hand while I lay here and cry.

June 17, 1965
San Diego

My grief is so big I'm no longer capable of feeling it. Like a landscape so vast you can't see it all at once. I feel blank. Empty. There's nothing inside me anymore.

June 19, 1965
San Diego

I was carrying twins. A boy and a girl. And now I'm not.

June 20, 1965
San Diego

The doctor says I can't have more children. Because of the miscarriage and what they had to do to save me. Which means I'll never have children at all.

June 21, 1965
San Diego

Why didn't they let me die? Why didn't they just let me bleed out on the operating table? Why did they "save me." Save me for what exactly?

June 22, 1965
San Diego

How do you mourn not just one lost baby but *two*? Plus all the children you will never have? A future that will never be yours? A family that will never exist? First steps and graduations and weddings and grandchildren that will never come. All those babies on our street with their clinging fingers and soft smiles. Never to hold one of my own.

I hadn't realized how much I loved these babies until these babies were no longer possible. I will never be a mother. And Dickie will never be a father.

Dickie says it's my fault. He says I caused the miscarriage by changing the oil on his car. He whispered it to me, as I lay here in my hospital bed.

"You did this, you stupid bitch. You don't deserve to be a mother."

Later, I asked the doctor if changing the oil on Dickie's car caused the miscarriage.

He frowned. "Where did you get that idea?"

"From my husband," I said in a low voice, unable to meet his eyes.

And he gave me a long look, full of sympathy. And suddenly I wanted to tell him everything, about the way Dickie screams at me, and finds flaws in everything I cook and the way I keep the house. In the way I look and talk and everything I do. The way he took away my shoes.

But I didn't because I'm so ashamed. Ashamed and stupid. And this is my punishment. For thinking I deserve a husband who looks like Paul Newman. For thinking I deserve a house full of babies. For thinking I deserve anything at all.

Chapter Thirty-Eight

KIERSTEN

Pink and orange light streaked the early-morning sky as Kiersten laced up her sneakers, then slipped through the side door and into the garage, where she grabbed a basketball.

She'd had a rough night. When she finally drifted off to sleep around 2:00 a.m., Dottie's husband plagued her dreams, appearing as a violent, faceless giant who pelted her with shoes. She shook her head, trying to dispel the strands of nightmare that still clung to her consciousness.

The crisp October air nipped her nose and fingers as she paced off the distance from the hoop mounted on a steel pole on the side of the driveway. She faced the basket, lined up her shot, then sent the ball flying through the air.

The net swished as the ball dropped through. She sprang forward to retrieve it before it bounced across the driveway.

She didn't want to wake her neighbors at 6:00 a.m. with the thunk, thunk, thunk of a basketball hitting the asphalt. But she needed to think, and she did that best while shooting free throws.

Growing up, she'd done this in the partially heated Quonset where her dad fixed machinery while she and her four siblings spent the long Minnesota winters playing H-O-R-S-E and pickup basketball.

She'd found peace in the repetitive process of shooting free throws, standing at the line her dad painted on the concrete floor, aiming for the hoop he'd attached to the corrugated metal wall. It provided an outlet for the slings and arrows of teenage life, a bad grade, a breakup, an argument with a friend.

And this morning she needed the balm of basketball again.

The diary entries last night disturbed her. The desire to help Dottie, and the futility of doing so, created a knot in her stomach.

It was like reading a history book and wanting to shout at Abe Lincoln to skip that performance at Ford's Theatre. She wanted to do the same with Dottie, to reach into the past and warn her, to tell her to leave immediately, but space and time made such advice impossible.

She didn't know even who Dottie *was*, where she lived now, or whether or not she still lived at all. Maybe she'd died peacefully in her sleep after a long and happy life. Or maybe she was alive and well, an active senior taking her grandkids for ice cream.

But Kiersten couldn't shake the feeling that Dottie may have had a different fate.

She gripped the basketball and tried to rid her mind of these disturbing thoughts, took aim, and sent the ball through the hoop again.

"That's a beautiful shot you've got there."

She whirled around. An older man who looked like Morgan Freeman smiled at her from the end of her driveway. Sweat stained the front of his sweatshirt as he ran a hand over short-cropped hair streaked with gray.

"Thanks,". she said, walking to the end of the driveway where he stood.

"Reggie Spade. Welcome to the neighborhood."

"Hope I didn't wake you up," she said, shaking the hand he extended.

"Oh, I've been up for hours." He dismissed this concern with a wave of his hand. "You probably have too. I've seen all those boys climbing out of your car. You've got a whole platoon. You're *busy.*"

She gave him a weak smile. "Too busy to exercise, unfortunately. I used to be a decent ball player, back in the day. Now I'm just a mom who shoots free throws in the driveway when she needs to think." She gestured at his sweat-streaked shirt. "It looks like you've already gone for a run."

His eyes narrowed as he gave her an appraising look. "You could run, too, you know. We're just a short hop from the bike trail. Nothing better than a jog along the Potomac to start your day."

"That's a good idea," she mumbled, looking down at her shoes.

Wake up an hour early *to run*? Was he mad? Running was something she'd only ever done as a form of punishment, like when her coach had ordered one lap for every free throw she missed. Her aversion to running had created the perfect shot her neighbor admired so much.

"Run with me," he said.

She shifted the basketball to her hip and tried to look her neighbor up and down surreptitiously. He appeared to be some kind of geriatric iron man, lean and wiry, but still muscular.

"I couldn't keep up with you," she said, attempting to hide the truth behind a lighthearted smile. "And I have to get the boys ready for school. We're going to start homeschooling today, and . . . well, there's just a lot going on. This is a bad time."

He raised an eyebrow. "On a scale of one to ten, I'd give that excuse a three."

She felt a prickle of irritation. "Look, here, Mr. . . ."

"Call me Reggie."

"Okay, Reggie. It's not an *excuse*, all right? You said it yourself. I have this whole platoon of boys, and I have to get them ready for school and—"

"Didn't you just say you were homeschooling?"

"Well. Yes. I did."

"So school is right here, isn't it? At home. You don't have to drive anybody anywhere. You just got the gift of *extra time*. Time you can use to exercise. If you really want to, that is."

Her mouth dropped open. "But—"

He held up his hand, stemming the tide of words about to flow from her mouth. "I am a retired Marine Corps drill instructor, and I have heard every excuse ever devised by the human mind to avoid physical exercise. I know an excuse when I hear one."

"But—"

He raised an imperious hand again. "And I see before me someone who used to be a damn good athlete. Someone who used to enjoy pushing her body to accomplish great things. And if you want to be that person again, I'll help you. But if you want to make lame-ass excuses, well, that's your business. But don't expect me to call those excuses anything but what they are. Lame. Ass. *Excuses.*"

Her eyes flared with surprise, followed by a surge of anger. People did *not* talk to their neighbors this way in rural Minnesota.

"Is that the official military term?" she asked caustically. "Lame-Ass Excuses?"

"Damn straight," he said with a sharp nod. "You are suffering from a terrible case of LAE."

She glared at this man. "And you're . . ."

"A neighbor man sent from God to call you on your bullshit?" he asked with a good-natured grin.

His smile melted her irritation, and she couldn't help but smile back. "I don't think we have those where I come from."

He grinned. "Welcome to the DMV, honey. I'll be here tomorrow morning at 5:00 a.m. to take you on a run. First we stretch. Then we run. Then we eat protein for breakfast."

"So you really want me to go running with you every morning at 5:00 a.m.?"

"I really do." He nodded. "And you can have Sundays off."

"How very kind of you," she said, inclining her head in a mock bow. "How far do we run?"

"As far as I tell you."

"Look," she eyed him warily, "I don't want to be Marine Corp fit. I just want to be . . . fit-into-my-old-pants *fit*."

"Leave that to me," he said.

And then a brilliant idea popped into her mind.

"How would you feel about taking on another role?" she asked. "In addition to being my new personal drill sergeant."

"What kind of role?" he asked, curiosity lighting his face.

She raised an eyebrow and smiled. "PE teacher."

Chapter Thirty-Nine

PIPER

Piper hated to admit it. But her mother-in-law was right. The Experiment was a disaster.

The first two weeks of school flew by in an exhausting, incoherent blur of long division, algebra, history, and *Island of the Blue Dolphins.*

Each day presented problems they hadn't anticipated, like timing. Some days they went too fast, and the kids were baffled and confused by the material. But if they went too slowly, the kids squirmed in their chairs, whined for snacks, begged for screen time, bickered, and stared out the window, yawning.

Luke was the canary in the coal mine. He became bored about fifteen minutes before everyone else. Once he lost focus, he took the rest of the school down with him.

Piper tried to remember how to solve for *x* with the older kids while Rosamund tried to teach the younger ones about nouns and verbs. Kiersten fluttered around like a distracted butterfly, trying to work one-on-one with anyone who needed extra help.

Meanwhile Luke made farting noises with his hands, Caitlin rolled her eyes and shot scornful looks at her classmates, Olivia and James fought over the same mechanical pencil, and Johnny begged for his fourth bathroom break in an hour.

Piper and the other moms finally threw in the towel at the end of the second week, right after lunch. They hustled the kids outside two hours before school was technically supposed to dismiss and declared an end to the school week.

The older kids headed for the basketball hoop in Kiersten's driveway, where they talked and shot baskets. Caitlin, she noticed with a sinking heart, stood on the sidelines, scowling with her arms crossed.

The younger kids sat on Kiersten's front porch with markers and a giant roll of butcher paper, elbowing each other and bickering over crayons.

Piper sat on the front steps, "supervising" the little kids with a cup of coffee that had gone cold hours ago because she'd been too busy to drink it. She tossed back two Tylenol and massaged her forehead.

"Lovely artwork."

She looked up, shading her eyes against the afternoon sun. A middle-aged man with brown hair, glasses, and a British accent stood on the sidewalk.

Eeyore Man. That's what the girls called this neighbor who never seemed to smile. He shuffled to his little white car with hunched shoulders as he headed off to work in the mornings, then came home again at the end of the day and shuffled back inside. He'd moved in two years ago, after the death of his wife.

Her youngest daughter stopped drawing and looked up at the man with wide eyes. "Do you know Mary Poppins?"

He turned to her with a patient smile. "I do, as a matter of fact. She's a lovely person. But that carpet bag of hers is heavier than it looks."

Her daughter nodded gravely, as though she had always suspected this to be the case, then returned to her coloring.

"A little after-school arts and crafts?" he asked, inclining his head toward the children.

"Sort of," Piper said. "We've dropped out of regular school for a while . . . and now our school is here." She gestured toward Kiersten's house with her coffee cup.

His eyes widened. "That's rather bold, isn't it?"

"*Bold* is one word for it," she replied with a wry smile as the front door opened, and Rosamund joined them on the porch.

"I'm a teacher of sorts myself, actually. A professor. At Georgetown." He extended his arm, and they shook hands. "Miles Townsend."

"Piper Mondello," she said, then introduced Rosamund as well.

"I've come to enquire about the potluck." He produced a piece of paper from his back pocket and handed it to her.

Her eyes narrowed as she read the flyer, which stated that Piper, Kiersten, and Rosamund had graciously volunteered to organize the potluck harvest feast, all children's games and concessions, face painting, the bouncy house, and the decoration of front porches for the Harvest Festival.

She felt her cheeks flush with irritation.

"Something wrong?" Miles asked.

She rolled her eyes. "I'm irrationally irritated because someone has apparently taken me up on my completely insincere offer to help organize the Harvest Festival."

"Ah. I see. So would this be a bad time for me to ask what I'm supposed to bring?"

Piper sighed. "What would you *like* to bring?"

He scratched his head and looked up at the sky. "Well. Um. My wife was our household chef. But she passed away. Two years ago, about this time. Ovarian cancer. And I'm afraid I haven't learned much in the way of cookery since she . . . left. I can make a lovely spotted dick, though."

Piper had watched just enough episodes of the *Great British Baking Show* to know this wasn't an inappropriate sexual innuendo.

"Can you remind me . . ."

"Oh yes, of course. Spotted dick is a steamed pudding. Quite lovely."

She pinched her lips together, stifling a juvenile desire to giggle. Why couldn't they have one of those English people who whipped up coronation cakes or a Victoria sponge with Italian meringue? It was like getting an American who didn't know how to make apple pie. Although come to think of it, she'd never actually made an apple pie herself.

"I'm sure your . . . spotted dick . . . will be perfect," she said, glancing at Rosamund, who was staring at their neighbor with a thoughtful expression.

"So what exactly do you teach at Georgetown?" Rosamund asked.

"Ah, yes. Well, I teach biology classes to freshman, of course, when it can't be avoided, but my real area of expertise is wildlife biology, with a particular interest in the North American red fox. In fact, I'm running a research study right now. A couple of our neighbors have just given me permission to place wildlife cameras in their backyards, and also here in the cul-de-sac, as I attempt to learn more about their habits in heavily populated areas. In fact, if you ladies would be willing . . ."

Piper's heart leaped. She would *love* cameras in her backyard. And more cameras in her front yard to augment the Ring camera too.

"Absolutely. Front yard. Backyard. Anywhere you like, as long as I can look at the footage every now and then . . . you know . . . just for fun," she added.

"Thank you *ever so much*," he said. "This is very helpful." He turned to Rosamund. "And would you be willing also, to donate your backyard to science?"

"How about a trade," Rosamund said. "You can put cameras in my backyard . . . but in exchange you become a guest lecturer at the Beaverbrook Academy for Inquiring Minds. You teach our kids about the scientific method, about wildlife biology and the North American red fox."

A smile creased his face. "I would be honored. But I'm afraid I must ask for additional compensation for my services."

Rosamund raised an eyebrow. "What kind of *compensation*?"

"Well, I don't need money. But I could use some cooking lessons."

Piper watched as Rosamund's face lit up, making her every bit as lovely as Sigrid Thovaldsdotter, the Shield-Maiden of Stamendahl from one of Rosamund's romance novels.

"Deal." Rosamund gave him a brilliant smile. "We'll start with sausage and mashed potatoes."

The corner of his eyes crinkled as he smiled back. "Bangers and mash?"

She inclined her head in a little bow. "I look forward to it."

Piper glanced from Miles to Rosamund as they gazed at each other for just a second longer than necessary for polite conversation.

Potluck suppers. Wildlife cameras. Secret diaries. And now, *romance*?

What could possibly happen next? An alien abduction?

She picked up her coffee mug and tried to hide a smile as her exhaustion temporarily melted away.

Chapter Forty

LILLIAN

A little more than a week later, Lillian Landry sat on her front porch, binoculars clutched in her hand. Major events were happening next door.

"Walter. I think they've started a commune."

That was the only explanation she could think of. The running of the minivans had ended. Instead of revving engines and yelling mothers, she now heard screams of laughter coming from the cul-de-sac at all hours of the day and long past dusk.

They all seemed to be gathering at the home of those new people from Minnesota, the ones with all those boys.

Reggie, the retired drill instructor down the street, appeared to be involved too. Every afternoon he led the kids to the end of the cul-de-sac, where they did jumping jacks and calisthenics, and some complicated game involving running, ducking, and dodging that brought broad smiles to the kids' faces.

She squinted through her binoculars and saw a small gang of children emerging from the Cleaver house, heading down the sidewalk. A little herd of neighbor kids, including those cute little Mondello girls, and the Cleaver boys and Rosamund Hensler's girl, the one who always wore a cape for some reason.

Lillian's eyes widened, and she almost dropped the binoculars as they approached her front gate and fiddled with the latch.

Good gracious. They were coming to see *her*, like a little band of underage Mormon missionaries.

She stowed the binoculars under the quilt that covered her lap.

The oldest Cleaver boy knocked on her porch post. "Hello, Mrs. Landry," he said politely.

"Are you selling Boy Scout popcorn?" she asked, squinting down at him from her chair on the porch.

"No ma'am."

She craned her neck and peered at the little group of children behind him. "Girl Scout Cookies?"

"No."

"Then why are you here?" she asked, sounding more unfriendly than she'd intended.

"We want to interview you," one of the little kids said.

"Me?" The words came out in a surprised squeak. In all her eighty-seven years, no one had ever interviewed her before. There was truly a first time for everything.

"We're working on a project for school," the Hensler girl said. She had blue hair, in addition to her cape. She looked like a forest elf.

"But not real school. It's *home school*," one of the kids said.

"I see." Lillian nodded gravely. "Well, sit down and tell me about it."

The kids sprawled across the floor or took seats on the porch swing. Her son had installed it two years ago, but she never sat in it. The motion made her seasick. This might be the first time anyone had actually swung on her porch swing.

The youngest Mondello girl gazed up at her from the floor. "You look like you're a hundred years old."

"Almost." Lillian smiled. "I'm eighty-seven. How old are you?"

"I'm seven." They all giggled.

"What do you want to interview me about?" Lillian asked.

"The olden days," the littlest boy from Minnesota said.

"The neighborhood," his older brother clarified.

"We're doing historical research," the Hensler girl added importantly.

"I see." Lillian settled back in her rocking chair. "Well, I've lived here for fifty-eight years, so I've seen a lot of changes. What do you want to know?"

It had been a long time since anyone had asked what she thought, or recognized that she had something valuable to offer. Sometimes, if you weren't on TikBook or Facegram, society kind of left you behind.

More and more lately, her family seemed to think of her as a project to be managed, not someone whose company could be enjoyed.

"Where should I begin?" she asked.

"At the beginning," one of the little kids said, and they giggled again.

"All right, then. I'll start at the beginning."

She described her first day on Beaverbrook Lane as a mother of six in 1967. She told them about the kids who lived on the street back then, including her own children, and what they did for fun. Kick the can and baseball and tag, how they rode their bikes to school and to visit friends, how she and the other mothers would stand on their front porches at sunset with a cowbell to ring the kids home for supper.

Their eyes went wide as she described the freedom her own children had, almost sixty years earlier.

"Enjoying a nice visit with your grandkids?" An adult voice brought her back to the present with a jolt. It was the lady who lived across the street with her sister. She'd moved here from some country overseas.

But what was her name again? Valerie? Veronica? She couldn't remember now, but she made very good banana bread. She'd brought a loaf over, after she first moved in. And now she was recently retired. She'd seen more of this lady lately, walking her little Yorkie and planting bulbs in the front flower bed.

"We're not her grandkids," the oldest Mondello girl said. "We're her neighbors."

"Shouldn't you be in school at 1:00 p.m. on Tuesday afternoon?" the woman asked.

Oh dear. Lillian clutched the binoculars hidden beneath the blanket on her lap. She seemed to remember that this woman had headed the local teachers' union, until she retired last spring.

"We go to the Beaverbrook Academy for Inquiring Minds," one of the girls said.

The woman narrowed her eyes. "The *what*?"

"Our moms are homeschooling us," the youngest Cleaver boy said.

"Homeschooling?" The lady looked aghast.

"We were all kind of stressed out," the oldest Mondello girl explained.

"Yeah," her sister added. "So we're dropping out. For a year. Just to see how things go."

"I see." She exchanged a glance with Lillian, who gave a shrug that said *Don't blame me—I'm just the living history lesson.*

"Are you a *teacher*?" one of the boys asked shrewdly.

"I am now a recently retired teacher," the woman said in accented English. "How did you know this?"

"You have that look," he said.

"And you look suspiciously like a third grader." She raised an eyebrow. "I can spot them in the wild."

"I *am* a third grader!" The little boy grinned with delight, as though the woman had just performed a magic trick.

Then he rose, jumped off the porch, and took the woman's hand.

"You should come talk to my mom," he said, pulling her down the sidewalk.

"Why?" The woman looked bemused, allowing the boy to tug her toward his house.

"Because our moms are pretty good," the boy said. "But we need a real teacher."

Chapter Forty-One

KIERSTEN

Kiersten surveyed the chaotic mess of her once and future dining room. Textbooks, crayons, Goldfish crackers, scissors, glue sticks, water bottles, and pencils lay strewn across the table.

Piper and Rosamund had gone to Costco for more snacks and supplies while Kiersten had stayed behind to clean up the classroom after sending the kids next door to interview Mrs. Landry. She needed to talk to Mrs. Landry herself, as soon as she found a spare minute.

They'd somehow managed to survive another week of homeschooling, but the Experiment was not the relaxing Shangri-la she'd thought it would be.

As it turned out, teaching was *hard*.

She thought she would just be supporting Piper and Rosamund. But they'd found that someone needed to work with the little kids while they worked with the older kids and vice versa. So in addition to scheduling field trips and making lunches and printing out worksheets and buying school supplies and filing paperwork, she was teaching too.

She'd been up until midnight watching YouTube videos on how to write a lesson plan. The night before she'd been trying to relearn how to divide fractions. Or perhaps just *learning*. Fractions had never been her strong suit.

And then there was Luke.

He wasn't reading at the level of the older kids, but he didn't want to be stuck with the younger ones either. And he had trouble sitting still. He'd get up, wander around, look out the window. He'd fiddle and jiggle and fidget, and this distracted the other kids.

It was becoming a huge problem. And Piper, who had the courage of a lion, cared enough to face the issue head on instead of letting it fester.

"Can we talk about Luke?" she'd asked at the start of the second week when the kids went outside in the backyard and Rosamund went home to work on her novel.

Kiersten hung her head. "I know. I know. I'm sorry."

"He's such a sweet kid," Piper said. "We just need to find a way to keep him engaged and interested, especially when we're working on material that's harder for him than it might be for the other kids."

"I'm trying to find a dyslexia specialist who can work with him until he's reading at grade level, but it's been really hard."

She'd been unable to find a reading specialist with the qualifications, flexibility, and time to work with a new student in a home school setting. It was like searching for a unicorn.

And then a woman she'd never seen before in her life walked into her dining room, or rather, was pulled into her dining room by her youngest son.

"Mom. This lady is a real teacher," Johnny said by way of introduction. "Not a pretend one like you and Mrs. Mondello and Ms. Hensler."

The woman smiled and extended her hand. "I am Valentina Lucia Rossellini."

She had curly dark hair, chunky red glasses, and a purple T-shirt with the word **COEXIST** written across it in flowers. She also had a little dog tucked under her arm. She looked like Dorothy from *The Wizard of Oz* en route to a rave.

"I'm Kiersten Cleaver. Please, come in," she said, even though Valentina was already inside her dining room.

"I understand you are homeschooling." Valentina spoke quickly, with an accent Kiersten couldn't quite place. She found herself leaning forward to make sure she caught everything.

"It's not a criticism of the public schools," Kiersten said nervously. "Our kids had wonderful teachers. It's more a matter of trying to achieve balance in our lives. And I have a son with dyslexia, and ADD, and he's struggling, so we decided to try something different."

"I was born in Italy," Valentina said. "Then I lived in Latvia, Scotland, and South America, teaching Italian all over the world. Ten years ago I moved here, to be closer to my sister. I became a certified reading specialist, working with children who have dyslexia."

"Really?"

"Yes." She flipped through the textbooks scattered across the dining room table. "And I disagree with everything you do here by *abandoning* public education."

Kiersten shrank back. She *knew* they'd end up offending someone.

"But I understand *why* you do it," Valentina continued. "And I will help you."

Kiersten's mouth dropped open. "You will?"

"Of course!" She gave Kiersten an indignant look that said any decent person would do the same. "I will work with your son. By spring, he will walk through your house, clutching Katniss Everdeen to his heart like a long-lost love."

"How much will you charge because I know this costs a lot and—"

Valentina cut her off with a wave of her hand. "You will pay me twenty-five dollars each week."

She gasped. "But that won't even begin to cover your—"

"This is true," Valentina conceded with a gracious nod of her head. "But it will pay for the expensive prescription dog food required by Luciano Pavarotti." She stroked the little dog tucked under her arm.

"Are you sure?" Kiersten asked. "Because it doesn't seem right—"

"Yes." She cut Kiersten off with an imperious wave of her hand. "I am sure."

"Gosh." Kiersten sank into a chair, blinking back tears. She'd wanted this experiment to work so badly. And it wasn't working. Not even a little bit. But with this woman's help . . . maybe things could change.

She swallowed back the gratitude clogging her throat. "I don't know how to thank you," she whispered, trying not to cry.

"This is true," Valentina gave a little shrug. "But not important."

Kiersten smiled and wiped away the tears that escaped her lashes and trickled down her cheek.

"Write down everything about your son and what you hope to accomplish with this"—she looked around the dining room with a skeptical expression—"with this . . . *school*. Tell me his interests and strengths. Give me the names of all books he is reading. Put this in my mailbox. I will write plans for him. I will start on Monday."

"Um. Thank you?"

"You are welcome. And remember . . ." She was a tall woman, and she had to stoop slightly to look Kiersten straight in the eye. "A good education is *priceless*."

And with that, Valentina Luciana Rossellini swept out of the room, leaving a whiff of perfume behind.

Chapter Forty-Two

KIERSTEN

Later that night, Kiersten collapsed on the couch with a cup of tea. The boys were in bed, the kitchen was clean, and Garrett would come home tomorrow.

Weariness made her limbs heavy, her mind dull. She'd been up since dawn, running with Reggie, and she was tired, but it was a *good* tired. The exhaustion of someone who has accomplished important things.

Is this what teachers felt like at the end of each school day? If so, why weren't they paid like hedge fund managers?

But instead of reaching for the TV remote to hang out with Ross Poldark in a Cornish tin mine on PBS, her usual escape, she reached for the diary she'd left sitting on the ottoman.

Dottie felt like a friend at this point, a friend she needed to check in with every day. She opened the black cover and began to read.

Chapter Forty-Three

DOTTIE

June 25, 1965
San Diego

We go home tomorrow. We've been here for two weeks. The nurses keep telling me what a lucky girl I am, to have such a wonderful husband. He smiles and gives me tender kisses and brings me magazines and candy.

"How's my beautiful girl today?" he asks when he arrives for a visit. The nurses smile and titter and he brings them little gifts. A bouquet of flowers for the nurses' station to thank them for taking such good care of me, or a box of chocolates for the break room.

In some ways, this helps. It proves I'm not crazy, that Dickie really was a different person when we got married. He was *this* person, the person the nurses see every afternoon during visiting hours. Handsome and charming and thoughtful.

But it also makes things worse. Because even if I admitted the truth, even if I told someone, they wouldn't believe me. Everyone loves him. The nurses here at the hospital. The girls in the office at the dealership. Our neighbors. Even Daddy. *Especially* Daddy. No one will believe me. And I'm as stupid as Dickie says I am to think otherwise.

June 26, 1965
Beaverbrook Lane

We flew back from San Diego today. The neighbors walked by as we pulled up to the house. Dickie smiled and waved and told them what a wonderful time we had, and how exhausted I am from the trip. Traveling for two, he said with a wink.

And then we went inside, and he started yelling again about how this is all my fault, how working on his car and changing the oil caused the miscarriage. He says that's why women aren't mechanics. He said I'm abnormal. Unnatural. Then he told me not to tell anyone about losing the babies.

June 28, 1965

Is he right? Did I cause the miscarriage? Cried so hard today I can hardly see. God, this is awful. He said I can't leave the house until I'm "feeling better." He said he doesn't want me bursting into tears at the meat market or the drug store. I don't care anyway. All I want to do is sleep.

July 9, 1965

I just can't seem to pull myself out of this. Today I slept until two o'clock, ate some toast, and went back to bed. Every time I look out the window I see mothers and children. In the cul-de-sac, on the sidewalk, mothers pushing strollers, children riding their bicycles, playing baseball in the street, little gangs of children roaming through the front and back yards.

I can't bear this. I just can't. Because if I'm not going to be a mother, then what am I going to be? Am I just supposed to roll around inside this big empty house, making three course dinners for Dickie and ironing sheets every day, for the rest of my life. Is this all there is, forever?

July 25, 1965

I know I should try to pull myself out of this, but I don't have the energy. I'm exhausted. My stomach hurts. My skin is gray. I don't have a purpose anymore. I can't be a mechanic or an engineer. And now I can't be a mother either.

Men can be fathers, plus anything else under the sun. But married women aren't supposed to have jobs. Married women can't *be* anything but mothers.

And maybe . . . maybe that's the answer. Maybe I shouldn't be married. Then I'd have the freedom to be a secretary again, or a teacher or a nurse. Something else. Anything else. Anything but Dickie's wife.

Chapter Forty-Four

KIERSTEN

Kiersten shut the black cover, heart aching.

Then she heard a strange sound. Coming from the basement.

A rustling sound, followed by a faint tapping. She froze, trying to listen over her heartbeat pounding in her ears.

Silence. Then the tapping sound again.

I watch you.

The message on the blood-streaked note flashed through her mind as she rose from the sofa, grabbed her phone from the kitchen counter, and called Piper.

"I hear something . . . in the basement," she whispered.

"Unlock the mudroom door," Piper said. "I'm coming."

Moments later, Piper slipped through the side door, Glock holstered at her side.

"The basement?"

Kiersten nodded. She followed Piper as they began to move silently down the stairs, backs pressed against the wall.

The bottom step creaked as Kiersten landed on it. Then a high-pitched scream punctured the air.

Chapter Forty-Five

PIPER

Piper rounded the corner of the stairs. Bella screamed again. Then she giggled.

Relief flooded Piper's body, followed by confusion as her eyes took in the strange tableaux spread before her in the Cleaver basement.

"What the *hell* is going on here?"

All eight kids stared back at her, guilt and surprise etched across their faces.

They knelt on the floor, huddled around the small fire safe Kiersten kept in the nook beneath the staircase that she and her husband used as an office.

A stethoscope protruded from Matthew's ears. Beside him, Caitlin pressed the round part of the stethoscope against the door of the safe.

"Are you . . ." Kiersten frowned. "Are you trying to *crack our safe*?"

The kids were clad in various shades of black, plus what appeared to be attempted disguises. Guinevere wore a Darth Vader mask. Olivia wore a Harry Potter cape, Bella an Elsa wig, and Luke sported a purple balaclava normally used for snowmobiling.

What the hell?

"Upstairs," Piper bellowed. "NOW."

The kids scrambled up the stairs, followed by their mothers. Kiersten called Rosamund, who arrived moments later to find all eight kids sitting in uncharacteristic silence on the couch.

Piper pointed to her youngest. Always start an interrogation with the person most likely to rat out her partners in crime. Bella was notorious for giving "hints" that revealed the contents of every Christmas present under the tree.

"You. Spill it."

"We just wanted our iPads back," Bella said plaintively.

"I can't take this anymore." Luke pulled off the balaclava. His hair stood on end, giving him the strung-out look of an addict in need of a fix. "I need *Fortnite*. I need it *now*."

Caitlin removed her black *Incredibles* mask. "People are, like, *texting things* about me. Saying I left school because I had some kind of *mental health episode*. And I can't set the record straight, because I can only text *one hour a week*. This is *ruining my life*."

"We used your iPad," Johnny confessed. He removed his goalie mask and looked up at his mother with a guilty expression. "We went on YouTube. We found a video about how to crack open safes. They said to use a *sethascope*. So we got the one you use when you're a nurse."

"We had no choice." Matthew removed the catcher's mask he'd been wearing. "The current screen time policy is *draconian*."

Rosamund shot him a small smile. *Draconian* was one of the vocabulary words they'd discussed this week.

"We want to negotiate a better deal," Matthew continued.

Piper's mouth dropped open. "Negotiate?"

"That's right." Guinevere removed her Darth Vader mask. "We pay attention. We behave. And you let us have screens for three hours every day. And *two* movies on Saturday nights."

Caitlin moved to stand beside Guinevere and Matthew with crossed arms. "These are our demands."

"And if we don't meet your demands?" Kiersten asked, eyebrows raised so high they disappeared into her hairline.

"Then we go on strike," James said. "We won't learn things."

Piper exchanged a glance with Rosamund and Kiersten. "Management needs to discuss this."

Matthew picked up the remote. "Great. We'll watch the *Minecraft* movie while you talk."

He turned on the TV, and the kids immediately sank into a tranquilized silence.

The mothers retreated to the dining room / classroom.

"I can't *believe* this," Kiersten spluttered.

Piper threw her hands in the air. "Completely outrageous. This is—"

"Smart," Rosamund said.

They turned to stare at her. "Smart?"

"We discussed this in history last week," Rosamund said with a bemused expression. "The Industrial Revolution. The Luddite movement. The newsboys' strike of 1899. The rise of labor unions. Believe it or not, I think they're actually *learning* things. And I think they're right. One hour of screen time once a week *is* draconian, by modern child-technology standards. I say we rethink our policy."

Piper put her hands on her hips. "Seriously?"

"Yes. Seriously," Rosamund said. "And it might actually be easier if we do it their way. If they expect screen time every day, we have a carrot we can use when their attention starts to wander."

Piper chewed on her lower lip and considered this. "I guess if we want them to have friends to go back to next year, they need time to text and play video games with those kids while we homeschool."

"I can get on board with a little screen time every day," Kiersten finally conceded. "I guess it's sort of like methadone for a heroin addict. But three hours is too much. Luke would turn into a *Minecraft* zombie."

"So we lowball them," Rosamund said. "We offer half an hour a day. They counter with two hours. We settle at screen time for one hour each day, plus a movie on Friday *and* Saturday nights."

Piper nodded. "I'm prepared to go as high as ninety minutes of screen time a day. But that's our final offer."

Kiersten nodded. "Agreed."

They returned to the family room, paused the movie, and began their negotiation. It took ten minutes, but the children finally agreed to an hour of screen time each day, plus a movie on Friday and Saturday nights. They ratified this agreement with handshakes.

The mothers made popcorn as a peace offering and let the kids stay up past their bedtime to finish watching the *Minecraft* movie as a demonstration of good faith.

As the kids snuggled on the couch with their movie, the moms retreated to the kitchen, where Kiersten made everyone a cup of chamomile tea.

"We are either the best moms in the world or the worst moms in the world," Piper said. "I'm not sure which."

"My parents never, ever negotiated with me about *anything*," Kiersten said, shaking her head.

Rosamund wrapped her hands around her steaming mug of tea. "I know, but it's a new era. I like to call it 'Parenting with Pragmatism.'"

"Speaking of eras," Kiersten said, "can I read you guys a couple more entries from Dottie's diary?"

"Sure," Rosamund said. "Are they interesting?"

Kiersten swallowed her tea. "They're heartbreaking."

Chapter Forty-Six

DOTTIE

August 22, 1965

Everything is different now, without the babies. It's like a film has lifted from my eyes and I can see clearly.

If there are no babies, there's nothing tying me to Dickie. And if I'm not married, I can get a job as a secretary again or go to college and become a nurse or a teacher. A divorce will cause a scandal of course, and Daddy will be mortified, but I have my whole life ahead of me, and I can't bear the idea of spending it barefoot and trapped inside this house with Dickie.

And honestly, I don't think he wants to be married to me either. In fact, I have this terrible feeling he only married me because he wanted Daddy's money and Daddy's connections. There. I said it. Out loud. On paper.

August 23, 1965

I sat down with Dickie last night and told him I want a divorce. I tried to appeal to his enormous ego.

"It isn't fair to you, Dickie, now that I can't have children," I said. "If you stay with me, you'll never have the family you've always wanted. The family you deserve. You'd be such a wonderful father."

He raised an eyebrow. I might have laid it on a little thick.

"You can have the cars, the house, the money in our joint accounts, everything," I added, trying and failing to keep my desperation from leaching into my voice.

His eyes narrowed. Then he reached across the table and took my hand. It took all my self-control not to flinch and pull it back.

"Unfortunately, Dottie, there's no future in politics for a man who's divorced. People want a family man with a loving wife and beautiful children. And your father is unlikely to keep his ex-son-in-law employed as his general manager."

He released my hand, and I broke down. He patted me on the back. "I'm afraid you're stuck with me, babies or no babies. But don't worry. I have a plan to make everything so much easier for you."

Even though the air was sticky and the night unbearably hot, I shivered.

Chapter Forty-Seven

PIPER

Kiersten closed the book. Her features hardened into an expression Piper had never seen before.

"What do you think he's going to do?" Rosamund whispered.

"I don't know. I only know that he's *awful*," Kiersten said with a quiet vehemence that startled Piper.

"What else do we know about him?" Piper asked, going into investigation mode.

"Not much." Kiersten's shoulders hunched. "We don't know his last name. Or Dottie's married or maiden name. Dottie's father owned a car dealership somewhere nearby. She was valedictorian of her high school class. And that's it. Dottie and Dickie, newlyweds who lived on Beaverbrook Lane in 1965."

"Anything else?" Piper asked.

"Those names didn't ring any bells with the old guy who lived in our house. He suggested we talk to Lillian. She's eighty-seven and sharp as a tack, according to him. And I've been meaning to, but I've been so busy with school and the Harvest Festival that I haven't had time to sit down with her. And she's leaving early tomorrow morning to visit her son in Chicago again."

"What about the Influencer?" Rosamund asked. "Weren't you going to talk to her husband's Grammy and Grampy?"

Kiersten nodded. "I was, but Grammy just had cataract surgery, and I didn't want to bother them until she's had a chance to recover. I plan to talk with them both, once we get this harvest extravaganza over with."

"Have you read anything beyond this diary entry?" Rosamund asked.

"No." Kiersten shook her head. "It takes time. A lot of the entries are devoted to recipes she's experimenting with, and mundane things like the weather and washing the curtains. And her handwriting is so small that it's hard to read."

Piper nodded. "It's been a long time since I've read anything in cursive."

"I've been going slowly," Kiersten said, "to make sure I don't miss anything, like a name or an initial or a reference to something that might help us figure out who she is. Like the other day I went back and reread early entries and realized that she referred to her school as 'good old SMA.'"

Piper frowned. "SMA?"

Kiersten nodded. "Dottie got married right out of high school, so it's not a college. I'm not sure what it stands for."

Piper sighed. "Someone on this street must know something about the past."

"I always thought the past was *better*," Kiersten said quietly. "Everyone knowing their neighbor. No social media. But now I'm starting to think . . . I don't know . . . like the fact that she needed permission to get birth control pills. I guess I thought the '60s were all drugs and free love . . . but this . . . well, this is very different from what I imagined."

Rosamund took a sip of tea. "I think the late '60s were different. But this phase, in the early to mid-'60s, right before the women's liberation movement . . . well, I think maybe these are the reasons there *was* a women's liberation movement."

Kiersten nodded. "I'd have burned my bra too. I mean, I've always wanted to be a nurse, and I could have done that in 1965, but there were no female police officers back then. What if I'd wanted to go into law enforcement, like you?"

Piper was silent for a moment. Then she said, "There's something else going on right now that isn't very nice and pumpkin spice either."

Kiersten frowned. "What?"

"Someone is leaving things . . . in my yard. On my front porch."

"What kinds of things?"

"A box of worms from a pet-supply company."

Rosamund shuddered. "Worms?"

"Yeah," she said grimly. "Someone also left a bloody piece of paper in my front yard."

Kiersten's eyes went wide. "I found one of those nailed to the tree in my front yard too. And in my backyard."

"Did it say anything?"

"Something like 'I'm watching you.' At first I just assumed it was one of my kids."

Piper felt her eyebrows shoot up. "Your boys would do that?"

"As a joke, yes. Boys are wonderful. And disgusting. But I asked them, and they didn't know anything about it. I thought about calling the police, but I wasn't sure if it was serious enough, and then with everything else going on, it kind of moved to the back burner."

Rosamund's eyes narrowed. "I've been finding . . . dead things . . . on my welcome mat."

"What kind of dead things?" Piper asked, leaning forward.

"Two or three mice. A frog. And last week, a squirrel. I thought it was our cat . . . but maybe it's not?"

Piper sighed. "Okay. I need to think about this. Do you want to keep reading?"

"Yes," Kiersten said. "I feel like Dottie's trying to tell us something. Something important."

Chapter Forty-Eight

DOTTIE

August 25, 1965

Stunning reversal. Dickie apologized. He actually cried. He told me he's so sorry for the way he's behaved and treated me. He says he loves me, and he doesn't want a divorce. He said he wants a chance to make it up to me. He said I just need more help around the house.

And he's right. I'm still exhausted and kind of . . . foggy inside my head, with an upset stomach and no energy at all.

He says he's going to bring someone in to do all the housework and cooking so I can rest and recover.

I'm surprised to find that I believe him. He seems so genuine, so contrite. I don't *want* to believe him. But I *do* believe him. And I'm so tired. The idea of leaving, fighting him in a divorce court, disappointing Daddy, dealing with the scandal, it makes me exhausted just thinking about it.

Maybe he really can change. And if he's willing to try, I'm willing to stick around awhile longer and see what happens.

He's even willing to let me work in the garage if that will help me "get over" my grief.

I'll never get over the loss of the babies, or my inability to have more. But I guess it would give me a reason to get out of bed in the morning. So Oscar is dropping off a '57 Chevy with a bad engine.

In exchange, Dickie has asked me to stay close to home and not tell anyone about the miscarriage until I get my strength back. He's afraid I'll burst into tears at the grocery store and embarrass myself. Which is true. I cry all the time. I'm in no shape to be out in public.

And I'm not ready to tell anyone about the babies. Especially Daddy. He'll be crushed when he finds out he'll never be a grandfather. I'm happy to stick my head under the hood of a car and delay those conversations with Ruby and my father and the neighbors and everyone else for as long as possible.

August 28, 1965

Oscar and Glen towed the old Chevy into the garage today and put it next to the space where Dickie parks his car.

Dickie asked me to wear one of the baggy maternity dresses hanging in my closet, to hide the fact that I'm not pregnant anymore. I burst into tears when I put it on, but seeing the guys again chased the blues away for a couple hours.

They brought me a whole chest of tools. It's almost as good as the garage down at the dealership, but this one is better because it's mine, right here, to use any time I want.

"Anything new at the garage?" We leaned against the car drinking iced tea after they set up the work bench and helped me hang all my tools on the wall.

"Well," Glen took a sip of tea. "Leonard threw out his back last week putting in a new tail pipe. Otherwise it's the same old, same old. Still trying to find someone who can replace Danny . . ."

His voice trailed off and a hush settled over the garage at the mention of Danny's name.

"But that's easier said than done," Oscar muttered in a low voice, almost to himself.

I rested my hand on his arm and swallowed the grief clogging my throat. "Some people can't be replaced."

Oscar nodded, then gave me a small smile. "We just miss him, is all . . . and good mechanics are hard to find. Too bad you're not a man, Dottie . . . before you got in the family way, we could've trained you up to take his place."

A vision flashed across my mind, accompanied by an intense longing, an almost physical pain. An image of a future where I could be a mechanic. Where I could be anything I want . . . even though I'm female.

Then he leaned over and gripped my hand. "It's good to see you again, Dottie. I know you'll get this thing running again . . . and hopefully before the baby gets here. Then you'll be too busy."

I managed a weak smile and thanked them for coming.

It was the nicest afternoon I've had in a long time. And Dickie has been wonderful. Kind, solicitous, tender, the way he was before we got married. I don't have much of an appetite, but he makes all my meals for me. He puts a sandwich in the fridge before he goes to work, and makes a bowl of soup or a burger every night when he gets home. Then we snuggle up on the couch and watch Johnny Carson together.

Maybe he really can change. For the first time in a long time, I feel hope.

Chapter Forty-Nine

KIERSTEN

Kiersten woke the day of the Harvest Festival to find blue skies and temperatures in the mid-fifties, cold enough to encourage picturesque fall sweaters, but not cold enough to keep people inside.

Garrett planted a good morning kiss on her cheek as she made her first cup of coffee.

"I see you've gone 'full farmer' in honor of the occasion."

He glanced down at his western-style shirt and cowboy boots. He touched the brim of his green John Deere cap and grinned down at her. "Gotta look the part for the city folk."

He'd been tasked with driving a small tractor and trailer up and down the cul-de-sac, giving hayrides. Richard Davis had used his contacts in local government to secure permission to close the street to traffic for the entire day.

"Knock, knock." Rosamund entered the house through the mudroom. "Guinevere could use some help setting up cornhole," she called out to Kiersten's boys.

She flattened herself against the kitchen island as they bolted out the front door to help.

"Morning, Rosamund," Garrett called.

She raised her coffee mug in greeting. "They just unloaded the tractor, and Miles needs you to sign something."

"Got it." Garrett headed out the door.

Kiersten turned to Rosamund with an innocent smile. When she'd taken the trash cans inside last night, she'd seen the wildlife biologist whistling as he left Rosamund's house.

"Looks like Miles had dinner at your place again?"

"Oh. Well. Yes," Rosamund stammered, her cheeks turning a becoming shade of pink. "The poor man is brilliant, but he's such a *terrible* cook. Guinevere and I take pity on him a few nights each week and invite him over to eat with us."

"I see," she said, arching her brow.

"Knock, knock," Piper called from the mudroom.

A warm sensation radiated through Kiersten's chest. She loved that her neighbors felt they could enter her home with a verbal knock from the inside, rather than a physical knock from the outside.

Homeschooling was going better too. The carrot of daily screen time and the coming of Valentina had made all the difference in the world. Piper wondered how they had functioned without her. It felt like they were slowly finding their rhythm.

"Did you see the camera crew?" Piper asked, a little breathless.

"What camera crew?" Rosamund asked.

"I think Aspen is filming . . . or taping . . . or whatever they call it. Come look."

They filed onto the front porch to witness the transformation taking place on Beaverbrook Lane.

Musicians set up microphones and speakers, while Garrett, Brendan, and Miles set up a semi-circle of hay bales in front of a stage to create seats under the supervision of Aspen's husband, Trey.

He wore waterproof zip-leg hiking pants and a Patagonia half zip. He looked like he'd just stepped out of an REI ad.

And in the midst of it all strode Aspen, blond curls cascading down her back, resplendent in cowboy boots and a chunky oatmeal-colored sweater.

Behind her trailed a man with a large professional-looking camera on his shoulder, a young woman recording with a phone, and a still photographer snapping pictures as they walked.

"Concessions over there," Aspen called to a group of high school kids who'd arrived to sell food in support of the high school crew team. "Right next to the Fort Hunt Presbyterians."

Three energetic middle-aged women wrestled with the metal legs on a folding table as they set up their chili stand. The high school rowers noticed their struggle and quickly helped them flip the heavy tables upright.

"It looks like a Hallmark movie," Rosamund said.

And it did, Kiersten realized. A true community, where everyone came together to celebrate a beautiful autumn day while supporting various worthy causes.

Aspen crossed the cul-de-sac and approached Kiersten's porch, camera people in tow. "What do you guys think?" she asked, a broad smile lighting her perfectly made-up face.

"I think it's amazing," Kiersten said honestly. "You've done an incredible job pulling it all together."

"I *know*." She turned in a circle with the gleeful expression of a kid in a candy store. "So much *content*."

"Well," Piper said with that bright, fake smile she always used around Aspen, "I guess we should get to work. Any marching orders?"

"Yes," Aspen said decisively. She then enumerated a long list of duties for each of them. "And when the festival ends at five, we start the harvest feast. Got it?"

"Yes ma'am," Piper said.

"Great. Let's get this party started." She waved goodbye and headed for the bouncy house, camera people following closely behind.

"Here we go," Piper said, looking grimly determined. "Time to manifest abundance like a . . ." She paused.

"Like a mother clucker?" Kiersten asked, smiling.

She grinned back. "Time to manifest abundance like a mother clucker."

Chapter Fifty

PIPER

The day flew by as Piper flitted around the cul-de-sac, parachuting in where needed. She mediated disputes at the surprisingly contentious pin-the-tail-on-the-donkey station, solved a Crock-Pot-extension-cord crisis for the Fort Hunt Presbyterians, and dealt with allegations of line cutting at the face-painting station.

"Why don't you take a break?" Kiersten said around 2:00 p.m. "Get some lunch. I'll take my break when you're done."

"Thanks." She actually *was* hungry, now that Kiersten mentioned it.

She purchased a bowl of Presbyterian chili and augmented it with a can of Coke and a bag of Doritos from the crew-team concession stand.

Then she sat down at one of the blue-and-white-checked tables in front of the musicians and looked around for her husband or the girls. As she squinted into the distance, something caught her eye.

Caitlin stood at the entrance to the bouncy house, arms crossed over her chest. A tall older boy obviously wanted to get inside, in defiance of the age limit they'd imposed to keep the little kids safe.

Caitlin raised her hand, pointing to the entrance of the cul-de-sac, clearly telling the boy to leave. The boy shook his head and widened his stance, refusing to move.

Piper rose from the table, eyes narrowed. She'd never seen this boy before.

Wait. Could this be Alex Orlov?

She sprang from her chair and moved at a fast walk toward the bouncy house, forcing herself not to run, not to alarm anyone, never taking her eyes off the boy.

Her stomach dropped as he pulled a phone out of his pocket and raised it to record Caitlin.

She increased her pace.

Suddenly Matthew Cleaver appeared beside Caitlin. He reached out and snatched Alex Orlov's phone.

Almost there.

Just as she approached the bouncy house, Luke and Guinevere appeared on Caitlin's left, Guinevere's velvet cape swirling like Wonder Woman's, if Wonder Woman were flat chested, wore glasses, and had blue hair.

"Everything okay here?" Piper asked, out of breath.

"Everything is fine, Mrs. Mondello," Matthew said evenly.

"He stole my *phone*." The tall boy spat out the words, his face red.

"I took Alex's phone because he was going to record Caitlin," Matthew explained, never taking his eyes off Alex Orlov. He had his father's unflappable Scandinavian demeanor.

"No, I wasn't," Alex argued.

"Yes, you *were*," Caitlin insisted. "And now you need to *leave*."

"That's right." Guinevere stepped forward. "And henceforth may you never darken the door of our cul-de-sac again."

Piper bit back a smile. Like mother, like daughter. Then she turned to Matthew. "I'll take the confiscated phone, if you don't mind."

Matthew handed it over. Piper jerked her chin at Alex Orlov. "Caitlin's right. You need to go."

Caitlin lifted her chin. "Now."

"I can stay if I want to," he said, his voice sullen. "It's a free country."

"Not here." Piper shook her head. "This is the People's Republic of Beaverbrook Lane, and I'm asking you, nicely, to go home. *Now.* Follow me if you want your phone back," she said, taking a few steps toward the entrance to the cul-de-sac.

He shot a parting scowl at Matthew, Caitlin, Luke, and Guinevere, then lumbered beside her, brows knit, mouth twisted in an ugly sneer.

She shot him a sideways glance. He was considerably taller than she was, with his father's thick build and small deep-set eyes.

"How old are you?" she asked when they reached the entrance to the cul-de-sac, where a black dirt bike leaned against a telephone pole.

"Almost fifteen," he said.

"Held back?" she asked.

"I repeated kindergarten." He scowled. "Not that it's any of *your* business."

She held out the phone, and he grabbed it.

"Leave now and don't come back," she ordered.

His upper lip twisted in a sneer. "You won't be able to kick me out when I *live* here."

She stifled a gasp. "What do you mean?"

He grabbed his helmet from the handlebars of his dirt bike. "My parents are gonna buy that new house. The one they're building on this street. I'll be Caitlin's neighbor."

Then he tugged the helmet over his head, jumped on the bike, and tore down the street, leaving her speechless.

Chapter Fifty-One

KIERSTEN

At five o'clock Kiersten waved as the last family herded their face-painted children out of the cul-de-sac. Then she rallied her flagging energy for the Harvest Festival potluck, the last event of this wonderful, exhausting day.

During a brief lull in early afternoon, she'd stood outside her garage and taken in the scene around her.

She'd watched her younger boys make change at their tepid chocolate stand, all by themselves, while her older sons patiently helped little kids at the bouncy house.

She'd seen Garrett laughing at something Piper's husband said as they worked together to manage the hayrides. She'd watched Guinevere and Caitlin giggle together as they painted faces under the tutelage of Valentina's artistic sister, Alessandra.

She'd watched Reggie and Valentina line dance in front of the stage, encouraging others to do the same, looking like Fred and Ginger in fleece zip ups.

And she'd witness Rosamund's smiles and flushed cheeks as she and Miles worked together in piñata management beneath the giant sweet gum tree in her front yard.

Now they all gathered together at a long table running down the center of Beaverbrook Lane, draped in burlap and decorated with pumpkins and mums.

The camera man walked the length of the street, shooting video of the spread while Aspen placed a pumpkin pie on the table.

"Time to eat, everyone," she called. She'd changed outfits again and now wore cowboy boots and a knee-length ivory dress trimmed with lace. If Kiersten had worn this, she knew she would have looked like an extra from *Little House on the Prairie*. But Aspen somehow managed to look both hip and vintage at the same time.

Aspen looked into the camera and began to speak.

"Family. Community. Abundance. We have it all, right here in our beautiful neighborhood on the shores of the Potomac River." She spread her arms, and the camera panned the street around her, taking in the tastefully decorated porches, the straw bales, and finally, the river sparkling in the distance.

Then she rang a cowbell, summoning her neighbors to the table filled with food.

"Can we eat now?" Johnny asked impatiently.

Kiersten planted a kiss on top of his head. "Yes, honey, we can eat."

"Can I interest anyone in some spotted dick?" Miles asked with a jovial grin, raising his dessert in the air and making everyone smile.

When the kids were settled, Kiersten sat down between Chip and Trey Davis and across from Rosamund in the only empty chair left at the table.

Trey's little girls sat beside him in matching pinafores as their mother directed them to smile into the video camera.

"Would either of you like some macaroni hotdish?" Kiersten asked, raising her contribution to the Harvest Festival potluck into the air.

"Hotdish?" Chip raised his eyebrows, like she was offering a Pyrex baking dish filled with anthrax. "No thanks."

"Your loss," she said cheerfully, trying not to take this rejection of food from her native land personally.

"Trey? How about you?" she asked, turning to his son. "Tomato soup. Macaroni. Ground beef. Corn. All mixed together. Nectar of the gods."

"No thanks." He held up his hands, as though defending his pristine body from the frightening ingredients in her casserole. "I'm on a keto diet right now. But I'll have one of those celery sticks."

She manufactured a bright smile to show there were no hard feelings, even though, deep down, *there were*, and passed him the veggie tray. Then she piled a generous helping of hotdish onto her own plate.

"Aspen did a wonderful thing for our neighborhood today," she said after swallowing a bite.

Delicious. She resisted the urge to moan with pleasure, just to give them an idea of what they were missing.

Chip swallowed a gulp of lemonade and gave her a bemused smile. "My daughter-in-law excels at making things look pretty on camera. My wife had a knack for this kind of thing too."

"I don't think I've met her," Kiersten said.

Chip lowered his eyes. "She passed away a few years ago, unfortunately. Right before Trey and Aspen got married."

"Heart attack," Trey said. "Everyone thinks heart disease only impacts men, but it actually claims thousands of women each year."

He rattled off some statistics, sounding a little bit like an infomercial for the American Heart Association. "I'm so sorry to hear that," she murmured.

Chip shrugged. "We're adapting. My mother has sort of stepped in and become a grandmother to these little girls. They call her Great-Grammy."

"We miss having grandparents next door," Kiersten said.

"Yeah, I'm sure everything is pretty different out here on the East Coast," Chip said. Then he frowned and leaned in closer. "You should keep your wits about you. This neighborhood isn't as safe as it looks."

"What do you mean?"

"New people moving in and out all the time. It's transient now," he said, waving his hand scornfully. "Not like it used to be."

She refrained from pointing out that *she* was one of those transient new people.

"Well, everyone has made us feel very welcome," she said stiffly. He had a Get Off My Lawn vibe that she found off putting.

"So how did the whole Instagram thing take off?" she asked, trying to bring the conversation back to a lighter subject.

Trey dipped another celery stick into a bowl of hummus. "Aspen worked in social media marketing before we got married. She wanted to keep working, and I wanted her to stay home and focus on our family."

Kiersten shifted in her seat. *I'll bet you did.*

"Daddy, will you cut my hot dog for me?"

"Mommy will be back in a minute," Trey said, glancing at his daughter.

Women's work, apparently. Kiersten crumpled her hands into fists. What if she choked?

"I can do it." She reached over and cut the hot dogs into safe bite-size pieces.

"Thanks," he said, munching on a celery stick. "Anyway, after Aspen quit working, she asked me if she could post a few videos, talking about homeschooling and baking with Grammy's recipes."

Kiersten's eyebrows rose, and she forced her face back into a more neutral expression. Aspen had to ask her husband for *permission* to post videos?

"I said sure, go ahead. I didn't think it would lead to anything," Trey added.

"And he was wrong about that," his father said with a look Kiersten couldn't read. There was an undercurrent here, a tone she couldn't identify.

"Yeah. I was wrong," Trey admitted, an edge to his voice. "I had no idea it would be come this huge *thing*. Our timing was perfect. The whole trad wife movement started trending just as we began adopting Grammy's lifestyle and recipes. So basically, we got lucky."

"Or you have a really smart wife who understands how social media works," Kiersten said, pushing her plate away.

"It's not like she's the primary breadwinner or anything." Trey's words had a defensive tinge. "There's not actually a whole lot of money in being an influencer at our level. The money comes when you parlay your followers into something else, like a TV deal. We get a lot of free stuff, but the property-development and real estate company where I work with my dad and grandfather are still our primary source of income."

"Until this HGTV deal goes through," his father said. "That's the big payoff. Then your wife will bring home the bacon."

Trey narrowed his eyes. "I'm the one negotiating that deal."

Chip clapped a hand on his son's shoulder. "I know you are, son. And you're doing a helluva job. And when the deal goes through, we've got big plans for that money, don't we?"

"We do," his son said. "Lots of changes coming when that money hits our account."

"What kinds of changes?" Kiersten asked.

A secretive look crossed his face. "We can't discuss details yet."

"By the way," Chip interrupted, abruptly changing the subject, "this morning Aspen told me you found some old diaries in your basement?"

"I did." Kiersten wiped her mouth on a lace napkin that seemed far too nice to actually use. "They belonged to a woman who lived here on Beaverbrook Lane in 1965, but I don't know her full name. And I was wondering if your parents would be willing to take a look and see if they can figure out who they belong to."

"I'm sure they'd be happy to help," Chip said.

"Great. I would have asked sooner, but I know your mother is recovering from cataract surgery."

He nodded. "She had both eyes done last week. But she's feeling much better now. Why don't you come over tomorrow after lunch and they can take a look?"

"That would be great. Thank you so—"

A vigorous clanking interrupted their conversation. Aspen stood at the head of the table, next to Richard and Margaret Davis, ringing the cowbell. She set it on the table as silence fell over the cul-de-sac.

Chip and Trey pushed their chairs away from the table. "Excuse us," Chip said. "Time for a little presentation."

Trey looked at his daughters. "Girls, you need to help Mommy, remember?"

They scampered to the far end of the table, where they stood beside their mother.

Aspen stepped back, allowing her husband and father-in-law to stand beside Margaret and Richard in the place of honor at the head of the table. Trey put his arm around Aspen and pulled her close. She rested her head against his shoulder, while their little girls stood beside them.

"What an extraordinarily picturesque family," Rosamund whispered.

Kiersten nodded, examining the three men at the head of the table. It was remarkable, almost like looking at photographs of one man over the span of a lifetime.

Richard Davis represented the final phase, his face creased and spotted with age, likely in his eighties, but retaining a full head of white hair and a pleasant smile, still handsome in a *Lion in Winter* sort of way. It was easy to imagine him as the charming politician he'd allegedly been sixty years ago.

His son, Chip, stood to his right. He looked like central casting's version of the CEO of a Fortune 500 company, managing to preserve his good looks as he entered his early sixties. She wondered if he used Botox. His jawline had blurred, and there was a hint of gray at his temples. But otherwise he remained tall and vigorous, obviously still in excellent shape.

And then Trey. Mid-thirties. Strikingly handsome. Dark hair neatly parted on the side. Preppy. Perfect. Ken to Aspen's Barbie.

She chewed her lower lip as she examined them. But that was too glib. There were depths here, beneath the surface. Trey was smart, ambitious. And given what she'd accomplished thus far in her young life, so was Aspen. It was a mistake to assume they were shallow and unintelligent just because they were both so good looking.

Chip raised a mason jar filled with iced tea. "I'd like to propose a toast to an extraordinary couple. My parents, Margaret and Richard Davis, who've been married for fifty-nine years, all of those years happy, and spent here on Beaverbrook Lane."

Everyone raised their mason jars in the air.

"Let's drink a toast to strong marriages, strong families, strong communities, and wonderful neighbors. Here's to another fifty-nine years of happy families on Beaverbrook Lane."

Everyone raised their glasses and drank, including the kids. She glanced at her boys, their young faces glowing. They obviously felt very mature and dignified being included in a real toast. Caitlin grinned at Matthew and threw her arm around Guinevere. Her little sisters gleefully clunked their plastic cups together.

Aspen handed her daughters two small bouquets of flowers, which they presented to their great-grandmother. Margaret bent in her chair so the little girls could kiss her wrinkled cheeks as the photographer leaned in close to snap pictures.

Kiersten's eyes began to sting, and she brushed away a tear, surprised by the genuine emotions generated by an event created by an influencer.

"Happy?"

She glanced up at her husband, who slipped into the empty seat beside her. He smiled, taking her hand.

She looked around at her neighbors and nodded, not trusting herself to speak.

Down the table, Piper caught her eye and grinned.

When they first moved here, she didn't know a single person. And now, just a few months later, she had friends.

Not acquaintances. Not internet friends. But real friends. Three a.m. friends, the kind of people you could call in the middle of the night, and they'd be there.

"You did a great thing today," Garrett said, leaning over to kiss her cheek.

"So did you. How did it feel to be back on a tractor?"

"Good. Normal." He looked out across the cul-de-sac. "But this . . . this community that you've created for us, for our kids. This feels good and normal too. It feels . . ." He paused.

She looked into his eyes and smiled. "It feels like home."

Chapter Fifty-Two

KIERSTEN

Hours later, after they'd deflated the bouncy house, unstrung the lights, folded the folding tables, and washed all the dishes, Kiersten climbed the stairs to bed.

Garrett was already there, reading the *Farm Journal.*

She squeezed his hand. "Ten more minutes?"

He peered at her over his reading glasses. "Just enough time for me to finish this riveting article on the latest innovations in pasture management."

She had only a few pages left in Dottie's first diary. She turned on the bedside lamp and began to read.

Chapter Fifty-Three

DOTTIE

September 6, 1965

I met the live-in help this morning. The doorbell rang and I found Peggy, the incompetent girl from the office, standing on the porch in scuffed shoes and a big overcoat, even though it was hotter than blazes by 9 a.m., holding a suitcase. She's different than I remember. Still very pretty, but pale, quieter.

I put her in the second-floor guest bedroom and showed her where everything is inside the kitchen, and she got right to work.

Then I went back to bed. But as I drifted off to sleep, I caught the scent of baking bread.

I hope it's edible. Because if she's as bad at cooking as she is at running the Selectric we're all going to starve.

September 13, 1965

It's been a week since Peggy arrived. She never seems to leave the house, but maybe she doesn't have time, with all the cooking and baking and gardening she does. I can't figure out if she got fired from the dealership, or if Dickie poached her from the office to be our domestic help.

I feel a little sorry for her. She wears scuffed shoes and these worn, shapeless dresses that hang on her petite frame. She seems troubled. Scared. But she makes me delicious meals. Scrambled eggs for breakfast, a small casserole with fresh fruit for lunch, and a lovely dinner that I eat on my own in the kitchen before Dickie comes home. Then I go out in the garage and work on the '57 Chevy until long after dusk. I come inside around 8 p.m. and fall into a deep sleep. I'd forgotten grief is like this. I felt this way after my mother died. Tired. Right down to my bones.

September 14, 1965

I learned a little bit more about Peggy today while eating my lunch. She grew up in a small town in Missouri, near Fort Leonard Wood, with six siblings. Put herself through secretarial school while working as a cook at a restaurant and a maid at a hotel. She's awfully pretty, and a much better housekeeper than I'll ever be.

She cuts flowers from the garden and makes the most beautiful arrangements. Hydrangeas and foxglove and some of those roses still blooming on the east side of the house. I have to admit, she's got a knack for making the house look pretty.

I shared my recipes with her to make her life easier and she's been making them. She adds too much salt, though.

September 15, 1965

I came in from the garage last night to find Dickie and Peggy eating together in the dining room. It made my stomach heave, almost like having morning sickness again, as I watched them laughing and talking together as they ate.

She's always so careful never to sit with me when I eat, to maintain this idea that she's the staff and I'm the mistress, even though it's just the two of us here all day together and we're basically the same age.

She looked beautiful. And even though I don't love Dickie anymore, something inside me twisted like a shard of glass.

Chapter Fifty-Four

KIERSTEN

The next day dawned harsh and cold. The Instagram-perfect fall weather from the day before had vanished, replaced by a gloomy fog. A gray curtain hung over the cul-de-sac, muting the crimson of the sugar maples planted at regular intervals along both sides of the street.

Kiersten slipped out of her quiet house and met Piper at the mailbox.

After church and pancakes at IHOP, Garrett had taken the boys to the big Air and Space Museum out by Dulles airport, giving her all of Sunday afternoon to exercise with Reggie, and then have coffee with Richard and Margaret Davis in their house at the end of the cul-de-sac.

A misting rain dribbled down from the sky. Kiersten pulled up the hood on her Minnesota Vikings sweatshirt in a vain attempt to protect her hair and stashed Dottie's first diary in the front pocket of her sweatshirt to keep it dry.

"Thanks for coming with me," she said as she balanced a plate of freshly made brownies in her other hand.

Piper walked beside her, unhurried and untroubled by the falling rain. "Is it just the old couple?" she asked.

"The old couple and their son, Chip."

Piper groaned. "That guy again? He totally ducked out of all the cleanup for the Harvest Festival last night."

"I know. He seems a little . . . slick," Kiersten admitted.

"And he's the Influencer's father-in-law?"

Kiersten smiled. Piper never called Aspen by her name. "That's right."

"And he's going to be there because . . ."

"I think he's just trying to be helpful. He said he'd join us, if he had time."

They glanced at the skeleton of the new home going up next to Richard and Margaret's house. It had a roof now, and shingles, but no windows or doors.

"Listen, I've been thinking about the Harvest Festival," Piper said.

Kiersten smiled. "It was great, wasn't it?"

"Sure, it was great," Piper said. "But I also think it was a commercial."

Kiersten frowned. "A commercial? For what?"

"I follow Trey's real estate company on Instagram and Chip's property-development company too. And they've already turned all that footage from yesterday into an ad for the two new houses they plan to build here on Beaverbrook."

"They had professional photographers shooting video and taking pictures all day long," Kiersten said with a shrug. "I guess we knew they were planning to use it for something."

"But I think *that* was the real purpose of the whole endeavor. We basically donated our time to organize an elaborate photo shoot promoting Chip and Trey's companies."

A feeling she couldn't identify washed over Kiersten as they walked up the front steps. Disappointment maybe, mingled with a flash of anger. She'd baked three dozen cupcakes, an apple pie, plus all that macaroni hotdish, all *for a commercial*?

"So it wasn't about . . . building community?"

Piper shook her head. "I think it's about cramming as many homes as possible onto those two lots and then selling them to the highest bidder, who may turn out to be Bruce Orlov and his equally sketchy son."

"What do you mean?"

She told Kiersten about the incident at the Harvest Festival with Alex Orlov.

Kiersten hunched deeper into the folds of her hooded sweatshirt. Piper's theory had a ring of truth to it.

"Maybe that's true," she conceded. "But we still had a wonderful day. The kids had a great time. *I* had a great time. And maybe these new houses they're building will bring us some lovely new neighbors who *aren't* the Orlovs."

Piper shot her a look that clearly said *You are so naive.* "Last night I asked them not to use any video of me, or my husband or my kids. I don't want our faces on the internet with Hawkeye Slaughter on the loose."

"Did they honor this request?"

"They did." Piper jutted her chin. "But I still don't trust Chip or Trey. So keep your powder dry, okay?"

"Keep my powder dry?" Kiersten pressed her lips together and managed to stifle a derisive giggle. "We're having coffee with our eighty-something-year-old neighbors, not heading into nuclear disarmament talks with the Russians."

Piper cocked an eyebrow. "Just . . . *be aware.*"

"Okay, Matlock." She pressed the doorbell. "I'll keep my wits about me."

A few moments later Margaret opened the door, her white hair perfectly coifed, wearing pearls and a floral dress. Behind her stood Richard, beaming at them with a welcoming smile.

"Here we go," she murmured to Piper under her breath. "Entering the *den of iniquity.*"

"Don't be a smart-ass," Piper muttered back.

"Come on in," Richard called from the foyer.

"Thank you so much, Mr. and Mrs. Davis, for making time to see us." Kiersten handed Margaret a plate of brownies she'd baked from scratch that morning. She'd decided she couldn't make brownies from a box for a woman whose recipes had sold a billion cookbooks. Margaret would *know* . . . she probably had a sixth sense for lazy baked goods containing maltodextrin and riboflavin.

The old couple led them to a kitchen table in an alcove overlooking a spacious backyard. Outside, birds darted from leafless November trees to the feeders beside the patio.

Inside, pictures of Trey and Aspen's two little girls hung from the refrigerator beside childishly misshapen drawings of houses, unicorns, and flowers.

"I made a fresh pot of coffee," Margaret said, gesturing to the kitchen table laid with a silver coffee pot, and delicate china cups and saucers. "And a pecan pie. Do you prefer ice cream or whipped cream?"

People didn't entertain like this anymore, Kiersten thought, remembering the first time she'd had Piper and Rosamund over to her house, and how they'd eaten pizza from a box chased with water from red Solo cups.

"I'd love some coffee," Kiersten said. "And I can't say no to pie with ice cream." She'd work off the calories later with Reggie.

"It's real whipped cream," Margaret said. "Not that stuff you buy at the grocery store."

"Well, in that case . . ." Kiersten amended. "I'd love pecan pie with whipped cream."

"Me too," Piper added. "Thank you."

Margaret handed them coffee cups, plus cream and sugar in matching china containers.

They sipped their coffee, ate their delicious pie, and discussed Margaret's recent cataract surgery, hot-water heaters, traffic on Fort Hunt Road, and the fact that you could find both Advent candles *and* poker chips at the neighborhood variety store down the street.

Kiersten got the impression that the old couple could happily have visited with them for hours. They seemed a little lonely, even with their son and grandson right next door.

She glanced at Piper, who darted a meaningful look at the clock.

Kiersten cleared her throat and managed to steer their meandering conversation back to the reason for their visit. "So we're here today because we need your help."

A slamming door and a thumping noise behind the kitchen interrupted her words. A few moments later, Chip entered the room.

"Good morning, ladies." He flashed a smile as he pulled out a chair and sat down at the kitchen table. "I just popped over to make sure my parents are staying out of trouble."

"They're delightful," Kiersten said truthfully. "And as I said last night at dinner, I'm hoping they can help me track down the rightful owner of the diaries I found in my basement. It's kind of a mystery."

"A mystery!" Richard pushed away his empty pie plate. "We'd be happy to help."

Kiersten removed Dottie's diary from the pouch in her sweatshirt and pushed it across the table. "I found them hidden inside some old encyclopedias. Someone donated them to a garage sale here on Beaverbrook about ten years ago. But no one purchased them, so they've been sitting in my basement ever since."

Richard gently picked up the diary and opened it, brushing his fingers over the page as he and Margaret squinted down at the handwriting.

"The lady who wrote them is interesting." Kiersten resisted the urge to help herself to a second piece of pie. "Her father owned a car dealership in this area, and she was a newlywed. Her name was Dottie, and her husband was Dickie. Dottie and Dickie. Does that ring any bells?"

Richard's hand trembled slightly as he turned the pages, but his expression didn't change as he stared down at the diary.

After a short silence, he looked up at Kiersten. "It doesn't ring any bells. I'm sorry."

"How many did you find?" Chip asked.

"Three diaries," Kiersten said. "Plus some cash. The others are back at the house."

"Well, we'd be happy to read through it and see if anything strikes us." Richard clutched the volume in his age-spotted hands.

"That would be really helpful," Kiersten said. "I'm not getting very far with just a first name to go on."

"How did you say you found them again?" Margaret asked.

She repeated her story about the box in her basement.

Richard reached for a brownie. "Have you read them all?"

"I finished this one last night." Kiersten scraped her fork over the last crumbs of pecan pie on her plate. "I haven't started on the others yet."

Chip took a sip of his coffee. "Anything interesting?"

"Well . . ." She paused. There were similarities between the "advice" Dottie got from Dickie in the diaries, and the advice Aspen dispensed in her trad wife workbooks. What if Dottie had been married to one of their oldest friends? Someone they knew and loved?

"It didn't seem like a particularly . . . happy marriage . . ." Kiersten said, attempting to be diplomatic. "But this was also a long time ago."

A saucer rattled as Margaret set her teacup down with shaking hands. "*Everything* was different back in 1965. The things that people did back then . . ." Her voice trailed off. "Well, they wouldn't get away with things like that *today*."

Chip laid his large, smooth hand over his mother's wrinkled one. "She's still recovering from cataract surgery, so I think we might need to wrap things up now. But if you want to leave the diary here, I'm sure Grammy and Grampy can figure out who it belonged to. And please, bring the other diaries over too."

"I will," Kiersten promised, "if I ever finish reading them. This homeschooling takes up more time than I expected. And the Harvest Festival kept us all busy, too, of course."

"I'll come by and pick up the diaries after Grammy and Grampy finish this one. I'm sure they'll get through it quickly."

"That's the nice thing about being retired," Richard said. "Lots of time for reading."

“Perfect. Thanks again for all your help.” Kiersten rose from her chair as Piper caught her eye, sending her a look she couldn’t interpret.

Chip walked them to the door, while the old couple remained in the kitchen. She glanced back and saw Margaret lift a napkin to her eye and wipe away a tear.

Chapter Fifty-Five

PIPER

They walked back to Piper's house in silence. "Come inside for a minute," Piper said in a low voice.

"I can't. Reggie and I are doing weight training in ten minutes. I can now bench press thirty pounds," Kiersten said proudly.

"That's great." Piper opened the side door to her garage and pulled Kiersten inside. Then she lowered her voice to a conspiratorial whisper. "But what did you think?"

"Of what?"

Piper resisted the urge to shake her friend. "Of their reaction when you told them about the diaries."

Kiersten shrugged. "I thought they were nice old people who were kind enough to volunteer to help."

Piper chewed on her lower lip. "They're hiding something."

"Like what?" The corner of Kiersten's mouth twitched, and Piper could tell she was trying very hard not to laugh. "Black market motorized wheelchairs? Fake AARP membership cards?"

Piper's eyes narrowed. "I'm serious."

Kiersten shook her head. "I'm serious too. They were the world's sweetest old couple. The only thing those people are hiding are unwrapped Christmas presents for their great-grandkids."

"Margaret was crying when we left. Did you see that?"

"Margaret just had cataract surgery. Her eyes are watering."

Piper went silent. "Is that a *thing*?"

"I don't know," Kiersten said with an exasperated sigh. "I have not yet had my hips replaced or my cataracts done, but I think that's a far more logical explanation than . . . stolen Geritol tablets."

"What's Geritol?"

"I don't remember exactly," Kiersten admitted. "My grandmother used to take them. It's a pill. For old people."

Piper ran a hand over her ponytail. "Just don't give them the other diaries yet. And hide them somewhere safe, okay?"

"Why in the world—"

"Look, the woman who wrote those diaries didn't feel safe leaving them laying around *her* house, did she? She had a reason for hiding them. We need to honor her wishes by keeping them safe, at least until we've read everything she has to say."

Kiersten went silent for a moment, brow knitted in thought. "Fine. I won't share the rest of the diaries until we've read every page. And I'll keep them someplace safe."

"Not in your underwear drawer."

"But that's—" Kiersten began.

Piper cut her off. "Put the diaries in a ziplock bag. Put the ziplock bag inside that big bag of birdseed you keep in your garage."

Kiersten tilted her head. "Are you serious?"

"That's what drug dealers do. It's a very effective hiding place. Or I can keep the diaries at my house. But I do not want to turn them over to Chip and Richard . . . at least not yet."

Kiersten frowned. "I think this is overkill."

Piper opened her mouth, then closed it again, struggling to find the words. "I don't trust them."

"Piper." She arched a brow. "I can understand not trusting Chip. Or Trey. Anyone with teeth that white probably shouldn't be trusted. But his eighty-something-year-old grandparents?"

"Yes, yes, I know." Piper rubbed her forehead. "My therapist would not approve. But learning to trust doesn't mean blindly trusting *everyone* all the time in every circumstance. It means using your discretion, your judgment. And in this situation, I say we proceed with caution and hold on to the diaries."

"Fine. You're the law enforcement officer. But you owe me a pan of brownies if it turns out that Margaret and Richard are *not* actually geriatric MS-13 drug mules."

"I will happily make you brownies if I'm wrong about all of this."

"And I will happily eat them. If Reggie gives me permission."

"Good," Piper said. "Enjoy your weight training."

"When was the last time *you* exercised?" Kiersten asked. "I mean, you're one of those people who actually finds running therapeutic. And we've been working pretty hard. You deserve some time of your own too."

Piper blew out a breath. "You're right. Maybe I will go for a run."

"How about this. When I finish with weight training, I'll go to the library and dig through old newspapers to see if I can at least figure out the name of the car dealership Dottie's father owned. That would give us her maiden name. From there, we might be able to find a wedding announcement and track down her married name. If she died recently, an obituary should turn up. And if she's still alive, Google should be enough to help us find her."

Piper crossed her arms. "Good idea."

Kiersten leaned in and wrapped her in a hug. She went stiff. Kiersten would be absolutely perfect, if it weren't for all the *hugging*.

"I'm sorry if I seem skeptical of your skepticism," Kiersten said, pulling away. "But I respect your judgment. I really do. And if you want me to hide things in a bag of birdseed, I'll do it."

"I appreciate that," Piper said.

Kiersten gave her a little salute, then darted across the street to Reggie's house.

Kiersten's words echoed in her mind as she changed into her running gear. There was an invisible line that separated casual acquaintances from true friends. Casual acquaintances told you what you wanted to hear, because it was easy. Real friends told you the truth, even when you didn't want to hear it.

Kiersten had the courage to question her assumptions, to tell her she was being paranoid, and she was grateful for this.

But deep inside a little voice whispered what she had long known to be true. Sometimes paranoia really did mean that someone was genuinely out to get you.

A little shiver caressed her skin as she bent to stretch her hamstrings. Then she pushed her fears away and began to run.

Chapter Fifty-Six

KIERSTEN

Kiersten climbed out of her car at the Martha Washington Library. Her entire body felt like a pool noodle, and she once again questioned the premise that exercise gave people more energy.

But all the tension in her sore shoulders evaporated when she entered the hushed building, where sound itself was absorbed by thousands of books.

She walked up to the front desk to conduct today's business: getting a new library card, finding some books on teaching and creating lesson plans, and figuring out Dottie's last name. She waited patiently while the librarian helped a mother with three small boys check out the greater works of Thomas the Tank Engine. Then she turned to Kiersten.

"How can I help you?"

"I'm looking for advertisements for a Chevy dealership here in Alexandria back in 1964 and 1965. Do you have any idea how I could find something like that?"

"Hmm. Interesting request." The librarian stacked three copies of *Harry Potter and the Half-Blood Prince* beside her computer. "You could try the *Fort Hunt Gazette*."

Kiersten frowned. "Never heard of it."

"That's because it went out of business in 1972," the librarian said, peering at her over reading glasses. "Our region used to have countless newspapers. The whole country did. Back when journalism was profitable. Now of course most of them are defunct. But the *Gazette* served readers in Alexandria from 1946 to 1972. I'd start with that. If you don't find what you're looking for there, you could go wider and try *The Washington Post* archives online."

"Okay, but how do I search a defunct newspaper?"

"Microfilm." The librarian picked up the Harry Potter books. "Follow me."

Kiersten trailed after her through a forest of shelves. The librarian stepped into a dark room tucked in a far corner and flicked on the lights. Then she pointed to a machine sitting on a table. It looked kind of like a computer monitor.

"Have you ever used microfilm before?" the librarian asked.

"Sorry." Kiersten shook her head. "I'm new to all this."

"Is this genealogy research?"

"Not exactly." She explained how she'd found the diaries in her basement. "All I have to go on is her first name and the fact that her father owned a car dealership in the area."

The librarian pursed her lips in thought. "You're on the right track. A lot of businesses back in the day bore the owner's name, like 'Smith and Sons.' If we can figure out her last name and the year she graduated, we can figure out where she went to high school and find a picture."

Her use of the word *we* made Kiersten feel lighter. She wasn't doing this research alone. "That would be great. I'll do the microfilm first and look through advertisements. Then I can try the yearbooks."

The librarian led her to a row of file cabinets, then opened a drawer and removed three boxes of microfilm. "Start here," she said.

They returned to the room with the microfilm reader, where the librarian showed Kiersten how to load the spool of film into the reader, how to move backward and forward, and how to zoom in and out.

"Good luck," she said with a smile. Then she left Kiersten alone.

It took Kiersten a few minutes to get used to using the equipment, but after some trial and error, she figured out how to scroll through the newspaper, zooming in to examine the many ads sprinkled throughout the pages.

Looking up at the screen, she read an advertisement for shoes that cost $2.99 a pair and girls' cotton play sets for just 99 cents, plus ads for flameless "electric heat," an amenity advertised as "not just for the rich anymore."

She had to force herself to focus because she kept reading the articles. The year 1965 didn't seem like the distant past, yet everything was so different back in an era before cell phones, social media, and the instant gratification of Amazon deliveries and DoorDash.

Leaning back in her chair, she stretched her tired muscles and glanced at the time on her phone. She'd gone through the first box of microfilm and started on the second, but she still hadn't found a single clue about Dottie. She'd try one more box; then she'd have to head home. Garrett and the boys would be back from the museum soon.

She loaded a new roll and started again, flipping through the images on the screen.

Suddenly she sat up straight and leaned forward.

There. On the lower left side of the page. An advertisement for Anderson Motors, a Chevy dealership with locations in Arlington, Fairfax, and Alexandria, Virginia.

She squinted at the ad, then zoomed in to make it bigger.

The Alexandria location was in Old Town, just a few miles up the parkway from Beaverbrook Lane. She'd seen no other ads for a Chevy dealership.

This had to be it.

But as she zoomed in further, doubt dampened her elation, and she slumped in her chair.

Anderson. Could there be a more commonplace last name than *Anderson*? It could be the right name but the wrong family.

She took a picture of the ad with her phone, stacked the boxes neatly beside the machine, and went to find the librarian again.

"Progress!" she whispered. "I think her last name is Anderson. Now can I see those yearbooks?"

The librarian smiled. "This way."

She led Kiersten into another small room lit with overhead fluorescent lights. "We have yearbooks from every high school in Alexandria right here, some of them going back further than others. Both public and private schools. Do you have any idea where to start?"

"She was the valedictorian of her class," Kiersten said slowly, "and she said something once about 'good old SMA . . .'"

The librarian frowned. "That could be a reference to St. Margaret's Academy. It was an all-girls Catholic high school back in the 1960s. Then it merged with an all-boys Catholic school in 1990. Today it's a coed high school called Bishop Ignatius."

"That could be right," Kiersten said slowly. "I think she got married the same year she graduated, so she would have been a senior in 1964."

The librarian moved around the room with precise steps. She knew exactly where everything was. Kiersten wished her home were as organized as this library.

The librarian pulled a volume from the shelf and handed it to Kiersten. "Try this."

Anticipation warmed Kiersten's cheeks as she opened the cover. A musty odor rose in the air as she carefully turned the yellowing pages to photos of the senior class of 1964.

A small class, all girls. She ran her fingers under each name. Then she inhaled sharply.

Dorothy Marie Anderson, Valedictorian

A strange pang of recognition pierced her heart. She knew so much about this woman, what she thought and felt, what she ate for breakfast. But she'd never actually seen her face. Until now.

Dottie Anderson looked back at her from the yearbook. Wide, intelligent eyes, high cheekbones. Smooth hair. Cat's-eye glasses. Not pretty exactly, but dignified, with a quiet integrity.

Kiersten sat down in a metal folding chair and went back to the very first page of the yearbook, working her way through it slowly, from beginning to end, seeking to confirm that Dorothy Marie Anderson was indeed the Dottie who'd penned the diary.

Bingo.

Her fingers brushed a picture centered on a page entitled "Future Homemakers of America Hone Their Skills in Home Economics Class."

Candid black-and-white photos filled the two pages. Her eyes rested on a snapshot of two girls in a classroom kitchenette, wearing aprons, holding a tray of gingerbread cookies. The caption read "Dottie and Ruby finally catch the gingerbread man."

She squinted down at the picture. Dottie was a full head taller than her best friend, and thinner. They stood beside a stove, grinning at the camera.

"This is her," she said softly, looking up at the librarian.

"Now that you have her first, middle, and last name, we can look for her engagement and wedding announcements," the librarian said.

Kiersten snapped a picture of Dottie's yearbook photo with her phone, then followed the librarian back to the microfilm machine.

"Do you know what month she got married?"

Kiersten squinted up at the ceiling, trying to remember what she'd read. "She graduated in May and met her husband the day after graduation. She got pregnant on her honeymoon, and the baby was due in October. So she would have gotten married in . . ."

"December or January?" the librarian supplied.

"Yes. That's right," she said, remembering. "They had a New Year's Eve wedding. The last day of 1964."

"So she got engaged at some point between May and December."

Kiersten nodded. "Correct."

The librarian left the room and returned with a new box of microfilm. "Start here. Let me know what you find."

The librarian left, and Kiersten resumed her search, flicking patiently through the black-and-white pages that filled the screen in front of her. Suddenly a headline leaped out at her. Her mouth dropped open as she read the words.

Dorothy Anderson Engaged to Wed Richard Davis.

The back of her neck prickled as she leaned closer to the screen, incredulous.

The sweet old man who'd given her coffee this afternoon . . . the kindly eighty-something-year-old gentleman who'd offered to read the diaries for her . . . Chip's father and Trey's grandfather. *He* was the monster who'd stolen his wife's shoes so she couldn't leave the house? *He* was the man who'd blamed his wife for having a miscarriage? *He* was the husband who'd threatened to kill his wife if she left him . . . ?

This couldn't be the same man.

Or could it?

And if the monstrous husband in Dottie's diary was alive and well and living at the end of the cul-de-sac with a wife named Margaret . . . then what happened to Dottie?

Chapter Fifty-Seven

PIPER

The doorbell chimed, and Piper heaved herself off the couch and into the foyer.

Brendan had just left for Andrews Air Force Base and a flight to Brussels with the secretary of state. Piper had told the girls they could order pizza for an early dinner. Must be the pizza guy.

She looked through the peephole in the front door.

A middle-aged man in a polo shirt and neatly pressed khaki pants stood on her porch. Clean shaven with wire-rimmed glasses and a slight paunch, he looked efficient and businesslike. He also had a canvas duffel bag slung over one shoulder.

But he was not holding a pizza.

Her forehead creased as she tried to figure out who he could be. Then she remembered.

The locksmith.

After the incident with the worms, she and Brendan had decided to have all the locks in the house rekeyed, just as a precaution. The locksmith was supposed to come tomorrow, but they'd promised to send someone sooner if they had a cancelation.

She opened the front door and stepped onto the porch. "Hi. Can I help you?"

"Are you Piper?" the man asked, looking down at his phone. "At 1405 Beaverbrook Lane?"

"I am."

"Great. I'm in the right place. I always double-check, just to make sure. Otherwise things can be . . . you know . . ." He gave her a conspiratorial smile. "Awkward."

"I understand," she said. "Please, come in."

He stepped into the foyer and closed the door behind him. "I've brought everything we need," he said, tapping the duffel bag slung over his shoulder. "I'm Winston, by the way."

"Hi, Winston. Nice to meet you."

He unzipped his bag, then looked around. "Would you like to record it? Or do you prefer not to use cameras? I'm fine either way."

She frowned. "I don't think we need to record anything."

"Works for me," he said with a shrug. "Voyeurism isn't my kink. But I did bring these, as you requested."

The nape of her neck began to prickle as he reached into his duffel bag and removed a roll of duct tape and an ostrich feather.

Her mouth went dry. These did not look like the tools of a locksmith.

She thrust her hands into the pocket of her sweatpants and wrapped her fingers around the small Swiss Army–style multi-tool she carried everywhere.

"What's all this?" she asked, working hard to keep her voice steady.

He frowned. "It's for our encounter."

Her heart dropped into her throat. "What *encounter*?"

His eyebrows shot up into his receding hairline. "Our *sexual* encounter. The one you placed an ad for on Craigslist." He removed a pair of handcuffs and two long rubber gloves from his shoulder bag. "I brought these, too, just as you asked."

She swallowed, struggling to force words out of her parched throat and into her mouth. "But I never . . ."

Time stood still as her mind began to pinball in a thousand different directions. Brendan wouldn't be back until the end of the week. Kiersten was at the library. Rosamund, Miles, and Guinevere had gone to a renaissance festival. None of her neighbors were home.

There's no one to hear you scream.

Except the girls, who were down in the basement playing Barbies. Which was why she needed to get this man out of her house and away from her daughters.

Now.

She gripped the multi-tool in her pocket and managed to surreptitiously unfold the corkscrew. She would blind her assailant, restrain him with the duct tape, and call the police.

"This *is* 1405 Beaverbrook Lane, is it not?" he asked, his face suddenly pale. "And you *are* Piper, are you not?"

She widened her stance, blocking the entrance to the kitchen, turning herself into a bulwark between him and her daughters. "I am. How did you get my name?"

He held up his phone, hand trembling. "It's right here. You said you wanted a BDSM sexual encounter today between the hours of 4:00 and 6:00 p.m. at this address. You asked me to bring handcuffs, rubber gloves, duct tape, and an ostrich feather. Your safe word is macaroni."

"Listen." Piper spoke slowly, forcing herself to remain calm. "I believe you. But I never placed that ad. I have no idea who you are or what you are talking about. And I need you to leave. Now."

The man's gaze began to dart around the foyer. "Is this a setup? Where are the cameras?"

She took one step toward him. "There are no cameras. You need to go. Now."

An ugly scowl twisted his features as he took a step closer. "Did Bernice put you up to this?"

"Turn around, open the door, and walk outside, or I call the police."

He craned his neck, looking up at the ceiling. "I know you're here, Bernice. I know you did this," he began to shriek. "You set me up. You set me up *again*."

In one fluid movement, she removed the corkscrew, placed it against his ribs, and opened the front door. Then she pulled him through the doorway, off the front porch, and to the Prius he'd parked in her driveway.

"I did *not* place this ad," she repeated. "I don't know Bernice. Never come back here again. Do you understand?"

His shoulders slumped as he pressed his key fob, unlocked the door, and climbed into his car.

"Craigslist is no longer the festival of carnal delights it once was," he muttered, shaking his head in disgust.

"I'm sorry to hear that. Good luck with your next . . . encounter."

He looked up at her from the driver's seat. "Even though you didn't place the ad, are you sure—I mean, I drove all the way down here from Bethesda."

"I'm sure. Thank you very much. Do not come again."

He backed out of the driveway, and she memorized his license plate as he drove away. She ran into the house, where she locked every door, all the windows, and retrieved her Glock from the gun safe. Then she slid to the floor in the foyer, resting her back against the front door, and tried to stop shaking.

Chapter Fifty-Eight

KIERSTEN

Kiersten leaned closer to the screen and began to read the engagement announcement.

> Mr. Gerald Anderson of 1102 Belle View Landing has announced the engagement of his daughter, Dorothy Marie Anderson, to Richard Davis, son of Mr. Glen Davis and the late Mrs. Eleanor Davis.
>
> Miss Anderson, also the daughter of the late Mrs. Marie Anderson, is a graduate of St. Margaret's Academy and is currently employed by her father's auto dealership, Anderson Motors.
>
> Mr. Davis, a graduate of the University of Virginia, is currently employed as Vice President of Sales at Anderson Motors.
>
> A New Year's Eve wedding is planned.

She snapped a picture just as the librarian poked her head through the door.

"Any luck?"

"Lots of luck. Now I just need to find out if she's still alive. And if she is, I need to figure out how to contact her."

"I suggest Google for that. If she's still living, you could also try a white pages search or even Facebook. If she died anytime in the last twenty years, her obituary will be digitized. And if she grew up in this area, her obituary likely appeared in *The Washington Post*. I'd try that."

"What if she died . . . earlier?"

"If she died before they digitized the obits, you'd have to hunt through microfilm for that. And if you don't have a death date, it could take quite a while," the librarian conceded.

Kiersten nodded, still shaken by what she'd found. "Thank you so much for all your help. I'd never have found all this on my own."

"That's what we're here for," the librarian said. "Take care."

Kiersten stumbled out of the library and into her minivan, a sick feeling twisting her gut as she argued with herself.

Maybe this meant nothing. Maybe it was all a coincidence.

Anderson and Davis were common last names.

Maybe the Richard Davis who lived next door was a completely different person from the Dickie Davis who'd made Dottie's life a living hell on Beaverbrook Lane in 1965.

And what about Peggy? Wasn't Peggy a nickname for Margaret?

She rubbed her hands over her face, then stared out the window. She had to face it. Richard and Margaret, her sweet next-door neighbors, had to be the Dickie and Peggy in Dottie's diary.

Her mind flashed back to the Beaverbrook Harvest Festival supper, where they'd toasted Richard and Margaret's fifty-nine-year marriage. What had Chip said last night? *We've been married for fifty-nine years, all of those years happy, and spent here on Beaverbrook Lane.*

How was that possible? Richard was living with Dottie on Beaverbrook in 1965. But in 1966 he was living on Beaverbrook with *Peggy*?

And they were still there. So what happened to Dottie?

She leaned back against the headrest. Garrett and the boys would be home soon. She couldn't sit here at the library for days, sorting through boxes of microfilm.

But she could search every obituary for Dorothy Davis on Google tonight. And she could listen to Dottie's words.

She drove home as fast as the law allowed, ran inside, and removed the second diary from its hiding place and began to read.

Chapter Fifty-Nine

DOTTIE

September 26, 1965

I am so stunned I can hardly breathe. Hardly move. Hardly *think*.

I got up last night around 10 p.m. to use the restroom. I tiptoed down the hall and realized someone was already using it. The door was open a crack and I could see Peggy brushing her teeth at the sink. She wore a cotton nightgown so thin it was almost translucent.

She spit into the sink, and then she leaned back, and that's when I saw it. Her belly, round and ripe beneath the white cotton.

Peggy is pregnant.

Chapter Sixty

PIPER

The girls in the back of Piper's SUV screamed with joy as she took the entrance to the parking lot a little too fast, sending gravel flying beneath her tires as she pulled up to the Potomac Pals pet shelter just off Fort Hunt Road.

After the . . . incident . . . with the man who *wasn't* a locksmith, she'd checked Hawkeye Slaughter's account on X. That morning, he'd posted a grainy picture of her in uniform, taken from an online flyer for a self-defense class she'd taught at Georgetown. He'd photoshopped antlers on top of her head. The caption on the picture made her blood run cold. "Happy Hunting Season!"

She glanced at the dashboard. Just in time. The shelter closed in fifteen minutes.

"Mom. Can we get a little dog that I can carry inside my purse like Demi Moore and Paris Hilton?" Caitlin asked.

"No." She shook her head emphatically. "We're getting a big dog. The biggest dog we can find."

They should have done this right after Scout died, but she and Brendan and the girls couldn't bring themselves to get a new dog while still mourning the loss of their old one.

But that situation today . . . well, it would never have happened if Scout were alive. His intimidating bark would have sent that man packing, mitigating Piper's incredible stupidity in bringing him inside the house without asking for an ID, without determining that he was indeed a locksmith before inviting him into the home where her children lived.

She did not want to spend another night alone in that house without a barking dog as a living addition to the alarm system.

It had been a couple of months since they've volunteered at the shelter, but hopefully the fact that they'd fostered puppies in the past would allow them to take a dog home today. They'd already been through the background checks, the home visit, and the approval process.

"But I want a *little* dog," Bella whined. "Like Toto." She'd been the Tin Man in a children's theater production of *The Wizard of Oz* last year and had developed a strange fixation with the old movie, even though she had to hide her face in a pillow each time the flying monkeys appeared.

"Big dogs are better," Piper said. "Because if he's really big you can . . . hook him up to your sled."

Bella beamed at her mother in the rearview mirror, revealing the gap between her two front teeth. Piper averted her eyes, suddenly feeling guilty for raising Bella's hopes of becoming a suburban dog musher.

Caitlin crossed her arms in the passenger seat beside her. "But after Scout died you said we weren't getting another dog until we had demonstrated our 'capacity for responsibility.'" She used her fingers to make indignant air quotes around the phrase.

Piper racked her brain for examples of responsible behavior in a home where children routinely left ice cream cartons sitting on the counter until the contents melted into dairy soup. But the girls would be terrified if they knew the real reason she suddenly wanted a new dog.

"We haven't lost a single hairbrush all month," Piper said, pulling into a parking spot. "Bella found her missing Hello Kitty raincoat. Olivia put an entire plate in the dishwasher instead of the sink, *without being asked.* And you threw an empty Cheez-Its box into the garbage recently instead of leaving it in the pantry, like you normally do. And you all used the Target gift cards Grandma gave you for Christmas last year instead of losing them under your beds. You guys are beyond ready for a new dog."

Caitlin pursed her lips and gave her mother a skeptical look. She wasn't buying it.

"I think *you* miss having a dog," she said in an accusing tone.

Piper repressed a deep sigh.

Sometimes the lies, deceit, and psyops involved in motherhood made her feel like a double agent. Pretending you didn't care if your toddler wore shoes while desperately needing them to put their shoes on *right now.*

Pretending you enjoyed standing in subzero temperatures at a card table outside a grocery store with a pack of overexcited Girl Scouts selling Thin Mints when you'd rather be at home in sweatpants watching *Bridgerton.*

She manufactured a solemn expression and tried to pretend Caitlin had forced her into an honest admission about the real reason for this sudden trip to the pound. "Okay. Fine. You're right. It's all about me, and I just really miss having a dog. So let's go inside and pick one out before I change my mind."

That did it. The girls catapulted out of the car and into the shelter. Soon they were sitting on the floor, where exuberant puppies attacked them with sloppy kisses.

She smiled for what felt like the first time all day. This was the right thing to do. And now that she was home on administrative leave, she'd have time to train a dog.

The girls needed this. *She* needed this. Plus, puppies added an extra layer of love to any home.

And since the Incident . . . since the death threats on X from Hawkeye Slaughter and the bloody notebook paper and the worms . . .

since the bizarre thing that happened today . . . they needed the extra layer of protection too.

It took about ten minutes to identify Scout's replacement, a light-brown mutt of no discernable breed with an outgoing but affectionate disposition and gigantic paws, suggesting he would eventually become enormous.

"What should we name him?" Piper asked as they drove home. After much fighting and three coin tosses, Bella provided the lap on which the puppy rode in his cardboard box.

"Travis," Bella said dreamily.

"Travis?" Piper shot her daughter a puzzled look.

Bella nodded. "Because our dog is a boy, just like Taylor's fee-onshay."

Piper sighed. It was Taylor Swift all day, every day in her house. In fact, Olivia had only managed to memorize the multiplication tables by setting them to Taylor Swift songs. Piper couldn't hear "Shake It Off" without automatically singing "In my mind six times four is twenty-four."

So she could handle it if they wanted to name their dog after Taylor Swift's football-player fiancé.

She'd sleep better at night if she had an actual NFL tight end guarding her home. But for now she'd have to make do with a guard puppy named after one.

Chapter Sixty-One

KIERSTEN

The beep-beep-beep of a delivery truck backing out of her driveway pulled Kiersten's attention away from Dottie's diary and to the window.

A delivery. Maybe *Lesson Plans for Dummies* had finally arrived.

She opened the front door, where a white box sat on the welcome mat. She picked it up, took it inside, and set it on the kitchen island.

Red letters stamped across the top announced that the package was **PERISHABLE**.

Frowning, she checked the label. Her name and address. Maybe her parents had sent one of those Edible Arrangements? Her mother loved those.

She slid a knife under the slats and removed the packing paper. Inside she found an oblong cardboard tube.

Odd. Could it be some kind soil testing kit? Or seeds? Something Garrett needed for work?

She opened it.

And began to scream.

Chapter Sixty-Two

PIPER

"Mom, can we show the Cleavers our new puppy?" Caitlin asked as they pulled into the driveway.

"Sure." She got out of the car, scooped up the puppy, and carried him toward the Cleaver house. The girls trailed behind, carrying the new dog dish, dog bed, dog leash, and many other puppy accessories they'd picked up at PetSmart on the way home.

An ear-splitting scream pierced the air as she approached Kiersten's porch.

Adrenaline spiked through her body as she ran up the steps. If only she were carrying a gun instead of a puppy.

She turned and handed the dog to Caitlin. "Take Travis out in the backyard." She resisted the urge to add *and then go inside and lock all the doors*, because it would terrify her daughter. "I think Mrs. Cleaver accidentally touched something hot," she lied.

Caitlin took the dog. When she disappeared into the backyard with her sisters, Piper opened the front door to the Cleaver house, flattened herself against the wall between the foyer and the kitchen, and peered around the corner.

At worst, she'd expected to see a masked man making off with the television set. At best, she'd expected to see a pot of boiling water spilled on Kiersten's shirt—or a chunk of potato, a flap of skin, and a bloody mandolin.

Instead, she found her normally calm, composed neighbor careening across the kitchen with a rolled-up *Washington Post* in her hand, frantically whacking the countertops while emitting little screams.

Piper crossed the room in two strides and grabbed her by the shoulders. "Kiersten. What's wrong?"

Kiersten's gaze ricocheted around the room. "The cockroaches. They're *everywhere*."

Piper released her shoulders and stepped backward. "Cockroaches?"

Then she went silent as her ears tuned to a soft hissing sound. "What's that . . . noise?"

Kiersten swallowed. "It's *them*."

Dear God.

Piper grabbed a Sharper Image catalog from the pile of junk mail on the kitchen counter and rolled it into an impromptu cudgel. A giant bug skittered across the kitchen island, and she brought the magazine down with a sharp thwap.

Kiersten dropped to her knees and did the same, whacking and slapping at gigantic cockroaches as they skittered across the floor.

For a solid twenty minutes the kitchen rang out with the smack of rolled-up reading material and small shrieks as they systematically killed every cockroach they could see. The hissing eventually faded to silence as they stared at each other with wild eyes, surrounded by the carcasses of dead insects.

Chapter Sixty-Three

KIERSTEN

Kiersten sank down on the family room couch with a box of Keebler Fudge Stripes cookies and shoved one into her mouth.

She'd been so good since she started running with Reggie. She'd lost six pounds since they started the Experiment, and she could now button the jeans she'd worn to chaperone one of Matthew's field trips when he was in *fifth* grade.

But the cockroaches . . . she shuddered and stuffed another cookie into her mouth. Her body screamed for sugar as her mind tried to block out the hissing . . . the legs . . . the antennae.

A new shudder convulsed her body as she watched Piper use a piece of cardboard to heroically collect each carcass, slide it back inside the cardboard tube, insert it into the box, and seal the whole thing shut with packing tape.

Only a true friend would gather *cockroach cadavers* in your kitchen and then dispose of them. She said a silent prayer of gratitude for Piper and the random forces that had brought them together.

After carrying the box out to the curb, Piper sank down on the couch beside her. "I'm so sorry about all this."

"Sorry?" Kiersten blinked. "How could Madagascar hissing cockroaches possibly be your fault?"

That's what the packing label inside the box said. **Live Madagascar Hissing Cockroaches** from the Happy Valley Farm Pet Supply Store.

Piper pinched the bridge of her nose and sighed. "It's Hawkeye Slaughter. My stalker. He's disappeared and joined some kind of antigovernment militia group."

"Is this the guy you told me about before?"

"Yes."

"I still don't see how this is your fault."

Piper ran a hand through her hair. "Hawkeye obviously intended to send those cockroaches to my house, and they were delivered to your house by mistake. He sent me worms, too, remember?"

Kiersten shook her head. "But this box had my address. And my name."

Piper frowned. "That's weird."

"Maybe someone with a similar name and address has an exotic pet? And they're ordering these things for their gecko or something? And they sent them to me by accident?" Kiersten asked hopefully.

Because surely that was a more plausible explanation than a crazy member of an antigovernment militia with a grudge sending hissing cockroaches to Piper's neighbor *on purpose*?

This wasn't a John Grisham novel, after all. Or an episode of *Ozark*. This was a nice, quiet neighborhood in the Washington, DC, suburbs.

Then her mind began to skim through the headlines she'd read over the years . . . about the Russian sleeper spies who'd spent years pretending to be a normal suburban family, until they were arrested by the FBI . . . or the double agent who left messages for his Soviet handlers while walking his dogs in a Northern Virginia park. Or the Cuban spies who passed stolen documents to their handlers at a Safeway in Georgetown.

Things like this didn't happen at home in rural Minnesota—as far as she knew—but things like this *did* actually happen out here.

Kiersten closed her eyes and forced her mind open, wide open, pushing herself to really consider the possibility that a dangerous person was targeting her neighbor.

What if Piper's fears were real? What if Piper *wasn't* paranoid?

"But why would someone go to all this trouble to do something so mean?" Kiersten asked.

"Because they're crazy." Piper shrugged. "And crazy people do crazy things. Something even creepier showed up on my doorstep this afternoon."

"What could be worse than Madagascar hissing cockroaches?" Kiersten asked, dread slinking up her spine.

"A man with handcuffs, an ostrich feather, and a bag full of sex toys."

Kiersten's mouth dropped open. *"What?"*

Piper explained what had happened that afternoon.

Kiersten gasped. "A *sex man* showed up on your doorstep?"

"That's right."

"Is that a . . . thing?"

"Apparently."

"Is that why you now have a puppy the size of a Shetland pony?" She gestured to Piper's backyard, where a chocolate brown puppy chased the girls around the swing set.

"Yeah. I just feel better having an extra set of ears in the house when Brendan is out of town."

Kiersten tossed the package of cookies onto the coffee table. Maybe the sugar rush was clouding her judgment. "Maybe . . . maybe this Hawkeye Slaughter guy is just trying to scare you. Maybe he has no intention of hurting anyone."

The corner of Piper's mouth curved in a faint smile. "Because most people are good?"

Kiersten's mind wrestled with the dichotomy presenting itself here. People could be angry, rude, impatient, and petty, but in her experience, most people were decent and kind.

Then her mind traveled back to Dottie's wedding announcement—if everything she'd just read in the library was accurate, then one of her neighbors was truly evil.

"Maybe he's . . . Hawkeye the Kindly Stalker?" she asked tentatively.

Piper shook her head. "I don't think so."

"Maybe he's just . . . lonely?"

"He's probably very lonely," Piper conceded. "But I don't think inviting him over for hotdish is going to solve his many problems."

"You can move in with us," she said impulsively, squeezing Piper's hand. "We'll protect you."

"With what? Dairy products?"

Kiersten's face broke into a smile. "I could kill him with Midwestern kindness."

"You could build a lethal hotdish bomb using nothing but cream of mushroom soup and your bare hands."

"I'm serious," she said. "Stay with us when Brendan travels. Until this . . . situation settles down. At least until they find this Hawkeye person."

Piper took a deep breath and exhaled slowly. "I'll talk to my old boss again and see what they can do, though I suspect the answer is nothing. I'll talk to Brendan and see if he can ease up on his travel for the next few weeks. He gets paid to protect diplomats from bad guys. He's more than capable of protecting his own family. And I'm more than capable of protecting my family too. But I'd feel better if he were home more often."

"Would that be enough to make you feel safe?"

"I don't think anything will ever make me feel safe." A wistful expression haunted Piper's features, and Kiersten's heart suddenly ached for her friend.

Her fingers clamped into a fist, and she longed for the power to wipe the past from Piper's mind. The drug dealers and human traffickers, Mr. Claussen and his shovel, the bomb threat and everything that followed.

It didn't seem fair, that keeping other people safe meant Piper could never feel safe herself.

"I just wish I knew what he was planning," Piper said quietly.

Kiersten rose to grab Dottie's diary from the kitchen island. "Speaking of bad guys, I have something else to show you."

"Now what?" Piper asked warily as she returned to the couch.

"I think . . ." She took a deep breath. She didn't want to say these words out loud, but in her heart, she knew they were true. "I think Richard Davis is the evil husband in Dottie's diaries."

Piper sank back against the couch cushions. "Seriously?"

Kiersten nodded. "And I also think his sweet wife who just had cataract surgery and fed us pecan pie is actually Peggy, the mistress."

Piper's mouth dropped open. "No way."

"Way." Kiersten handed her the diary. "Read this."

Chapter Sixty-Four

DOTTIE

September 27, 1965

I confronted Peggy in the kitchen today after Dickie left for work.

She was standing at the sink, washing raspberries she'd picked from the garden.

"Is Dickie the father?" I asked, point blank.

She burst into tears and damn it, but I actually felt sorry for her.

She shook her head emphatically. "No. He was a mechanic. From the garage." She swiped at her tears with the back at her hand. "He skipped town when I told him about the baby."

The hair on the back of my neck stood on end.

She's lying.

I knew every mechanic in that garage. If one of them had quit suddenly, Oscar and Leonard would have mentioned it.

I swallowed and made a sympathetic noise in the back of my throat. "When are you due?"

She lowered her gaze. "October."

October.

Just like me.

I turned away quickly so she couldn't see my expression.

I want to believe her. I really do. Because if she's lying, then Dickie seduced her days after our honeymoon, or maybe days before the wedding itself. If this baby is his, then he never loved me, not even for a moment, not even at the very start of it all, and for some reason, this knowledge still has the power to break my heart.

"What will you do?" My words came out parched and dry.

"I was hoping . . ." She lowered her eyes, then raised her gaze to mine. "I was hoping that you and Dickie would take my baby."

I suddenly felt disoriented and breathless, like I'd fallen from a tree, knocking all the air from my lungs. "That's insane."

"No, it isn't." Words rushed from her mouth, her expression both calculating and desperate. "I'm due in October, just like you were . . . no one knows I'm here. No one knows I'm pregnant. And no one knows you've had a miscarriage, except for that doctor out in San Diego. I can't support a child as an unwed mother. But you could raise my baby. I'd feel so much better knowing the baby was here, in a good home, with you and Dickie."

I opened my mouth to speak but no words came out. I couldn't steal another woman's child and pretend it was mine. This was wrong.

Wasn't it?

I pressed my fingers into my forehead, trying to put my thoughts in order. "I . . . I need to talk to Dickie," I finally said.

"He knows," she interjected, refusing to meet my eyes. "He knows all about it. That's why he brought me here. I left the dealership just before I started to show. But before I left, I told Dickie the truth. He offered to pay my rent and my expenses if I promised to stay out of sight and tell no one about my pregnancy."

"And you agreed to this?" I asked, incredulous.

Her features hardened, and it changed her completely, squaring her jaw, narrowing her lips. She looked like a boxer. Determined. Exhausted. Dangerous.

"My only other option was one of those homes for unwed mothers." She gazed at me, eyes challenging. "And I'll never do that again."

I swallowed. "Again?"

She nodded and turned away. "I was sixteen. In high school. It was like a jail. But worse."

"Worse in what way?" I asked, once again feeling sympathy in spite of myself.

"The shame." Her thin shoulders slumped forward. "They made us put on fake wedding rings anytime we left the home. They told us we were neurotic, crazy, unfit for motherhood. They forced me to give up my baby. I held her once and then gave her to strangers." She looked up at me again, her gaze so fierce that I drew back. "I'll never do that again. *Ever.*"

I'd heard of these places. Sometimes during high school a girl would just disappear for a while. Her parents would tell everyone she was going to visit her aunt, or that she wanted to try boarding school.

And then six months later she'd return, spouting vague stories about her fun stay with relatives in Cleveland or Dallas or Sacramento.

But whispers clung to these girls like spiderwebs as they moved through the halls, nebulous and sticky, about where they really went, and why they went there.

"I won't go back to a place like that," she repeated, jutting her chin. "I'll have the baby here, and then I'll leave. You will raise my baby." She stroked her stomach. "It's almost time now. And that's why Dickie brought me here."

My mouth dropped open. Dickie couldn't swap wives without being tainted by the scandal of divorce and losing Daddy's money and influence. So he's arranged to *swap babies* instead, trading my dead twins for this woman's living son or daughter.

"But . . . you can't just . . . *give us* your baby."

"Of course I can," she argued. "That's exactly what I'd be doing in the hospital or a home for unwed mothers . . . I'd be giving my baby to strangers. At least this way I know where my baby is going." She looked around her wistfully. "You have a nice house . . . lots of money. And you're a kind person. I know that. Everyone at the office loved you . . . my baby will never want for anything, here with you."

"How well do you know Dickie?"

She lowered her eyes. “I don’t know him well, but he’s always been nice to me. And fair. If he hadn’t suggested this . . .” She shuddered. “I don’t know what I would have done.”

She looked up at me, eyes hard. “This is the only way.”

Chapter Sixty-Five

KIERSTEN

Piper lowered the diary, and her gaze met Kiersten's.

"Holy shit," Piper said.

"I *know*."

Piper rose from the couch and began to pace in front of the fireplace in Kiersten's family room. "What do we do now?"

"We need to figure out if Dottie is still alive."

"How do we do that?"

"Google." Kiersten rose from the couch and grabbed her laptop from the kitchen counter. "If she died anytime in the last twenty years, it should be easy to find."

She sat down and opened her laptop. Then she began to type, saying the words out loud for Piper as she typed them.

"Dorothy Davis Obituary."

Her heart fell as pages and pages of listings came up. "I wish she had a more unique name."

"We need to go through them all," Piper said.

"That's easier said than done." Kiersten chuffed a sigh that lifted the hair on her forehead. "*Not* finding her obituary could mean we aren't looking hard enough. Or it could mean there is no obituary to find because she's still alive and well and living who knows where. And maybe she divorced Dickie, got remarried, has a new name."

"Then we need to keep reading the diaries," Piper said.

Kiersten glanced at the clock on the microwave. "Garrett and the boys will be home any minute."

Piper retrieved her purse from the floor beside the couch. "I ordered pizza before we left for the shelter and then completely forgot about it. It's probably been sitting on my front porch for hours."

"How about this." Kiersten stood. "You read the diary out loud while I make dinner. You guys can eat with us."

"Are you sure?" Piper shot her a skeptical look. "Sounds like you're getting the short end of that deal."

"Look, I know you don't want to hear this." Kiersten opened her pantry and removed a bag of potatoes. "But Aspen's Table of Sustenance actually works. I've done my meal prep, planned my menu two weeks in advance, and ordered all my groceries online."

Piper crossed her arms over her chest and raised an eyebrow. "How Betty Crocker of you."

"I'd rather be Betty Crocker than Kiersten who used to run to the grocery store five times a week and *still* had nothing for dinner," she said, pulling a potato peeler from a drawer.

"So what are you making tonight?" Piper asked. "Filet mignon and a soufflé?"

"No, but I can whip up mashed potatoes and stick a pork tenderloin and some chicken nuggets in the oven."

"Fine." Piper pulled up a stool at the kitchen island. "I'll be the Audible version of Dottie's diary while you cook. I can't say no to mashed potatoes."

She opened Dottie's diary and began to read.

Chapter Sixty-Six

DOTTIE

September 27, 1965

I violated every rule on The List. When Dickie returned home from work today, I did not put a bow in my hair or make any effort to appear attractive and "fresh." I did not attempt to be gay and interesting. Instead, I accosted Dickie the moment he entered the house.

"We need to talk," I demanded.

He seemed to expect this. Had they coordinated it? Was Peggy supposed to break the news first, to soften me up, and then he'd follow up with the hard sell?

"Let me change first," he said abruptly.

I waited on the back porch in a rocking chair. Peggy made a gin and tonic for him. The drink sat on the little wicker table, sweating beads of moisture onto my mother's monogrammed linen cocktail napkin, a silver bowl of mixed nuts placed thoughtfully beside it.

I heard his footsteps and glanced inside. She said something I couldn't hear, and his laughter filled the room. The knot in my stomach twisted a little tighter.

He came out on the porch and sat down in the other rocking chair.

"Have a nice day, darling?"

"Why didn't you tell me?" I asked.

"Tell you what?"

I heaved an epic sigh and rolled my eyes. "That Peggy is pregnant."

He shrugged. "I was going to. I just hadn't gotten around to it yet."

"Is the baby yours?"

"What a ridiculous question," he said mildly.

"Just answer the question, Dickie."

"The father is a mechanic from the garage. A coward who abandoned Peggy as soon as he found out." His voice was rote, expressionless, like a child reciting a poem he'd memorized.

"What was his name?"

"The mechanic?"

"Yes, the mechanic."

He waved his hand dismissively. "Oh gosh. I don't know. But he's long gone. Took his last paycheck and skipped town or something."

I willed myself not to react, keeping my face carefully neutral. I've known every mechanic in that garage since I was ten years old. Danny was the only new addition to that group, and he died in Viet Nam shortly after Peggy arrived. If someone else left suddenly, Oscar would tell me. That means Dickie is the father of this baby.

I kept my face blank. "And you want us to adopt her baby?"

"Yes. Don't you?" he asked, looking puzzled.

"Do I have a choice?"

He turned to me with his most earnest expression. "This is your opportunity to do something good. For Peggy. And for her poor infant. She's giving her child up for adoption no matter what we do, and you and I can give him a loving family, a good home. You can be a mother, and I can finally have a son."

He seemed to assume the baby would be a boy, I noticed.

"You'd do that, for me?" I asked, attempting to hide my loathing for him, for his schemes and his lies.

"I just want you to be happy, darling." He took my hand. "That's all I've ever wanted."

I swallowed my revulsion and forced myself to smile. "I think it's a wonderful idea. But I'd like to sleep on it. Think about it just a little bit more. Is that all right?"

"Of course, darling. Anything to make you happy. I'm doing all of this for you."

My fingers itched to slap him.

Instead, I rose from my chair, kissed the top of his head, and went up to my room. I shut the door, locked it, and collapsed onto the bed, trying to think.

Is Dickie the father of this child? Does it even matter?

For some reason, it does.

Is my husband bringing his pregnant mistress into my home and then demanding that I raise their child and pretend it's my own?

Or could this really be an act of kindness? Helping an unwed mother find a home for her child? Finding a way for me to become a mother?

Which explanation is true?

I need to find out if Dickie is the father.

Chapter Sixty-Seven

PIPER

"Holy *shit*!" Piper exclaimed, looking up from the diary and meeting Kiersten's gaze.

"Don't stop now!" Kiersten gesticulated wildly with her potato peeler. "Keep going!"

"We need to call Rosamund. She needs to hear this."

"Good idea. But tell her to come right *now*," Kiersten demanded.

Piper picked up her phone. Rosamund answered on the first ring.

"Listen," she said. "The diaries are getting juicy. And we got a new dog. And someone is sending us cockroaches and middle-aged sexual perverts. So bring Guinevere and come over for dinner. You need to hear all this."

Her face broke into a smile. She covered the phone and looked over at Kiersten. "Rosamund wants to know if Miles can come over for dinner too?" She resisted the adolescent urge to make kissing noises.

Kiersten grinned back. "*Of course* Miles can come. Tell him we'll eat in an hour. And call Reggie and Valentina too. And Lillian next door, if she's back from her trip. I'll peel another bag of potatoes."

A few minutes later Rosamund and Guinevere showed up. Guinevere immediately ran out into the backyard, where the girls were playing fetch with Travis.

"I'll make the vegetables," Rosamund said.

"Oh." Kiersten looked crestfallen. "I forgot about vegetables. Other than the potatoes, of course."

"You are an unreconstructed Midwesterner." Rosamund smirked as she removed four gleaming purple eggplants from a canvas *New Yorker* bag. "But don't worry. I'll make these."

Kiersten wrinkled her nose. "Eggplant?"

"It's *good* for you."

"That's what I'm afraid of," Kiersten said, opening a new sack of Yukon Gold potatoes.

Rosamund removed a can of breadcrumbs from her purse. "I will prepare them in a way that makes you forget you're eating vegetables. I promise."

"Go for it." Kiersten handed her an apron. "Make me believe in the power of roughage."

"Ladies, are you ready?" Piper asked, after bringing Rosamund up to speed on everything that had happened.

Kiersten nodded vigorously. "Keep going."

Piper opened the diary and began to read.

Chapter Sixty-Eight

DOTTIE

September 29, 1965

I drank four cups of coffee last night before bed to keep myself awake. Then at 9 p.m. I told Dickie I was turning in.

But instead of going *to* bed I crawled *under* the bed, under Peggy's bed, in the guest room.

I wriggled under the dust ruffle and lay there, awaiting the creak of bedsprings, the sound of voices.

My mind drifted and wandered in those long dark hours as I waited to find out if my husband had really moved his pregnant mistress into my home. To find out if she carried his child in her swollen belly.

I was about to drift off when a noise stirred my consciousness. Hushed voices, muffled footsteps on the carpet, the mattress sagging as two people climbed onto the bed.

They made love inches above me. Each soft grunt and quiet sigh carved a new channel of pain through my heart. When they finished, the whispers came, indistinct and muffled, occasionally punctuated by soft laughter. I caught the word "baseball," and Dickie's name. I caught my own name once or twice, and the word "baby." After a few minutes they became bolder, louder and then she admonished, "Shh . . . she'll hear us."

The voices lowered again, then lengthened into silence, followed by the sound of Dickie snoring. I stared into the empty blackness for a long time, begging God to strike me dead as I contemplated my life with no baby, no husband, no future.

But God didn't take me.

So I crawled out and returned to the room I share with my husband and sank into our bed, alone.

Chapter Sixty-Nine

KIERSTEN

Kiersten stood frozen in place with the potato masher clutched to her chest.

"This is so *awful* . . ."

Rosamund transferred a slice of eggplant to a Pyrex baking dish. "It's like . . . a soap opera."

"Mrs. Claussen used to watch *Days of our Lives* religiously," Piper said. "It reminds me of one of those episodes."

"Maybe that's because things like this actually used to happen." Rosamund dredged another slice of eggplant through the tray of breadcrumbs.

"They did?" Kiersten raised her eyebrows in surprise.

"Think about the world back in 1965, before the internet and cell phones and modern computers," Rosamund said, pausing her work for a moment. "Long-distance telephone calls cost a fortune. Medical records were kept on paper. If you wanted to find someone, you had to look them up in a printed phone book. And they certainly didn't have 23andMe or easy access to highly accurate paternity testing like we do now. They didn't have Find My Friends or Find My Phone or people posting pictures on Instagram every time they traveled. And they didn't have Google. Without a digital trail, you could hide a lot more than we can hide today."

Kiersten put down the potato masher. "Assuming they're hiding something. Maybe Dickie and Dottie simply got divorced. He married Peggy, and Dottie moved to Florida, and they all lived happily ever after . . . with different spouses. The end."

Piper raised an eyebrow. "Or maybe he killed her."

A heavy silence settled over the kitchen.

"We don't know them very well, do we?" Kiersten scraped the mashed potatoes into a casserole dish and smoothed the top with a spatula. "I mean, we all hang out with each other . . . but the Davis family doesn't really hang out with *us*."

"True." Rosamund tapped fresh breadcrumbs into a pan. "It's like when someone is murdered and the reporters show up and interview the neighbors. They always say, 'We didn't know them very well. *Because they kept to themselves*,'" she added in an ominous voice.

"Although Richard and Margaret *did* just have us over for coffee," Kiersten conceded as she covered the potatoes with tinfoil and put them in the oven to stay warm.

Piper's eyes went wide. "A coffee visit where we *gave them* the first diary. And told them we have two more sitting right here in this house."

An uneasy feeling swept over Kiersten, raising goose bumps on her arms.

"There's nothing . . . incriminating . . . in that first diary," she said, casting her mind back to the early entries. "Mostly she's just complaining about Dickie."

Piper looked down at the diary in her hand, frowning. "But Richard probably doesn't want it widely known that he was an abusive jerk to his first wife."

"Or maybe that he even *had* a first wife," Kiersten added.

"I think that all depends on *what happened* to the first wife," Rosamund said quietly.

They went silent again.

"Keep reading," Rosamund ordered.

Chapter Seventy

DOTTIE

September 29, 1965

I'm leaving. I just need a little more time to get that old car running again. And then I'll sneak out after they go to bed.

Together, apparently.

I was going to wait for Daddy to come home from Florida, but I can't. I need to leave now. I can't live like this. I can't stay here another second.

Because I think Peggy and Dickie are trying to kill me.

Last week, I sat down at lunchtime to eat the au gratin potatoes Peggy served in my favorite cornflower CorningWare casserole dish.

It was picture perfect, like something out of the Betty Crocker cookbook. And it's so much work, to make me an individual casserole each day for lunch when I'd be happy with a peanut butter sandwich and an apple, like she has.

But every day, she goes to all that trouble just for me. And she never eats a bite of it. Never saves the leftovers. Never heats it up in the oven and gives it to Dickie for dinner. In fact, she scrapes anything I don't eat directly into the garbage.

Yesterday, I watched her like a hawk.

She brought flowers in from the garden, the last hydrangeas and foxglove of the season, and put them in one of those Hull vases that belonged to my mother.

I went into the den and pretended to watch *Days of our Lives*, but I could see her making my lunch out of the corner of my eye and then I noticed it.

She reached up and snipped a tiny fragment from a foxglove leaf. Then she chopped it up really small and put it in my casserole.

I looked up foxglove in the encyclopedia. Every single part of that flower is poisonous, from the flowers to the stem to the leaves. Eating it causes nausea, headache, skin irritation, and diarrhea. It can also cause foggy thinking and disorientation.

This explains why I've been so tired. Why I sleep so much, and why my stomach is upset.

I thought it was grief, when it's actually poison, in a very small dose.

A large dose stops your heart.

Chapter Seventy-One

PIPER

The doorbell rang, and Piper looked up from the diary, fighting the sense of disorientation that came from being abruptly ejected from Dottie's mind.

"Poison?" Kiersten whispered.

"She must be wrong . . ." Rosamund said, shaking her head. "I know he's awful . . . but would he really try to kill her?"

"*People* magazine and *Dateline* always have stories about people trying to kill their spouses instead of just divorcing them," Kiersten said, clutching the meat thermometer. "And that's *now*."

Piper gripped the diary so hard her knuckles turned white. "And back in 1965, Dickie had even more motivation to kill his wife. Plus he had means and opportunity. His father-in-law's money, business, and political connections, the fact that his wife was infertile, his political ambitions, and the social stigma of divorce. It would all make murder a far more palatable option than divorce."

"If you happened to be a monstrous person with no conscience," Rosamund added. "Which Dickie obviously was."

"Or *is currently*," Kiersten added.

The doorbell rang a second time.

"Rosamund, can you get the door?" Kiersten asked. "I've got to make the rolls."

"It must be Miles and Valentina and Reggie," Piper said.

"Wait." Rosamund wiped her hands on her apron. "Do we tell people about this? Or not?"

They all looked at each other.

"No." Piper shook her head. "We don't."

"Why not?" Kiersten asked.

"Because we don't know the whole story," Piper said. "And we don't want to impugn the character of a living person with diaries written sixty years ago. Maybe Dottie was trying to tarnish his reputation. Maybe she was crazy. First, we get all the facts. Then if it looks like something . . . bad . . . happened on Beaverbrook Lane back in 1965, we go to the police."

"Do we confront Richard and Margaret Davis with what we know?" Kiersten asked.

"Definitely not. We tell no one else. For now," Piper said firmly.

"Okay." Rosamund raised a breadcrumb-caked hand. "Blood mother's oath of silence."

The doorbell rang again, and Piper opened the door for Miles, Reggie, and Valentina.

Simultaneously, a thundering sound reverberated through the house as Kiersten's family returned home from the Air and Space Museum and came in through the mudroom.

Matthew, Luke, James, and Johnny flung their shoes, coats, and hats into the air, disrobing as they moved through the house, only to find the neighbor girls in the backyard with a new puppy, causing them to stampede out the back door into the frigid dusk in their stocking feet.

"In case you're wondering," Kiersten called out to Piper as she gestured toward the shoes and coats strewn across the floor. "*This* is how I end up with socks in my trees."

They called the kids inside, and everyone gathered in Kiersten's kitchen to serve themselves, buffet-style, from the food laid out on the kitchen counter. The kids took plates of mashed potatoes and chicken nuggets onto the screened-in porch, where they ate with the dog, despite the autumn chill.

The adults crammed into the classroom / dining room and gathered around the table, where they discussed childhood pets, Las Vegas, the six new homes going up on Haskel Avenue, and recent news stories about unidentified flying objects in the night sky over New Jersey.

"And speaking of anomalies, I noticed something else odd the other day," Miles said, plucking a dinner roll from the basket on the table.

"What's that?" Garrett shifted his chair, making room for Piper to sit down after getting a second helping of mashed potatoes.

"Someone's been tampering with my wildlife cameras."

Kiersten and Piper exchanged a look.

"Tampering in what way?" Piper asked.

"The cameras aren't complicated," Miles explained. "They're solar powered with a simple on/off switch on the side. Someone keeps flipping it to off."

Reggie looked up sharply. "I could have sworn someone was poking around my backyard yesterday morning. It was about 4:30 a.m. I lift weights out in the garage before I come over and get you for our run." He gestured at Kiersten with a forkful of pork loin. "Something bumped into the trash cans behind my garage. I thought it was a raccoon. I went out back to check, and whatever it was ran away, but it sounded big. Bigger than a raccoon."

"I also found a strange thing," Valentina said, leaning a little closer to Reggie. "This morning, I go out to get my newspaper, and there is a notebook paper, nailed to the tree in front of my house."

Piper swallowed. "This paper . . . was it blank?"

Valentina shook her head, curly dark hair undulating as she moved. "No. It had nasty things on it." She made a motion with her fingers. "Like someone painted on it . . . with *blood*."

Kiersten swallowed. "At the Harvest Festival, Chip told me the neighborhood wasn't as safe as it used to be. He told me to keep my wits about me, or something like that."

Piper narrowed her eyes as her mind churned through the possibilities, searching for a link, a connection. Hawkeye Slaughter, the sick bastard actively making threats against her on X. Alex Orlov, the fourteen-year-old kid who continued to stalk her daughter. And Richard, the eighty-something-year-old man next door who tried to kill his wife sixty years ago.

And what about Chip and Trey Davis, with their own career and political ambitions? Did they know what had happened sixty years ago? How far would they go to protect family secrets?

She looked at her neighbors. Good, decent people, all of them. They deserved to know about the threats she could identify . . . with the exception of Richard, for the time being.

She took a deep breath and told them about the traffic jam she'd created and the threats from Hawkeye Slaughter, about the worms and the cockroaches and the man who'd shown up at her house with a bag of sex toys. About the strange papers nailed to the tree in front of her house and the Cleaver house.

It felt cathartic, to say it all out loud. Now they knew. Now they could protect themselves . . . but from who?

Chapter Seventy-Two

KIERSTEN

Rosamund and Piper moved to the kitchen to help Kiersten clean up while the kids played a rousing game of Pictionary in the dining room with Garrett and the rest of the neighbors.

After they finished loading the dishwasher and wiping down the counters, Kiersten picked up the diaries.

"A couple more entries, before you guys go home?"

They nodded. She opened the diary and began to read.

Chapter Seventy-Three

DOTTIE

October 1, 1965

Today Peggy served me breakfast in the dining room as usual. As soon as she went upstairs to make the beds I scraped my scrambled eggs into a pail and buried them in the back flower bed. I did the same thing at lunch. I grabbed an apple from the pantry and ate that instead. I'm starving, but my stomach is better today. No nausea or diarrhea. And I no longer have a headache.

October 4, 1965

Three days without eating any food prepared by Dickie or Peggy and I feel almost back to normal. My skin looks better. I have energy again, and best of all, the fuzziness in my brain is gone.

It all makes sense, now that I can think straight again. Dickie can't divorce me because the scandal would end all his political ambitions. And it would turn Daddy against him forever. He'd be back where he was before he married the boss's daughter. Just another salesman at a car dealership, trying to make his quota each month. Instead he's living in a big house in a new development, with a new car, lots of money, and big political ambitions. All because of me. And all of that goes away if I divorce him.

But if they poison me and somehow pretend I died in childbirth, Dickie is a sympathetic widower left to raise his child alone. Then a few months later he "bumps into" Peggy somewhere and they get married. She becomes the kindly stepmother. And together they go on to have more children. He has his political career with Daddy's money and connections to help him. I'm the only thing standing in the way.

October 5, 1965

Dickie has to be the one behind all this. Peggy isn't smart enough to think of it by herself. And I wouldn't have thought her ruthless enough either. But I guess desperate times call for desperate measures, and Peggy is desperate.

Pregnant and unmarried, alone with no money and no prospects. She's in a bad situation and she knows it. And everything gets better for her, too, if I'm out of the way.

She marries a respected pillar of the community and becomes a wife and mother. This is why she never leaves the house. No one can know she's here until she returns as Dickie's new wife and the stepmother of her own child.

So I'll give them what they want. I'll get out of their way, but not in the way they think.

I've almost got that old clunker running. I just need a little more time. Dickie doesn't know it, but when he allowed them to tow that beat up Chevy into the garage, he provided the means of my escape.

October 6, 1965

I was out in the garage until midnight. I'm almost there. I got it running, then it conked out again. But now I know what's wrong, and I can fix it.

I suppose I could just run out the door right now and tell the neighbors everything. About the miscarriage and pregnant Peggy and the casseroles poisoned with food from my own flower bed. I could ask the neighbors to take me to the police.

But I'm afraid.

I'm afraid of Dickie and his ability to charm and manipulate people. I'm afraid he would convince everyone, even Daddy, that I'm crazy. I'm afraid he'd have me locked up somewhere. I'd rather be a prisoner in my own home with someone trying to poison me than drugged and restrained in a mental hospital. And he'd do it. I know he would.

And if people *did* believe me, it would become a huge scandal. I can see the headlines now. Infertile Car Dealership Heiress Poisoned by Husband's Pregnant Lover.

That would make it difficult to start a new life. And I don't want to put Daddy through something like that. He worked so hard to build his business. I can't do that to him.

I just want to slip out, divorce Dickie, and get on with my life. People will still whisper, but we'll keep the whole thing quiet. I'm only 19 years old, for Pete's sake. I have my whole life ahead of me.

I've packed a few things. I'll retrieve my diaries from inside the encyclopedias in the den on the way out, after they've gone to sleep.

I've been stealing money from Dickie's wallet at night while they eat dinner. I've got almost a hundred dollars now. That's more than enough for food and motels and gas to get me to Florida.

It's funny, but I now realize that in less than a year of marriage, Dickie has managed to isolate me from everyone. All my relatives and friends from high school and the dealership. He even discouraged me from getting to know the neighbors. He didn't even want me spending time with Daddy. And now there's no one left to help me.

But unfortunately for Dickie, I'm still smart enough to help myself.

Chapter Seventy-Four

PIPER

The cul-de-sac rang with high-pitched screams and laughter as the kids did PE outside with Reggie, while Valentina took a break on the front porch with a cappuccino, completely absorbed in one of Rosamund's Shield-Maiden of Stamendahl Viking romance novels.

Inside the house, the moms prepared lunch in the Beaverbrook "cafeteria."

"Do you think it's true?" Piper asked, jutting her chin toward the third and last diary sitting open on the counter as she cut open a package of baby carrots.

"Listen to us." Kiersten shook her head in disgust as she spread peanut butter over a slice of bread. "We're doing *exactly* what Dottie predicted people would do. We're calling her a liar. We're wondering if she's crazy, if she's making it all up."

"I never called her a *liar* . . ." Piper protested. Well, not in so many words anyway. Maybe Kiersten had a point.

Kiersten reached for the grape jelly. "But we're questioning whether or not it could be true."

"I believe her." Rosamund's voice had a slight edge as she sliced a knife through an apple.

"Why?" Piper asked.

"Because Dickie sounds like Guinevere's father."

Piper froze as a sympathetic ache rose in her chest.

Rosamund set her knife down on the cutting board and lifted her chin. "His name was Adam, and he was a controlling narcissist. At the time, I didn't know what that was. After a lot of therapy and reading many books, I eventually figured it out."

"How did you . . ." Piper began.

"Get away?" Rosamund asked.

Piper nodded. "Yeah."

"I disappeared." Rosamund's fingers moved quickly as she carved the apple into slices. "When I found out I was pregnant, I left. He doesn't know Guinevere exists. He's the reason I do radio and podcast interviews but never appear on TV."

She sank the knife into another apple with more force than necessary. "*He's* the reason there's no mention of my daughter on my website or in my bio. *He's* the reason you will never see my face on social media."

She slammed the knife through the apple each time she referred to her ex. "*He's* the reason I write under a pen name, and *he's* the reason I have no picture on my book jackets."

Kiersten set her peanut butter knife down on the cutting board, moved around the island, and wrapped her arms around Rosamund. "I am so sorry, Rosamund. I had no idea."

Rosamund rested her head on Kiersten's shoulder for a brief moment, then pulled away, dabbing her eyes with the back of her hand. "Thank you." Then she looked over at Piper. "Don't worry, Piper, I don't expect you to hug me too."

Piper smiled. "I appreciate that, but I'm going to do it anyway."

Piper crossed the kitchen and enveloped Rosamund in a quick, stiff hug. "Sigrid of Stamendahl's got *nothing* on you. You're a total badass."

Rosamund looked at her with red-rimmed eyes. "Thank you," she said, returning to her apple slices again. "But there are so many details in Dottie's life that strike me as familiar. Which is why I think she's telling the truth."

"Can you give us an example?" Piper asked, tilting her head. "I'm trying to understand this, but it's hard, not having been through it."

She understood physical terror, like the kind Mr. Claussen used to control and terrify Mrs. Claussen. But this was something different. This type of abuse was far more subtle, leaving bruises and wounds on the inside, scars no one could see.

Rosamund grabbed another apple and cut through the skin. "Calling her belittling nicknames, like Dottie the Dimwit. Telling her what she can and can't say. Isolating her from everyone in her life. And the fact that he's charming to everyone else. That's classic. Narcissists are often charismatic people. And they use their charm to isolate their victims."

"How awful," Kiersten whispered.

Rosamund lifted her chin. "*This* is why we need to keep reading. This is why we keep going through pages and pages of obituaries on Google, to see if she's alive or dead. We have an obligation to figure out what happened to her. And if something bad happened, then we have an obligation to make sure that bastard doesn't get away with it."

"One more entry?" Kiersten asked.

Piper glanced at the clock on the microwave. "Okay. One more."

Chapter Seventy-Five

DOTTIE

October 8, 1965

Today is the day. Peggy is completely preoccupied.

I've managed to pack a small bag. I'll grab my diaries and the money after Peggy goes to bed.

I think the baby must be getting close because Peggy has become a domestic demon. Last night she pulled all the corn and squash out of the garden and carried them into the house. Now the kitchen is covered in mason jars and she's canning preserves.

She looks exhausted. Sometimes she stands there in the kitchen, stretches backward, and winces. I think she might be having contractions. Her skin is pale and she has big circles under her eyes.

She doesn't try to hide her pregnancy, now that I know about it. An apron splashed with old raspberry stains covers her enormous belly, and her long, thick hair is piled in a bun.

I forced a smile, determined to pretend everything is normal. Or as normal as it can be when you're living in a house with your husband's pregnant mistress who is trying to poison you.

"Looks delicious," I said when I entered the kitchen.

She shrugged. "My family didn't have much money, but we had a huge garden. My mother made our fruits and vegetables last all through the winter by making preserves. I used to help her."

She dabbed the sweat beading on her forehead with the back of her hand and reached for a crate of newly canned corn.

Something about her heaving that heavy crate of mason jars off the counter tugged at my heart.

"Let me carry that," I said, grabbing the crate.

She'd stolen my husband and tried to poison me, but for some reason the idea of her lifting something heavy and having a miscarriage was more than I could bear. No one should go through that kind of pain. Even Peggy.

She gave me a shy smile and I felt a twinge of guilt. Was I wrong about her? Maybe she didn't know foxglove was poisonous. Maybe she was just doing what Dickie told her to do.

"Thank you," she said. "I'm putting them in the fallout shelter. It's dark and cold down there . . . the perfect root cellar."

I descended the steps to the basement as she followed behind me.

Chapter Seventy-Six

KIERSTEN

The doorbell rang, and Kiersten stopped reading. "I'll get it," she said, putting the diary down and rising from the table.

"Wait," Piper said. "I'll come with you . . . just in case."

"Just in case it's another . . . *sex man*," Rosamund said as she grabbed a pair of children's blunt-tipped Hello Kitty scissors, prepared, apparently, for anything.

They moved through the foyer together and clustered around the front door, where Kiersten looked through the peep hole. Her body stiffened.

She swallowed. "It's Chip Davis."

"Pretend everything is normal," Piper muttered.

She nodded. Easier said than done with the son of a murderer standing on your front porch.

Then she took a deep breath and opened the door. "Good morning!"

He gave her a wide smile. "Did I catch you at a bad time?"

"Oh no," she said. "Just taking a little break while the kids have recess."

"Looks like they're having a great time," he said, jutting his chin toward the cul-de-sac, where the kids did jumping jacks with Reggie.

"Anyway, I don't want to disturb you. I'm just here to pick up those other diaries. My parents finished reading the first one. They still don't have a clue who wrote them, but they'd be happy to read the next two and see if they can learn anything helpful."

She twisted her fingers, stalling for time as she tried to come up with a suitable excuse. "Oh. Gosh. That's really kind."

"But unfortunately, you're too late," Piper said, coming to her rescue.

"She donated them," Rosamund added.

Kiersten nodded vigorously. She couldn't lie on the fly, but she could back up the lies told by more capable liars.

"That's right," Piper said. "To the Fairfax County Historical Society."

"A friend of mine runs it," Rosamund said.

"But he's traveling right now," Kiersten interjected.

"He's in *Japan*," Piper said.

"For the next three months," Rosamund added.

His eyes narrowed as he scanned their faces. "I see."

"We've sort of given up . . ." Kiersten added nervously. "On trying to find out who wrote those diaries. It's just so long ago . . . and I'm sure whoever wrote them is dead by now."

"You're probably right," he said with a smooth smile. "Well, I hope the historical society puts them to good use."

"I'm sure they will," Kiersten said firmly. "You know historical societies . . . they love . . . things . . . that are . . . historical."

For a brief moment his eyes went cold, and Kiersten caught a glimpse of the man behind the affable mask. Ruthless. Angry. Manipulative.

Like father, like son.

A prickle of fear caressed the back of her neck.

Then that smooth smile appeared again. "I've come here for another reason, as well," Chip said.

"What's that?" Kiersten asked. Her face felt like a plaster cast, capable of cracking at any moment.

"I'm here to extend an invitation, on behalf of my daughter-in-law, Aspen. She's throwing a little party tomorrow afternoon, at her place.

Wine, champagne, and a few of her influencer friends. And she'd love it if you all could drop by."

"What's the occasion?" Piper asked.

"She gets so many things for free," he said, with a bemused shake of his head. "Beauty products. Clothes. Shoes. Sometimes she invites friends over for spa days or makeovers, things like that. She's going to have a masseuse. And a tarot-card reader. And one of those people who analyzes your skin tones and tells you what colors to wear."

"Oh gosh. We'd sure love to be there," Kiersten said, cranking up the dial on her Minnesota accent. "But unfortunately, we have the kids so . . ." She shrugged and spread her arms in an oh-well-too-bad-maybe-next-time gesture.

"That's not a problem. The kids are welcome," he said, waving this concern away. "We'll have childcare. Games. All kinds of activities. It would mean the world to Aspen."

He took a step closer, and Kiersten forced herself not to shrink away. He lowered his voice. "Frankly, I think she's a little worried no one will show up. You see, she has a lot of online friends, but she doesn't have many friends *in real life*. And she's pretty stressed out right now, with the homeschooling and content creation and this TV deal in the works."

He looked up at the sky and blinked rapidly, as though seeking answers from the heavens. Then he turned back to Kiersten. "She could really benefit from the friendship and wisdom of some *older* moms . . . moms who aren't all wrapped up in the number of followers they have. If you could just stop by for one glass of champagne, she'd be grateful. I'd be grateful too."

Kiersten shot a look at Rosamund, whose nostrils had flared at the phrase *older moms*. Then she glanced at Chip again. He looked so earnest, his brow creased with concern about his young daughter-in-law. His eyes were even a little red. Was he on the verge of *tears*?

She felt a flash of disgust.

Kiersten knew she could be naive, that she was sometimes kind and generous to a fault.

But her open, trusting nature had given her one tool that fake and insincere people lacked.

She had a finely calibrated bullshit meter. And Chip's crocodile tears tripped every alarm inside her body. It blared like a World War II submarine caught in a torpedo strike. AWOOGA AWOOGA.

She shot a look at Piper, who gave her an almost imperceptible nod.

Aspen needed extra bodies to build a crowd and make the party look good on Instagram?

Fine. They'd allow Aspen to use them as props again, just like they did at the Harvest Festival.

But this time, they'd use Aspen's event to investigate Richard, Chip, and Trey.

"We'd love to come." Kiersten managed to infuse her words with warmth. "Wouldn't we?" she asked, turning to Piper and Rosamund.

"Sure," Piper said with enthusiasm.

"We'd be delighted," Rosamund added.

"Wonderful." A giant smile creased Chip's handsome face. "I appreciate this. I really do."

He headed across the street, to the construction site next door to his parents' house. Then he entered the skeletal structure of the new home and disappeared inside.

Chapter Seventy-Seven

PIPER

Kiersten sank to the rug in the foyer, resting her back against the closed door.

"You were awesome," Piper said, sinking down beside her.

"I don't feel awesome. I feel terrified. He *knows* we're lying about the diaries."

"It doesn't matter," Piper said. "You kept them out of his hands. That's the important thing."

"I'm kind of excited," Rosamund said, settling onto the bench in the foyer. "I've always wanted to go *undercover*."

"Do you think Aspen will tell us anything useful?" Kiersten asked.

Piper chewed on her lower lip, thinking. "She spends a lot of time with Margaret. Remember how she told us Grammy is really popular on Instagram? She's gotta know something about the family she married into. Something about Margaret's early years as a wife and mother. It's worth a shot."

"Do you think Chip knows . . . about his dad?" Kiersten asked.

"I do. I think he is literally a chip off the old block in every possible way."

"You mean . . . he's capable of murder too?" Rosamund asked quietly.

Piper paused. She didn't want to scare Kiersten and Rosamund. But they also needed to understand the possible consequences of what they were about to do.

"There's an inverse relationship between the consequences of a crime and the length people will go to cover it up."

"So if Richard murdered Dottie . . ."

"He and Chip will do everything in their power to keep Richard from going to prison. To keep the truth about sweet old Grammy from derailing Aspen's Happy House Life HGTV deal. And to keep Chip's and Trey's political and career ambitions on track."

"You think they would . . . kill again?" Kiersten's face had gone pale.

"I think we need to be really careful," Piper said.

Kiersten rose from the floor and extended a hand to pull Piper to her feet. They moved to the dining room.

"We still haven't spoken with Lillian about this." Kiersten squirted cleaning spray on a dry-erase board filled with algebra problems. "But she came home from her trip yesterday, and she's lived here for decades. And she might know something that points us in a completely different direction."

"Before we do anything else, we need to finish Dottie's last diary," Piper said, handing her a paper towel. "We only have a couple entries left."

"Where is it?" Kiersten asked.

Piper frowned. "Where's what?"

"The *diary*."

Her heart dropped. "I thought you had it."

"I don't have it," Rosamund said.

Kiersten went into the kitchen and returned a few minutes later. "Sorry. It was buried in a pile of LEGOs. Ready?"

Piper sat in a dining room chair, prepared to listen with an open mind, hoping she was wrong about her neighbors, wrong about Dottie's fate, wrong about everything. But the tiny whisper of intuition that had guided her through a long law enforcement career told her she was right.

Chapter Seventy-Eight

DOTTIE

October 8, 1965

We opened the door in the far corner of the basement and entered the fallout shelter with one last load of mason jars.

Suddenly, Peggy cried out, doubled over, and dropped a jar of beet pickles on the hard-packed dirt floor. The jar broke open. The liquid inside seeped into the dirt.

She moaned softly, then sank onto one of the cots we keep inside the shelter.

I set my crate of preserves on the table next to the shelf holding the blankets, board games, and first aid supplies. Then I sat beside her.

"Are you okay?"

She closed her eyes, then nodded. "The baby's coming."

"Right now?" I asked, alarmed.

"The contractions started at dawn."

"But you aren't due until the end of the month," I argued, as though this would somehow make the contractions stop.

"Sometimes babies come early," she said, wincing.

"Shouldn't you go to the hospital?"

"I can't."

My mouth went dry, and I swallowed. "Why not?"

"Because I'm giving birth to your baby. Remember?"

"This is crazy." I took her arm and attempted to pull her up, off the cot. "You need a doctor."

She waved this advice away with a sharp groan. Then she turned to me, her pale face urgent. "We don't have much time."

"Time for what?"

"Time for saving your life."

I turned to stare as her mask fell away. And suddenly I saw her for what she truly was. A young woman, poor, scared, desperate. And all my jealousy fell away. The fear and the anger dissolved, too, leaving only the truth behind, like a residue after all the lesser elements have burned away.

"You're trying to poison me, aren't you?"

She shook her head. "The foxglove was designed to make you feel sick and weak and lethargic. To keep you from running away. To keep you here until I went into labor. I'm sorry about that. I truly am. But I can't . . . I can't help Dickie with the rest. I won't."

The top of my scalp prickled. "What do you mean . . . *the rest*?"

"The locks." She grimaced as she waved a limp hand toward the door. "He reversed them."

I rose from the cot and examined the door to the fallout shelter. The dead bolt, the throw bolt, and the hook and eye bolt. Everything used to be on the inside. Now the door to the fallout shelter locks from the *outside*.

I shuddered. "Why would—"

"He wants to lock you inside the fallout shelter. Then he'll shut the garage door and start the car. There's this small hole, above us, in the corner of the garage. He'll kill you with carbon monoxide poisoning."

My body froze. "And then tell everyone I died in childbirth."

She nodded, eyes enormous in her pale face. "After you're . . . dead . . . he'll haul your body upstairs. He'll stage it all. Everything . . . that comes out of my body will bolster his story. The bloody sheets . . . the afterbirth . . . the placenta. He'll call the doctor, and it will all look so convincing. So obvious. No one will bother to examine you. No one will doubt his story. Not when there's a dead woman and live baby lying in his bed."

"What happens to you?"

"I stay. We get married." Her lip twisted and her face went hard. "And then we live happily ever after."

I rubbed my hands over my face and sat down beside her on the cot. "I'm so incredibly stupid."

"No, you're not." She reached out to touch my arm and I flinched and pulled away. "You're kind and trusting and good, so it would never occur to you to do something this depraved."

"Why are you telling me this?" I turned to face her. "Isn't this what you wanted? With me out of the way you get to raise your own child. You have a husband to claim your . . ." I can't bring myself to say the word.

"I have a husband to claim my bastard?"

"Yes."

"I was fine with giving you my child. I was fine with you raising my baby and pretending it's yours. But I'm not fine with murdering you and then taking your place as Dickie's wife."

"Why?"

"Because it's wrong," she said simply.

"Ah yes. And you're such a moral person."

"I'm not a bad person." She looked hurt.

"You sure fooled me. You're sleeping with my husband."

"That's not . . . it's not what you think."

I thought back to the mattress above my head. "What else could it possibly be?"

"Look, when I started having contractions this morning, Dickie told me to lock you in the fallout shelter. And I think we should still do that."

"Why on earth would I let you—"

"Just listen. Please." She winced and pressed her hands into her back. Then she turned her pale face toward me. "I lock you in here. I have the baby. And then I leave."

"How does that help me?"

"If I'm gone, he can't kill you. He needs a wife. And he needs a mother for the baby. You'll be safe, once I give birth."

"No." I shake my head slowly. "I'll be safe until the next pregnant mistress comes along. Then he'll do the same thing again. I'm not staying here with him. I can't."

"You don't have to stay forever. Just a couple days. Then you take the baby and run."

"And then what?"

"And then you raise my baby as your own. You have money. You have a nice place down in Florida. You can raise him there."

"But it's your *baby*. Don't you want to raise this baby yourself?"

"With what? Love and fairy dust?" Her face twisted in anguish as tears began to roll down her cheeks. "I have no money. No husband. No job. I don't even have a place to live anymore. And I can't get a job with a baby to care for, even if someone were willing to hire an unwed mother. No." She shook her head. "I'll leave. And you take the baby."

Silence filled the space between us as a kaleidoscope of ideas bloomed inside my mind.

"We'll go together."

"How?"

"We lock *Dickie* in this stinking room. We take the baby and head to Florida. When we get there, we call the police and tell them everything. He'll go to jail, and we'll never have to worry about him again. And *we'll* raise your baby. I'll get a job. I'll help you."

She looked up at me with those big eyes. "You'd do that, for me?"

"I'd do it for your baby."

"The baby isn't Dickie's."

I sink back against the cinder block wall behind the cot. *"What?"*

She nodded, a small smile creasing her face. "He thinks he's the father. But he's not."

"Then who—"

"The baby's father died in Viet Nam."

A quick intake of breath. "Danny."

"Yes."

"You're the girl with the green eyes."

"He talked about me?"

"All the time. In his letters from basic training."

She smiled. "We met when he was at Fort Leonard Wood. I moved up here to work at the dealership before he shipped out. We were going to get married. But then his orders came, a week after I arrived. And then he died . . . over there. I don't know if my last letter ever reached him . . . telling him about the baby."

She stroked her swollen belly. "When I realized I was pregnant, and Danny was dead . . . I panicked . . . and Dickie . . . well, he was always making passes at me. Always touching me. Always asking me to bend over and pick up the pencil he'd just dropped on the floor. So I stopped fighting him off. It was impossible anyway, trapped in that office with him after everyone else had gone home, on those days when he asked me to stay late to take 'dictation.'" Her lips curled downward in a sneer as she said the word.

Her expression hardened. "I let him do what he was going to do anyway, whether I wanted him to or not. I figured I could get some cash out of him if he thought the baby was his. Figured he'd put me up somewhere while I was pregnant. And he did. Paid my rent and all my expenses these last few months once I started to show and had to quit working . . . and then he told me if I just stayed here until the baby was born, you would raise it . . . and I was fine with that . . . but I never in a million years imagined that he'd try to kill you."

"When did you find out?" I asked.

"This morning, when the contractions started. He told me what I needed to do . . . and I can't. A tiny trace of foxglove to keep you here until the baby came is one thing. But this . . . this is murder. And I won't do it."

She gasped as another contraction gripped her body. "We don't have much time . . ."

I grabbed her hand, and she squeezed so hard I thought she'd break my fingers. "After the baby comes, I'll send him out to get something, something to get him out of the house. He has no idea, about babies or childbirth or what a woman needs after. I'll tell him we need talcum powder for the baby. Or aspirin or orange juice or pickles for me. Something. He'll be so happy when he sees it's a boy. He'll do anything I ask."

"How do you know it's a boy?"

"Danny told me."

My mouth dropped open and all my words dried up.

She looked sheepish. "He comes to me sometimes. Just before I fall asleep. He tells me things. He told me to trust you."

Another agonized cry erupted from her body.

"Tell me you'll do it." She squeezed my hand so hard I thought the bones would break.

"You're asking me to let you lock me up in here?"

She nodded. "And then I'll let you out, after he leaves."

"And if I don't?"

"Then Dickie will hunt you down and kill you. You know he will."

The accuracy of her prediction sank into my skull. She was right. He couldn't get remarried if I was still alive and well and living in Florida. He couldn't claim this baby as his own, marry Peggy, pursue his political ambitions, or continue with his life as Daddy's son-in-law. None of this worked with me alive.

But if Peggy and I left together, we could go to the police. It wouldn't be just my word against his. Peggy could prove he'd been unfaithful. I could divorce him. And they could arrest him for attempted murder.

"Does that car of yours actually run?" she asked.

I smiled. "It does now."

She squeezed her eyes shut and grimaced. "The minute he leaves . . ." she panted out the words. "We take the baby and go."

"We could go now—"

"This baby . . ." She let out a low moan as her gaunt face twisted in pain. "This baby is coming . . . and I can't give birth alone . . . in the back seat of a car . . . while you drive."

My mind rushed ahead, sprinting through my options. I could push her away, run up the stairs, jump in the car, and leave.

But what would Dickie do to her when he realized I got away?

I shuddered as the truth washed over me.

Dickie will kill her. And he'll kill the baby too. He'll cover the whole thing up. Pretend Peggy and the baby never existed. And then he'll hunt me down. His story only works if he has my dead body *and* her live baby.

I can't leave them here to die at the hands of Dickie. Her plan is the only way to save all three of us and send Dickie to jail for the rest of his life.

Did I trust her?

I looked into her eyes and saw my own fear of Dickie reflected back.

I nodded. "Okay. I'll do it."

"Pack a bag. For us both. Don't take too much from the closet, or he'll notice."

"He'll be home in an hour."

"I know. We don't have much time."

"I'll put the bag in the trunk of the car. Then you lock me in."

"Okay," she grunted through gritted teeth. "I'm gonna stay here a minute. Catch my breath. Do you trust me?"

"Strangely, I do."

We sat there for a long moment, me stroking her back, her squeezing my hand.

Dickie thinks we have no power because we are women. But oddly, we have power together *because* we are women.

But just in case something goes wrong, I'm leaving these diaries behind, leaving them hidden.

If all goes well, I'll come back for them. After we're divorced, after Dickie is arrested and locked up in prison, away from all women, where he belongs.

But if Dickie succeeds in killing me, I will leave a clue, buried in the past, leading to the truth.

Chapter Seventy-Nine

KIERSTEN

Dottie's last words hung in the air after Kiersten stopped reading.

"Is that all?" Piper whispered.

"That's it. That's the last entry from the three diaries I found." Kiersten closed the small black volume and handed it to Piper.

"Could there be more diaries hidden in the encyclopedias?" Piper asked, leafing through the remaining diary pages, all of them blank.

Kiersten shook her head. "I double-checked last night. This is the last one."

"It's like watching a show on Netflix and then they cut off your subscription before you can watch the season finale," Rosamund said.

"Do you think she got away?" Piper asked, sinking down in her chair.

Kiersten chewed on her lower lip. "We need to talk to Lillian next door. She must know *something*."

Rosamund nodded. "And we need to find out if Evil Dickie and Pregnant Peggy—"

"You mean Richard and Margaret," Kiersten interjected.

"Right. We need to find out if Richard and Margaret have a fallout shelter underneath their garage."

They all looked at each other.

"And if we find one . . ." Rosamund began softly.

Piper swallowed. "If we find one, that's a coincidence we can't explain away."

"Let's take it one step at a time." Kiersten began to gnaw on her thumbnail. She couldn't bear the idea of not knowing what had become of Dottie. But she also couldn't bear the idea of learning that she'd been murdered.

"Unfortunately, I can't do anything more right now." Rosamund got up from her chair. "I have to take Guinevere to the orthodontist. Time, tide, and braces wait for no man."

"And I have to take Travis in for his shots," Piper said.

"I can take the kids with me to see Lillian," Kiersten offered.

"No. I'll take them with me," Piper volunteered. "We'll call it career day at the veterinarian. You talk to Lillian and report back, okay?"

"All right." Kiersten nodded. Clearly she was getting the better end of this deal. She shuddered at the idea of taking seven children and a puppy *anywhere*, much less to the vet.

"By the way, tomorrow might be rough," Kiersten warned, unable to keep an ominous undertone from her voice.

"Because?" Rosamund asked expectantly.

"Because Valentina and Reggie are going to a line dancing convention."

They both turned to look at her. "A *what*?"

"A line dancing convention," she repeated. "At the Dulles Expo Center. And then they're going to the Blue Diamond Bingo Emporium."

"Reggie the retired marine corps drill instructor is doing *line dancing*?" Piper asked.

Kiersten nodded. "He says it keeps his mind sharp."

Rosamund looked perplexed. "And they are doing this because . . ."

"Because apparently they've started going to the Scoot Your Boot country and western bar in Lorton on Thursday nights for line dancing lessons, and now they're going to take a two-hour workshop to further refine their technique."

"Are Valentina and Reggie . . ." Rosamund waggled her eyebrows. "You know . . ."

"A thing?" Kiersten asked. "I'm not sure. I tried to ask last week. He made me run an extra mile for, quote, 'expressing curiosity about things that are none of my damn business.'"

"Wow," Piper said.

"I know." Kiersten grinned. "But that's the problem with having a faculty made up of mostly unpaid retired people who may or may not be conducting a romance outside of school hours. If they want to take the day off to hang out at a line dancing convention and play bingo, we obviously can't say no."

"So who watches the kids while we go next door to the Influencer's party?" Piper asked.

Kiersten frowned. "I supposed we could just let the kids hang out here, unsupervised. We'll be right next door."

"Absolutely not." Piper shook her head.

"Chip said they'd have childcare available," Rosamund said. "We could bring them along."

"No way." Piper shook her head again. "I'd rather leave them home alone for an hour than trust them to the tender mercies of Evil Dickie's son."

"You mean the man Evil Dickie *thinks* is his son but who is actually the offspring of a mechanic who died in Viet Nam," Rosamund added.

Piper exhaled loudly. "Holy soap opera, Batman."

"No kidding," Kiersten said. "I think I've lived a very sheltered life."

Rosamund patted her hand. "Welcome to the big city."

"But this *isn't* the city," Piper argued. "It's a quiet, respectable suburb. Or at least we thought it was, back then."

"Maybe nothing is the way I thought it was back then." Kiersten attempted to swallow her sorrow for Dottie, for the past, for a sweeter, simpler time that apparently never existed.

Piper rapped her knuckles on the table. "Dudes. Focus. Childcare for this damn party . . . to which I have nothing to wear. Maybe I should stay here with the kids while you guys go to the Influencer's house."

"Oh no you don't." Kiersten eyed her with a determined expression. "We *all* need to go. And if Grammy and Grampy are there, maybe one of us could sneak next door and check their basement for a fallout shelter while the other two keep them distracted."

"Excellent point," Piper conceded with a sigh. "So is the least terrible option really leaving the kids here by themselves for an hour?"

"They're good kids," Rosamund said. "They're responsible. And we will literally be next door. Plus Miles is working from home tomorrow. He'll be right across the street."

Piper cast a sideways glance at Rosamund. "By the way, are you and Miles . . ."

Rosamund rolled her eyes. "Every man is surrounded by a neighborhood of voluntary spies."

Piper grinned. "Shakespeare?"

"Jane Austen," Rosamund said with a sphinxlike smile. "And I have no further comment at this time."

They rose from the table to go in their separate directions. After helping Piper load seven children and Travis the puppy into an SUV, Kiersten headed two doors down to find out what her neighbor remembered about Beaverbrook Lane in 1965.

Chapter Eighty

KIERSTEN

Kiersten rang the doorbell and then waited for what felt like a very long time before Lillian eventually stumped into the foyer with the help of a cane and squinted at her through the storm door.

Her wrinkled face broke into a wide smile, and she pushed the door open. "It's Johnny's mom."

Kiersten smiled back. Johnny and Bella, Piper's youngest daughter, had latched on to Lillian like barnacles. When she came out to sit on her porch in the afternoons, they usually ran over to swing on her porch swing while Lillian told them stories about her childhood during and after World War II.

Whenever one of the kids tattled on someone, Johnny shot them a scornful look and informed them that *loose lips sink ships*.

Kiersten held up the plate of cookies she'd made that morning. She actually had both unexpired baking soda *and* baking powder in her pantry, thanks to Aspen's Happy House Life Table of Sustenance system.

"Chocolate chip," she said. "A small thank-you for all the hours you've spend playing UNO with Johnny and Bella these past few weeks."

"They are delightful companions." Lillian led her into the kitchen and gestured toward the table with her cane. "Even though Johnny does have a propensity to make a person draw four the moment you utter the word *UNO*."

Kiersten felt like she'd walked into a museum or her grandmother's house.

Colorful braided rag rugs dotted the floor, and brown paneling enclosed the seating area in the kitchen, where a large picture window looked out on the enormous yard on the backside of the house.

Framed photos adorned the paneled walls depicting the many phases of a long life. A black-and-white photo of a bride and groom, faintly colored pictures of that same bride a few years later, holding babies, and then toddlers on her lap. Color graduation photos with hairstyles that ran the gamut from the straight tresses of the 1970s to the permed pyramids of the 1980s. Then more baby, first-day-of-school, graduation, and wedding photos. Photographic proof that while hair, clothes, music, and politics changed, the chapters of family life remained the same.

"I just made a pot of coffee," Lillian said. "Would you like some?"

Kiersten smiled. Her own grandmother also insisted on drinking coffee every afternoon at four o'clock and refused to listen to modern theories about good sleep hygiene and avoiding caffeine in the afternoon.

"I'd love some. Thank you."

Lillian set a delicate teacup in front of Kiersten with trembling hands.

Once again she was struck by the little grace notes that older people brought to life.

Why did she only drink coffee from the garish and indestructible mugs they seemed to buy every time they visited a tourist attraction, like the Grand Canyon? Why didn't she ever use the beautiful old teacups and china plates she'd inherited from her grandmother?

Another thing Aspen was right about. Slowing down. Finding beauty in old things. Making time to add a few lovely touches to an afternoon cup of coffee. She silently resolved to do better.

Lillian eased herself into a chair beside the ancient kitchen table with a chrome base and a yellow Formica top.

"Is this the kitchen table you had when your kids were young?" Kiersten asked.

"It is." Lillian ran her hands over the scratched yellow surface. "That young real estate man tried to buy it the other day. He's always over here, asking me to sell my stereo or my dining room set. Says they're mid-century something or other and they're worth a lot of money. He wants my house too. But I'm not selling. They can wait until I'm dead."

"Who's that?"

She gestured east with a wrinkled hand. "The young man. Not Chip. But the other one. His son. Trey, they call him."

"He wants to buy your house?"

She nodded. "He says the neighborhood isn't safe anymore. He found this hanging on the knob on my front door when I was in Chicago."

The old woman rose from the table and rummaged in a drawer; then she pulled out what appeared to be a coat hanger, yarn, and a scrap of cloth, and tossed it onto the Formica tabletop.

Kiersten held the hanger aloft by the tips of her fingers. "A . . . noose?"

Chapter Eighty-One

KIERSTEN

A tiny cloth doll dangled from a noose made from string. The noose dangled from the top of the triangle on the coat hanger.

"Apparently," Lillian said.

Kiersten shuddered at this crude tableau of violence made from innocent objects. Cloth from a dish towel. Kitchen twine. Wire. "But why in the world . . ."

"Beats me." Lillian raised her shoulders in a shrug. "Trey said someone tried to break into my house while I was away. He says you and Piper have gotten some strange deliveries too. He says it isn't safe anymore, here on Beaverbrook, and I should go live in a nice retirement community."

Kiersten frowned. How did he know about the packages she and Piper had received? They'd told the other neighbors at dinner on Sunday night. But they hadn't told Trey or Chip or Richard.

Maybe he heard about it from Miles or Reggie or Valentina?

"Did you call the police?" she asked.

"Trey said he'd take care of it. But he told me they were unlikely to do anything because it's not a hate crime."

"It's not?"

"Well, I don't see how it *can* be. I mean, I'm an Episcopalian."

"I can see how that would rule out a hate crime designation," Kiersten admitted reluctantly.

"I do enjoy eating meat. And bread and pasta," Lillian said thoughtfully. "I sometimes think *that* makes me a member of a marginalized group."

"Does your family know about this?" she asked.

"Not yet. I'll let my son know. But he's on one of those Viking riverboat cruises. I'll bother him when he gets home next week."

"I was wondering if you could tell me a little more about the Davis family," Kiersten said, leaning forward. "I found a diary belonging to a Dottie Anderson, who lived here on Beaverbrook in 1965. Does that name ring any bells?"

The old woman frowned. "We moved here in '67, and I don't remember ever meeting anyone named Dottie. But I do remember hearing something about Richard's wife . . . Margaret. About how she was Chip's stepmother, not his biological mother. I vaguely remember people talking about how wonderful she was, how she loved that little boy like he was her own. They never had other children. Just Chip. And then Chip and his wife had Trey. She died a couple years ago. Heart attack. Poor thing."

"Do you happen to know if Richard and Margaret have a fallout shelter underneath their garage?"

Lillian pursed her lips, considering the question. "When these homes were built, the developer gave people the option of a fallout shelter. Some people paid extra for that, and some didn't. Ours doesn't have one. But our friends Herman and Agnes had one. They were the original owners of the house where Reggie lives now."

"What did it look like?"

She made a dismissive gesture with her teacup. "Just a cinder block room with one door, no windows, and a light bulb in the ceiling. And usually a dirt floor. That made it a little more affordable, if you skipped the cost of concrete and linoleum for a finished floor."

"Do you remember anything else?" she asked.

"Those shelters were cold and dark." She tugged at her sweater, pulling it tighter. "I don't think anyone would have survived for long down there. But you know how it was back then . . . we had the Cold War and the Cuban Missile Crisis. We were all on edge, worried the world was about to end. Kind of like my grandkids now with all that global warming. Every generation seems to invent a new way to bring us all to the edge of extinction."

"Did people use the shelters for anything?"

"Oh sure." She nodded, taking a sip of her coffee. "Made a perfect root cellar. We all canned fruits and vegetables from the garden back then, and it was a perfect place to store those mason jars full of pickled beets. And they put emergency supplies in the fallout shelter. You know, things like candles. Board games. Rice and beans. Everything you'd need to survive the collapse of civilization. They came in handy, those fallout shelters, even without a nuclear apocalypse. When people remodeled their basements over the years, they usually left the fallout shelter alone."

"Why?"

"Well, the walls were thick, and that made it really expensive to retroactively add heating and air-conditioning and plumbing. Like Agnes and Herman, the couple who owned Reggie's house. They left their fallout shelter alone when they redid the basement. They used it to store camping gear and canned goods. That's what most people did."

"Is there any way to tell, from the outside, if someone on Beaverbrook has a fallout shelter under their garage?"

She considered the question. "Not that I know of. The only way to find out is to go down to the basement and see if it's there. It would be on the north side, right under the garage."

Kiersten nodded, then glanced at the clock shaped like an owl above the kitchen sink. "Gosh. I'm sorry to have taken up so much of your time. I should get going."

"Before you leave, I have a suggestion to make. For a field trip."

Kiersten leaned forward. "I'd love to hear it."

"There's a cemetery in Old Town. One of the oldest in the state. Dates back to 1795. The kids and I have been talking about the fact that soldiers from the Revolutionary War once lived on the land where our houses sit today. Some of them are buried in this cemetery, and the kids would like to see their graves. It's open to the public tomorrow morning from nine to noon. And I think it would be a fun outing."

Kiersten paused. This was not in their lesson plan for tomorrow . . . but then again, isn't this why they were homeschooling? To take advantage of opportunities like this?

"I'll need to double-check with Rosamund and Piper, but I love the idea. I think we should do it."

Lillian grinned. "I have a handicap placard for my car. We can park right at the front gate. I can be ready to go by nine."

"Thank you, Lillian, for helping with this project."

Lillian smiled. "I've thoroughly enjoyed it. Things are different, here on Beaverbrook, since you started that experiment of yours. It's nice having the kids around all day. And it's nice getting to know your family and the other neighbors. I was seriously considering Trey's offer to sell the house and move into one of those retirement places, until you guys came along. Now I plan to stay put awhile longer."

Kiersten rose to leave. "I'm glad to hear that. And if you find other strange things in your yard, will you let me know?"

Lillian nodded. "I promise. Now you go home and make dinner for your family. It's time for me to watch *Wheel of Fortune* while I eat the rest of these cookies you made."

Kiersten smiled. "I wish I could eat chocolate chip cookies for dinner."

Lillian winked. "It's one of the many perks of being eighty-seven years old. You don't give a hoot what you look like. And you don't give a hoot what anyone else thinks of what you look like either."

Kiersten rose to leave. "Can I ask you one more favor?"

"Sure," her neighbor said.

"Rosamund, Piper, and I have been invited to a little get-together at Aspen's tomorrow afternoon, after we get back from our field trip. We'll just be down the street, and we'll only be gone for an hour, so we're going to leave the big kids in charge of the little ones. Would you mind just keeping an eye out? If you see blood or broken limbs, will you call me?"

"Write your number down, and I'll keep a discreet watch on things from my porch."

"Thank you." Kiersten wrote her phone number on a pad next to a phone that was actually hooked to the wall. She ran her fingers over the long curling cord. "I haven't seen one of these in *years*."

"Your Johnny and little Bella think I have a time machine in my kitchen."

"You do."

"I have one of those cell phones, too, like everyone else." Lillian made a disparaging gesture with a chocolate chip cookie. "But I'm always losing it. And I forget to charge it. But you can't lose a phone that's attached to the wall."

"See you tomorrow morning. And thank you, Lillian. For everything."

Lillian smiled. "That's what neighbors are for."

Chapter Eighty-Two

PIPER

They parked at the end of a quiet street in Old Town, near the entrance to the cemetery, and gently pushed against the wrought iron gates. Piper squinted up at the cloudless blue sky as the gates opened silently on ancient but well-oiled hinges. A perfect fall day, unseasonably warm for November.

She redirected her attention to the kids, roving through the cemetery with notebooks and pencils, searching for the tombstone of Cavan Boa, a Revolutionary War veteran who found his place in history as George Washington's tailor, and Pierre La Croix, a drummer boy from the French and Indian War who eventually joined the American Revolution.

Next door to the cemetery, on the other side of an ancient brick wall, children laughed and shrieked during recess at St. Margaret's, the local Catholic school. Piper smiled. It seemed appropriate somehow, for life and death to coexist side by side.

Lillian sat in a lawn chair, absorbing the autumn sunshine. The kids ran back and forth to show her their historical discoveries.

Piper shaded her eyes with her hand and gazed across the cemetery, past the beautiful stone angel at the entrance and toward Kiersten, who stood in front of a headstone.

Suddenly Kiersten slumped to her knees.

Piper sucked air into her lungs as the darkest part of her mind manufactured a thousand terrifying scenarios. Sniper. Bomb. Heart attack. Seizure. Sinkhole. Snake bite. Mad dog. Murder hornet.

Her legs worked like pistons as she sprinted across the cemetery, heart throbbing inside her chest, her ears, her skull. She skidded to a stop beside Kiersten.

"What's wrong?" she puffed. "Are you okay?"

Kiersten looked up, tears streaming down her face. "I found Dottie."

Chapter Eighty-Three

KIERSTEN

She reached out and touched the moss-covered indentations on the large white stone.

In Loving Memory
of
Dorothy Marie Davis
September 5, 1946–October 8, 1965

Piper laid a hand on her shoulder. "Look." She pointed at the two stones flanking Dottie's. Marie Anderson and Gerald Anderson, Dottie's parents.

"Her dad died two years later," Piper said, kneeling beside her. Rosamund joined them, sitting cross-legged on the other side of Kiersten.

Kiersten scrubbed her hands across her cheeks. All the things she didn't want to believe about human nature, about greed and desperation and selfishness, settled over her like a shroud. "Look at the death date."

Piper ran her fingers over the engraving. "October 8, 1965."

Kiersten's eyes burned as a fresh round of tears trickled down her cheeks. "Same date as the last diary entry."

Rosamund's shoulders slumped. "He really did it. He killed her."

"So what do we do now?" Kiersten asked, voice raw. Once, as a child, she'd become briefly separated from her family in the Boundary Waters of Northern Minnesota, surrounded by trees, with no idea which direction led to safety. She felt that way again now. Lost. Surrounded by dangers she couldn't see.

Piper rubbed her hands over her face, exhaustion etched into the lines around her mouth, across her forehead. "It's a sixty-year-old cold case, except it's not even a case, because everyone assumed she died in childbirth. We could go to the police, but it's not enough. We need more."

"More what?" Rosamund spit the words into the air, each syllable laced with anger.

Kiersten put her arm around Rosamund's shoulder, and Rosamund clutched her hand, blinking back tears. She suddenly realized how much they all loved Dottie, in different ways and for different reasons.

"More *information*," Piper said with a frustrated shrug. "From someone in that family. Aspen, Trey, Chip. Someone other than Margaret and Richard must know what happened back in 1965. We just need to figure out who."

Kiersten was silent for a moment. "Dottie knows."

"Yes, but we can't just summon the Ghost of Dottie to come forward and tell us what happened," Piper said, angrily plucking at a blade of grass.

"We need to read her last entry again." Kiersten rose abruptly, brushing the dirt from her knees. "Dottie left us a clue. And we need to go to that party and find it."

Chapter Eighty-Four

PIPER

The moms sat in Piper's dining room, preparing to leave for the Influencer's party while the kids made themselves peanut butter and jelly sandwiches in the kitchen. They'd temporarily relocated the cafeteria to Piper's house so the kids could keep Travis company while he slept in his crate.

Piper removed her feet from the uncomfortable taupe-colored heels she planned to wear to the party and wiggled her toes.

There was a reason law enforcement officers didn't wear heels. What if they managed to get into Richard and Margaret's basement and Chip pulled a gun and demanded the diaries? What if she needed to tackle someone?

Kiersten picked up the diary sitting on the table while Piper applied a Band-Aid to her heel. These damn shoes always produced blisters.

"Let's read her final entry again," Piper said.

Kiersten read the last sentence. *"But if Dickie succeeds in killing me, I will leave a clue, buried in the past, leading to the truth."*

"A metaphor?" Rosamund asked.

Kiersten shook her head. "I think it's literal."

"Literal how?" Rosamund asked.

"Lillian told me a lot of the fallout shelters had dirt floors because it was cheaper. I think Dottie buried something in the floor," Kiersten said.

"So we just have to find the nuclear-fallout shelter under Richard and Margaret's garage," Piper said.

"Right." Kiersten nodded.

"And then we just have to get inside and dig up the floor," Rosamund said.

Kiersten's face fell. "Well. Yes."

"And we have to do that without letting them know we're doing it," Piper added.

Kiersten looked crestfallen. "Look, I didn't say it would be easy. I just said this is what we need to do next."

Piper sighed, then froze, arms in midair. She was about to run her fingers through her hair, as she always did when frustrated. But she couldn't do that today, because Caitlin had fixed her hair with hairspray. She wasn't allowed to touch it.

Instead, she lowered her arms and ran her sweating palms down the side of her blue shantung silk sheath dress. This was her baby shower, bridal shower, dance-recital, and kindergarten-graduation dress, because these were the only occasions that caused her to pull it reluctantly from her closet. But those were spring events. It was November now. Shouldn't her outfit be more autumnal?

"I think you look lovely," Kiersten said, as though these wardrobe insecurities were written across her forehead in lipstick.

"That's because you've never seen me in anything but yoga pants and a sweatshirt." She curled her toes inside her taupe pumps. "I *hate* wearing clothes like this."

But it wasn't just the outfit making her uncomfortable. It was her conscience too. She did dangerous things for a living. It was part of the job description. But she'd never forgive herself if something happened to Kiersten and Rosamund.

Piper glanced at Rosamund, who looked stunning in a full-skirted, knee-length purple dress.

Then she double-checked the safety and tucked her Glock, and a knife, into her purse. "You both look fantastic . . . but . . . I think you guys should stay here. I'll go snoop around and report back."

"Absolutely not," Rosamund said emphatically.

"Look," Piper said. "They know we have the diaries. They know we've read to the end. They know we've probably figured out what happened to Dottie. They have to be getting desperate. And desperate people do . . . dangerous . . . things."

Kiersten shook her head vehemently. "One of us needs to distract Richard and Margaret while the other person searches their basement. One of us needs to question Aspen and be a lookout. You can't do this alone."

"I don't know." Piper frowned as they moved from the dining room into the kitchen. "I really think you guys should stay home with the kids."

"No!" eight kids shouted with one voice as they turned to look at their mothers with mutinous expressions.

"You *promised* that Matthew and Guinevere and Caitlin could be in charge of us for a *whole hour*," Bella said in a deeply aggrieved voice.

"And we promise not to leave the cul-de-sac, no matter what," Olivia said.

"And we won't turn on the stove," Johnny added.

"And we won't fight," Caitlin promised.

"And in case of a catastrophic injury, we will start the breathing, stop the bleeding, protect the wound, and treat for shock," Guinevere recited.

Guinevere had paid very close attention to Kiersten's first aid demonstrations. Piper suspected she wanted to be prepared should she ever be called upon to compete in the Hunger Games, play Quidditch, or enter a military academy for dragon riders.

"We won't open the door if a stranger rings the bell," Matthew promised.

"We won't open any packages," James said.

"We won't shoot Nerf guns in the house," Johnny added. "Only the backyard."

"If we need anything, we'll ask Lillian next door or Miles," Luke said, reciting yet another rule from the list Piper had given them an hour earlier.

"We won't let Travis out of his crate until you come home, even though it seems really mean to keep him locked up," Bella said.

"And we will stop, drop, and roll if we accidentally immolate ourselves," Matthew added. "But that won't happen, because we will *not* play with matches."

"I think they've got this," Kiersten said, glancing at Piper. "We will literally be down the block. For an hour. We have cell phones. They can call us."

"Caitlin, Matthew, and Guinevere are very 'sponsible thirteen-year-olds," Bella added earnestly.

Rosamund smiled. "I think they'll be fine."

"Okay. Okay." Piper raised her hands in surrender. She couldn't fight the mothers *and* the kids. "Just be *good.* You know how I—"

"Worry," all the kids said in unison.

She gave the group a sheepish smile. "Fine. I am now turning my default setting to semi-relaxed."

Caitlin rolled her eyes. "Mom. You came from the factory without that setting."

She rolled her eyes back at Caitlin, who giggled and trouped into the backyard with the other kids to play Red Light, Green Light, Dynamite, Boom, a retro game from Rosamund's childhood that they had appropriated.

"Let's get this over with." Piper lifted her chin, forcefully expelling from her mind the ten thousand worst-case scenarios housed there, involving everything from kidnapping to natural gas explosions.

Kiersten ran next door to her own house and stashed the diary in the bag of birdseed. Then they headed down the sidewalk toward Aspen's house as Piper tried to ignore the fact that her feet already hurt.

Every time she wore these shoes, she regretted it. And yet every time she wore this dress, she wore these shoes because they looked nice.

If doing the same thing over and over again and expecting a different result was the definition of insanity, then high-heeled shoes were proof of mental instability.

Her eyes narrowed at the long line of cars parked up and down Beaverbrook Lane as she minced forward in her heels. So much for Chip's fears that no one would show up for Aspen's party.

A burst of anxiety knifed at her gut, driving away petty concerns about her clothes, her hair, her damn shoes.

Just because you're paranoid doesn't mean they aren't out to get you.

Someone had even parked their Mercedes in front of the fire hydrant due to the scarcity of spaces.

"Let's hope the kids don't play with matches," Rosamund muttered under her breath.

Piper gripped her purse, feeling the comforting outline of the handgun stashed inside. Then they climbed the steps, walked through the already open door, and entered the Influencer's house.

Chapter Eighty-Five

KIERSTEN

Kiersten suddenly felt as though she'd been thrust into an advertisement for something she was not qualified to sell. Hipness, maybe. Or youth. Or cellulite-free thighs.

Young women wandered through the house, teetering in impossibly high heels, while cell phones recorded each step, raised above the gathering by long skinny arms or with selfie sticks, snapping photos of everything . . . the buffet, the other guests, the balloons spilling around the fireplace mantle, teapots filled with flowers, a young woman dressed like the Mad Hatter, and another like the Queen of Hearts.

Small groups posed for pictures, knees bent, lips puckered, cheeks sucked inward. And on the backside of the house in a white tent, she spotted Aspen wearing a blue dress with a white apron, her long blond hair held back with a headband, a picture-perfect Alice in Wonderland.

A waiter appeared holding a silver tray filled with champagne flutes containing a red liquid. A little tag hung from each flute with the words *Drink me* spelled out in Edwardian script.

"Champagne punch?" he asked.

Kiersten immediately grabbed one and took a long sip. Rosamund and Piper did the same.

"This is *good*," she whispered. Like Kool-Aid, with a kick.

She cast a furtive glance at the woman standing beside her in a short, low-cut Queen of Hearts dress and instantly felt out of place. Her own dress, her favorite, purchased a few years ago at Ann Taylor for a Rural Hospitals Medicaid Reimbursement conference in St. Cloud, Minnesota, suddenly felt dowdy, like something her grandmother would wear to church. During Lent.

It was as though she'd traveled through time and space and had somehow become a freshman in high school again, a freshman who had wandered into a party with all the cool seniors.

But unlike high school, the cool kids here were cool not because they were old, but because they were young.

She raised her flute and took another sip as her gaze darted around a room filled with unfamiliar faces. Her heart sank down into her sensible shoes. She'd lost Rosamund and Piper. They were probably making small talk with George and Amal Clooney. Or a lesser Kardashian.

She drained her champagne glass and grabbed a second one from a tray offered by a waiter who magically appeared at exactly the right moment.

So far this party was terrible. The punch, however, was terrific.

But she wasn't here to have fun. She was on a *mission*, like Trixie Belden, her favorite literary sleuth. She just needed to find Aspen. Ask questions. Figure out if Grammy and Grampy were here or at home.

Craning her neck, she spotted her target in the center of a little group taking selfies beside an archway made from giant playing cards. Aspen's eyes widened when she saw Kiersten. She excused herself from the other guests and came forward.

"It's a *really* lovely party," Kiersten said, suddenly aware of a slight difficulty in pronouncing the word *really*. "Guess you didn't have to worry about *numbers*."

Aspen frowned, although absolutely no wrinkles appeared on her Botoxed forehead as she did so. "What do you mean?"

"Your father-in-law." She gestured in the direction of Chip's house with her champagne flute. "He said you were *concerned* . . . that nobody would *show up*."

It suddenly seemed very important to *emphasize* all the *words*.

"He asked us to *come by* and . . . *make sure* you had a *full house*."

"Really?"

Kiersten nodded emphatically. Then she frowned. "Wait. So you didn't . . . *invite* us?"

"Um. This is like . . . *so awkward*." Aspen wrinkled her nose in adorable embarrassment, like Cinderella slipping her foot into the glass slipper her ugly stepsisters couldn't cram onto their enormous feet. "I actually didn't ask him to invite you. But I'm, like, *so glad* you came anyway."

Kiersten's mouth went dry as a trickle of fear slid down her spine.

Chip lied.

With effort, she managed to re-reorganize her face into a mask of polite nonchalance. "Is this a *special occasion*?"

"I'm trying to produce a lot of cool content right now while we're in negotiations for this HGTV show. I figured everyone loves Alice in Wonderland, right?"

"It's a *great* idea for a party," Kiersten said with a somewhat wobbly smile. She was supposed to ask her something. Something important. But it was so hard to *focus*.

"Yeah. Super-cool visuals. Anyway, I've gotta circulate, but thanks so much for coming. Did Rosamund and um . . . what's her name again?"

"Piper?"

"That's right. Piper. Are they here too?"

"They're here too," Kiersten repeated, working hard to smile through the layers of worry building inside her gut with each word Aspen spoke.

"Are Grammy and Grampy here?" she asked, articulating each syllable with fierce concentration.

Aspen shook her head. "Grammy's been under the weather lately. She hasn't left the house much since the Harvest Festival. It's such a bummer. I made her *the cutest* Queen of Hearts costume."

She hasn't left the house much since the Harvest Festival. Since the day she and Richard read Dottie's diary.

"I'm *really* sorry to hear that," Kiersten said, slurring slightly.

"I'm sure she'll be up and around soon," Aspen said. "Anyway, I need to mingle, but thanks again so much for dropping by. And sorry about the confusion. I'll send a personal invite next time. Enjoy the punch," she added with a smile, "since you have the luxury of walking home."

Kiersten nodded, then clenched her champagne flute so hard her knuckles turned white.

Was Margaret in danger too? Was Richard planning to kill her the same way he'd killed Dottie?

A waiter appeared beside her and offered another glass of punch. It was like he had a sixth sense and knew exactly when her glass was empty.

She grabbed it and took a short sip. She had to find Piper and Rosamund.

Chapter Eighty-Six

LILLIAN

Lillian sat on her front porch and pulled the blanket around her waist a little tighter. It would be Thanksgiving soon, too cold to sit out here in the afternoons. She'd have to take a break until the warm weather returned in the spring.

It had been lovely today, at the cemetery with the kids. A nice outing. They'd had cookies at her house afterward, where she told them stories about George Washington's dogs.

She was about to rise from her chair and go inside when her arms and legs began to tingle.

"Walter . . . I feel . . . funny," she called to her dead husband.

She tried to move her leg . . . but she couldn't . . . because it had gone numb . . .

Then she began to sweat, profusely.

This didn't make sense. It was autumn, and chilly out here.

She suddenly felt as weak as a newborn kitten. She slipped from her chair and crumpled to the floor.

An excruciating pain flashed through her skull. She squeezed her eyes shut against the late-afternoon sunlight.

Then she heard voices coming from next door.

Help me! she cried out over and over again. *I'm right here. Help me!*

But she couldn't make her lips move. Couldn't push the words out.

Voices again. In the yard. Next door.

"Hey, kids, I've got a treat for you."

A man's voice.

Her heart hammered inside her rebellious body. Who was this man talking to the kids? Where was Kiersten? And Piper and Rosamund? Where were the *mothers*?

"A few weeks ago your moms asked if I could give you a tour of the new house we're building. Unfortunately it wasn't safe then, with all the work going on. But we've hit a lull in the building process while we wait for the windows to come in. So you guys can come over now and learn all about construction work."

Now she remembered. *This* was why she was sitting outside. The mothers were just down the street. At Aspen's house. She was supposed to keep an eye on things. Protect them. *Keep them safe.*

"We can go inside?" a little boy asked. Her heart softened. Little Johnny. So much like her youngest son. George. Curious George. Remember those books, about a monkey and a man in a yellow hat . . .

Stop it, Lillian. *Listen.*

Her mind felt clumsy . . . like a boat. A big boat . . . in the water . . . unwieldy . . . Walter, help me turn it. Help me turn the boat so I can listen . . .

"That's right," the man said. "I'll meet you there in ten minutes. Just go inside and wait. I've got the architectural plans so you guys can see what it'll look like when it's all done."

No. No. No. Don't leave the yard. Don't do it.

The boat started to turn again . . . to drift in another direction . . .

Help me, Walter. Help me warn them . . .

Tears of frustration rolled down her cheeks as she whimpered and tried again and again to cry out, to push the words out of her mind and into her throat, through her mouth, into the open air.

But she couldn't.

The boat turned again . . . and turned again . . . swirling under the sky-blue sky . . .

Chapter Eighty-Seven

PIPER

Piper glanced at her watch and set her empty champagne flute on a small side table. A waiter immediately appeared at her side and offered another glass.

She took it and scanned the room, holding the drink like a prop. She'd been nodding and smiling so long her face hurt, as she stood on the periphery of little groups, sipping champagne punch and pretending to be interested in conversations about algorithms, makeup artists, clothing brands she'd never heard of, which influencers had agents and which ones didn't, the best selfie sticks, and lighting tricks to reduce neck shadows.

They'd been here for almost an hour. She'd made a loop of the party, twice. No sign of Chip, Grammy, or Richard. Which meant the old couple must be at home, probably watching TV next to their fallout shelter in the basement. No sign of the "childcare" Chip had promised either.

For some reason, she found this lie more troubling than all the others. She clenched her jaw and eyed the exit. They'd been here long enough.

She glanced across the room to where Rosamund seemed to be having better luck. Someone had discovered that one of her books was trending on BookTok, and she'd become the center of a little group of women who listened with rapt attention as she discussed her real-life experiences with the extremely handsome actor who'd played Bold Ragnar in her *Shield-Maiden of Stamendahl* Netflix series.

She raised her glass, took a sip, and made her way to Rosamund's side.

"Let's get out of here," she whispered.

Rosamund nodded and slipped away from the little group. "I feel like I'm 107 years old. In fact, I think we are the only people in this entire room old enough to remember 9/11."

"Where's Kiersten?"

"At the buffet."

They made their way into the dining room, where they found Kiersten, standing in the corner stuffing mini crab cakes into her mouth.

"Did you . . . have any luck?" Piper asked, suddenly feeling a little unsteady on her feet. That punch was *strong*. Plus high heels and alcohol were always a bad idea.

Kiersten swallowed another crab cake. "Grammy is at home . . . she's been *sick* since the Harvest Festival," she added in a loud whisper, putting air quotes around the word *sick*.

Piper's eyes widened. What was she talking about? And was Kiersten *tipsy*?

"These crab cakes are *so good*." Kiersten grabbed another one from the buffet and stuffed it into her mouth. "You should eat some too," she mumbled with her mouth full, pointing at the table with her napkin.

"I'm ready to go home," Piper said. "I think you are too."

Kiersten nodded gravely, then leaned in closer as though she were about to impart an important secret. "The crab cakes are excellent, but this party *sucks*."

Piper and Rosamund exchanged a look. Piper gently took Kiersten's elbow and steered her toward the foyer. But she found it unexpectedly difficult to walk in a straight line.

What the hell was in that punch? Had someone slipped a roofie into her drink at an Alice in Wonderland tea party?

They opened the front door and stepped onto the porch. A flash of light in her peripheral vision made her turn her head in the direction of the half-constructed home next to Richard and Margaret's house.

Flashing lights.

Police cars.

Then she saw them. Through the skeletal beams of the home under construction, deep inside the structure, engulfed in shadows.

The kids.

She ripped off her high heels, leaped off the porch, and ran.

Chapter Eighty-Eight

KIERSTEN

It took about half a second for the fog of alcohol shrouding her brain to lift as Kiersten pulled her addled thoughts together.

Something is wrong.

Piper ran down the sidewalk, barefoot, hair streaming behind her, oddly elegant with her athletic gait and long strides, toward the flashing police cars in front of the half-constructed home.

She squinted. Through the beams, inside the house, a flash of red.

Then she knew.

Johnny.

Johnny's entire wardrobe was Minnesota Twins red.

She ripped off her shoes, too, jumped off the porch, and began to run, legs working like pistons, catching up to Piper.

She arrived at the building site, out of breath, sides heaving as Rosamund skidded in beside her a few seconds later.

The house stood on the left side of the lot, near Richard's house, framed, with a roof, beams delineating the eventual rooms, and empty squares awaiting the installation of doors and windows.

Anyone could wander inside, and she knew many of her neighbors had. People were understandably curious. Where would the dining room go? How many bedrooms did it have? But she'd told the kids never to venture onto someone else's property without permission.

Her heart lurched. So why did she hear children's voices coming from inside the half-constructed house?

She entered and squinted into the dim light, following the sound. The house had no electricity yet, and the only light came from the gaping openings where the windows would eventually go.

Suddenly Luke slammed into her, hugging her around the waist. "Mom. We didn't do anything wrong. *Tell them.*"

She rounded the corner and found Chip and Trey Davis talking with two police officers, while the kids stood huddled a few feet away.

"Here they are," Chip Davis said, shooting a look at her, Rosamund, and Piper as they entered a large open space likely designated as the kitchen and family room. "Maybe *they* can explain why their kids are allowed to roam free in the middle of the day, vandalizing building sites when they're supposed to be in 'school.'"

His lip twisted, mocking the word *school*, as his face contorted into a scowl.

Piper scowled back. "What in the hell are you talking about?"

"See for yourself." Trey extended his arm and pointed at the Sheetrock wall where the kitchen cabinets would eventually go.

Kiersten's gaze followed his pointing finger as her stomach plummeted into her shoes.

Lewd pictures. Graffiti. Curse words sprayed across the Sheetrock.

Caitlin gripped Piper's hand. "Mom, we didn't do this."

"Officer, this is obviously a misunderstanding—" Piper began.

"I can smell the alcohol from here," Chip muttered, waving his hand in front of her face.

One of the officers approached Piper.

"Ma'am, are these your children?"

"They are. I mean, some of them are."

"Where are the parents who are supposed to be supervising these kids?" he asked.

Kiersten and Rosamund stepped forward.

"Officer, this is clearly some kind of a mix-up—" Rosamund began.

"Please, ma'am." The officer raised his hand. "If you could just remain quiet while we try to determine what happened here."

"It's obvious what happened here," Trey said, coming forward to stand beside his father. "These moms are day drinking *again*, leaving their kids completely unsupervised. They do it all the time."

Piper's nostrils flared. "That's a lie and you know it."

Kiersten's mouth dropped open. "We were at *your house*," she protested. "At a party hosted by *your wife*."

"These kids are never in school," Chip said, throwing his hands up in apparent frustration. "They roam the cul-de-sac day and night like a band of hoodlums, terrorizing their neighbors, leaving weird things on people's doorsteps. Breaking into people's homes. They noticed our building site is unattended today, so they came in with their spray paint and vandalized the place."

"But you invited us to come over." Matthew lifted his chin, eyes blazing with indignation. "You *told us* to meet you here."

Trey narrowed his eyes. "You're a cool liar for someone so young."

The officer glanced over at Trey and Chip. "I think you two can head home now. We'll follow up with you later."

"This is our property, officer," Chip protested. "And we will not leave our property while these kids—"

"I understand that, sir," the officer said, patient but with an authoritative edge to his voice. "But I need to ask these kids some questions, and your presence isn't helpful right now. We'll handle things from here. And we'll be in touch shortly."

Chip turned on his heel with a derisive snort, muttering something about his tax dollars at work. Trey scowled at the officer, then followed his father out of the house.

Matthew turned to his mother when they left, a panicked expression on his young face. "Mom, we're telling the truth. We didn't vandalize anything. It was like this when we got here."

Kiersten looked into his eyes and saw the truth. Her kids would never do something like this. And suddenly she knew the phrase *her kids* included Rosamund's and Piper's girls too. They were *all* her kids.

She pulled him into a hug. "I know that, honey. Everything's gonna be fine." Then to her mortification, she *hiccupped.*

The officer looked over at Kiersten. "Ma'am, have you been drinking?"

"Drinking? I . . . well, yes, actually, but I've only had a couple . . ."

The officers exchanged a glance. "Maybe we need to get social services involved here," one muttered to the other.

Kiersten twisted the skin on her upper arm. A nightmare. This had to be a nightmare, and if she just pinched herself hard enough, she'd wake up.

Pain prickled her flesh, yet everything remained the same.

She already had a black mark next to her name after the incident on the Turnpike.

What if they took her kids away?

Her knees went weak, and she gripped a sawhorse for balance, trapped in the worst kind of nightmare.

The kind you have when you're wide awake.

She'd tried to give her children what she had growing up. A childhood filled with love and freedom, with enough space to read and explore, to become bored, to tinker and experiment, to learn independence by roaming the neighborhood with a troop of other kids for companionship and protection.

Would her children be ripped from her arms to grow up in foster care as a result?

"We need to ask these children some questions." One of the officers bent down to speak with Bella. "Does your mommy ever leave you home alone?"

Kiersten held her breath as Bella looked up at the officer and shook her head. "No. But sometimes she locks Travis in a cage. I don't like it when she does that. Travis doesn't like it either."

He exchanged a glance with the other officer as bile coated Kiersten's throat.

Piper took a step forward, "Officer, you don't understand—"

"Ma'am. Another outburst and I'll ask you to leave."

"Where do you go to school?" the officer asked, turning back to Bella.

"The Beaverbrook Academy for Inquiring Minds."

"Where's that?" he asked.

"In Mrs. Cleaver's dining room. It's home school. But Mr. Reggie does PE. And Miss Valentina reads us stories. Mr. Miles helps us find fox poop. He's from *England*, and Mary Poppins is his cousin. We call that science."

"What else does your mommy do?"

"One day we had worms in our house," Bella said.

"We had cockroaches," Johnny put in helpfully. "And we go to the cemetery sometimes and look for dead people."

"Does your mommy ever drink?" the officer asked, turning back to Bella.

She nodded. "She drinks *a lot* . . ."

"I see."

"She calls it her 'cup of ambition.'"

"What does your mommy like to drink?"

"K-Cups mostly," Bella said. "She drinks *a lot* of those."

The officer lifted his eyebrows. "Your mother drinks a lot of . . . coffee?"

She nodded. "She puts a whole scoop of sugar inside her coffee, but she won't let me have a whole scoop of sugar on my strawberries. I don't think that's fair."

"I see. Does she drink anything else?"

"Water. She says it's important to stay hy-rated."

"Does your mother ever forget about you when she's doing other things?"

Johnny nodded. "My mom forgotted me at a truck stop once. The patrol people brought me home."

"Tell me more about Travis," the officer said. "How old is he?"

"He's like . . . just born," Bella said. "He's still a puppy."

"Wait. Travis is a *dog*?"

"'Course, silly," she said with a little giggle. "You don't lock *people* in cages. And his real name is Travis Kelce Mondello. After Taylor's fee-onshay."

"Where's your daddy?" the officer asked.

"We never know where Daddy is," she said with a cheerful shrug. "He's with Deborah. The secretary."

"His secretary?" the officer asked.

She nodded. "I think so. He travels with her. They go *all over* together."

"My daddy is gone with his secretary a lot too," Johnny added helpfully. "They go to Oklahoma mostly. Or Kansas."

"The secretary of *agriculture*," Piper cried out. "And Deborah Templeton. The secretary of *state*. My husband is a DS agent."

The officer glanced over at her. "What's his name?"

"Brendan Mondello."

The officer's stern face betrayed a hint of a smile. "I know Brendan Mondello."

"You do?"

"Sure. I did a stint in DS, too, till my wife threatened to divorce me because I was never home. So I switched to local law enforcement."

"Then you understand—"

Suddenly Valentina and Reggie burst into the building.

"This is all my fault," Valentina bellowed dramatically. "I am an addict. And *bingo* is my drug of choice."

The officer sighed. "And you are?"

"Valentina Lucia Rossellini. And I promised to watch these children today, but instead I left them unattended because the jackpot at the Blue Diamond Bingo Emporium has reached $10,000."

"That's right," Reggie nodded. "And I had to haul her ass out of there *again*. Shameful. Truly shameful."

The officer rubbed his forehead. "I'm sorry. Who are you?"

"He's our PE teacher," Johnny said.

Reggie extended his hand to the officers. "Reggie Spade, United States Marine Corps. Retired. Nice to meet you. Kids, get into formation."

The kids immediately lined up in two neat rows and saluted. The sound of feet stomping on plywood echoed from the entrance, and then Garrett and Brendan rushed in.

"Honey, I'm so sorry I was late getting home to watch the kids. You told me how important it was for me to be home by four o'clock today to help watch the kids, but traffic was terrible on the Fourteenth Street Bridge, and I just couldn't get here in time."

Kiersten mustered a smile. Someone had called the cavalry, and they'd ridden to the rescue, armed with semi-plausible excuses.

"Same here," Brendan said, casting an apologetic look at Piper. "I'm really sorry I'm late, honey."

One of the officers looked up at Brendan. "Brendan Mondello?"

"Sam Elridge?" Brendan took his outstretched hand as the officer slapped him on the back. "Hey, man, great to see you again."

Suddenly Miles strode through the doorway and joined the group.

"Let me guess," the other officer said, lifting an eyebrow. "You promised to watch the kids too?"

"No, actually," Miles said. "But I can provide this."

"What is it?" the officer asked.

"Video." Miles came forward with his phone. "From the wildlife cameras I've placed throughout our neighborhood. The time stamp is in the corner. If you look here, you can see Chip Davis approaching the children, right here, between their home and Lillian's house, about an hour ago. You can see him gesturing to the house where we are currently standing."

"Okay."

"And if you rewind . . ." He moved his finger across his phone. "If you rewind, you find this taking place around 2:00 a.m. this morning."

They crowded around Miles's phone. Kiersten squinted at the image of a tall person in black, entering the partially constructed home, carrying a can of spray paint, his features obscured by the hood on his dark sweatshirt, and a baseball cap.

"Excuse me, officer," Matthew said, his voice authoritative but respectful.

The officer looked over at him. "Yes, young man?"

"If you look at the very beginning of that video, you can see our neighbor, Lillian Landry, in the corner of the frame, sitting out on her front porch. She would have overheard the entire conversation. I'm sure she can vouch for the fact that he invited us to come over here."

"I'll go get her," Rosamund said.

The officer ran a hand through his hair and exhaled loudly. "You guys need to know something."

Kiersten's eyebrows rose in alarm. "What?"

"This isn't the first call we've gotten about the kids on Beaverbrook Lane."

Piper looked stunned. "It's not?"

He shook his head. "We've been getting anonymous calls for the last couple months from someone in this neighborhood, claiming kids are roaming around unsupervised, terrorizing the neighbors. But every time we've come over to check things out, we find them jumping on the trampoline, or playing tag in the backyard, or shooting basketball in the driveway, or doing PE out front with Reggie here, or sitting on the front porch, talking to the old lady across the street. We realized these reports were unfounded, and we asked the person to stop. And then today they called us again and accused the kids of vandalizing this construction site."

"Do you have the name of the person making these calls?" Piper asked.

"Not until today, when Chip called, and gave us his name and met us here. But it's a pretty good bet Chip is behind the other calls too. If I were you all, I'd keep a close watch on your kids. Someone is unhappy with what you're doing here."

"So you're not going to call social services?" Kiersten asked, holding her breath.

"I think we'd all be lucky to have this many good people looking out for our kids. Just watch your backs, okay?"

"Thanks for the heads-up," Brendan said. "We will."

Kiersten raised her face to the open beams in the ceiling and said a prayer of gratitude. Then a scream from outside pulled her back to the present.

"Ambulance! We need an ambulance! *Now.*"

The officers reacted first, running outside the half-finished house and across the street. Kiersten followed behind them and looked across the cul-de-sac where Rosamund knelt beside Lillian's crumpled body.

Chapter Eighty-Nine

PIPER

Piper slumped beside Kiersten in the hard plastic chairs in the waiting room at Alexandria Hospital. The air around her held a faintly antiseptic smell, heavy and oppressive with the anticipation of bad news.

When the paramedics had loaded Lillian into the back of the ambulance, she and Kiersten jumped into Reggie's car to follow Lillian to the hospital. Through the passenger window, she'd watched Brendan scoop Bella into his arms. The little girl sobbed into her father's shoulder as the ambulance pulled away. Then she opened and closed her little fist, waving goodbye to the old lady who'd taught her how to make elegant ladies in ballgowns out of hollyhock blooms and toothpicks.

Blinking back tears, Piper had watched Garrett and Brendan load all the kids into her SUV and Kiersten's minivan.

We're taking everyone to Chuck E. Cheese for dinner Brendan had texted.

She'd grimaced but hadn't argued. This choice of dining establishment guaranteed they'd all have norovirus and strep throat within a week. But it might help distract the kids from the hospitalization of the woman who'd become their beloved living history lesson.

Kiersten had called Lillian's son on the way to the hospital, and now Lillian's local children and grandchildren filled the critical care waiting room upstairs, waiting to see if the eighty-seven-year-old woman would emerge from her stroke diminished, or if she would somehow remain the funny, independent person her family adored and her neighbors had come to love.

She and Kiersten had moved downstairs to the main waiting room to give Lillian's family privacy as they waited for news from the doctor. Reggie would be back any minute to give them a ride home.

Piper sat in her chair, shoulders slumped in defeat.

She had done everything in her power to keep her daughters safe and happy. She'd pulled them out of school. Out of all their activities. She'd become an actual *teacher*, spending her entire day with her kids.

And yet she'd failed. Repeatedly. Epically. Because her kids were still not safe. And neither were Kiersten's. They could have been arrested today and charged with vandalizing their neighbor's property. Social services could have gotten involved, enmeshing her family in an invasive investigation, with the threat of removal and foster care.

All because she'd failed at her one and only job. *Protecting her kids.*

She ran her hands over her face. Maybe it was time to cry uncle. Time to pack up and move. To start fresh with a new address. One that Hawkeye Slaughter didn't know. One that Chip and Trey Davis and Alex Orlov didn't know either. They could purchase a different house and put the title in her in-laws' name. Hide their identity. Start over in a new neighborhood, a different suburb.

She glanced at Kiersten. Her neighbor. Her friend. Her best friend.

The friend she'd have to leave behind.

Kiersten's mascara had run, streaking her face, clumping her lower lashes. Her blond hair lay flat and lank around her shoulders as she stared at the wall, blue eyes glassy.

"You look like the Shield-Maiden of Stamendahl after losing the battle of Stiklestad," Piper said gently, suddenly aware that she had no other female friends to whom she could make such an honest and completely unflattering statement.

Kiersten turned to her with a thousand-yard stare. "What *the hell* is the battle of Stiklestad?"

"I don't know exactly." She shrugged. "Something Rosamund was teaching the kids about the other day in history."

Kiersten raised a weary eyebrow. "Well. You look like a postapocalyptic Talbots model."

"I'm going to take that as a compliment," Piper said, sitting up a little straighter.

An exhausted but comfortable silence fell between them.

"We've been successful failures," Kiersten finally said.

Piper turned to look at her. "What do you mean?"

"The Experiment worked. We've created a community. A village. Our kids were happy. I was happy. We were surrounded by loving people who have our best interests at heart. And those people came through today, in a huge way."

Piper rubbed her temples, trying to ward off a colossal headache. "With the notable exception of Chip and Trey."

Kiersten swallowed. "If Brendan hadn't known that cop . . . if Miles hadn't produced footage that exonerated the kids . . ."

Her voice trailed off. Piper squeezed her hand, letting her know she didn't need to speak the unspeakable.

Kiersten shook her head, blinking back tears. "I just wanted peace and freedom. And instead, I have *this*."

She gestured at the hospital waiting room and all it represented.

"Maybe it's time to go back to Minnesota." Her voice was flat. Defeated.

Piper said nothing. The giant lump in her throat made it impossible to speak.

Kiersten blew her nose into a disintegrating tissue. "This situation obviously calls for chocolate." She rose from her chair and grabbed some cash from her enormous purse. "You want anything from the vending machine?"

Piper shook her head. "I'll watch your bag."

Kiersten tossed her phone into her purse and slumped down the hall.

As soon as she disappeared around the corner, Piper's phone rang. Her shoulder muscles tensed as she picked up the call.

"Brendan?"

"You need to come home."

The undertone of despair in his voice sent her stomach plunging. She dug her nails into her palms and fought to remain calm. "What's wrong?"

"We just got back from Chuck E. Cheese."

"And?"

He took a deep breath. "And . . . you know how it looks after the DEA tosses a house, looking for drugs?"

Her mouth went dry. "Yeah."

"That's how our house looks right now."

Her brain froze, unable to process the words coming through the phone. At the end of this long, dramatic, terrifying, exhausting day, her mind had finally shut down. Stopped working. Gone on strike.

"I don't understand," she finally managed.

"Wait. Garrett's at the front door. Hold on."

She massaged her forehead and tried to think.

Hawkeye Slaughter?

No. Chip and Trey Davis. *Searching for the diaries.*

An indistinct rumble of voices came through the phone, but she couldn't make out what they were saying. Then Brendan came back on the line.

"Same thing at Garrett and Kiersten's house. Someone ransacked their place too."

She shook her head, trying to corral her wild, scattered thoughts.

"How fast can you get home?" he asked.

"Reggie's on his way. Send me pictures. And don't touch anything. Tell Garrett the same thing."

An exasperated sigh came through the phone. "Honey. I know better than to tamper with a crime scene."

"Sorry . . . I know . . . I just . . . make sure Garrett knows that too."

"I already told him. We sent the kids over to Rosamund's. And I just called Sam, the cop who was here earlier today. He's on his way over with a detective. They're gonna want to talk to you. And Kiersten."

"We'll be there as soon as we can," she said and ended the call.

She gnawed on her cuticles, waiting for the ding of an incoming text. Then Kiersten came around the corner carrying a Kit Kat and a Diet Coke.

She took one look at Piper, and her face fell. "Oh no. *Now* what?"

"Do I look that bad?"

"You look horrible." Kiersten sat down beside her and rested a hand on her shoulder. "What's wrong?"

A ping alerted her to a new text message. She looked down at her phone; then she held it up to show Kiersten the picture Brendan had texted.

"This."

Chapter Ninety

KIERSTEN

Kiersten stood in her kitchen, fists curled at her sides as she tried, and failed, to fight back the tears burning her eyes.

The cannisters that had belonged to her great-grandmother lay smashed on the floor, sugar and flour strewn across the hardwood. Yellow stuffing pushed through slashes in her sofa cushions, like exposed flesh from an open wound.

It would take days to clean this up. And thousands of dollars to replace the items the vandals had broken or damaged. They'd left the kids' bedrooms untouched, and most of the basement. But they'd trashed the main floor and the master bedroom.

"I'm sorry about this, ma'am." A female police officer with a sympathetic smile touched her arm before heading for the door. Kiersten nodded, not trusting herself to speak.

It was almost midnight. The detective had left a few minutes ago, and the other two officers were leaving now. They'd dusted for fingerprints but found nothing. The animal who'd done this had worn gloves.

Garrett put his hands on her shoulders and planted a gentle kiss on her forehead. "C'mon. We're not sleeping here tonight."

He led her outside. The crisp November air sent a shiver skittering along her skin as they crossed the street to Rosamund's house.

The moment she'd heard about what happened, Rosamund scooped up the kids, bringing them all over to her house, preventing them from seeing any of the damage, from realizing that bad guys had been inside their home, ripping their things apart.

Now the boys were asleep in Rosamund's basement while the girls slept in Guinevere's room upstairs, an impromptu block-wide slumber party.

Garrett opened the front door without knocking. He and Kiersten made their way through the lamplit foyer to the kitchen on the back-side of the house. Brendan and Piper sat with Valentina and Reggie at a kitchen table spread with a cheerful yellow tablecloth. Rosamund moved around the kitchen, putting food on a tray. And Miles stood at the island, pouring steaming tea into a line of mugs.

"Tea?" Brendan asked with a wry smile. "At a time like this? Maybe we need something a little stronger."

"Tea was *created* for times like this," Miles said as he handed Brendan a cup of chamomile.

"Sorry it's not an elegant charcuterie board." Rosamund leaned over to set a bowl of popcorn and a plate of brownies on the table, along with a bag of Hershey's Kisses, a hunk of cheese, Ritz Crackers, pretzels, and a bunch of grapes. "This is all I have on hand at the moment."

"You obviously haven't been using your *Table of Sustenance* meal-planning workbook," Piper said, her voice bitter.

Kiersten and Garrett squeezed around the backside of the kitchen table to sit on the banquette beside Piper and Brendan.

"Thank you, Rosamund. This is perfect." Kiersten reached for a Ritz Cracker. "I'm starving."

"We have some good news," Reggie said, looking over at Kiersten and Garrett.

"About Lillian?" Garrett asked.

Reggie nodded. "Her son just called. She's awake and alert. Her speech is slurred, but they think it's temporary, and they expect her to make a full recovery. She could be back home by the end of the week."

"Thank God." Kiersten sagged against the banquette in relief.

"We've been talking"—Piper glanced at Garrett and Kiersten—"and we think they must have trashed our houses while we were at that stupid party."

"I can confirm that," Miles said, setting his mug on the table. "I checked my cameras, and one person entered each of your homes right after the kids walked down the street to meet Chip at the house under construction. Both of the intruders wore ball caps and hooded sweatshirts, but they each had a very different build. One was big, sort of hefty. The other skinny. They emerged about twenty minutes later."

"Chip Davis and Trey Davis?" Piper asked.

Miles shook his head. "Chip and Trey were talking to the cops while the person who ransacked your house was still inside."

"That doesn't make sense." Kiersten frowned. "Because the person who broke into our home only took one thing."

"What's missing?" Piper asked.

She lifted her gaze and met Piper's eyes. "Dottie's diaries."

Piper inhaled sharply. "Did you—"

"Yes. I hid them both in the bag of birdseed. And now they're gone."

She watched as Piper exchanged a look with her husband.

"This rules out Hawkeye Slaughter," Brendan said.

Piper nodded. "It had to be Chip and Trey Davis, or someone connected with them. Those diaries have no value for anyone else. And they had to tear our houses apart to find them because we hid them so well."

Kiersten rubbed her hands over her face. "*That's* why he invited us to that stupid party. That's why the waiter kept plying us with drinks. He wanted us to stay as long as possible to buy them time. Aspen didn't even know we were coming."

"That's also why he offered childcare." Rosamund set her mug down with a disgusted clunk. "To get the kids out of the house so they could search it."

"And when we declined, he lured the kids away." Kiersten reached for another brownie.

Piper took a thoughtful sip from her mug. "And that gave him an opportunity to frame the kids, make us look like unfit day drinkers, *and* search our houses."

"I'd bet you my next royalty check they're behind everything that's happened on Beaverbrook Lane," Rosamund said in disgust.

"But why exactly?" Kiersten asked. "What do they gain from all this, *besides* getting their hands on the diaries and covering up Dottie's murder?"

"I can tell you why," Reggie said. "They're trying to force us to sell our houses."

They all looked at Reggie. "What do you mean?" Brendan asked.

"My daughter's been getting calls from Chip over the last couple months. He says he's *concerned* about me." He rolled his eyes. "Says he sometimes finds me wandering the cul-de-sac, looking confused. He said I drove up on the curb the other day and knocked over his mailbox, which is a damn lie. He told my daughter she should think about selling my house and moving me to assisted living . . . before someone gets hurt."

Kiersten's mouth dropped open. "But you're in better shape that I am!"

"I *know*," Reggie said indignantly, spinning his finger in the air. "I'm in better shape than all y'all."

Valentina nodded vigorously. "My son Paolo and my nephew in Milan get emails from Chip. Just last week they got an email saying I am bothering you"—she pointed at Piper and Kiersten—"when you are doing home school. He says I am a pest. A nuisance to my neighbors. And he says this neighborhood is not safe for me and my sister. He says we have crime and vandalism, that Paolo and my nephew should sell our house and find a nice, safe retirement home for us."

Kiersten's mouth went dry. "I heard the same thing from Lillian's son just now at the hospital. He said he'd gotten some concerning phone calls from Chip about his mother and asked if she's a burden to us. Apparently Chip claims he goes over there every day to check on her."

"That's a damn lie. I can tell you that for free," Reggie said indignantly.

Kiersten swallowed a bite of her brownie. "Lillian told me that Trey comes by frequently to ask her about selling her house. And the day of the Harvest Festival, Chip tried to tell me our neighborhood isn't safe, that I should be careful and keep my wits about me."

"So what do we do with this information?" Garrett asked. "I mean, I'm not a cop or a lawyer, but expressing concern about your elderly neighbors isn't against the law. Even if those concerns are actually lies."

Kiersten glanced at the people sitting with her in Rosamund's kitchen. Two hours ago she'd been ready to pack her bags and leave Beaverbrook Lane behind.

But as she looked at her neighbors, she realized she couldn't leave. Not now. These people were more than neighbors. They were *family*. And you didn't abandon family when times got tough.

"But terrorizing and harassing people *is* against the law," Brendan pointed out.

Piper's forehead creased in a deep frown. "Do you remember that story a few years back, about those executives at eBay who harassed a couple by sending them sick things in the mail."

Miles looked at her over the rim of his mug. "I do remember that story."

Kiersten nodded. "They sent things like *cockroaches*."

"And spiders," Rosamund said.

They all looked at each other.

"Those bastards," Reggie whispered.

Kiersten's eyes narrowed. "He's trying to drive us out of our houses so he can tear them all down and build new ones. Like he's doing with those two million-dollar homes he's putting up at the end of the cul-de-sac."

Never in a million years would she have thought of doing something so nefarious to another human being, much less a *neighbor*.

Rosamund frowned. "But Miles hasn't gotten any hissing cockroach deliveries or weird things in his trees."

They all turned to look at Miles. "True," he said, swallowing a sip of tea. "But I'm renting."

"What?" they all asked in unison.

He nodded. "After my wife passed away, I couldn't bear to be in our home. Too many memories. So I sold my house and looked for a rental. I figured eventually I'd buy another place, but I just needed some time first. So I went on Zillow, and I found my house here on Beaverbrook."

"So who actually owns your home?" Kiersten asked.

"It's not a person," Miles said. "It's an LLC."

Piper leaned forward. "What's it called?"

"Dynamo Development Group. Something like that."

Piper pulled out her phone and began typing furiously. Then she held up her screen, showing Miles the logo for Dynamo Moscow, a Russian Premier League soccer team.

"Does this look familiar?" she asked.

He squinted across the table. "It does actually. There's a similar logo on my rental agreement."

Kiersten's head swiveled back and forth between Piper and Miles. "I don't understand."

"Bruno Orlov." Piper gestured with her phone. "He's that shady parent at school, Alex Orlov's dad. When I met with him, he was wearing a Dynamo Moscow soccer jersey. He named his real estate development company after his favorite Russian soccer team, in addition to running some kind of illegal sports-betting operation."

Reggie drummed his fingers on the table thoughtfully. "I've seen that name somewhere before."

He and Kiersten exchanged a look. "Me too."

Piper smiled. "You see it every morning when you run. Dynamo Development Corporation is doing that massive project a couple streets over on Haskel Avenue."

Kiersten's face lit up. "Where they tore down that one old house and they're building six new ones on the same lot."

Piper nodded. "It's right there on the sign. Chip and Trey Davis are listed as his business partners."

Valentina frowned. "I like you all very much, but if they made me a good offer, I would sell. No cockroaches or bloody papers are needed for this. So why go to this *trouble*?"

"Because they don't want to make a good offer," Piper explained, leaning forward. "It eats into their profit margin. And cockroaches and scary notes are cheap. They want to scare us into selling our houses way below market value. Then they turn this whole cul-de-sac into a new housing development with river views."

"If you chop down all the trees," Reggie added.

"That's exactly right." Piper snorted. "If you chop down all the trees."

"And if they price these new homes like the ones going up a few streets over on Haskel . . ." Rosamund began.

"And put multiple houses on each lot . . ." Garrett added.

"They'd make tens of millions of dollars," Brendan concluded with a low whistle.

"And they'd advertise this new development to the Influencer's hundreds of thousands of Instagram followers. And document the whole teardown and rebuild process on her new HGTV show," Piper said.

"Dottie is the wild card," Kiersten said softly. "And now she's come back from the dead to derail the whole project with her diaries."

Piper nodded. "Richard would be arrested. Probably Margaret too. So much for the sweet little old lady who bakes pies in a frilly apron."

"It would destroy Aspen's wholesome trad wife brand if sweet old Grammy on the 'Gram is the pregnant mistress who murdered her husband's first wife," Kiersten said.

"Which would scuttle her HGTV deal," Rosamund added.

There was a moment of silence as they processed this.

"So what do we do?" Garrett asked. "Go to the police?"

Piper exchanged a glance with her husband.

"We need more," Brendan said.

"I agree." Piper nodded. "Without those diaries, we have no evidence of foul play. No murder weapon. No motive. No confession. The police could ask a few questions, but that's it. They need more to build a case and make an arrest."

"Then we have to get those diaries back." Kiersten gripped her mug. "They *prove* that Richard murdered Dottie."

"But he'll destroy them," Rosamund said. "He could be burning them as we speak."

"He'll finish reading them first," Piper argued. "To find out how much we know. That buys us a tiny bit of time."

"We need to get into that nuclear-fallout shelter," Kiersten said, snapping a Ritz Cracker in half. "I *know* Dottie left something for us. Some kind of clue."

Piper gave her a grim nod. "And then we take him down."

"This is even more exciting than bingo," Valentina whispered.

"But, honey"—Brendan put his arm around Piper—"how do we actually get inside their house and do this?"

Piper looked at her neighbors and smiled. "I have an idea."

Chapter Ninety-One

PIPER

Piper stood on her front porch the next morning holding a steaming mug of coffee. She'd come to love Miles, but she doubted she would ever come to share his love of tea.

Kiersten emerged from Rosamund's house across the street and climbed the porch to stand beside her. A belt cinched the waist of her baggy jeans, and her cheeks had no color. Between running with Reggie and the stress of the last few days, she looked like she'd lost weight.

"Are you sure you want to do this?" Piper asked.

Kiersten nodded. "We built something here. And I am not going to let those *bastards* tear it down."

Piper shot her a smile over the rim of her coffee mug. "If you keep using language like that, they're going to revoke your Minnesota Nice badge."

"I don't need my badge at the moment. Because right now, *this* is my home." Kiersten looked over the quiet cul-de-sac as the morning sun climbed over the river, behind the naked trees.

"Amen, sister." Piper clinked Kiersten's mug with her own. "Let's go over the plan again."

"Okay." Kiersten took a deep breath. "The stonemason arrives at noon to give us an estimate on fixing the sign at the entrance to the cul-de-sac. Our husbands lure Richard, Chip, and Trey out to join this meeting. When the Davis men leave their homes, I head over to Richard and Margaret's house to search the fallout shelter in their basement and find the clue Dottie left behind. If I don't find anything there, I go next door and search Chip's house and try to at least recover the diaries he stole so we can go to the police.

"Meanwhile," Kiersten continued, "you're here on the porch, keeping watch. If Chip, Trey, or Richard tries to return to the house while I'm still inside, you'll delay them by accusing them of stealing the diaries. Which they will deny, but the argument will buy me time to get out of the house."

"And Reggie and the kids will be stationed right in the center of the cul-de-sac doing PE," Piper reminded her. "If Richard, Chip, and Trey head back to their houses while you're still inside, the kids will make a racket. And that's your signal to leave."

"*If* I can hear all that noise down in the basement," she added, her voice tight with worry.

"Remember," Piper said, "their door must be *unlocked*. No breaking and entering."

Kiersten nodded. "I knock softly—then I enter and do what needs to be done."

Piper ran her hand over her ponytail. "I still think I should be the one to search the houses."

"We discussed this." Kiersten shook her head. "If I get caught, it's not the end of the world. But if they charge you with trespassing or breaking and entering, you'll never work in law enforcement again."

Piper sighed. "It's not a perfect plan."

Kiersten gave her a weak smile. "But it's the best plan we've got."

Rosamund's front door opened, and the kids ran out of her house and across the street to Kiersten's backyard for "recess" before school started.

The adults had been up until 4:00 a.m. restoring order to the main floor of the Cleaver house so the kids could have school as usual this morning. Though they were starting an hour later than normal, it still felt like a victory to have school today at all.

Garrett, Brendan, Reggie, and Miles planned to spend the morning cleaning up the Mondello house. Hopefully everyone would be able to sleep in their respective homes tonight.

Rosamund crossed the street and waited for them in front of Kiersten's house while Valentina joined them on the sidewalk, clutching her morning cappuccino.

"The Beaverbrook Academy for Inquiring Minds soldiers on," Rosamund said, "even in the midst of drama, upheaval, and cul-de-sac-wide intrigue."

"But it needs one vital element to continue," Valentina said.

Piper frowned. "What?"

"Food," Valentina said. "For lunch. For the children."

Kiersten whacked her own forehead with her palm. "Ugh. I completely forgot. I was going to do a giant Costco run yesterday, but with all the drama and the hospital trip, I completely forgot."

"We also need peanut butter," Valentina said.

"And paper towels," Rosamund added.

"And Goldfish."

"Sorry," Piper said as Kiersten added item number twelve to the Costco list on her phone. "I guess we let ourselves run a little short on supplies. So much for the infallible Table of Sustenance."

Kiersten shot her a tired smile. "I'm actually glad to run to Costco. It'll calm my nerves before our mission. I'll be back before you miss me."

Chapter Ninety-Two

KIERSTEN

Kiersten grabbed her purse and keys from the mudroom, exited the house through the side door, and approached her minivan.

She opened the driver's side door, tossed her phone and keys into her enormous purse, and dropped it down on the passenger seat. She was about to climb in, when clawlike fingers wrapped around her arm.

She spun around. A tiny woman with enormous eyes stood beside the car.

Margaret.

The old woman blinked up at her through the lenses of her bifocals. A black handbag dangled from her wrist, with a gold clasp on top, like Queen Elizabeth used to carry.

Kiersten blinked back at her as the name *Peggy* lodged in her throat. She swallowed. "Margaret?"

The woman nodded, then plucked at Kiersten's sleeve. "Come with me."

"Come with you where?"

"To my house. We don't have much time."

Her mind raced. In just a few hours she was planning to sneak into this woman's home. And now Margaret was *inviting her inside.*

A trap?

Dottie's words swirled through her mind. If the diaries were true . . . and she believed every word she'd read . . . then Margaret . . . or Peggy . . . or whatever this woman called herself . . . had suffered as much as Dottie had.

"We don't have much time," the tiny woman whispered, tugging her arm. "Please. Come now."

Kiersten chewed on her lower lip, contemplating this request. She'd seen chickens that looked more dangerous than this frail, elderly woman.

She reached inside her purse and grabbed her phone, just in case, shoving it into her back pocket. Then she allowed Margaret to slip her age-spotted hand into her own, and pull her out of the minivan and down the street to Margaret's house.

"What do you need to show me, Margaret? Can you tell me?"

The old woman glanced over her shoulder, gaze darting around the cul-de-sac. "Please. Just come."

Margaret clung to the railing as they climbed the front steps of the house she shared with Richard . . . or Dickie. Then she opened the door, which was not locked, she noted, and led Kiersten back to the kitchen, just like she'd done on her first visit.

"Is your husband here?" Kiersten asked, casting a nervous glance over the kitchen for Evil Dickie.

Margaret glanced over her shoulder. "Richard's over at Trey's house, making a video with Aspen."

This was the chance she'd been waiting for.

Kiersten tried to give her a reassuring smile. "I need to see the fall-out shelter in your basement. Okay? It'll only take a second."

Margaret pursed her lips in exasperation, then shuffled through the kitchen and stopped at the head of the stairs. "These steps are hard on my hips. But there's a door on the north side. It's under the garage. Hurry. We don't have much time."

Kiersten wrapped her fingers around the railing and descended into the basement.

A musty smell tickled her nose. She moved through the rec room, which didn't look like it had been updated in decades. The tile on the floor reminded her of the tile in her elementary school.

She found a door in the wall on the north side of the basement. Taking a deep breath, she extended her hand, turned the knob, and pushed it open.

The musty smell intensified. She stepped inside, and darkness enveloped her.

Something brushed her hair, and she bit back a scream as she reached up to slap it away.

Her fingers brushed a string.

The ceiling bulb.

She tugged the string, and the room filled with light.

Her gaze roamed the room. Shelves with paint cans. Nothing else. She looked down at the floor.

Concrete.

Concrete?

How was this possible?

She dropped to her knees and ran her hands over the smooth floor.

But Dottie promised to leave a clue . . . *If Dickie succeeds in killing me, I will leave a clue, buried in the past, leading to the truth.*

But there was nothing here. Nothing at all.

She headed upstairs, shoulders slumped in defeat.

Could she be wrong? Maybe there was no clue to find.

Margaret waited at the top of the steps, still clutching her black handbag. "Did you find what you're looking for?" Margaret asked.

"No," Kiersten shook her head. "I didn't."

"That's because you're looking in the *wrong place*," the old woman hissed.

The hair on the back of Kiersten's neck stood at attention. "I am?"

Margaret nodded. "I told you. *We don't have much time.* Come with me."

She followed the old woman through the sliding patio door, out of Richard and Margaret's house, and across the backyard to the house next door.

Chip's place.

The old woman knocked on the sliding glass patio door, then listened.

"He's still at Aspen's," Margaret said. "But he'll be back soon."

She slid the glass door open and grabbed Kiersten's hand.

"This way." She tugged Kiersten into the basement level of her son's home, her grip insistent, urgent.

Someone with money and good taste had recently remodeled this basement. It smelled fresh and clean, with a sleek, modern look. Gray porcelain tile covered the floor, a pool table commanded the center of the room, and a giant TV dominated the far wall. A well-equipped home gym with a Peloton and a bench press took up the rest of the space in the open main room.

"*This* is our original house," Margaret said. "The house where Chip was born. Chip wanted this one when he got married because it's bigger and has better views of the river. So we bought the house next door and gave him this house as a wedding gift. And we bought the house on the other side and gave that to Aspen and Trey when they got married."

The old woman gazed up at Kiersten, but she couldn't read the expression in her eyes.

"So where is—" Kiersten began.

"The fallout shelter." The old woman beckoned with her hand. "I wouldn't let them touch it. This way."

Margaret took her hand and led her through the exercise room to a bolted door on the far side of the room.

"This?" Kiersten asked.

The old woman nodded, and Kiersten slid the bolt open and turned the dead bolt lock. Then she tried to open the door, but it stuck. Kiersten pushed against it with her shoulder, and it finally opened with a loud creak.

A dry, earthen smell filled her nostrils as she stepped inside the shelter. Once again, she raised her hand above her head and felt for the string. Her fingers grasped it, and she pulled.

Light flooded the room as she gazed around in wonder. It felt like entering a time machine and stepping into the past.

Two cots. A table and chairs. A rough shelf held ancient cardboard boxes, canned goods, board games, first aid supplies, everything covered in dust.

Nailed to the wooden shelves, a yellowing calendar displayed the month of October in the year 1965. And across the bottom ran the words *Don't forget your next oil change! Thank you for being an Anderson Motors customer!*

"She was smart," Margaret said. "Smart as a whip. She left something behind."

"In the floor?" Kiersten asked.

The old woman shook her head.

"Where?"

Margaret pointed to a stack of board games on a shelf in the corner. "Yahtzee."

Yahtzee?

Kiersten frowned, then knelt by the shelf and unstacked the neat pile of ancient cardboard boxes. Scrabble. Monopoly. Checkers. Then she removed the cover from the board game at the bottom of the pile.

Memories flooded her mind at the sight of the dice, the black plastic cup lined with green felt in which to shake them, the pad of white scorecards, and little pencils. She'd played this game at her grandparents' house countless times, after Thanksgiving dinner or on Christmas Eve.

Then she paused. *Scorecards. Pencils.*

She pulled a pad of blank scorecards out of the box and turned them over.

Dottie's handwriting covered the backside of the pages.

Chapter Ninety-Three

DOTTIE

October 8, 1965

Peggy's water breaks, right here on the doorframe. A small puddle. Soaking into the dirt floor.

I reach for a towel. She grabs my arm.

"Leave it." Her voice is ragged, exhausted.

We embrace, then she pulls the door shut and locks it. I hear the bolt slide into the lock on the far side of the door and my skin twitches.

It's a small room. About 12 x 20 with a little table, four chairs, two cots. Daddy supplied everything we'd need to survive a nuclear disaster. Canned goods. Water. Medicine. Blankets and clothes. Even board games. But no windows. No sound.

It's like being buried alive.

My watch says I've been in here for three hours. Writing while I wait, writing it all down. Has Peggy given birth? What if she dies? What if the baby dies? What if she has complications and Dickie refuses to take her to the hospital?

Nothing I can do about it now. Only wait. And try not to scream.

Chapter Ninety-Four

KIERSTEN

Kiersten looked up from the pad of paper in her hand. Margaret met her gaze.

"Richard killed her," Margaret said. "Right here. In this room. I tried to stop him. But I failed. She failed. We failed. And Richard won. Richard always wins."

Footsteps sounded. Kiersten whirled around and found Chip standing in the doorway with Richard . . . Dickie . . . behind him.

Then the door slammed shut.

Chapter Ninety-Five

KIERSTEN

Kiersten felt like she'd fallen from a tall building and landed on her back as the air rushed from her lungs. She gasped, sucking in nothing but silence.

Dead quiet screamed inside the room like a Klaxon as she gripped Margaret's hands, staring into her faded green eyes.

Then the air rushed back into her body. She scooped panicked gulps into her lungs and launched herself at the door, screaming, pounding until her knuckles bled.

When the rage and shock drained away, she sank to the dirt floor. Margaret rose from the cot and sat beside her, dropping the scorecards into her lap.

"Read," Margaret whispered.

There was nothing else she could do.

Chapter Ninety-Six

DOTTIE

October 8, 1965

The tapping noise starts around 7 p.m. Then concrete fragments flake off and fall from the ceiling.

The pounding gets louder, goes on for a long time. And now that little hole in the corner of the ceiling is bigger. That damn hole I asked Dickie to fix so many times.

Eventually someone in the garage above pokes a screwdriver through the hole, then the shaft of a hammer, like they're measuring the size of the opening.

Then everything goes silent. It's silent for a long time.

Then I hear the bolt pull back. The door swings open.

Peggy.

Standing in the doorway, wearing an old dress, legs streaked with blood.

She carries a bundle of towels. Then she steps into the room, gets closer. I look down.

It's a *baby*. Beautiful. Newborn. A tiny, pristine *person*.

"Richard wants to name him Richard . . . and call him Chip—Chip off the old block—as a nickname." She shakes her head vehemently. "But his name is Daniel."

"Daniel." I repeat the name as she transfers the bundle into my arms. The baby blinks up at me. Enormous blue eyes. Perfect rosebud mouth. My eyes burn as I fight back tears.

"I sent Richard to People's Drug to fetch talcum powder for the baby." She looks ravaged, terrified. "We don't have much time."

We leave the shelter and creep up the basement stairs. Peggy grabs the doorknob at the top of the steps.

And then it's like God presses a button and sets everything in slow motion.

The door swings open . . . and Dickie is there.

A scream rips from my throat as he looms at the top of the stairs, eyes gleaming, my dad's shotgun . . . the one he uses for skeet shooting . . . cradled in his arms.

I clutch the baby tighter with one hand and reach for the handrail to keep from falling backward with the other.

"Where do you ladies think you're going?" His voice is smooth, like water. Then he smiles. I almost throw up.

"I was just . . . checking on her." Peggy's voice quivers.

"Just checking on her," he repeats in a mocking tone.

Then he descends, shotgun in the crook of his arm. Each step slow. Deliberate. Dangerous.

Thunk. Thunk. Thunk.

Peggy reaches back and grasps my hand. We retreat backward, one step at a time until we reach the bottom.

"Get back in the fallout shelter, Dottie."

I shake my head and clasp the baby tighter.

He points the shotgun at my chest. "Give the baby to Peggy."

My body shakes, but I force myself to lift my chin, look him straight in the eye, to pretend I'm not afraid. "You can't shoot me. How do you explain a gunshot wound on a woman who died in childbirth?"

He seizes Peggy by the hair and jerks her close.

"True. But I can shoot *her*. I can dispose of *her* body. And no one will ever know."

I can hardly breathe, much less speak. I inhale a slug of air, then force the words out. "Calm down, Dickie."

"Put the baby down or she dies," he repeats.

"Let her go."

He shakes his head, eyes glowing, mouth set in a grim line. "Put the baby down or I kill her. Now."

"Please, Richard," Peggy begs, tears streaming down her face.

Still gripping Peggy's hair, he raises my dad's shotgun with his other hand.

He points it at me.

My thoughts ricochet around the basement, searching for a weapon, a way out. Then they ping back . . . to the baby in my arms, to the gun in Dickie's hand. And to Peggy, whimpering beside him.

No choice. I have no choice.

I set the baby on the floor. Little Daniel starts to cry, a terrible, urgent, siren-squall and I feel like I'm going to shatter. The gun. The screaming baby. Peggy cowering, babbling, begging Dickie to release us.

"Please let us go," I whisper. *"Please."*

"I don't think that's going to work." Dickie gives me a sad smile, raising his voice above the cries of the newborn.

"You can't do this, Richard," Peggy begs.

He yanks her hair, and she shrieks.

"Enough!" he snarls. "Into the shelter or I pull the trigger."

I scuttle backward, into the small room. Peggy sobs, clinging to Dickie's leg while the baby screams, mouth wide, face purple.

That's the last thing I see. The baby on the floor, howling in a bundle of towels, Peggy, babbling and pleading, with Dickie's fist embedded in the hair at the top of her scalp, his other hand clutching the gun. And Dickie's face. Blank. Expressionless.

He releases Peggy's hair, pulls the door shut, and bolts it from the outside.

Then I hear the blast of a gunshot on the other side of the door. Followed by a heartbeat of quiet. Then curses streaming from Dickie's mouth.

I sink to the floor, shaking, suffocating in the awful silence.

And now a tapping sound as fragments of chipped concrete fall from the growing hole in the ceiling.

Chapter Ninety-Seven

KIERSTEN

"It's happening again," Margaret muttered.

Kiersten looked up. Concrete fragments, dead leaves, and a yellow piece of insulation fell through the hole in the upper corner of the ceiling.

"Margaret, is this how it happened?" Kiersten asked, pointing to the writing scribbled on the back of the yellowed scorecards.

"Peggy. I'm *Peggy*," she said vehemently, pointing a clawlike finger to her chest. "That's what everyone called me. Until I became Richard's wife. He said 'Peggy' wasn't dignified enough. Too lower class. Then I had to go by my given name. I've been Margaret ever since."

"What happened to Dottie?" Kiersten forced herself to take a deep breath, trying to stave off the panic rising up through her body, leaching into her mind. "After Dickie locked her in this room?"

"I tried to save her." Peggy's hands twisted in her lap. "I reached for the gun. It went off. Missed him. Missed me and the baby too. He was too strong. Too evil. All these years, living with that *monster*. And then you came along."

The tiny woman turned to look at Kiersten. "I didn't know Dottie kept a diary. And then you came over that day and brought the first one. I recognized the handwriting the minute I opened it. From her recipes. Richard recognized it too. He told Chip and Trey everything. And they redoubled their efforts to drive you away from Beaverbrook Lane. To get your children into trouble. To make you sell that house and go away. And to get the diaries back."

"Have you ever told anyone about Dottie? About what Richard did?"

She hung her head. "I was too scared of Richard. He told me I imagined it all. That I'd made it up. That Dottie died in childbirth. He threatened to have me locked up in a psychiatric hospital if I told anyone. And my son . . ." The rims of her watery eyes turned red. "He's not Richard's biological son. They don't know that. But it doesn't matter. He grew up to be just like Richard. And my grandson too. This was my punishment . . . to watch the son I conceived with Daniel turn out just like the man who made my life a living hell . . . the man who killed Dottie."

"And this room?" Kiersten asked.

Margaret wiped away the tears that trailed down her wrinkled cheek. "This room was the price of my silence. I said I wanted to keep it just like it was, for her. And he agreed to that. He and Chip. It was my only demand in fifty-nine years of marriage. They shut the door and locked it, and no one has been in here in sixty years, except me. I came down here sometimes, when Richard was at work. Just to sit and feel close to Dottie, the only one who understood the hell of living with Richard."

"Is that when you found her writing, on the back of all these scorecards?"

She nodded. "I knew she'd leave something behind. She was so clever. So smart." She held up the scorecards in her lap. "This *proves* what he did. This. Plus the diaries."

"Do you know where the diaries are now?" Kiersten asked.

"I stole them. From Chip." She patted her black purse. "They're right *here*."

Kiersten didn't know whether to laugh or cry. They had the diaries. They had Dottie's final clue. But they were locked in an underground bunker with no way to escape.

Except she had something Dottie didn't have back in 1965.

She reached into her back pocket and pulled out her cell phone. Bile rose in her throat as she squinted at the screen.

No signal.

She dashed around the tiny room with her phone raised in the air, willing the little bars that indicated a strong, or even a weak, signal to appear in the right-hand corner of her screen.

But a nuclear-fallout shelter built to block out radiation could also block a cell phone signal.

She lowered her arm and tossed her useless phone onto the cot.

Despite over half a century of technology and progress, she'd ended up in exactly the same position Dottie had been in sixty years ago.

Right before Dickie killed her.

Gently, she pulled the yellow scorecards from Peggy's hand and began to read Dottie's last entry.

Chapter Ninety-Eight

DOTTIE

October 8, 1965

I climb the shelf. It's tippy. Precarious. But I manage to stuff a rag into the tube Dickie inserts through the hole in the ceiling.

He pulls the tube back up through the hole. He plucks out the rag and shoves the tube back down.

I try a blanket.

Same thing. Dickie pulls the blanket up and through the hole. I watch, helpless, as it disappears into the garage.

I try again with another blanket. A strange tug of war ensues. He pulls the blanket from the garage above, while I tug from below.

Eventually he pulls that blanket up too. It disappears into the garage overhead.

I have nothing left. Except these words. Scribbled with a little wooden pencil on the only paper I can find, a whole pad of scorecards from a brand-new game of Yahtzee, purchased by my father to help us while away the apocalypse.

It's quiet for a long time. Then a voice calls to me through the hole in the ceiling, like some kind of muffled prophet.

"Are you awake?"

I jump at the sound. "I'm awake, you evil bastard."

"No need to be bitter, Dottie." I can't see the eye roll, but I can hear it in his voice. "It's not my fault you had a miscarriage. It's not my fault you can't give me the things I need."

"No one can give you the things you need, Dickie."

"That's not true. Peggy is going to make me very happy. She's going to be the perfect wife."

Relief floods my body. She isn't dead then. He didn't shoot her.

"You're evil." It's not an insult. It's simply true.

"You never knew your *place*, Dottie. That was your problem." He says this patiently, like a teacher explaining a complicated problem to a particularly dim-witted student.

"I hope you live a long life. I hope you live long enough to see a different world."

"I'm going to turn your car on now," he says. "Clever girl, getting it to run again. It will be a peaceful death. Like falling asleep."

"You don't have to do this." I know it's useless, but I have to try, one more time, to talk him out of this.

"Yes, I do actually. You had all the things I needed. Money and car dealerships. A rich and politically connected father. But you were plain and insufficiently committed to making me happy. Peggy does as she's told. She's beautiful. A wonderful cook. She's fertile. Peggy is the wife I need to get where I want to be."

"You won't get away with this."

"I'm pretty sure I will. I did last time."

That brings me up short. "Last time?"

"I was married before, you know. Only for six months, but I had to kill her in order to marry you. That's when I learned about the efficacy of foxglove. My father was a florist. Poor man, lost everything in the Depression, but he managed to pass that one piece of useful information along in lieu of an inheritance."

"Someone will figure out I didn't die in childbirth." It's not a threat. It's a vow I make to myself as I document his words, taking dictation one last time.

"Actually, I'm pretty sure they won't. The baby will serve as proof. No one will bother to examine your body too closely. They won't perform an autopsy. We'll dress you in Peggy's nightgown, put you in our bed, smear blood in strategic places and the doctor will declare you dead when he arrives."

"And you'll marry her."

"Yes. But first I'll weep at your funeral while holding my poor, motherless infant."

Bile burns my throat, and I swallow it back. "A grieving widower with a new child to care for."

"Exactly. I'll remarry quickly, as any man would in those circumstances. Peggy will be an angel, loving your poor, motherless child as though it were her very own. Your father will be grief stricken but devoted to the grandson you left behind and he'll leave everything to my son when he dies."

My mouth twists in a bitter smile as I record these words.

He'd thought he was lying to me, back when I asked if Peggy was carrying his child. He'd thought he was feeding me a cover story, about the mechanic who'd gotten Peggy pregnant.

He doesn't know it's the truth. Daniel's son will inherit the dealerships and Daddy's money. The son of a mechanic killed in Viet Nam will inherit Daddy's fortune. And Richard will have no idea he's raising another man's son.

"You'll never get away with this, Dickie."

"Thanks for the memories, my dear."

And now . . . the smell of exhaust and gasoline. Smells I once loved . . . the odor of grease . . . and the garage . . . andfriendship.

My . . . . . . Chevy is Dickie's murder weapon.

So strongs,mell

Alldone now and

hide th e words

I lost

my

chanc

Rollin.g

th

die . . . silence flows

through.

the

ceiling

like sky

Chapter Ninety-Nine

KIERSTEN

Maybe the thumping of her heart would serve as a signal . . . a beacon . . . a distress call . . .

Help me. *Help* me. *Help* me.

A feeble hope, but the only hope she had left.

She'd been down on her hands and knees, digging through the ancient boxes filled with emergency supplies, searching for a weapon of some kind. A shovel. A knife. A tool to dig under the door, out of the basement.

She found a spoon, a can opener, a corkscrew. These tools would have to do.

Tiny pebbles of concrete cascaded down the wall, and she looked up. Then someone pushed a flexible black rubber tube downward, through the hole in the ceiling.

It's happening again.

Peggy's words reverberated through her mind.

She grasped the end of the tube and tugged hard, just as Dottie had done with the blanket. The person above pulled back harder, and the tube slipped from her hands.

The person in the garage readjusted it, leaving it flush with the opening in the ceiling. Not enough pipe to tug on, but enough to channel the carbon monoxide directly into the fallout shelter from the exhaust pipe of the unseen car.

Panic clawed at the edge of her mind. She dug her nails into her palms.

Stop. Stop. Stop. Think. Think. Think.

How long had she been down here? What time was it?

She checked her phone. She'd been gone for over an hour. She'd left her purse sitting on the front seat of her car with her keys. Surely they'd start looking for her soon?

She'd taken the diaries out of Margaret's black Queen Elizabeth purse and hidden them and the scorecards with Dottie's last words inside a game of Monopoly, beneath the money and the gameboard. Then she placed everything back where it had been for the last sixty years, the board games obscured by candles, first aid supplies, and rusting canned goods.

Margaret—or Peggy, as she preferred to be called—had curled up on the cot in the corner, as tiny and vulnerable as a child taking a nap.

Kiersten adjusted the woolen blanket she'd spread over Peggy when she'd started shivering from the cold in the underground bunker.

What had Peggy's life been like, all these years, shackled to a monster like Dickie?

Suddenly, the muffled sound of voices came from the garage above. "Just stick it through and connect the hose to the back of your car," someone said.

"Chip!" she yelled. "Is that you?"

The voices lowered to a whisper, followed by silence.

Then, minutes later, the locks on the outside of the door began to rattle. The dead bolt clattered back.

She grabbed her phone, pressed the record button, and slid it under the blanket on the cot.

Then she fisted the corkscrew as someone fumbled with the knob.

The door opened, and she sprang forward, lurching through the doorway, lunging with the weapon in her hand. Someone grabbed her shoulders and slammed her to the ground.

A gray film crossed over her vision as she gasped, struggling to breathe.

Above her prone body, Chip scowled. She gulped a mouthful of air as he pulled her to her feet and tugged her hands behind her back.

The hard plastic of a zip tie bit into her wrists, and she twisted, straining to see behind her.

"Get back in there." Chip pushed her, and she stumbled into the bunker again.

Peggy sat up on the cot, her tiny body trembling. "You can't do this again."

Richard entered the fallout shelter and smiled at his wife. "Actually, I can."

Chapter One Hundred

KIERSTEN

He stumped around the room with a cane, looking at the shelves and the hole in the ceiling where a black tube now protruded.

"Let me go, Dickie," Kiersten pleaded.

He froze for a long moment, then turned to stare at her. "Dottie was the only person who ever called me that," he said softly. "It was her pet name for me. A nickname. Odd that you should use it, too, just before you die the same way she did."

A hyperawareness filled her body, like a useless superpower. The dank smell. The sweat on her upper lip. The papery folds above Richard's eyes. "I won't tell anyone. I'll pack up and go back to Minnesota. You'll never see or hear from me again."

He tilted his head, eyes wide behind his bifocals. "You don't strike me as the kind of person who would overlook a murder. That's why you read all of Dottie's boring diaries. Went to the library. Did your homework. Tried to figure out what happened to her. I very much doubt you would retreat to your dairy farm and forget this ever happened."

"What are you going to do with me?" Her voice came out shrill, an octave too high.

"The same thing I did with Dottie," he said simply. "Margaret was right to demand that we leave this room exactly as it was back in 1965. Who knew it would come in handy again, all these years later?"

"It won't work." Kiersten swallowed, tried to sound calm. "We know what you did. We know what Chip and Trey are doing with the houses, how they're trying to scare us into selling."

"And you can prove nothing without the diaries," Dickie said. "Which we now have."

She forced herself not to glance at the pile of board games stacked on the lower shelf.

"If I'm not home in an hour, they'll come here looking for me."

"And you'll be dead by then."

She needed to stall for time, to keep them talking. If she hadn't returned by lunchtime, they'd look inside her car and realize she'd never left. Piper would know something was wrong.

"Is Aspen in on this too?" she asked.

"Aspen is a useful and beautiful idiot, like my own wife." Dickie jutted his chin in Peggy's direction. "Like most women."

"They'll know what you did," Kiersten repeated.

Trey snorted. "It won't matter, because they can't prove it. And in an hour you'll be buried under the concrete foundation we're pouring for the second house next door."

Keep them talking. Stall for time.

"We have you on video. Entering our houses. Vandalizing the construction site."

"That wasn't us," Chip sneered. "And you know it."

"Who was it then?"

"Our business partner, Bruno Orlov." Dickie smiled.

"Dynamo Development," Kiersten whispered.

Chip smiled. "You've been paying attention. We launder his money through our building projects."

"He's got a son named Alex Orlov," Trey said. "Talented kid, especially considering he's only fourteen years old. We hired him to harass

Caitlin Mondello. And to pick a fight at school with your son Luke. And to bully that weird girl with blue hair who's always wearing a cape. And to show up at the Harvest Festival and plant the idea that his family was going to move in next door. You were supposed to get so frustrated that you'd move to a different school district. I never thought you'd start *homeschooling*."

Kiersten's eyes narrowed as she struggled to understand so much evil. It was one thing to target adults . . . but children too? "All in an effort to drive us away."

Chip nodded. "The bloody papers nailed to the tree. The noose on Lillian's porch. The cockroaches and sex ads on Craigslist. You guys were supposed to become so scared and anxious to get out of here that you'd take the first lowball offer that came your way from a buyer who is actually Dynamo Development."

"Then we tear down those old houses you guys live in and build three new McModern Farmhouses on each lot," Trey said. "And make millions."

"Where does Aspen come into all this?" Kiersten asked.

"Aspen documents the construction process on Instagram. She picks out the tile and the flooring and the fixtures, all that dumb stuff. In a couple months, she signs her HGTV contract for her new show, *Happy House Life Block Party*. By the time those houses are finished, we'll have millions of views on Instagram and a season's worth of free advertising on HGTV."

Chip nodded. "People will get into bidding wars to buy a home on the block she made famous. And then we do it all over again in a different neighborhood. Orlov gives us dirty money. We launder it through our building projects, and it comes out clean. We sell the houses. Aspen gets a TV show and makes even more money, which adds an aura of legitimacy to the whole thing. It's a win-win-win."

"For everyone but you," Trey added. "Sometimes getting to know your neighbors is deadly."

"C'mon, Margaret, time to go," Dickie said, attempting to pull his wife up from the cot.

Kiersten froze as the blanket shifted, leaving the bottom edge of her phone visible.

Peggy brushed his arm away. "I'm not leaving."

Dickie rolled his eyes. "This? Again? Sixty years later?"

She shook her head vigorously. "I'm not leaving. Not this time. If you kill her, you have to kill me too."

Dickie rolled his eyes. "Suit yourself."

Chip's eyes widened in horror. "I am not going to murder my own *mother*."

He went over to Peggy and took her hands. "Please, Mom. It's time to go."

"Peggy, you need to go with them." Kiersten wanted to pull her up from the cot, but she couldn't with her hands zip-tied behind her back. "Aspen and those little girls need you . . . given what the men in this family are like."

Peggy shook her head. "I'm staying with her."

Trey heaved a sigh, then strode across the room and picked up his tiny grandmother and carried her out of the room.

Dickie turned and left the bunker. "Let's finish this."

The door slammed. Kiersten was alone.

Chapter One Hundred One

PIPER

Piper glanced at her watch as Bella whined, "Mommy, I'm *hungry*."

"I know, honey. We'll eat lunch soon."

"We didn't get a snack," Luke pointed out.

"I'm *starving*," Johnny said.

"I'm pretty sure not giving us a snack violates child labor laws," Guinevere added.

Rosamund rolled her eyes. "We do not have a contractual obligation to give you Goldfish." Then she gestured to Piper with her phone. "Did you text her?"

Piper nodded. "I've called and texted. No answer."

Rosamund walked into the foyer, opened the front door, and stepped onto the front porch. "She's back. Her car is here."

"Great." Piper jogged down the steps and toward the minivan parked in the driveway. "I'll help her carry everything inside."

At the back of Kiersten's vehicle, she pressed the button to open the rear hatch. It rose, revealing an empty car.

Her eyes narrowed. It should have been filled with boxes of granola bars and Goldfish, with pretzels and clementines and apples and grapes.

She frowned and moved to the front of the car, where the driver's side door stood open.

She poked her head inside.

Kiersten's purse sat on the passenger seat. But no Kiersten.

Her stomach dropped as she grabbed Kiersten's purse and dug around inside.

No phone.

No Kiersten.

Bile rose in her throat as she scanned the cul-de-sac.

Everything was quiet at 11:00 a.m. on a Wednesday morning. Brendan, Garrett, Miles, and Reggie had gone to Home Depot while she, Rosamund, and Valentina were teaching the kids.

She squinted toward the building site. The *tap, tap, tap* of hammers echoed through the neighborhood as men crisscrossed the roof of the soon-to-be-finished home, adding shingles to the first house while a cement truck sat parked in front of the second building site. It looked like they planned to pour the foundation for the second house today.

The sound of an engine tugged her attention toward Chip's garage a few houses down.

The hackles rose on the back of her neck as the garage door lowered and closed while the engine kept running.

Chapter One Hundred Two

KIERSTEN

Kiersten stopped the record button on her phone and played the conversation back.

Elation surged through her body as Dickie's voice filled the room again. It *worked.* Then she looked up at the ceiling, and despair displaced this temporary rush of hope.

A recording was useless if no one ever heard it.

Frantically, she pulled the cot over to the corner of the room and did exactly what Dottie had done. Her fingers shook as she stuffed the wool blanket into the end of the hose protruding from the ceiling.

The person on the other end simply hauled the tube up through the hole and removed the blanket.

She had nothing left except her clothes, and there was no point in sacrificing those. Trey and Chip would just pull the tube up again, remove the blockage, and shove it back through.

She may as well remain fully clothed and die with dignity. She sat down on the cot and buried her face in her hands.

This was it.

The air around her took on a blue quality, and her head began to throb.

Don't fall asleep. She began to bargain with her mind and body. *Don't fall asleep.*

Someone would come. Piper would come. She'd be suspicious when she saw the purse sitting on the passenger seat of the empty car that had never made it to Costco . . . because Piper was suspicious of everything. And that was smart.

She still believed most people were good . . . she'd just chosen to trust the bad ones . . . and that was stupid.

And now she would die because of that stupidity.

She lay down on the cot and closed her eyes . . . just for a minute . . . as images floated through her mind. Garrett smiling . . . the ripple of yellow wheat under a vast cerulean sky . . . the face of each son . . . smiling . . . running into the light . . .

Chapter One Hundred Three

PIPER

Piper ran next door to her own house, where she tore through the many gun-safety measures they had in place to protect the girls. She retrieved her Glock from the gun safe and removed the trigger lock. Then she ran out to the garage and opened the second safe, where they stored the ammunition.

She needed a badge. She needed handcuffs. But she had neither.

She loaded her weapon, strapped on her holster, and approached Chip's house from behind, cutting through her neighbors' backyards.

When she reached his house, she crouched and approached the single door on the backside of the garage.

She turned the knob.

Locked.

Damn it.

She pulled the multi-tool out of her pocket, flipped open the screwdriver attachment, and removed the screws around the doorknob. The knob fell into her hand, and she quietly set it on the ground. Then she tripped the mechanism to unlock the door.

She entered the garage, climbed into the car, turned off the ignition, and put the keys in her pocket.

Then she smashed her hand against the garage door opener. It lifted, filling the garage with fresh air.

She moved to the backside of the car, where a black rubber tube protruded from the exhaust pipe. A sour taste coated the back of her throat as dread flooded her body.

No. No. No. No. No.

Hands trembling, she followed the length of hose to the hole in the corner of the garage and tugged it free.

"Kiersten. Kiersten, are you there?"

No answer.

She whimpered as fear, grief, and rage tore through her body. She staggered out of the garage and moved to Chip's backyard. Then she slid the basement door open and entered his house.

Chapter One Hundred Four

KIERSTEN

Someone called her name. Over and over again.

But she was dead.

Wasn't she?

A lifetime of Lutheran church and Sunday school had prepared her for the hereafter, the place where all tears would be wiped away, a paradise with many mansions, and a room prepared just for her.

Her eyes felt sticky, but she forced them open, blinking. Surely heaven was not a cinder block bunker with a dirt floor?

A headache zigzagged across her befuddled mind as she tried to sit up. Suddenly a metallic scratching came from outside. Then the door flew open.

Piper stood in the doorway, holding a gun.

Chapter One Hundred Five

KIERSTEN

Piper crossed the room and wrapped her arms protectively around Kiersten's shoulders.

"Are you okay?"

Kiersten squinted through one eye. Her mind felt blurry, like her eyes before she put her contacts in each morning. "Maybe?"

Piper rose and tugged at her hands. "C'mon. We gotta move."

"Move . . . where . . . ?"

Everything was so hazy . . . words drifted and broke apart before they could coalesce into thoughts . . . into action.

"Away from here." Piper put her arm around Kiersten's waist to support her, which helped because her legs were wobbly, just like her thoughts.

With Piper's help, they left the fallout shelter, crept through the sliding doors and into Chip's backyard, where they broke into a hobbling run toward Kiersten's house.

"Where did they go?" Piper asked once they reached Kiersten's front porch.

Jo. Mo. Go. Slow. Ho. Kiersten squeezed her eyes shut and tried to marshal her thoughts into some kind of order . . . it felt important . . . though she couldn't remember *why* . . .

"Aspen's house." The words came out thick and mushy, like marshmallows. "They're making . . . a video."

"Go inside," Piper ordered. "Tell Rosamund. Call 911. Send the police to Aspen's house. Keep the kids inside and lock all the doors. Can you do that?"

She nodded and drew a gulp of fresh air into her lungs. Each breath added focus, made things sharper.

"Garrett and Brendan are coming." Piper's fingers dug into her arms. "Send them to Aspen's house."

"Garrett and Brendan," Kiersten repeated as the fog continued to lift. "Wait. Where are *you* going?"

"I'm arresting these bastards."

Chapter One Hundred Six

PIPER

Piper ran to Aspen's house and pressed herself against the vinyl siding. At the corner of the house, she stopped, peering into the backyard.

The Davis family sat on Aspen's patio, smiling into the phone held by the same young woman who'd shot video at the Harvest Festival.

Piper pulled out her phone and thumbed across the screen. Aspen was live. On Instagram.

There would never be a safer time to take the Davis family into custody.

Taking a deep breath, she strode forward, weapon raised.

"Hands in the air!"

Aspen screamed while the men immediately lifted their hands over their heads.

"You are under arrest for the murder of Dottie Davis and the attempted murder of Kiersten Cleaver."

Richard's mouth dropped open. Chip recovered the ability to speak first. "You can't do this."

"Actually, I can," she said. And it was true. She was a law enforcement officer, and it felt so good to arrest bad people again.

Behind her a voice called out. Brendan's voice. "Keep your hands in the air."

Police officers swarmed the area, slapping handcuffs on Trey, Chip, and Richard.

Aspen's gaze flitted from one officer to the next, her beautiful mouth a perfect O of horror and surprise.

Then she leaped from her chair and lunged toward the young woman with the phone, who stood frozen, broadcasting the Insta-worthy arrest of the extended Happy House Life family.

"Turn it off, you idiot. Turn it *off*."

Chapter One Hundred Seven

KIERSTEN

June

Kiersten, Rosamund, and Piper sat on Kiersten's front porch, celebrating the first day of summer vacation.

Rosamund flipped through the print edition of *The Washington Post*. "Did you see the latest?"

"About the investigations into the death of Chip's wife and the murder of Richard's first wife?" Kiersten shook her head in amazement. Each morning *The Washington Post* delivered fresh revelations about her former neighbors.

"That was *yesterday*," Piper corrected. "Today they have a story about Bruno Orlov making large 'donations' to the school, and in exchange, Mr. Vex agreed to look the other way when Alex Orlov bullied kids in order to drive their parents into selling their homes at a loss and leaving the school district."

"Isn't his sentencing hearing coming up?" Kiersten asked.

"It is, and based on the sentences Chip and Trey got, he'll be in prison for a very long time," Piper said with a satisfied smirk.

"It says here that Evil Dickie is trying to claim he's too senile to stand trial?" Rosamund said, flipping to page A12.

"While simultaneously attempting to tamper with the jury from his jail cell." Piper snorted. "I know the prosecuting attorney, and she's a badass. Good luck to Dickie with *that*."

"Maybe he'll end up in the cell next to Hawkeye Slaughter?" He'd finally been arrested three weeks ago, attempting to smuggle a bomb into a data center in Loudoun County.

Piper grinned. "They deserve each other."

Kiersten gestured toward the **For Sale** sign in Aspen's front yard with her glass of iced tea. "Looks like Aspen's house is on the market."

Piper nodded. "She closed down all her social media accounts too."

Inadvertently streaming the arrest of her entire family live on Instagram made Aspen go viral, for all the wrong reasons. She'd filed for divorce from Trey and moved to Florida two weeks ago with Peggy and her girls. In her last text, she'd told Kiersten she planned to become a certified energy healer with a side practice as a life coach.

Rosamund folded the newspaper and turned to Piper. "How did your interview go today?"

Piper smiled. "They made me an offer, and I accepted."

"Congratulations!" Kiersten pulled her into a hug. "I *knew* they'd hire you."

Piper gave her a tolerant smile before disentangling herself from Kiersten's embrace. "It's noble work, and I'm excited to be part of it."

"What is it again?" Rosamund asked. "Some kind of shelter?"

"It's a home for runaway teenage girls, providing education, counseling, and a safe place to live. Everything they need to put the past behind them and move toward a better future."

"And the governor's wife is doing this?" Kiersten asked. "And that TV-anchor lady?"

"That's right." Piper leaned back in her chair. "Nikki Lassiter and Ainsley Bradley. They started it last year. It's called Project Runaway, and I think it'll be a great place to work."

Kiersten grabbed a chocolate chip cookie from the plate on the patio table. "Remind me how you heard about this job?"

"My friend Edna Chavez. She's a detective with a small department out in Maryland. Nikki and Ainsley wanted someone with a law enforcement background on staff to help build a case against the traffickers. And they need someone to develop security protocols to protect the building and the girls themselves. Bad guys aren't happy they've created a shelter for runaway teenage girls, and they've had threats."

"Listen to you, on a first name basis with television anchors and the first lady of our fine state," Rosamund teased.

Piper raised her iced tea with her pinky extended. "I'm sure I'll become far too cool for Beaverbrook Lane potlucks."

"Do you have any regrets about turning down that promotion?" Kiersten wiped her fingers on a cloth napkin. She'd started using her grandmother's lace napkins during "high iced tea" every Friday afternoon on her front porch with Rosamund and Piper. "Wouldn't it give you a lot of satisfaction to boss around the people who put you on administrative leave in the first place?"

Piper's reinstatement had been expedited, thanks to her role in uncovering an illegal sports gambling ring and a money-laundering operation, not to mention solving a sixty-year-old murder. She'd been offered a promotion and turned it down.

"No regrets," she said with an emphatic shake of her head. "I'll be doing important work in an office full of moms with a flexible schedule. It's perfect. And that's not all."

"There's *more*?" Rosamund asked.

Piper grinned. "This morning, I also received a backhanded semi-apology from my mother-in-law."

"No *way*." Kiersten had met Piper's mother-in-law at Christmas. This was quite possibly the most shocking development of all.

"She wants to take the girls to Europe this summer and build on the interest they've developed in history during our home school experiment, thanks to you, Rosamund."

"It takes a village," Rosamund said with a modest shrug as she reached for another cookie. "How about you, Kiersten? Are you going to be our new school nurse?"

Kiersten nodded. "Head lice and strep throat, here I come."

"Sounds like the hardest job on the planet," Piper said.

"Oh, I don't know." Kiersten smiled. "I like taking care of people. And little people with tummy aches at school need all the care they can get. Plus the hours are perfect. I'll have the same schedule as the kids. And if we get one of those giant tourist-bus passenger vans, I can drive all our kids to school in the morning and home again in the afternoon. You guys will never have to sit in the pickup line again."

"I'm going to miss the Beaverbrook Academy for Inquiring Minds," Rosamund said wistfully. "But Guinevere is excited to go back to school in the fall. Now that she has friends."

They gazed out at the street where the older kids played kickball while Johnny and Bella whacked each other with pool noodles.

"Do you think . . ." Piper's voice trailed off.

"That we'll be able to hold the line?" Kiersten finished.

"Yeah." Piper nodded.

"I do." Kiersten set her iced tea down on the table. "Because I learned something from the Beaverbrook Academy too. I learned about this crazy, old-fashioned concept called *balance*."

"Easy to say now, before the next school year has even started," Rosamund warned.

"True," Kiersten admitted. "But all those things I did before . . . I did them because I was afraid. Afraid of the future. Afraid my kids would be left behind if I strayed from the path taken by everyone else. But now I know my kids are resilient, loyal, curious, and strong, no matter what their report cards say. That fear is gone. You guys erased it."

"I feel the same way." Rosamund stirred a packet of sugar into her iced tea. "We dropped out, and the world kept spinning. The kids not only survived, but they *thrived.* So I feel confident about dropping *back in*, but slower this time."

"With balance and boundaries," Kiersten said. "My kids will play on a travel team for one season. Then they play a different sport on a rec team the rest of the year."

"Balance and boundaries," Piper repeated. "Amen to that."

"Isn't that what you're doing too?"

Piper nodded. "We're still doing dance but at the studio down the road. No more epic trips across time, space, and the DMV to study at a certain studio or with some special instructor."

"How about Guinevere?" Kiersten asked.

"She's going to audition for some plays," Rosamund said. "As you may have noticed, she has a flair for the dramatic."

Silence fell over the porch as they watched their kids play together in the cul-de-sac. Then Rosamund asked, "When does Lillian's granddaughter move in?"

"Tomorrow," Kiersten said. "She starts her junior year at George Mason in the fall. And she's a nursing student, so it's perfect."

"Rent-free off campus housing for her, and Lillian has someone there every day, just in case."

"And Lillian insists on seeing Bella and Johnny once a week to work on their spelling words," Piper added.

"She will still be very much involved," Kiersten agreed with a smile. "As will Valentina. Luke will work with her two days a week after school. She's finally going to let me pay her the going rate. And while she does that, Reggie is going to launch a personal-training business. I'm his first client testimonial."

"And Minnesota?" Piper took a sip of iced tea. "Anything new with that?"

"We thought about it," Kiersten said. "And we decided to stay out here until the end of the ag secretary's term. We'll be here three more years."

"So you're not going back home?" Rosamund asked, her expression hopeful.

Kiersten looked out at the cul-de-sac, where her children played. "We're already home. Home is where your friends are."

Acknowledgments

First, to you, the reader of this book. Thank you for choosing to spend your time and money on something I created. You make my job possible, and I am beyond grateful that you've chosen to put my book on your Kindle or your nightstand or your phone as you walk the dog.

If you read my first book and are now reading this one, then DOUBLE thank you. Thank you for taking the time to leave kind reviews and for reaching out with thoughtful emails. Thank you for inviting me to your book clubs, for subscribing to my newsletter and then hitting reply so we can have a conversation. Your emails make my day and keep me going when I get stuck.

Thank you for making *Friends with Secrets* a bestseller, for reading this one, and for planting the seeds for the third book, coming out in 2027.

If you'd like to stay in touch, you can subscribe to *Notes on Love and Laundry* at www.christinegunderson.com, where I promise a short essay each month designed to make you smile and possibly laugh out loud.

You are the very best part of being an author, and I truly hope you enjoyed the time you spent inside these pages.

And speaking of pages . . . diaries and timelines and multiple characters made these particular pages *hard*, and I'd like to thank the many patient people who put up with me while I wrote it.

First, always, is my agent, Michelle Grajkowski, for brainstorming, therapy, cheerleading, career advice, plus the whole actual *agenting* part. Thank you for everything you do for me, and for my characters. Kiersten loves you especially, because you understand about hotdish. :-)

To Chantelle Aimee Osman, for believing in my books and making my literary dreams come true. To Laura Van der Veer and Megan McKeever for helping me wrestle this giant file of words into a cohesive story. Good editors shine a light on the things writers are too close to see. Thank you for shedding your light on this manuscript.

To the entire Lake Union team. Thank you for producing this beautiful book and for all you do to help my books reach so many readers. Thank you for your reach and expertise on everything from fantastic proofreading to beautiful covers. I am so grateful to be part of this incredibly talented and supportive team.

To my writing buddies, the Omegas, the Serious Writers Seriously Writing, the Washington Romance Writers, the Virginia Writers Club, the Women's Fiction Writers Association, my Lake Union sisters, and the Sisterhood of the Traveling Pen. I am so grateful I never have to do this alone.

To the beta readers who bravely read this book as a terrible first draft and then told me with love and patience how to make it better. Thank you to Linda Kramer, Colleen Scott, Susan Heisler, Clay Shields, and Sonia Stozek. Thank you to Jo Ann Moore for her insights into life as a female Diplomatic Security agent, and to J. and F. for educating me on pitch counts, field size, and travel baseball tournaments. Any mistakes are my own.

To Molly Shields Uehling, Dr. Lydia Thomas, Kate Carr, Marilyn Dabagi Harris, and Vicki Weil. Thank you for sharing your time, your insights, and your memories of 1965.

Thank you to the many moms I've met in book club meetings all over Northern Virginia in person, and all over the US on Zoom since *Friends with Secrets* came out in 2024. Thank you for your ideas and anecdotes, for the fantastic discussions about motherhood, and for the hysterical laughter. And to all the children left behind at rest stops and restaurants over the years, please know you're *not* the only one.

Thank you to Nicole DiLorenzo for bidding on a character name to support the fabulous and fun charity auction for our school. Henry DiLorenzo, I hope you love seeing your name in the pages of this book, and happy Father's Day!

To the merry band of moms at BSSM and BI. Special thanks to Terra M. for liberating me from the car pool line. You are the reason I finished this book on time.

To Sharon Ritchey, Alison Fife, Checka Trigiani Noone, Adriana Trigiani, Aggie Blum Thompson, Camille Pagan, Hadley Leggett, Kristin Kisska, Jennifer Jabaley, Gibson McMahon, Maureen Allen, Meghan Campione, Holly Piper, Julie James Umstead, Paige Ralston Fromer, Jeanie Mamo, and Susan Whitson, for everything.

To my family, Corrine Iverson, Melissa Silvernagel, Gene and Judy Rose, Anna Marie Hernandez, Deb Moen, Greg Gunderson, and Susan Heisler. Thank you for believing in me on the days when I'm pretty sure I should give this whole writing thing up and become a professional dishwasher unloader.

To Erik, Mark, and Kari. Thank you for being the greatest kids on the planet and for putting up with a mom who forgets everything, except how much I love you.

To Brian. Thank you for knowing there is zero correlation between the depth of my love and my ability to remember anniversary dates. You make this possible.

Discussion Questions

1. How have expectations for women changed since the 1960s? Do you feel more or less is expected from mothers today? How have housekeeping expectations changed over the decades? Which expectations have remained the same?
2. What are your thoughts on travel sports? Do you feel they enhance childhood? Make it more difficult? Why do you think travel sports are now so prevalent?
3. What is your definition of *balance*? Do you think most families have balance in their lives? If not, why?
4. Think about your own childhood. Compare it to the experience children have today. Do you think things are better or worse for kids today? Why?
5. What is your neighborhood like? Is it a true community? Do people know their neighbors? Or is your sense of community based on something other than the place where you happen to live?
6. Have you ever thought about "dropping out"? If so, why? What prevents people from doing this, even if they find the concept attractive?
7. What did we learn from COVID? Were there any positive parts of that experience? What were the drawbacks?
8. Is your impression of the 1960s different after reading this book? If you lived during the 1960s, is there anything from this era you'd like to see explored in more depth?

9. Discuss the trad wife movement. Why do you think this lifestyle is appealing to some young women today?
10. What do you think life will be like for women sixty years from now? Will it be better? Worse? Do you think advances in technology will make motherhood easier or harder in the future?

About the Author

Photo © 2023 Renée C. Gage Photography

Christine Gunderson grew up on a fourth-generation family farm in rural North Dakota where she read Laura Ingalls Wilder books in her very own little house on the prairie. She's a former television anchor and reporter and former Capitol Hill press secretary. Her debut novel, *Friends with Secrets*, was an Amazon bestseller, an Amazon First Reads pick, and a Women's Fiction Writers Association STAR Award winner. She currently lives in the Washington, DC, suburbs with her three children, Star the Wonder Dog, and a very patient husband. When not writing, she's sailing the Chesapeake Bay with her family, playing Star Wars Monopoly, rereading Jane Austen novels in the school pickup line, or unloading the dishwasher. Christine loves to hear thoughts and ideas from readers or, best of all, delightful emails telling her that you laughed out loud while reading this book. You can reach her at www.christinegunderson.com.